MY WICKED EARL

The Wickeds Book 3

KATHLEEN AYERS

Copyright © 2019 by Kathleen Ayers

All rights reserved.

No part of this book may be reproduced in any form or by any electronic or mechanical means, including information storage and retrieval systems, without written permission from the author, except for the use of brief quotations in a book review.

❀ Created with Vellum

I

LONDON 1830

"Really Colin," Viscount Lindley leaned forward, widening his mismatched eyes in mock horror. "The fact that you haven't had a woman in nearly a year is *appalling*, the death of your beloved Uncle Gerald notwithstanding. Having met the man, I'm certain he wouldn't wish you to live the life of a hermit with nothing but your scribblings to keep you company. You've been in London for nearly a fortnight without so much as a glance at a female."

"You exaggerate." Colin Hartley shot his friend a murderous look before turning to take in the sumptuous furnishings of Hastings, Viscount Lindley's very discreet, very exclusive club. Hastings was reserved for only the very wealthy of London, or the incredibly powerful. Viscount Lindley was both. The club was even more exclusive than Whites or Brooks.

The paneled walls gleamed in the mellow light of the wall lamps, their glowing patina likely the result of the scrubbings of dozens of maids. Each wall was covered with portraits of past patrons and benefactors. Various dukes, earls, and such, covered every square inch, all looking appropriately disapproving. Had any of those august men been alive they would have routed Colin from their midst with a mere curl of their upper lips.

Large comfortable chairs circled the room, in settings of two and four, so that the powerful could decide the fate of lesser beings in relative privacy. Plush Persian carpet, so thick and lush it put the fields of Ireland to shame, cushioned his worn boots. Servants dressed in blue and silver livery wandered between the wealthy gentlemen, discreet and quiet so as not to disturb their betters.

The room was rich and decadent, much like Viscount Lindley himself.

Nick's lip curled. "Living in a hut—"

"Bugger off, Nick. My uncle's estate in Ireland was not a hut. My God, just because a person isn't a duke, or a bloody marquess, doesn't mean one lives in a hut."

"A farm then."

"Estervale is an *estate* whose tenants cultivate sheep, you snob."

His friend shot him a wolfish grin showing a gleaming line of teeth.

"Had," Colin waved his hand looking for the word, "*needs* not necessitated my trip to London, I would never have left Ireland." *A half-truth.*

"*Needs?* As in a woman?" Nick wiggled his brows lasciviously.

"No." Colin rolled his eyes. "Other, *needs.*"

"Well then here's to Uncle Gerald," Viscount Lindley raised his glass. "I liked your uncle, by the way. A fine man, Gerald McBride was, despite his taking you to live on a sheep farm."

"*Estate*. My uncle was a gentleman. Please rest assured not a *bit* of manure ever touched me."

A deep chuckle bubbled up from his friend's chest and the room quieted almost immediately. Glances and raised brows were thrown over stiffened shoulders.

"I should hope not, after all, you are the son of the Earl of Kilmaire."

"*Third* son. Thank God. I've no desire to ever wear the burden of a title. Sheep farming may suit me quite well." Another half-truth, for while there were sheep, they no longer belonged to Gerald McBride, or his nephew.

"Indeed?"

"Besides, I would never have been able to finish at Eton had Uncle Gerald not taken financed the remainder of my education. My parents could certainly not afford to, I believe they spent all they had sending my brothers. Uncle Gerald was a godsend."

Colin wished desperately that Uncle Gerald hadn't mortgaged Estervale to the hilt. While he was grateful for his uncle's sacrifice he was certain that the bulk of the money had gone to Runshaw Park and the Earl of Kilmaire, not Eton.

"Yes, it is fortunate Uncle Gerald took you in. I often wonder how it is that he and your mother had such...*different* in opinions of you."

How Colin detested Nick's habit of picking apart a person's life, his odd eyes piercing him as he brought up the odds and ends that made up Colin's existence.

Colin had no wish to discuss the Mad Countess, as Nick well knew.

"Membership here must cost a bloody fortune." He steered the discussion away from the Countess of Kilmaire.

"I'm certain of it, though I wouldn't know." Nick

shrugged his large shoulders, causing the expensive and expertly tailored coat he wore to pull a bit at the seams.

The bloody coat probably cost more than Colin's passage to London. And that was the problem. The very rich didn't know what it felt like to count *every* penny.

Estervale, the house Colin had called home for ten years, was his home no longer. What a shock it had been to have a solicitor waiting on the front steps shortly after Colin laid his uncle to rest. The Bank of Ireland owned Estervale now. He must find an alternate means of support, one that did not involve sheep farming. For though he certainly wouldn't admit such to Nick, Colin didn't care a bit for sheep or the smell of wet wool.

"Are you familiar with Lord Wently?" Colin pretended to study the amber liquid in his glass.

"Wently? Do you have an invention to share or perhaps you've written a treatise on sheep farming? While he is still funding the restoration of some Grecian marbles, marbles I'm quite sure will be shown to be fakes, I'm told he has thrown his weight behind William Howell and they've started a publishing house. Howell is the author of those lurid novels involving murder and young innocent ladies. Arabella is quite addicted to them, I fear."

"Your sister has always been rather bloodthirsty." Colin sipped at his drink trying to appear nonchalant.

Nick's eyes slid over him with a look meant to force Colin to give up all of his secrets. "What are you up to Hartley?"

"I may have a proposition for Lord Wently, though I need an introduction."

Nick held his glass up, pretending to study the amber liquid. "I'm not acquainted with Lord Wently, although Lord Robert Cambourne is his close friend." Nick shot him a speculative look. "But, I'm sure you knew that having spent so much time with the Cambourne family at Gray Covington. Perhaps that's why you've come to London?"

"Possibly."

"Why don't you tell me what this is all about?" Nick said. "I may be able to help."

The last thing Colin wanted to do was explain his reasons for seeking an introduction. In addition to picking apart a person's life, Nick had a terrible habit of rearranging other's lives in a manner Nick thought would suit them best. The results were often mixed.

"I was hoping to beg an introduction to Lord Wently from the Marquess but I understood Lord Cambourne was not in town at the moment."

"Well, not presently. But, as it happens, the Marquess of Cambourne is scheduled to make an appearance at my grandfather's ball tomorrow night, as is most of the *ton*. He would be delighted to see you, I'm sure. Cam's father was quite fond of you. Lord Cambourne is a man whose opinion I trust. Much more of a father to me than my own sire. I've often sought his advice, when I didn't wish my grandfather's."

Before Colin could respond, a harsh whisper drew his attention. A large man, his round form barely squeezed into the poor chair on which he sat, glared at Colin and Nick, while relating something to his companion. The fleshy face burned red with outrage as the beady eyes looked over an upturned nose at Colin.

He looks like an enraged pig.

Mr. Pig's companion was just the opposite, all sharp angles with a chin that looked as if it could cut through cheese. *This* gentleman was a bit more reserved in his perusal, only nodding in agreement with each word his friend spoke.

"What do you think," Colin waved his glass of whiskey towards Mr. Pig, "that we have done to offend those two?

Possibly we attended Eton with their sons and our reputation as the Wickeds precedes us."

"Humph." Nick regarded the men with hooded eyes. "I cannot fathom why such a ridiculous nickname has stuck so soundly over the years all because the three of us managed to encounter some old gypsy in the woods. Though, at the time I did appreciate her gracing us as such, for it was a useful tool in keeping the spoiled brats at Eton from threatening us with their fists."

"You mean threatening Cam and I," Colin corrected him. "No one dared go after you." Colin waved his hand over Nick's large frame. "Too bloody big." He nodded towards the men. "Probably my father owes them money. If so they will need to look elsewhere for recompense. Do you see that the large one resembles a wild boar of some sort?"

Nick's lips twisted into a grimace. "It's me." The words left his lips in a quiet hiss. "It's *always* me."

Colin sipped his drink. "Oh yes, *that*. Sometimes I forget you're the bloody Devil of Dunbar. I for one shiver in my boots every time I am in your company. You're terrifying," Colin pretended to tremble in fright.

Nick stayed silent, only sipping at his whiskey.

"Nick," Colin apologized, "I'm sorry. I shouldn't have made light of such a thing."

"It's of no import."

"I'm certain no one still thinks on the rumors. The war has been over for a very long time."

Accusations of theft and treason, though unproven, still cast a shadow upon the Dunbar family. Nick's father, Phillip, had taken his own life over the false accusations, as well as that of Nick's mother.

"You'd be surprised. The deaths of my parents didn't actually absolve them of the act my father was accused of. Most view it as proof of his guilt. I still find it baffling.

Anyone that knew my father personally knew he was too much of a drunkard to pull off such a complex scheme." Nick's eyes grew hollow and cold. "Someday I will find the person who is truly guilty. Neither they nor their family will be safe from the Devil of Dunbar. The Dunbars serve the Crown."

It was a phrase Colin had often heard repeated while he attended Eton with Nick. *'The Dunbar's serve the Crown.'* His gaze fell to his friend's large hands, the knuckles covered with scars and bruises. He'd never asked Nick *how* exactly the Dunbars served the Crown. Probably better off not knowing.

"The actions of my parents," Nick waved a hand in front of his mismatched eyes, "and these, are enough to make me a bit of a pariah. Were the *ton* not all afraid of Dunbar, I'm certain I would be hunted down with pitchforks and set aflame. Look at him," Nick lifted his chin to the quivering servant who stood to the left of their chairs. "He can barely hold his tray he's shaking so badly."

At Nick's perusal, the servant paled and blinked.

"My family is a founding member of this bloody club, so you'd think at the very *least* I would be waited on by someone who isn't trembling like a virgin on her wedding night." His friend sounded more amused than angry now and Colin relaxed.

"Well, you *are* the Devil, Nick." Colin chuckled taking the sting out of his words. The whiskey was going to his head. How long had they sat at Hastings drinking? No more than an hour. His eyes fell to the nearly empty bottle sitting on the table next to Nick's knee. *Well, possibly more than an hour.*

A mischievous grin crossed Nick's hard features. "I should bloody well start acting the part, don't you think? You," he pointed to the servant, "who are those two gentlemen? I think I'd like to make their acquaintance."

The servant's Adam apple bobbed as he swallowed

anxiously. "The Baron of Taunton and Viscount Sistern," his voice shook, "my lord."

"Well, send them a bottle of your finest brandy, won't you? Compliments of the Devil of Dunbar."

"Yes – yes, my lord." The servant's eyes grew round as he looked at Nick.

"And stop acting as if I'm about to turn you into a frog," Nick commanded. "Good Lord, you appear about to faint. Like a woman whose stays are too tight. I haven't turned anyone into a frog in ages. Mr.Hartley finds it very off-putting."

Colin nodded in agreement, the act of moving his head causing the room to spin a bit. "Very off-putting."

The servant bowed and scurried off, pausing only to look over his shoulder at the Devil of Dunbar.

"Probably won't come back."

An amused smile crossed Nick's lips, but he said nothing. The only sign of his agitation was the drumming of his fingers against his chair arm. An ancient pitted ring on his thumb glinted dully in the room's mellow light.

Colin often thought that the history of Nick's family would make for an excellent novel. His friend certainly looked the part of the Devil. He always appeared a bit menacing, as if he'd just come from a fight he'd won, and the bloodlust still ran through him. The eyes, of course, could be rather disturbing to those who first viewed them.

Just now those eyes, one blue and one brown, watched Mr. Pig and his friend with a bland look.

"Ah, there he goes." Nick lifted his glass in the direction of the servant who was making his way to Lords Severn and Taunton who appeared a bit chagrined that they'd gained the notice of Viscount Lindley.

The servant, poor man, tentatively approached the pair,

bowing slightly as he presented the brandy. He murmured something in a low voice and spared a glance at Nick.

Colin took another sip of his drink, gratified to see the flush that crept up the fat one's neck. Dislike for Nick colored his face. And fear.

His companion, obviously the wiser of the pair, stood, bowing deeply to Nick before averting his eyes.

"Colin," Nick continued in a half-whisper, "shall I go over and tap the fat one on the shoulder? Tell him Old Scratch has advised me that his time is up? That the brandy was just a beginning of the warmth he'll soon feel?"

Colin giggled again. He really should stop now lest he spend tomorrow in bed with his head aching. Whiskey spilled down his sleeve and he frowned. "Now see what you've done, Nick. I've so few good shirts left and now I fear this one is ruined."

"That's no way to speak to the Devil," Nick growled, loud enough so Lords Sistern and Taunton could hear. "I could make your blood curdle with a look."

The servant stopped as he made his way back to Nick and Colin. He nodded in their direction before hurrying away through a small door set into the paneled wall.

"Probably heading off to pray somewhere," Nick added sardonically, sitting back in his chair, a deep chuckle humming from his chest. "That was great fun."

Colin could see that it was not.

A shadowed look hovered in Nick's eyes, as if his friend were taking a moment of self-pity. All the money and power in the world wouldn't make Nick acceptable to the *ton*. Ever.

Wisely, Colin stayed silent.

"Now, where were we? Ah yes, discussing your lack of female companionship."

"We weren't, *you were*," Colin replied a bit defensively. Bloody hell, why couldn't Nick just leave it alone?

"You need a woman, Colin. It will do wonders for your ill humor. Perhaps even assist you with whatever little project you wish to discuss with Lord Wently."

So, they were back to Lord Wently again. "I am not in ill humor." Colin ignored his friend's curiosity.

"Nonsense, of course you are. A good tumble will help ease your mind before you are welcomed into the bosom of your family. You are going to Runshaw Park, are you not?"

Colin thought of his mother's hate-filled visage. It was doubtful the Mad Countess had ever clasped Colin to her meager breast in welcome.

"Possibly." His brothers wished him to come home, had in fact been begging him since they learned of Uncle Gerald's passing.

Nick frowned. "Hmm. Well, I'm only looking out for your best interests. Regardless, you need a woman. Celibacy has made you all dour and thoughtful." The big shoulders shivered in revulsion. "Christ, you're as pale as the sheets the maids use to make my bed. Unless, it's not a woman you need," his friend left the words hanging in the air.

"You're an *ass*, Nick. If you weren't so bloody big I'd call you out for that." The whiskey sloshed out of Colin's glass again. Good Lord he couldn't seem to keep the glass from tipping in his hand. "Not every man is lead around by his cock, as you are."

"I do agree that it has caused me to make some poor choices in the past. Many poor choices. I see a lovely pair of tits and I fear I lose all control. Can't help myself."

"I'm rather more selective."

Nick leaned forward. "I know a widow. Delightful woman. Rounded in all the right places and quite lovely."

"A former mistress of yours? No thank you." Colin drained his glass.

Nick shot him an insulted look. "I should say not. As it

happens, she's just come out of mourning, rather like yourself. Her husband was a business associate. Quite ancient. Died shortly after the wedding. Since you will be at my grandfather's ball—"

"I never said I would go." Just the thought of being amongst the *ton* filled Colin with dread. "I don't dance."

"Have you not just told me you need an introduction to one of Lord Robert Cambourne's closest associates?"

"Yes."

"Perhaps if you told me why—"

"No. Stop pestering me."

Nick held his hands up in supplication. "As you wish. Though I'm not sure why you would want the assistance of a stranger rather than myself."

Because you would try to manipulate things. "I'll tell you in good time. I promise."

"Well then, Lord Cambourne will be at my grandfather's ball. As will everyone else in London. No one dares defy Henry's invitation. And I will make sure my widow friend is in attendance as well. She adores brooding men awash in anguish. Which you most definitely are. The Irish are such a dreary race." Nick wiggled his eyebrows suggestively. "She's a lovely bosom as well."

"Shut up, Nick. God, you can be annoying. Why have I never noticed before now?"

"Careful, you've only got two friends, Hartley, and you can't afford to insult me since Cam is absent."

"My glass is empty and so is the bottle."

"Very helpful, Colin. Where do you suppose that little rodent's gotten off to?" His shaggy head turned slowly about the room until it stopped. "Never mind." He lifted his glass in the air to signal to another servant who stood near the far wall.

"Have you heard from him?" Colin asked.

"Who? The rodent?" Nick gave a short laugh. "I'm sure he's giving his notice as we speak."

"I meant Cam." Colin rolled his eyes. "God, you *are* awful."

"Not for some time. Cam is terrible at letter writing as you well know. I suppose there's a lack of paper and ink in the jungles of Macao. I do hope he hasn't gone and gotten himself killed, although I'm certain that was what *she* was hoping. I certainly can't fault you for not wishing to call on Cam's father at Cambourne House with that *bitch* in residence."

The bitch in question being the Marchioness of Cambourne, wife to Lord Robert. Cambourne. Cam's stepmother made his life a living hell, and Nick was certain she'd had something to do with her stepson's sudden journey to Macao.

"Cam will be home soon, rest assured. If he's still—," Nick sighed "—and I'm certain he *is*. The Dowager has asked my assistance and the use of a Dunbar ship. He's coming back even if I have to go and bring him back myself."

"Indeed. No one dares disappoint Cam's grandmother." Colin smiled at the thought of the Dowager Marchioness of Cambourne. "I would enjoy renewing my acquaintance with her."

"You'll get your chance. Miranda's just made her debut so I'm certain the Dowager will be in attendance."

"Miranda? In a gown making a debut?" Colin snorted thinking of Cam's younger half-sister. "God, she was so incredibly annoying as a child. Always covered in mud and chattering incessantly until one wanted to put cotton in their ears. Trailing behind me and begging for attention. If she's grown into anything like her mother, I'll keep my distance."

"I'm sure you will." An odd smile crossed his friend's face.

Another servant, this one made of sterner stuff than the previous man, returned with a fresh bottle, setting it gently on the table between Colin and Nick, before bowing and sliding away.

"Now," Nick filled Colin's glass before his own, "let me tell you more about my widow friend."

※

"I can't believe I let Nick talk me into this."

The ballroom before Colin was filled with the overindulged, pampered gentlemen and ladies of the *ton*, hovering in groups around the vast room like the vultures they were. He had a distinct dislike for society, having always been a member of it, but only allowed to exist on the fringes. The Earl and Countess of Kilmaire were certainly not sought after. Their third son, even less so.

It didn't matter a bit to Colin. He found the people humming about him like wasps about to sting to be dreadfully boring. The gentlemen spoke of their horses and their mistresses, usually in that order. The women were vapid bits of flesh encased in silk and taffeta who gossiped and pouted while flapping their fans and filling their dance cards.

Colin's arrival aroused little fanfare in the ballroom. The barely murmured announcement of his arrival from a dutiful footman didn't even merit a glance from the crowd.

He immediately took a glass of wine from a passing servant and slid into a deep alcove where he could observe the ball unseen. His only companion in the alcove was a rather large urn which looked appropriately ancient and priceless. A large potted plant sat inside the urn. A closer inspection of the large green fronds springing from the plant indicated it was a palm.

"Thank God I don't have to make attending affairs such as these a habit," he whispered to himself. "Ian or Thomas must fetch punch and converse with these nitwits."

There were few advantages to being born a third son, and even fewer if you were the third son of an *impoverished* earl and his addled wife. But one obvious advantage was that the continued lineage of the Kilmaire's would not be Colin's responsibility, but the responsibility of his brothers. Ian, the heir, and Thomas, the spare, would have to dance attendance on some virgin with a large dowry.

A *very* large dowry.

The state of Runshaw Park, the ancestral seat of the Earl of Kilmaire was a well-known fact amongst the *ton*. Every piece of property not entailed had been sold in bits over the years, probably to many of the people in this room. The Kilmaire jewels were gone. The paintings and tapestries that once hung in splendor had been sold to the highest bidder. Even the once magnificent Kilmaire library had been sold, book by book, to a London bookseller.

The sale of the library especially pained Colin.

But being an impoverished title wasn't the reason the Kilmaire's were considered beneath most of the *ton*. After all, plenty of titles needed the infusion of a rich dowry. No, it was more the Irish blood running through their veins. While the earldom was English, the origins of the title were Irish, and the Kilmaire earls continued to show a marked preference for women from Ireland. And of course, most of the Irish were papists. The taint was nearly more than the *ton* could tolerate.

And, of course, there's Mother, the Mad Countess.

Carefully tugging at a loose button hanging from his nearly threadbare coat, Colin grit his teeth at the thought of his mother. He wondered how he could possibly avoid her if he visited Ian and Thomas. There likely wasn't a way to do so. Just the sight of Colin would set off the Mad Countess, terrifying everyone on the premises.

Why did Rose McBride Hartley detest her youngest child? Even in hindsight, it still remained a mystery to Colin.

MY WICKED EARL

When he'd been younger, before he'd simply grown to accept her hatred, Colin would lie in bed and replay every action he'd had with his mother. How had he angered her to the point where she could no longer stand the sight of him? Her distaste for Colin increased during his years at Eton, to the point where he stopped visiting Runshaw Park all together, instead spending the holidays with the Cambourne family at Gray Covington.

On the rare occasions that Colin did visit Runshaw Park and his brothers, the Mad Countess would sit perfectly still, dark eyes so like his own, tracking his every movement. She barely blinked, reminding him of a cat stalking a defenseless mouse.

Bloody unnerving.

Lord Kilmaire, on the other hand, ignored his youngest son, only taking notice of Colin's presence if Colin managed to truly disturb Lady Kilmaire's mental state. Uncle Gerald took Colin's father to task once over his treatment of Colin, but Lord Kilmaire refused to defend his son or show him an ounce of affection. The earl would brook no disparagement of his wife, even from her younger brother. For though the Mad Countess was...well, *mad*, Colin's parents had been a love match. Lord Kilmaire's adoration for his wife bordered on obsession.

Colin's glance fell back to the ballroom and the entitled swirl of the *ton*. Mulling over his parents and his lack of finances was depressing. While Colin never expected much from Lord and Lady Kilmaire, Uncle Gerald was a different story. Uncle Gerald mortgaged away the only home Colin had ever really known, without so much as a warning to his nephew.

I must succeed, for there's no other way for me.

"Damn." Colin poured the remainder of his wine into the dirt around the palm, wondering if the liquid would have an adverse effect on the plant, for wine certainly did on Colin. He detested wine, no matter how fine and French the vintage. Possibly one of the servants would bring him a whiskey.

Not bloody likely.

Why hadn't his uncle told him the true state of affairs? They'd been close, close enough that Uncle Gerald did not mince words when speaking of the madness of his sister. Uncle Gerald even hinted that Mother had accidently killed a housemaid in a fit of rage and Colin's grandfather shushed the incident. Upon bringing Colin to Ireland, his uncle had taught him how to defend himself with a knife. He'd gifted Colin with a wicked long blade that could easily be stowed in the front pocket of a coat, or in one's boot.

'Just in case, lad. My sister's as mad as they come. And you might end up in London one day, a city full of murderous intent. Not one of them fops can be trusted.'

Rose McBride Hartley was indeed as mad as they came. A beautiful woman whose appearance was completely at odds with the chaos that dwelled within her mind. Though Uncle Gerald always spoke of his sister with love, there also was an everpresent undercurrent of fear.

A stir at the end of the ballroom ended Colin's musing. A hum, the sound of many voices all whispering at once, filled the air as if a hive of bees had been let loose. Several men bowed low, the ladies at their sides falling into deep curtsies. The musicians put aside their instruments and lowered their heads as if the king himself were making an appearance.

Not the king, of course, but close.

His Grace, the Duke of Dunbar, entered the nearly silent ballroom, daring anyone with an icy blast of his azure blue eyes, to notice the slight limp in his stride. Stubbornly, he made his way to the dance floor, slowly moving towards the center of the room, enjoying the homage he was paid.

None dared to meet his eyes.

The ballroom was eerily silent, the guests struck mute with respect for and fear of their host. The curse that lingered over the Devils of Dunbar gave one pause, for who among them knew if it was true or not? Treason hovered like a filmy cloud over the Dunbars. One would think London society would cut the entire family.

Nick once told Colin that his grandfather knew the secrets of everyone in London. *Horrible* secrets. Secrets that would ruin a family. While the *ton* may wag their malicious tongues behind the duke's back, none were foolish enough to incite his wrath or risk his displeasure.

The Duke, his large form towering over the mere mortals who packed his ballroom, looked out from a once handsome face made craggy by old age, lips twisted downward in disapproval. His hand clasped that of a pretty dark-haired woman wearing a gown of midnight blue silk. Tiny diamonds sparkled across the dress, reminding one of stars in the sky, as well as the wealth of the woman who could afford such a garment. The Dunbar jewels, sapphires and diamonds, dripped from her ears and throat.

Lady Cupps-Foster. The Duke's thrice widowed daughter.

Nick's aunt, Colin mused, was still a handsome woman in her prime, though there wasn't a man alive in all of England who would marry her. Not anymore. She'd buried three husbands, all of whom had died prematurely. Nick's cousins, Lady Cupps-Foster's two sons, inherited titles from their fathers and were an earl and a baron, respectively. Her last husband, Lord Cupps-Foster, died before an heir could be produced.

Lady Cupps-Foster smiled merrily up at her father with eyes just as blue as his, but where the Duke surveyed all those around him as if inspecting an inadequate supper buffet, hers were warmer. Graciously nodding to her guests, she gave the musicians leave to begin playing and gave her father a stern nod. Lady Cupps-Foster was a force to be reckoned with in the Dunbar family, and indeed in all of London. Her father rarely denied her anything.

The Duke grimaced.

A man, taller than the Duke but with a build so similar none could doubt they were related, sauntered in behind the pair. He surveyed the crowd with odd mismatched eyes, one brown, one azure blue. Nick's lips twisted in amusement, for he knew the stir his appearance caused, and he gave a mock bow to the room.

Viscount Lindley, the Devil of Dunbar had arrived.

The lords and ladies of the *ton* murmured among themselves, pushing back from him as if he were a leper and not the heir to Dunbar. Several ladies opened their fans with a flick of their wrists, hiding their faces behind the painted façade, some flicking their eyes up and down the man's expensively clad form.

"Finally. Bloody big idiot. Leaving me here to fend for myself when he knows how much I detest it."

Following behind her brother, chin tilted arrogantly, was Nick's sister, Lady Arabella. Arabella wore a gown of light rose and matching ribbons threaded through her dark hair. She looked young and sweet until one caught sight of her face, for Arabella wore a perpetual grimace.

Colin had yet to ever see Arabella smile. Humor was not her strong suit.

Arabella tried unsuccessfully to lead her brother to the dance floor, tugging on his sleeve as Nick shook his head.

"The Devil of Dunbar does not dance." Colin informed the palm. "Only Cam."

Cam was the dancer.

Would he ever see his friend again?

Regardless of Nick's determination to retrieve him, if

Cam didn't wish to come back, he wouldn't. Not unless he were forced.

Colin peered out from his hiding place, searching for the Marquess of Cambourne. He only needed a few moments with Lord Robert, to prevail upon his connection and secure an introduction to Lord Wently.

Pulling at his too tight neckcloth, Colin only succeeded in poking his finger through the thinning silk. Hastily, he twisted the silk so that the hole wouldn't show. *Good God, my clothing is falling apart even as I wear it. If I'm not careful I'll end up partially naked in the Duke's ballroom.*

Desperation was a horrible feeling. Nick would advance him funds, of course, any amount Colin wished. But then what? How to ever pay it back? Would he spend his life dependent on his friends?

"No. No. No." He repeated to himself.

Nick *assured* him last night that Lord and Lady Cambourne would be in attendance. Lady Miranda's debut would insist upon their presence. With so many eligible bachelors hovering about the ballroom, Lady Cambourne would be salivating over the sheer opportunity offered her eldest daughter.

Poor Miranda, who preferred catching frogs to learning deportment, had often trailed her older brother and his friends. Fascinated with stories that Colin told her of the wee folk, she became convinced the woods of Gray Covington were full of fairies and trolls. She could often be found crawling about the woods on her hands and knees, all the better to spy a stray fairy that might be hiding. She had also adored sweets, Colin remembered, particularly raisin cakes, which led her to be a bit chubby.

Lady Cambourne had not cared to have her daughter dirty *or* plump. How well Colin remembered her ladyship declaring at an evening meal when Lord Cambourne's business kept him in London, that Miranda not be served anything but water and boiled turnips. Miranda was *stout*, Lady Cambourne decreed in her silken voice as she patted down her wheat-colored coiffure. While Colin, Cam and Lady Cambourne dined on roast, Miranda sat silent in her chair, tears running down her cheeks. When dessert was brought to the table, Lady Cambourne made sure the tray was set directly before her daughter. On the tray lay at least half a dozen freshly baked raisin cakes—Miranda's favorite.

'You are a little piglet, Miranda. You already possess an inordinate amount of detriments to your deportment and character without looking like a cow. You'll see someday that I am doing this for your own good.'

Cam objected, of course, and threatened to tell his father, but Lady Cambourne whispered something in his ear, silencing him.

"Bloody bitch," Colin hissed out loud. The first time he'd seen her, Colin imagined her to be a fairy princess. Lady Jeanette Cambourne sparkled and shone like the finest diamond. Unfortunately, her ladyship was akin to a perfect, flawless apple, which once bitten into, revealed a rottenness that caused you to fling it away in horror. Her cruelty to Miranda was the least of the woman's sins. Colin well remembered the discovery of her cuckolding her husband with Gray Covington's head groom.

The night her ladyship had withheld the raisin cakes from Miranda, Colin had waited until the Marchioness retired to her rooms, then went directly to the kitchens and wrapped half a dozen raisin cakes in a napkin. He wasn't sure why he'd done it, only that Lady Cambourne's treatment of her daughter reminded him of the Mad Countess.

Unfortunately, his act of kindness held consequences.

Miranda's round, plump face lit up with a toothless grin and her eyes turned worshipful as she thanked him. The next day she marched up to him, Nick and Cam while they were building a fort and asked Colin to marry her.

For the next several years, Miranda followed Colin every time he visited Gray Covington. Talking incessantly, she buzzed around him like a gnat he could not rid himself of. Miranda begged for more tales of the wee folk and as she grew older, Greek or Roman myths. He would never have admitted it to Cam, but Colin secretly enjoyed the way she worshipped him. It had made Colin feel important. Needed.

"I suppose she's grown up to be one of these annoying creatures," Colin said under his breath as he watched a group of twittering young ladies circle the ballroom in a cluster of silk and lace, as if an invisible thread linked them together. How could she not be?

"Well, there you are, finally. I've been searching everywhere for you." The elegant, cultured voice teased softly from behind the Grecian urn.

Colin turned a bit cautiously, comforted by the feel of the knife tucked in his coat—a habit Uncle Gerald had instilled in him.

'It takes too long sometimes to load a pistol. But a knife is always ready.'

"I can't imagine why such an urn would be looking for me," he said lightly, "especially since we haven't received a proper introduction. I am acquainted with the palm, however, as we were introduced earlier this evening."

A soft giggle, as light as soap bubbles floating up from a bath, emanated from the urn, or rather from the person behind it. The palm waved slightly, as if a gentle breeze blew through the fronds.

"I said, I've been looking for you." The words were soft and suggestive, as if the speaker were bent on seduction.

The greenery parted, and Colin's first thought was that he *prayed* the speaker was bent on seduction.

A young woman stepped blithely in front of the urn, one gloved hand pressed to her lips as if she were about to burst into laughter. Glossy black hair, the color of a raven's wing, coiled about her head in an elaborate coiffure. Peridots winked at him from within the dark dresses, matching the gems that dangled from her delicate ears.

Colin's heart stopped at the sight of her. *So beautiful.*

Her gown was the color of the Irish hills and decorated with dozens more peridots, twinkling about her lush form in such a fashion that she appeared to shimmer in the weak light of the wall sconces. Almond shaped eyes, the same color as her dress, watched him in expectation. She was the most gorgeous thing Colin had ever seen. Like a fairy come to steal him and take him to the Otherworld.

Lovely, lovely.

Lust slammed into him so fiercely that for a moment he didn't breathe. How was it possible that this amazing creature was looking for *him*?

She moved closer, revealing a generous, but tasteful display of bosom. The top of her breasts gleamed pale and white in the candlelight, like fine alabaster.

Colin's eyes immediately took in the expanse of honeyed flesh and the gentle swell of her hips. She seemed not to notice the effect she had on him. Her plump red lips held an impish smile.

"I beg your pardon?" His throat went dry. Something about this woman seemed vaguely familiar, as if he'd seen her somewhere before, perhaps walking along Bond Street as his hackney passed.

The scent of sweet honey and lavender surrounded him as she neared.

Cocking her head to the side, she dipped into a polite half curtsy. As she did so, an ebony curl slid over her silk clad shoulder to settle in the crevice between her breasts.

Colin couldn't take his eyes off that curl. It seemed to beckon him, pleading with him to wrap the glossy strand around his finger. How would her hair look unbound, pouring over her shoulders, down to her–

"I've been sent to fetch you," she lowered her voice to a husky whisper. "Viscount Lindley thought you would probably be hiding, and, as usual, he was quite right. I find it an annoying habit of his. Always being right. Just once, I would like him to be incorrect about something, or someone, though he rarely is."

Colin nodded in agreement, his eyes never leaving the curl which beckoned him to come closer. He longed to press the curl to his lips.

Her head cocked to the side. "Although, if I could hide from all that fuss in the ballroom, I *certainly* would. The unnecessary flapping of fans," she rolled her eyes as her slender gloved hands waved in the air, "the tedium of making pleasant, meaningless conversation just so someone you don't even particularly care for will call on you the next day. I find it a terrible waste of time. I'd much rather read a book, wouldn't you?"

A smile tugged at Colin's lips. "Indeed. I adore books."

"I'm ashamed to say that I spend most of my time during calls attempting to keep from yawning in the caller's face. No one ever has anything interesting to say. Weather. Fripperies." She shrugged, moving the mounds of her ample breasts. "Although, I do adore the dancing, truly. I mean the dancing at balls," she giggled, "that sounded rather like I dance when gentlemen call on me. Do you dance, Mr. *Hartley?*"

She said his name in such an odd, familiar way, as if they'd known each other for years. There was something about the way she spoke, her words darting about like fish in a stream, that reminded him of something. Or someone.

"I do not." *God*, he wanted to touch that curl, possibly place one finger into the delectable crevice where it lay.

She pursed her lips, drawing his attention. She had a rather sinful mouth, one that made him think all manner of wicked things. Her lips were the color of summer berries and would likely taste as sweet.

"Well, that's rather unfortunate," a soft smile crossed the luscious lips. "I was so hoping that you danced, for I do adore it. The way the music floats about you while you're spinning around is delightful. I'm reminded of the ballet. Do you enjoy the ballet? Oh, don't answer, I doubt that you do. Most gentlemen do not. I'm not certain many young ladies do either, for that matter, though I've often wondered how one dances on their toes." The gown floated about her trim ankles as she turned back and forth for his benefit, pointing her toes at him in an imitation of a ballerina.

"Would I be able to make you reconsider? Not the ballet of course, but the dancing in general?"

A tightening in Colin's breeches told him that yes, there was much she could do to make him reconsider. There was no doubt that this was the charming widow Nick told him of last night. Nick's description did not do the woman justice. She was younger than Colin expected, though Nick did say she had been married to a much older man. It was not uncommon for a young girl to marry a lord many years her senior in order to gain a title.

He started at the feel of her fingers against the fabric of his coat, the action sending a wash of heat from his forearm down to the tips of his fingers. The boldness with which she approached him enticed him, for he didn't care at all for the false shyness many women affected. Colin much preferred a woman who was direct. Confident.

"I could teach you the steps," she leaned forward, the top

of her bodice lightly glancing off his chest. "Don't worry. They aren't hard."

Yes, but I am. She was so close that if he moved only an inch, he only need bend his head to press his lips against the scented flesh pushing out of her bodice.

"Come," she said as the musicians started up again in the ballroom, the muted strains just reaching the darkened alcove. Taking his hand in hers, she entwined their fingers. "I will turn a bit." Lavender and honey floated into his nostrils as she expertly spun about. "You barely have to do anything but stand there while I pirouette like a top. It's really quite simple, though I wouldn't like it if you stepped on my feet. Lord Bagley did that just the other night, unintentionally of course. He's too nice to do something like that on purpose. But," she came about so that their faces were only inches apart, "it still hurt quite a bit."

She had the most amazing eyes, like grass after a summer storm and flecked with gold.

"I feared he'd broken my toe. That happened to someone I knew once. A broken toe. Not by dancing, but when a horse stepped on her foot." She made a neat half turn and looked back at Colin, her brow crinkling in thought. "Now I don't mean to say that Lord Bagley is a horse. He's a rather delightful man. Truly."

She spun the remainder of the way around, until they were facing again. A smile of satisfaction crossed her lips. "See how easy that was?"

Desire rolled through Colin, and his cock hardened almost painfully as his eyes traveled down her form. She was slender, but not with the reed slimness of so many of the *ton's* beauties. Instead, she looked soft and plush, with welcoming curves that begged for his touch. He nearly salivated at the beauty he knew lay just beneath the silk and lace.

"I don't think I have it down," he murmured. "Would you show me again?"

Cheeks pinking like the buds of a rose she replied, "I suppose, but it's really not that difficult. She took his hand again, stepped forward, and then suddenly stopped, her eyes widening.

"You don't know who I am." It wasn't a question but a statement. A spurt of laughter escaped the plump lips. "This is rather unexpected. I just assumed—"

"Viscount Lindley sent you to find me, didn't he?"

Her mouth begged for a kiss. And he *was* going to kiss her. In fact, he didn't think he could stop if he wanted to.

She nodded her head, the curl bouncing across her lovely skin until it settled once again between the swell of her breasts. "Yes, of course, he did. He insisted I be the one to fetch you."

Colin tightened his fingers around her waist, pulling the luxuriant body closer to him, until he could feel the warmth of her skin. He reached out to tug at that teasing curl, allowing his fingers to brush intimately against the tops of her breasts.

A delicate tremor went through her at his touch. "You'll destroy my coiffure." She took a halting breath, causing her breasts to surge deliciously against the confines of her gown. "Have a care."

"Duly noted." The sound of the ballroom faded away and all he could hear was the breathing of the woman before him and the rapid beat of his own heart. Candlelight played against her beautiful cheekbones and across her shoulders.

He reached out to run a fingertip against her lips, watching as her mouth parted with his touch.

"You aren't," she said haltingly, "wearing gloves."

"Are you outraged at my lack of decorum?" He knew she wasn't, else she'd be screaming by now.

"No. I – I just find it unusual." Her tongue, tiny and pink, darted out between her lips.

"Jesus." Gently he touched his lips to hers, brushing lightly against her mouth as an adorable squeak sounded from her.

"Dear God, you smell delicious." He kissed the corner of her mouth as the fleeting thought that someone could chance upon them urged caution.

"As do you." She fell against him then with a relieved sigh, crushing those gorgeous breasts against his chest. One gloved hand lingered over his shoulder as if she were considering whether to accept his kiss before her silk clad fingers sank into his shoulders.

Moving his mouth lightly over hers, he teased and toyed with her plump lips, before deepening the kiss. He felt the shift in her body, heralding her surrender to him. Slanting his mouth against hers he devoured her, as if he were a starving man at a feast. Flicking his tongue against her bottom lip, he heard her purr, like a small voluptuous kitten, against him.

Emboldened, his hand slid down the length of her back, feeling the soft, warm skin hidden safely beneath her gown. How he wanted to peel away the fabric that kept him from touching the scented flesh beneath. He wanted to taste her. Inhale her scent. Sink himself into her.

Nipping at her lower lip, he whispered roughly against her mouth, "You are magnificent."

Her lips parted at his words.

She shivered slightly as his tongue moved through her parted lips, seeking hers. He felt her reticence at the intimacy, but she did not push him away; instead she shyly twined her tongue about his, and attempted to match his movements.

Colin groaned, wanting her. Lusting for her.

Her fingers ran up the back of his neck to the base of his skull, shifting through his hair. It was a delicious feeling.

He suckled her tongue while his hand moved up the front of her gown, lingering just below the curve of her breast. Leaving her lips, he ignored her protest to place his mouth against the satin of her neck.

Her pulse raced beneath his lips. Trailing a lingering kiss up the length of her neck, he paused to nuzzle against the lobe of her ear before drawing the bit of flesh between his teeth.

She struggled to pull him closer, clinging to him as if she were drowning. Her silk clad breasts slid across his chest, the tiny peridots decorating the bodice catching on the buttons of his coat.

Colin pushed her gently, but purposefully, against the wall, covering her smaller form with the hard length of his body. This was madness, for if it continued he would take her in this alcove, the Duke's ball be damned. He'd forgotten everything, even his reason for being at the Dunbar ball. The only thing that existed was the feel of this woman in his arms. The absolute *rightness* of her.

She broke off the kiss, "Colin."

The familiarity with which she used his given name surprised him even as the way she spoke, with a languid sensual sigh, sent another bolt of longing through him. His fingers moved to tickle the lace at the edge of her bodice, then stopped abruptly.

"Dear God."

Lips swollen from his kiss, her lovely green eyes regarded him with desire and some emotion he didn't recognize. *Green eyes.* The same as every other member of her family.

Her fingers ran down the side of his face until he caught her hand in his.

"Don't be angry," she murmured.

The last time he'd seen her, she'd been shoving a frog into a tart that the cook at Gray Covington was making for supper. He should have accepted her proposal of marriage years ago, but she'd been only eight at the time.

"Well," Nick's amused voice sounded behind him, "I see Miranda's found you."

2

LONDON 1836

Colin Hartley, the eighth Earl of Kilmaire, climbed the steps until he stood before the enameled black door gracing the home of the Marquess of Cambourne. He didn't wish to be there. His gloved hand hovered over the snarling lion that served as the knocker.

The bloody thing looked as if it would bite off a finger.

He'd only wished a bit of help from the Dowager, *guidance* of sorts, to help him find a wealthy heiress to wed. It would have been so much easier if her ladyship had simply sent a list of suitable young ladies to his rented residence which he could peruse at his leisure. *Alone.*

Unfortunately, the Dowager had other plans.

She had insisted, rather *firmly* in a note sent to him that morning, that he call on her at his earliest convenience. Meaning *immediately*.

One did not ignore the Dowager Marchioness of Cambourne if one wished her assistance in making a match. One in which the bride was possessed of a large dowry and whose family would overlook the scandal that was attached to the Earl of Kilmaire like a fattened leech. A bride who didn't mind the tragedy of the Kilmaire family, of which Colin was the sole remaining member.

Knocking twice in rapid succession, he lifted his chin to the rapidly darkening sky above him. Tiny drops of rain started to fall, peppering his cloak like gunshot.

"Bloody wonderful." He couldn't wait to greet the Dowager looking like a drowned rat. A more perfect day he could not have imagined.

He wouldn't be here at all, if it weren't for the crumbling heap of stone that was the home of the Earl of Kilmaire. The responsibility of the estate, as well as the title, fell squarely on his shoulders, at the death of his brother Thomas almost two years ago. Even though Colin gave not a fig for either. His business venture, if one could call it that, was no longer enough to support Runshaw Park according to his solicitor. Only a large infusion of money would set things to rights.

Ignored for years by Colin's parents, Runshaw Park had been allowed to rot. Decay oozed between the bricks instead of mortar. The vast woods surrounding the house were rapidly reclaiming the land on which the structure sat because there was no groundskeeper. Last summer's rainstorm battered the dilapidated roof, scattering the shingles and ruining a portion of the west wing. The gardens, once the envy of the neighboring estates, had become so overgrown with weeds and tangled wisteria that one could no longer see the steps leading to Runshaw Park's front door. A front door covered with peeling paint.

The tenants who farmed the land did so without modern tools and implements, their meager harvest barely enough to feed their own families. A new well needed to be dug. An illness had recently swept through the pigs decimating their numbers. The list continued to grow with no end in sight.

Had the bloody place not been entailed, Colin would have sold it immediately. Not that there would have been any bidders on Runshaw Park. Not after what transpired there.

"Probably couldn't give it away if I tried. Damn you Ian and Thomas." He cursed his deceased brothers, both of whom had loved Runshaw Park far more than Colin himself did.

Rain fell harder, the dampness sliding underneath Colin's cloak to send a chill up his spine.

He knocked again and shifted his booted feet.

It should have been one of his brothers, who needed to scour the ton for a wealthy heiress for Runshaw Park. Why must he sacrifice himself to keep that pile of shit whole? He took a deep breath feeling keenly the loss of his brothers, both of whom he'd held in great affection. The unfairness of both of them dying and leaving him to carry on alone was a lingering pain. Especially Thomas who forced a promise upon Colin from his deathbed.

A vision flashed before him, his brother pale and sweat-stained as he lay dying, begging Colin to do his duty to the family. The wasting sickness, the doctor called it. A horror of blood-soaked handkerchiefs and his brother coughing out his life into them.

Why hadn't it been Colin? The least loved?

The irony of outliving his entire family was not lost on Colin. He'd never thought to inherit, never wished a moment for the title and was ill-prepared in assuming the earldom. The only satisfaction he gained, and it was very little, was that his parents were likely turning in their graves that Colin was now the earl.

Oh, the irony of it all. Like the makings of a fine Shakespearian tragedy.

His father barely acknowledged Colin and chose to only shower affection on Ian and Thomas. And the Mad Countess?

The proof of *her* affection stared at him in the mirror every morning. A parting gift from his dear mother before she took her life.

Absently his fingers touched the scar that neatly bisected the left side of his face, starting at the corner of his eye and ending at the top of his lip. The jagged line shined stark white against his cheek. Thankfully, the Mad Countess had poor aim, or he would have lost an eye along with his looks.

Thinking of his mother only served to further agitate Colin, and he was quite irritated enough what with standing in the rain like a beggar waiting for someone to open the fucking door. His scar itched terribly in damp weather, as if a stream of ants were marching across his cheek.

Ian had been first. A stomach ailment to which the local doctor could find no cause. His elder brother suddenly fell to the floor in pain, clutching his left side. Lord Kilmaire drank brandy. The Mad Countess prayed. Colin arrived just in time to witness Ian writhing in agony, his hands clutching the bedcovers as he died.

The Mad Countess was next.

His mother's mental state had always been questionable, but grief over Ian's death destroyed what little remained of her mind. She wailed like a banshee as her eldest son died, frightening the staff as well as her remaining sons and husband. A week after Ian was laid in the ground, the family sat down to dinner. A footman, one of the few left at Runshaw Park, began to circulate the table pouring wine before bringing in the main course, a goose on a silver platter surrounded by potatoes and onions.

As the footman began to carve the goose, Lady Kilmaire suddenly stood on her chair. Lifting her skirts, she took a leap across the table, taking the knife from the startled footman's hand. In her haste to grab the knife she upended the gravy boat, splattering the contents over Thomas and Colin, as she began to slash at her youngest son's face.

'Why couldn't it have been you? The son I wished I'd never borne.'

Even now Colin could not bring himself to eat goose.

Shortly thereafter, the Mad Countess was found in her bath, wrists cut with her husband's shaving razor, her naked body floating in a tub of water stained crimson from blood. Her lady's maid, poor girl, ran screaming from Runshaw Park without collecting her wages.

The Earl of Kilmaire followed his dearly loved, insane wife to the grave, but not before spending what was left in the Kilmaire coffers on drink. His lordship would disappear for days, only to be discovered in an unused drawing room, or the attic, a bottle of liquor clutched in his hands. The last time the earl disappeared, every room in the house was searched, even the old priest's hole. It was Thomas who found him dead, sitting upright in a leather chair in the downstairs drawing room, surrounded by several empty bottles of madeira.

Colin did not drink madeira either.

Thomas and Colin went on as best they could given the circumstances, until the previous year. Thomas fell ill and died, but not before wresting a promise from Colin to restore Runshaw Park and care for the tenants. A promise Colin didn't wish to make but did for the sake of his brother, whom he'd loved.

Death shall surround you. Only you shall remain. No woman's love shall keep you warm, my Wicked. Certainly not your mother's. Nor the only one you are foolish enough to give your heart to. None shall love you. You are cursed to roam the earth alone until the end of your days.

The damned gypsy and her curse. Even now, so many years later, he could smell the smoke of the fire and feel the damp chill of the woods. The press of her lips against his cheek as she whispered the prophecy into his ear. What a lark it seemed at Eton to be cursed by a gypsy. To be named along with his friends, the Wickeds.

Not such a lark to be the *Cursed Earl*, as the gossips now christened him.

Sometimes, at night, when Runshaw Park grew silent, and he worked over the trail of numbers in the account books that all told of his dwindling fortunes, it seemed he could hear the crone whispering to him. There were terrible nights when the gypsy's words intertwined with the hateful ravings of the Mad Countess until he could no longer tell them apart. On those nights, Colin thought perhaps he was as mad as his mother.

'*None shall love you.*'

"Damn it." Must he bang at the door like a tradesman? As he raised his hand to knock again, the door suddenly swung open.

"May I help you?" A large, elderly butler stood in the doorway, guarding it like an aging mastiff. He lifted his nose in the air, his watery eyes alight with recognition as he took in Colin's wet clothing and the length of the scar on Colin's cheek. The butler was too well schooled to show any overt interest at the injury, but Colin still recognized the curiosity in his eyes.

Not that it was unusual. The ton was endlessly fascinated as well. Not so much for the scar itself, of course, but for the story surrounding the wound. After all, not many titled gentlemen were attacked by their mother over a roasted goose dressed with onions and potatoes.

"Lord Kilmaire to see the Dowager Marchioness." A drop of rain dripped off Colin's hat to land on his chin. His nose wrinkled with disgust as the smell of damp wool met his nostrils. Nothing worse than wet wool. He felt like a bedraggled dog.

The butler cocked his head and raised a hand to his ear. "I beg your pardon?"

Good God. The man was not only ancient, but deaf. And, familiar, though Colin couldn't remember the butler's name.

"Lord Kilmaire to see the Dowager Marchioness," he spoke louder into the butler's cupped hand.

Bushy gray brows drew up to the butler's hairline. "Greetings, Lord Kilmaire. Lady Cambourne is expecting you." Bowing as much as his age would allow, he waved Colin inside and slowly shut the door, grunting a bit with his efforts. Lifting trembling hands, the butler took Colin's cloak and hat, handing the dripping garments to a waiting footman. Moving at a snail's pace towards the double staircase at the end of the foyer, the butler turned his head slightly to make sure Colin followed.

Christ, I can hear his spine creak. Colin ran a hand through his hair, droplets of rain falling from the shoulder length strands to sprinkle his coat, while he surveyed the foyer. It had been many years since his last visit to Cambourne House. He'd not even visited when Cam and his wife were in residence the month prior.

The hall still smelled of beeswax from the battalion of maids who kept Cambourne House spotless. He could hear them even now, scurrying about like mice within the walls, ensuring that not a speck of dust would mar the bannister or a cobweb hide in the corner of any room. The foyer was painted a mellow cream color instead of the pale green it had once been, but the fine carpet covering the floor was the same. An expensive looking vase filled with pink roses, probably cut from the extensive garden behind the house, filled the air with their perfume.

He remembered the Marquess of Cambourne's garden well.

I choose you, Colin Hartley.

The seductive words lingered in the air like the scent of the roses.

"This way my lord. I am Bevins, by the way." Bevins dipped his head as he started up the stairs, his knees popping with each step.

Bevins. How could Colin have forgotten?

Pausing halfway up the stairs, Bevins stopped to catch his breath. "Lady Cambourne will receive you in her private sitting room." A spiderlike wave of his hand urged Colin forward.

Colin took a hesitant step. The last time he'd been in this house had been just before the gypsy's curse began to unravel his life and his family. He'd been very successful in avoiding London since, and had no intention of ever returning, but for the fact that his financial situation required such.

And he missed his friends.

The solitary life he'd embraced at Runshaw Park grew tiresome. He had assumed, wrongly, that she would no longer be at Cambourne House. That she would be a duchess just as she wanted. Married to another man with a passel of brats around her skirts.

I was too much of a coward to ask Cam.

Seeing her in the Duke of Dunbar's study was akin to being punched in the gut. Hungrily his eyes trailed over the curves of her body as her scent, lavender and honey, filled the air around him. The silk of her skirts whispered to Colin seductively, a delicious plea for him to come closer. Her lovely green eyes, the color of a fresh grass in spring widened in surprise, and for an instant he saw his own hunger reflected. It wasn't until one of the footmen addressed her that Colin realized something.

Not married.

"My lord?"

Bevins opened a carved oak door with no small amount of

effort and ushered Colin into a sitting room that faced the gardens of Cambourne House. The view was stunning for the Cambournes were known to employ the very best gardeners both in London and Gray Covington, the family estate outside the city. His eyes searched out the tiny white gazebo. Colin wondered if the bench was still there.

Bevins beckoned Colin to enter the room, bowing slightly as he did so.

The entire room was painted in pale yellow, the exact color of buttercups lining the fields every spring. Whimsical butterflies and birds hovered against the walls, so realistically painted that when combined with the view, it gave one the impression that the room was just an extension of the gardens.

Bowls were placed at strategic intervals around the room, all filled with roses and lilies. Two comfortable, slightly worn chairs sat before a merrily crackling fire. One chair held a discarded embroidery hoop and a book of poetry while the other sat empty in invitation. There was no doubt that this room was the private abode of the Dowager Marchioness, for the room carried the very essence of her.

Colin had always adored Lady Donata, the Dowager Marchioness of Cambourne and his friend Cam's grandmother. The Dowager lavished Colin with affection when he visited Gray Covington, seeming to know that the Mad Countess cared little for her son. She treated Colin as a member of the family, fussing over him and never forgetting his birthday.

She was also quite *fierce*.

Turning to ask Bevins how long the Dowager would be, Colin was instead greeted with the oak door shutting behind him with a discreet click.

Colin moved towards the empty chair and the warmth emanating from the fireplace. Perhaps he could dry himself out a bit before the Dowager received him. He could think of worse places to await his fate then this cozy room.

Halfway across the room Colin stopped, nearly upending a side table with a large vase of hyacinths.

A cloud of hair, as black as ink, cascaded over the arm of a small, green tufted couch set off to the side of the room. Unbound and unruly, the curling tendrils nearly brushed the floor.

Colin's hands splayed against his thighs of their own accord, remembering the feel of those dark strands trickling through his fingers like silk.

A small table sat just behind the head of the couch's occupant holding a tray laden with tea and a plate of raisin cakes. The tray was pushed up against the arm of the couch so as to be within easy reach.

She's still enamored of raisin cakes.

Colin's breath caught painfully.

Why hadn't she married St. Remy? After all, that had been her plan six years ago. To marry the heir to a duchy. Become a duchess. Stroll about uselessly like every other titled lady of the *ton*. Spend her days deciding on which gown to wear to some ridiculous ball.

Indeed, why hadn't she married at all?

Colin had done a wonderful job of steering clear of London and in doing so, avoiding *her*. But as luck would have it, his first night in London, she appeared in the Dunbar town house. In the confusion of the disappearance of Nick's betrothed and his sister, Arabella's role in the kidnapping, Colin found himself face to face with the one thing he'd been desperately trying to escape for so many years.

Miranda.

The bitterness rose up again at what she'd done. He didn't wish to see her. Or speak to her.

He turned, meaning to leave and call on the Dowager another day.

A giggle sounded from the couch, halting his movement toward the door, as potent as a siren's song.

It wouldn't hurt just to look at her.

Unlike so many ladies of the *ton* who eschewed books as if they were the plague, Miranda was reading. A pillow embroidered with a spray of butterflies lay across her stomach, a book propped up against it. A pair of discarded slippers lay on the floor beside the couch, as if she'd just kicked them off. Her stockinged toes wiggled as she read, sliding over the couch and into the space between the cushions in a sensuous motion.

A gentle flip of his stomach at the sight of her filled him with the most intense longing, a not so subtle reminder that time did *not* heal all wounds.

There was not a bit of Miranda that did not call to Colin, beckoning his mind and his body. The fluttering of her hands, waving them about in excitement as she told him of a lecture on ancient Greece. The way she spoke, her topics and words winding into each other in such a way that one must pay close attention or be confused. The way she breathed his name in a litany as she came apart in his arms.

The delicate, feminine hand in which she wrote the words that destroyed him.

'While I've enjoyed our flirtation, Colin, we both knew this would end. I find that while I bear you no small amount of affection I am ill-prepared to become only Mrs. Hartley. The daughter of a Marchioness cannot possibly marry a third son with no prospects. I've decided to accept the suit of Lord St. Remy at my mother's urging. He's to be a duke one day and I shall be a duchess."

Colin swallowed, his eyes still on her dark cloud of hair, remembering the shock as his grandmother's ring, the one he'd left for her, rolled out of the envelope and into his palm.

Miranda was so absorbed in her book that she still hadn't sensed his presence. What in the world was she reading that held her interest? He told himself he was only curious about the book she held. After all, he considered it research of sorts.

Colin stepped carefully across the sitting room's plush rug until he stood directly behind her. The vantage point gave him an exceptional view of her bodice and the crevice between the mounds of her breasts. He narrowed his eyes, at a disadvantage without the glasses he sometimes used.

Miranda was reading the latest Lord Thurston novel.

Colin had to bite his lip from laughing. How delightfully ironic.

She giggled again, a light musical sound, and snuggled deeper into the couch.

What in the world could she find so amusing about Lord Thurston? The tales of a disinherited earl turned pirate and his ladylove were thrilling. Romantic. Some would say slightly lurid. But, certainly not amusing.

Tempting fate and himself, Colin leaned over Miranda, watching in fascination as the dark blonde tips of his hair mingled against the ebony curls. Closing his eyes, he took a deep silent breath, allowing her scent to permeate his senses. He knew men who had an addiction to opium or drink. It must feel like this. The almost insane need for the very thing that would destroy you. He should never have asked the Dowager's help, nor come to Cambourne House. A dreadful miscalculation on his part.

Opening his eyes, he bent down to whisper in her ear, loving the way her hair tickled his nose.

"Lord Thurston? How scandalous, Lady Miranda."

3

"*Marcella!*"

Marcella tried to wrench her arm away from the pirate captain but succeeded only in tearing the sleeve of her dress. A feeling of desperation filled her as she realized that Captain Mohab might well use her as he had the poor women now cowering in the ship's hold.

Captain Mohab leered at her while she fought back his advances. She looked up into the rigging hoping for a glimpse of the one man who would be her salvation.

Lord Thurston.

She had not seen him in several days, not since Captain Mohab had taken her captive in Jamaica. Lord Thurston had danced with her at the Governor's Ball, then disappeared into the night mist as if he'd never been there. Captain Mohab and his crew snatched her from her father's carriage as she made her way home.

But she knew Lord Thurston would come for her. He had to. He was her only hope.

"Capt'n!" A shout came from the front of the ship. "It's the Gorgon! She's closing fast."

Marcella wrenched herself away from Captain Mohab and ran to *the railing. A ship was closing fast. The Gorgon. Lord Thurston's ship.*

"He'll not save you." Captain Mohab pressed his lips against her neck. "You'll be mine."

The crunch of wood splintering met her ears as the Gorgon scraped against Captain Mohab's vessel. A cry reached her ear, the sound of men boarding the ship.

"I told you he would come for me." She spat at Captain Mohab.

"Leave her!" A lusty roar echoed from the flapping sails as men scattered before the angry avenging angel who threw himself atop the deck.

"Marcella." Lord Thurston, his features, grim with worry, searched her face for any sign of injury. A firm arm wound around her waist, pulling her behind Lord Thurston as he thrust out with his sword. She melted into him, overcome with relief and something else.

Miranda sighed and turned the page, relieved to hear the storm intensifying outside. Thank goodness for rainy days. The inclement weather would keep all but the most obstinate ladies from calling to pay homage to the Dowager Marchioness of Cambourne.

If the day was relatively free of rain, a steady stream of fashionably garbed ladies, their bland daughters trailing them, would arrive to engage her grandmother in what passed for witty conversation. Grandmother would receive them all in the formal drawing room, a room whose furnishings were so rich as to leave no doubt as to the power of the Cambourne's and the Dowager Marchioness. The visitors would be appropriately grateful the Dowager was home to receive them.

Most of the titled ladies wished to advance themselves by associating with the Dowager Marchioness or sought advice on how to find a suitable match for their dull daughters, for Grandmother was known to be an expert matchmaker. Some ladies, braver than the rest, fairly ran up the steps to call at Cambourne House hoping to catch a glimpse of Miranda's brother, Sutton, a man whose very presence caused the ladies of the *ton* to swoon.

How her sister-in-law, Alex, tolerated such nonsense, Miranda would never understand.

Miranda, if forced, and she often was, would sit beside Grandmother, wearing her mask of carefully cultivated politeness. She would nod graciously, pretending to be enthralled by a discussion of what Lady Halstead wore to the opera, even though Lady Halstead could have arrived naked to her box and thrown herself at the stage and Miranda would still not be the least interested.

There were other callers, male and female alike, who came to gawk at Miranda, a woman who had once been the most sought after young lady in London during her first Season. A woman who now had one foot firmly on the shelf. A beautiful spinster with only a handful of suitors because of the scandal.

Lady Miranda, the *ton* twittered, had *shot* a man.

That last part, unproven, but scandalous in the extreme, was enough for Miranda to be considered, *unsuitable*.

So Miranda would sit, hands clasped and displaying perfect posture, on the edge of the couch and listen while the *ton's* titled ladies touted the many attributes of their insipid daughters while sipping their tea and stealing smug glances at Miranda.

The satisfaction displayed by these ladies was, Miranda admitted, probably justified, though not wholly directed at her. The superior attitudes displayed had much more to do with Miranda's mother, a woman who had lorded over these very ladies as if she were a queen. How many young ladies had Mother ruined with just one cutting remark? One small bit of gossip? Many a young girl's reputation had been questioned. Chances for a brilliant match ruined Invitations had been *denied*.

It was only fair, Miranda supposed, that these fine ladies

gloated a bit. Mother had been rather unkind.

At any rate, Miranda would much rather spend the afternoon with Lord Thurston. Books were so much easier than people, especially the people and circles within society whom Miranda was to embrace. Honestly, there were times she felt as if she were an oddity in a circus, a poor freak trapped in a cage while the world looked on her in muted, sympathetic horror.

Sutton did everything in his power to quell the talk regarding the *incident*, as the Cambourne family called it, but to no avail. If a young, unmarried woman possibly shot a man, even in defense of one's brother, sooner or later the gossips of the *ton* would find out. Young ladies of good breeding did not handle firearms, let alone shoot their mother's cousin.

Even though Cousin Archie had been a horrible person and had certainly deserved shooting.

One of the retainers at Helmsby Abbey officially took the credit for Archie's death, claiming he did so in defense of Lord and Lady Cambourne. But somehow the truth, in the form of innuendo, blazed like wildfire through the *ton*. Lady Cambourne herself was likely the culprit, for upon learning of Archie's death, Mother fell into a heap of silk skirts, screaming out her hatred for Miranda before collapsing like a wounded animal.

Until then, Miranda had thought her mother incapable of love, when in fact, it was only that the Marchioness was incapable of loving Miranda.

It no longer mattered *who* repeated the tale. The damage to Miranda's reputation was swift and unrelenting. No matter that she was the granddaughter of one of the reigning matrons of the *ton*, the Dowager Marchioness of Cambourne. Not even Grandmother could fix society's opinion of Miranda.

Miranda returned her attention to the page before her.

Lord Thurston deserved better than to have her attention wander. Truthfully, her mood today was not due to her mother nor her decision to marry one of the two rather desperate gentlemen courting her.

No, it was the sudden appearance of one specific gentleman.

Colin Hartley, now the Earl of Kilmaire and the object of her ruination, had finally returned to London. How casually he'd greeted her weeks ago in the Duke of Dunbar's drawing room as if they were nothing to each other but family friends. Frowning slightly as if her presence gave him a headache, he'd guided her from the room before dropping her arm as if the very touch of her disgusted him. Colin disappeared before she'd had an opportunity to speak to him, though he clearly had no desire to speak to *her*.

The page blurred before her for a moment and she angrily blinked back the tears starting to form.

The Earl of Kilmaire was obviously taking great pains to avoid Miranda at every turn, so she returned the favor, fleeing his sight whenever possible. She took comfort in assuring herself he wasn't the same man. Not anymore..

Colin was still beautiful, a sleek, golden lion stalking about the salons and ballrooms of London. The scar, angrily bisecting the left side of his face, did not detract from his looks but only added to the aura of suppressed danger that surrounded him. He remained aloof. Cold. If you *did* catch the Earl of Kilmaire smiling, you would see that the smile did not extend to the deep velvet of his eyes. This Colin was not the one that Miranda had loved so fiercely.

Unfortunately, Miranda's heart refused to see the difference.

Determined, as she often was, to push Colin from her mind, she gave her full attention to her two suitors, Lord Ridley and Lord Hamill. She'd gone nearly a whole day without thinking of Colin when Lady Dobson appeared for tea the day before.

Lady Dobson was not a favorite of the Cambourne family, particularly the Marquess and his Marchioness. She'd once chaperoned Miranda's sister-in-law, Alexandra, and it had not gone well. Grandmother still received Lady Dobson on occasion when she wished to hear all of the latest gossip; after being in bed for the last week with a nasty cold, Grandmother *had* received her.

Lady Dobson, thin lips sipping at her tea, confided to Grandmother that the Earl of Kilmaire might *do* for Lady Dobson's unfortunate niece, Miss Margaret Lainscott. Cursed and damaged though he was, Lord Kilmaire was still an *earl*. Lady Dobson cautiously broached the topic to Grandmother, the enormous peacock feather decorating Lady Dobson's ridiculous blue turban waving in the air as if hailing a hackney.

Turbans. The style was outdated. Miranda herself could never fathom why turbans became a fashion to begin with. Something to do with India, Grandmother claimed. Regardless, Lady Dobson seemed not to care. She was never seen without one perched on her head. Odd that one never saw the lady's own hair. Ever. Not so much as a wisp ever escaped the confines of the turbans.

Perhaps she doesn't have any of her own hair.

Miranda giggled out loud, imagining Lady Dobson bald, sitting at tea and conversing with Grandmother. She'd have to tell Alex, her sister-in-law, what she suspected.

'Lord Thurston wrapped one arm about Marcella's waist, his touch as assuring as it was alluring.'

Her neck prickled in sudden awareness just before she felt the press of lips against her hair.

"Lord Thurston? How *scandalous,* Lady Miranda."

Shocked, Miranda attempted to sit up but only succeeded

in banging the top of her head against the edge of the table behind her and unseating a tepid cup of tea she'd long since forgotten about. Crumbs from a half-eaten raisin cake scattered down the front of her gown and into the crevices of the couch. Horrified that he'd taken her unaware and found her in such a state, she pulled the pillow and Lord Thurston against her, as if either would protect her from the man looking down at her.

The seductive whisper against her ear must have been imagined, she thought, for certainly there was nothing but a look of annoyance in Colin's cold, dark eyes. No matter how hard she looked, she never saw any indication that he cared or even remembered that he'd broken her heart. Ruined her.

Bastard. Cursing him, even if only in her mind, felt empowering. And just then, with Colin Hartley staring her down, Miranda needed all the courage she could muster.

Lifting up her chin and composing her features, she summoned up the superior manner that had been her mother's trademark. Difficult to be haughty with bits of raisin cake crumbs clinging to her bodice and the tea-soaked strands of her hair sticking to her neck, but, still, she thought her look appropriately frosty. Pursing her lips as if sucking a lemon, she gave a brief nod.

"Lord Kilmaire. What an unexpected pleasure."

"Yes, I'm certain it is."

Colin did have the most amazing eyes, deep and fathomless. Difficult not to get lost in them, even under the present circumstances. Framed by sooty lashes that any woman would envy, his eyes tipped up slightly at the corners, almost catlike. The dark eyes and lashes were a sharp contrast to the color of his hair, which shone like a burnished gold guinea. The other Colin had worn his hair cropped close to his skull. The thick strands of the Earl of Kilmaire's hair scraped the top of his broad shoulders, as if he couldn't be bothered to cut it. He probably couldn't. It was unfashionably long. Very un-earl like.

A lock of gold fell across the scar, as he inspected her, clearly annoyed with her caustic welcome.

Did he expect to be greeted with open arms?

He moved a bit closer, a large, gorgeous male hovering over her, and Miranda's heart tripped. She could smell the soap he'd used, a clean scent she found intoxicating.

"I beg your pardon for startling you. My *deepest* apologies."

Well that was something, the sarcasm in his tone. *That* sounded like Colin Hartley and not the Frost King better known as the Earl of Kilmaire.

"If you are here to see my brother, Lord Kilmaire, I'm afraid you'll be disappointed." Why wouldn't her heart be still? "Sutton and Alex left for Gray Covington several days ago with the children. I'm so sorry you've braved this dreadful weather for nothing." Good Lord, she sounded just like her mother. "Allow me to ring for Bevins to show you out."

"I'm not here to see Cam, though I would like to discuss why your brother feels the need to employ ancient butlers. The man is eighty if he's a day. I became concerned that he would expire before he made it up the stairs."

"Bevins has been with us for many years. I'm sure you've encountered him before," she said pointedly. Bevins had chanced upon Colin and Miranda once, and it was only due to the poor lighting that the butler didn't see Colin's hand cupping her breast. A miracle made possible only by a servant who neglected to light the lamps in the front drawing room.

A hungry look caressed the tops of her breasts.

He *did* remember.

"Bevins's loyalty and devotion to our family is treasured. You may not value such things, Lord Kilmaire, but I assure you my brother does."

Colin's mouth twisted in a mocking grin.

"You find loyalty amusing?" How dare he show such a lack of respect towards Bevins.

"No. I find the word on *your* lips amusing."

Any hint of humor disappeared as his mouth drew tight. It was as if a someone opened the door on a cold winter day, blowing away any hint of the hunger displayed before. The Earl of Kilmaire fairly vibrated with anger. At her.

Whatever did *he* have to be angry about? *I am the injured party. I was the one who was ruined and abandoned as if I were some lightskirt.* Perhaps it wasn't anger but only concern that she would bring their past association to light? Miranda declined to respond.

The room grew silent except for the occasional burst of thunder and the rattling of the glass in the windows that followed.

Finally, Colin spoke. "I'm here at the invitation of the Dowager Marchioness. I would ask for refreshment, but it appears," his eyes fell on the spilled tray, "that I'm late for tea. Or raisin cakes."

"You never cared for them anyway as I recall," Miranda snapped back, watching the way the scar pulled at his upper lip as he spoke. A week after he'd left her, no, *abandoned* her, Father relayed the information of Colin's brother's death and the attack by the Mad Countess. She'd written of course, even though she'd not heard from him. All she received was a short, curt note, telling Miranda to stay away. Then nothing for six long years.

"It is impolite to stare, Lady Miranda. If you care for the details, I'll be happy to go over them with you," he spat. "You see, we were having goose and—"

"I was wondering," she interrupted, nodding to the expertly tailored charcoal coat and gray trousers, "what you could possibly have to discuss with Grandmother. Perhaps she is recommending a new wardrobe? You resemble an undertaker. Not a splash of color to be found anywhere. Not even your neckcloth, which, I might add, looks so tightly wound I wonder that you aren't choking." She smiled politely as if to say that she *wished* it were choking him.

"I prefer not to be considered a dandy." His tone was acid.

"Oh surely, Lord Kilmaire," Miranda allowed a small laugh to accompany her words, "none would *dare* find you as such. Well, they do say a man's clothing reflects his personality."

"Do they?"

"Austere. *Severe*. You are the very furthest thing from a dandy. No one would dare accuse you of merriment, I assure you. Why, there's probably a bet in the book at White's on whether you will ever crack a smile, or God forbid, burst into laughter."

The dark eyes narrowed on her. "What would a young *lady*, like yourself, know about betting books and White's? Has one of your many suitors filled your head with such? I should speak to your brother. I'm sure he wouldn't be pleased."

She did not care for the way he said 'lady' as if she weren't one. If her morals had been loosened it was due to *him*. Her many suitors? That was rather deliberate and *unkind* considering she was certain Colin knew of the *incident*. Doubtless he knew the reason why the drawing room wasn't packed with young gentlemen regardless of the storm outside.

"I find the weather is inhospitable to those wishing to pay calls," she answered pointedly. "It keeps away those we would rather not have visit Cambourne House." She lifted a brow. "Imagine my surprise that you found your way here."

"I am *here* at your grandmother's request. The Dowager and I have business to discuss." The words left his mouth in a slight hiss even as the velvet of his eyes hardened on her.

'You taste delicious, Miranda. A banquet for a starving man.'

Colin had once whispered those words against her neck and just the memory of them caused warmth to creep over the tops of her breasts. Even now, as he stood glowering at her, no hint of caring in his dark eyes, Miranda allowed desire to wash over her. Desire Colin taught her.

Mother once told Miranda that if a man wished to bed a woman, he would pretend any amount of affection or pretty speeches to get what he wanted.

How disappointing that Mother had been right.

"Why in the world would Grandmother request you to call on her during a thunderstorm?" She'd often thought of what she would say to Colin, were they ever to be alone together again, but found she couldn't quite form her questions. An ache started in her temple, a symptom of verbally sparring with Colin.

Colin begin to stride back and forth across the carpet, a big, golden cat, trapped by the rain in grandmother's private drawing room. Even agitated as he was, Colin moved gracefully. If he'd ever design to dance, he would dance beautifully.

"Lady Cambourne is assisting me in a personal matter."

Miranda nearly choked. There was only one thing Grandmother could be helping him with.

Colin was looking for a wife. How foolish to think Colin came to Cambourne House for *her*. A knot formed in the pit of her stomach even as she grew angry with her grandmother. Which was ridiculous given that Grandmother had no idea that Miranda and Colin were once...*something*. Or that the Earl of Kilmaire had taken her virtue. No one knew.

Colin stopped pacing and settled himself with a jerking motion into the chair across from her. Muscles rippled beneath the smooth dark trousers as he stretched out the length of his legs and crossed them at the ankle. His mouth tightened as he looked at her, almost daring her to say more.

His tailor should be fired. The fit of his trousers was *inde-*

cent. Miranda knew the warm skin that lay beneath the fabric. She had traced her fingers down the curve of his thighs to brush against the thatch of golden hair that lay between them. Her entire body flamed even as she pressed her fingers firmly into the leather binding of Lord Thurston. No amount of time would erase the memory of this man, unclothed before her, in the light of the fire.

She allowed it. All of it. There had been no hesitation in giving herself to Colin. It had been the most beautiful night of her life.

And now, he'd caused her to regret it.

Her fingers tightened along the edge of the book. She longed to toss the tome squarely at his golden head. She had a good arm for throwing, she mused, and was very good at skipping rocks and such. And she'd proven herself a crack shot as well though that's not at all the same as throwing a book. But still, she thought she could hit his temple and—

"That would be unwise, Miranda," Colin growled, guessed at the train of her thoughts while dropping all pretense of formality.

She still adored the way he said her name. *Damn him.*

"Do you really think I would risk damaging my new Lord Thurston novel by tossing it at *your* head? I wouldn't wish to damage the spine. It was quite expensive. A first edition."

"Yes, I recall *well* your reluctance to risk anything, especially where the finer things are concerned. You do so adore all that society offers as well as your place in it."

It sounded like an accusation, but what, exactly, was he accusing her of?

"Is there something you wish to discuss with me, Lord Kilmaire? For I would have you speak plainly instead of with innuendo I cannot make sense of."

"We have nothing to discuss, not now or ever." The scar darkened until it resembled a crimson bolt of lightning shooting across his cheek. A hint of Irish had entered his words, a sure sign that Lord Kilmaire did not have a firm grip on his emotions.

'You belong to me, Colin Hartley.'

'Yes. All of my days."

Miranda felt as if she were suffocating under the force of her emotions. How could that have been a lie? In addition to lovers, Colin had been Miranda's best friend. The person she was closest to in the world. They'd gone to museums and lectures. Bookstores. Walks in the park. And now he wanted nothing to do with her. Perhaps he feared that Miranda would suddenly cry ruination to her brother, though it was a bit late for that.

Miranda was appalled to realize she was close to tears.

"In case you are concerned, I would never remotely insinuate that we once bore each other any affection, especially to Sutton. It is not something I wish to admit to."

Looking into her lap, she blinked rapidly to stay the tears that threatened to spill. She was clutching Lord Thurston so tightly she was likely damaging the leather. Anger at his rejection warred with the pain she felt. He wished never to discuss the past, so be it.

"Miranda."

Did she imagine the longing with which he whispered her name?

Whatever he had been about to say was cut short by the appearance of a lanky, ginger-haired lad, dressed in the Cambourne livery, swinging open the drawing room door.

"Lady Cambourne," Harry, her grandmother's personal footman announced as he made a short bow. Turning slightly, he held out his arm to lend his assistance to the elderly woman behind him, her cane thumping as she made her way into the room.

4

Well, it appears I've interrupted something.

Donata Reynolds, Dowager Marchioness of Cambourne, held tightly to young Harry's arm, her other hand firmly grasping the head of her cane as she moved forward. A burst of impulsiveness led her to instruct Bevins to put Lord Kilmaire in her private sitting room instead of the more formal drawing room. Miranda often hid herself here on rainy days to read.

Inspiration had a way of striking when least expected.

Only someone who was completely obtuse, and Donata was far from obtuse, would miss the tightly controlled manner in which Lord Kilmaire treated her granddaughter. It had not always been so. Colin Hartley was nearly a member of the Cambourne family, having spent many summers at Gray Covington. Miranda had lavished her childhood affection on Colin, calling him her prince and stating rather firmly that she would marry him one day. The two had been close. The older Colin growing ever more protective of the much younger Miranda, whom he viewed as a younger sibling. Many years later, when Colin visited the Cambourne family in

London during the time of Miranda's debut, Colin squired Miranda about and the two formed a friendship of sorts.

Well, perhaps more than a friendship, she suspected.

Lord Kilmaire's arrival over a month ago was very welcome by the Cambourne family, with one exception. Miranda. Now the two kept their distance from one another. No one seemed to notice. Except Donata.

Odd. Colin and Miranda had suddenly become *averse* to each other.

Curious.

Add to that the fact that Miranda had never looked at Colin with anything but adoration since she was eight years old, and the whole of it was quite mysterious.

Or was it?

The air in the drawing room fairly crackled with tension between the two. Good Lord if she lit a match the entire room might burst into flames.

Lord Kilmaire, coldly polite and distant, so different from the Colin that Donata once doted upon, viewed her granddaughter with longing in the depth of his eyes. He was angry as well. Pained. The scar, that horrible reminder of his Mother's hatred, shone dark pink across the left side of his face.

Miranda resembled a wounded doe. Defiant, she clutched a book to her stomach so forcefully Donata worried she would tear the leather.

"Lord Kilmaire," Donata smiled in greeting as Colin stood and bowed over her proffered hand.

"Lady Cambourne." The ends of his hair brushed pleasurably against Donata's arm.

What a beautiful man Colin was. He'd always been handsome, of course, even as a lad he'd turned a lady's head. Unfortunately, she sensed that there was nothing left of the boy he'd once been, nor the earnest young man who'd visited her son, Robert, in this very house.

Easy to blame the scar, of course. The wound was dreadful, there was no getting around it, but it did not detract from Colin's masculine beauty. She rather thought it kept him from being too beautiful. Women still admired him. The tragedy of his family would certainly lend one to be rather dour, but Donata sensed that was not the reason for his manner, though she did wish he would stop dressing as if he were in mourning. Thomas, his final family member, had been dead for nearly two years. Although, Donata had to admit, the dark colors accentuated his coloring and gave Colin an air of melancholy that few women could resist.

"It is a pleasure to see you." A hint of Irish graced Colin's words. Purposefully, she thought. While he normally sought to suppress the accent, he'd learned early on that women in particular, adored the sound of it.

So, the scamp seeks to charm me.

And Colin was *exceedingly* charming when he *wished* to be. Had he wished to charm the ladies of the *ton*, he certainly could. He just didn't wish to.

"I did wonder, Lord Kilmaire, when you would decide to grace me with your presence."

"I received your note only this morning, Lady Cambourne. I came as soon as I was bid."

Donata raised a brow. She disliked having to summon people. They should anticipate that she requested their presence.

"Poor of you to make me chase you down, Lord Kilmaire. You asked for my assistance at His Grace's wedding. I would have thought the request would have prompted you to call on me much earlier. After all, His Grace has been married for some time now."

A lazy smile crossed Colin's lips. "I have been trying to reacquaint myself with society, as you suggested. It has been a challenging adjustment."

Donata pursed her lips in rebuke. "Doubtful. I know you've been invited to any number of homes and balls, and are now a member at White's. At any rate, I spent last night considering your choices. We have much work to do."

And, indeed Donata *had* been thinking of Colin last night.

One of the curses of old age was not sleeping well, or in her case, sometimes not at all. Last night, even after reading a particularly boring treatise on Greek architecture borrowed from Sutton, Donata found sleep eluded her. Believing a glass of sherry would help, Donata decided to rise and fetch herself one. No reason to summon the maid at such an unreasonable hour. She slowly made her way to her grandson's study, once her son's study. The room comforted her and so she thought to take her repast there.

Unfortunately, there was not a drop of sherry in her grandson's study, so instead Donata opted for a small snifter of brandy.

Lord Kilmaire, approaching her just after the Duke of Dunbar's wedding, had tasked Donata with finding him a wealthy, suitable bride. There was little time left in the Season, and Lord Kilmaire wished to marry as soon as possible. The wealthier the better.

Donata did not judge him for his haste. She knew what a muck of things his parents made of Runshaw Park. So, as she sipped her brandy, Donata pondered potential brides for Lord Kilmaire. Her mind drifted to the lackluster pair of men who were pursuing Miranda. She'd always found it strange that Miranda had not married after her first Season, after all she'd been most sought after. Even stranger that Robert, Donata's son, had not insisted his daughter marry. Miranda was rather a bookish sort and still was, which put many gentlemen off, no matter her beauty or her dowry. She was always asking to be taken to the museum, or a lecture, rather than the opera. With Robert often busy and Sutton having run off to Macao,

Miranda had been escorted to various intellectual offerings by her brother's dear friend, Colin Hartley, who had been visiting London at the time. Colin dined so often at Cambourne House that Donata joked it was as if he lived there.

The truth struck her so forcefully at that moment that she dribbled brandy down the front of her dressing gown. *Right in front of me, and I couldn't see it.*

The press of Colin's hand on her arm as he assisted her to the couch brought Donata's mind back from the previous night's discovery. "I was concerned, Lord Kilmaire, that the poor weather would dissuade you from calling upon me, no matter my summons." She watched in appreciation as his large form slid into a nearby chair.

"Perish the thought, Lady Cambourne. A bit of rain would never keep me away from your company."

Again, the lilt came up in his words and Donata allowed herself to enjoy his gentle flirtatious manner. She did *adore* Colin. Her eyes lingered over the scar on the left side of his face. How could such a thing have occurred? To be attacked by one's own mother? Lady Rose Kilmaire had been an unbalanced woman, prone to flights of fancy. She'd once been found wading about in a fountain during Lady Meuring's garden party. At the time, Lady Kilmaire claimed her feet were too warm in her shoes and the goldfish darting around the fountain wished to play with her toes.

The woman was completely mad, though Donata never thought she would injure her own child. *Never*.

It was one of the rare times Donata had misjudged someone.

"Good afternoon Granddaughter. The day is so lacking light I didn't see you lolling about my favorite couch."

"Good afternoon, Grandmother." Miranda appeared ready to flee at any moment, her distress evident, reminding one of a trapped bird waiting rather impatiently for a cat to pass by.

Donata raised a brow at the tea stains on Miranda's bodice, the overturned tray, and the spilled bits of raisin cake on the floor. A crumb was caught in the dark locks of Miranda's hair. "It appears that you've had an accident of sorts. I do hope you didn't stain my couch, though happily it appears most of the tea landed on you."

"I was startled and—"

Donata turned from her, giving Miranda no time to excuse herself from the room.

"I've taken to heart your very specific needs, Lord Kilmaire and given the whole of it *very* careful consideration. It's a bit late in the Season, of course, but that will likely only make things easier in some respect."

A small choke sounded from Miranda.

"I appreciate your efforts, Lady Cambourne."

"You *should*. I am known far and wide for my matchmaking skills."

Another sound emanated from Miranda. It sounded as if she were being strangled.

"Why, did you know that a steady stream of young ladies and their mothers consult with me on a regular basis? My opinion is relied upon in these matters."

"Grandmother, please excuse me as it appears you and Lord Kilmaire have business to discuss." Miranda stood, frowning as several crumbs rolled down her dress to dot the carpet around her stocking feet. She bent and reached for her discarded slippers.

"Nonsense, Miranda. Do sit. I feel certain you can be of assistance to Lord Kilmaire as well." Donata winked at Colin. "After all, *who* better? I feel she owes you."

A small thump sounded as Miranda sat back down forcefully against the couch cushions. The slippers slid from her hands. "I—"

"I am not aware of any debt that Lady Miranda may have incurred." Colin's gaze, the color of molten chocolate, wandered over Miranda, following the path of an errant curl moving against her bodice. He seemed oddly fascinated by it.

"Do you not recall, Lord Kilmaire, how Miranda used to trot after you at Gray Covington? It was good of you to indulge her. After all, she could be quite a nuisance. You were so kind to her, chattering little sprite that she was. Do you not remember when she made you a crown? Declared you her prince?"

Miranda was beginning to turn an alarming shade of red.

"I believe her adoration was not for me but for the pastries I stole for her from the cook at Gray Covington, my lady."

Donata ignored him. "And, I do recall, during her own first Season, when you offered your assistance in escorting her about to the Royal Museum in order to view," Donata fluttered her hand, "something *ancient* when no one else offered."

"A mummy." Colin murmured.

Miranda blinked, clutching the book she held tighter.

"How *kind*. I believe you endured a boring lecture or two as well."

Donata leaned over her cane and leaned towards Colin. "No doubt you refused many more interesting invitations in order to squire Miranda about. Now it is her turn to offer *you,* assistance. High time. After all it is a debt many years in the making." Donata put her finger to her lip as if she couldn't quite remember, which of course was ridiculous. She remembered everything. "Three years does seem to go by in the blink of an eye."

"Six." Colin's gaze never moved from Miranda and that dangling curl. "Begging your pardon, Lady Cambourne."

Was there a hint of anguish in his answer?

Miranda squared her shoulders and turned away, suddenly absorbed by the rain pelting the Cambourne garden.

Donata nodded and gripped the head of her cane. "My word, so long ago? I'm afraid that's one of the failings of old age, the days and months roll into one another so quickly. Of course, my own debut feels as if it were just yesterday. My father, the Duke of Shefford, sought to marry me off at the beginning of the Season, before I'd even enjoyed myself. But my mother wouldn't have it." She winked at Colin. "Oh, how I danced. The drawing room of our house on Mayfield Square was full to bursting with my suitors. As a duke's daughter I had my pick, of course. The Marquess of Cambourne pressed his suit most forcefully and the match was advantageous. A duke's daughter and the owner of an ancient title like Cambourne. Two powerful houses combined. Such are the makings of a successful marriage."

Lord Kilmaire shot her a look of what one could politely call resignation. "Your assistance is deeply appreciated, Lady Cambourne. With all that has happened—"

"Yes. You've stayed away from your duty for far too long, Lord Kilmaire. First brooding at your kin's house in Ireland ... "

"Not brooding. Uncle Gerald took me in after a disagreement with my father."

"Slaving away like a common day laborer."

"Since I expected never to inherit, I thought it best to learn a trade."

"Sheep farming." She could not keep the distaste from the words. The thought of this handsome earl before her shoveling sheep dung was beyond her comprehension.

"Farming is an honorable profession."

"Humph. An earl does not work with his hands. He has tenants which do such for him."

"I was not the earl at the time."

She did not care a whit for his impudence. "You've spent these last few years rattling around Runshaw Park, alone except for a handful of servants. You should be here, with us, in London. Especially now that Sutton is thankfully home from Macao. And furthermore—"

"I am here now, Lady Cambourne."

"Cease your interruptions. I am speaking."

Clutching the head of her cane, she stomped it against the Persian carpet beneath her feet. Canes were a wonderful accessory as one grew older. Useful in a variety of ways.

The golden head dipped in acknowledgement of her rebuke.

"As I was saying, it cannot be considered healthy, Lord Kilmaire. Constantly *brooding*, your family's unfortunate circumstances notwithstanding, of course."

The dark eyes narrowed, but he did not refute her claim.

"I am pleased to see that you *do* seem to have perked up a bit since your arrival in town, for which I am much relieved, though it would be preferable if you would cease to dress as if you are still in mourning. I find the whole of it," she waved her cane to his somber attire, "somewhat *macabre*. Most young ladies of my acquaintance would prefer to marry a man who is not dressed as if he were attending a funeral."

"I prefer dark colors. I suppose I've grown used to them over the last several years, but I will take your advice under consideration."

"As you should. One would think you enjoy being referred to as the Cursed Earl."

"It is no worse than some of the other odious nicknames the *ton* likes to bestow upon those whom they gossip about."

Donata frowned at the thinly veiled reference to her grandson's undesirable nickname. "No one refers to Sutton as such anymore." At least, not within Donata's hearing.

"As you will, Lady Cambourne."

"Humph." The cane pounded on the floor again. "You should wear blue." She waved the cane towards the edge of his left eye where the scar took root. "That healed quite well. Better than I anticipated." She leaned forward. "I think it makes you look quite dashing. Don't you, Miranda?"

Miranda turned back from her perusal of the rain-soaked garden but stayed silent.

"And you should smile more often, Lord Kilmaire. In fact, I insist upon it. There is no point in looking dour. You wouldn't wish to scare away a potential bride."

"I find that I smile often in your presence, Lady Cambourne. If I may say so." The lilt this time was much more pronounced.

Donata's heart fluttered. Even a woman as ancient as herself was not immune to the teasing of a handsome gentlemen.

"You may say." Her fingers curled in the air, then settled over the head of her cane once more. The maids at Gray Covington ogled her grandson, Sutton, but it was Colin who they would allow to steal a kiss.

"Harry," she said gently to the young footman hovering over her, "would you have tea brought? Make sure there are some of those delicious raisin cakes my granddaughter adores. And send someone to clean up." She waved to the contents of Miranda's spilled tray. "There's been a bit of an accident."

"Yes, my lady." Harry bowed and went to do her bidding.

Donata found Harry to be such a good lad. So devoted.

Miranda looked at Harry's departing back. "If you'll both excuse me, I am rather tea soaked and—"

"Nonsense, Miranda. There's only a bit of tea on you. Perhaps a raisin caught in your hair. Lord Kilmaire is in dire need of your assistance." Donata looked towards Colin.

His nostrils flared slightly, but he nodded tersely in agreement. "Of course."

Donata smiled. "Just so. So much has changed since your last visit to London, sadly before all the," she struggled to find the right word to convey the respect for all that Colin had endured, "*troubles* visited upon your family. I'm sure you find the city much changed. It's astounding to me that eight years has flown by so quickly."

"*Six*, Lady Cambourne. Six years." His gaze once more settled on Miranda with startling intensity.

Miranda appeared oblivious to his attention.

In Donata's experience, gentlemen did not typically remember with such clarity the exact passing of time, especially as it related to something mundane. Like the debut of your friend's younger sister. Unless, of course, there was something more.

"My word, of course you're correct." Donata smiled. "I keep forgetting." She raised a brow and gave a pointed look to the tome clutched on Miranda's lap. "Do you approve of such reading material for young ladies, Lord Kilmaire? Lord Thurston! Miranda seems obsessed with this series of books though I cannot imagine being interested in such...*drivel*. A peer turned pirate by circumstance, as if any man of good birth would do such a thing. Miranda is filling her head with nonsense."

Miranda shot her a look that could best be described as *hostile*.

"You do not approve of the Lord Thurston novels?" Colin asked with a mischievous twinkle in his dark eyes, as if he was amused by her diatribe.

"Not in the least." Donata shook her head. "Filling the heads of impressionable young ladies with outlandish romantic notions is irresponsible."

"I'm given to understand that Lord Thurston and his

adventures are all the rage amongst the ladies of the *ton*. I visited Lord Bumont's box at the opera, and I overheard Lady Bumont professing her adoration."

"The fact that Lord Thurston is *fashionable* does not mean one should read such," Donata hesitated to make her point, "*tripe*. And Lady Bumont is a featherwit." Donata could not think of anything less entertaining that reading about pirates. "Young ladies *especially* should not read such things. It gives them unrealistic romantic notions."

"You've read Lord Thurston, my lady?" Colin mused, one finger pressed against his lip.

"Good heavens, *no*. I'm certain there is nothing in those books that would interest me. I'm much more partial to poetry." Her dear friend Lady St. Claire, in a shocking display of disobedience to her husband, had purchased one of the tomes from a bookstore on Bond Street. She'd been regaling Donata with the shocking details ever since. "Poetry is much more suited to a lady."

Miranda flicked a raisin off her lap. "I think I'm rather old to have you monitor my reading material, Grandmother. Alex reads Lord Thurston as well. She adores the books."

"Humph." Donata's eyes watched as another raisin made it to the floor. Now it was time to truly set her snare.

"Enough of Lord Thurston. We've much more important matters to discuss." She bestowed a wide smile on Colin. "Lord Kilmaire has asked my assistance in finding the future Countess of Kilmaire. And since you are like a sister to him," she let the words hang in the air, "I feel certain that your opinions of the young ladies I've selected could be crucial. Isn't that so, Lord Kilmaire?"

Colin's light mood fled, and his handsome face contorted into displeasure. He appeared as if facing a firing squad. "Yes. Of course."

Miranda pressed a hand to her stomach. Possibly the

pastries she'd eaten earlier were about to join the collection of raisins on the floor.

Splendid.

Now that Donata was certain of her assumptions concerning Colin and Miranda, she refused to acknowledge the flood of guilt that filled her at the look on Miranda's face.

Time was of the essence. How could Donata allow Miranda to marry either one of the gentlemen vying for Miranda's hand now that the truth was sitting across from Donata in the form of the Earl of Kilmaire? And, Colin who was notoriously stubborn, would never seek Miranda out of his own accord. He would marry a woman he didn't want just to prove a point.

"Miranda?" Donata thumped her cane.

"I am happy to help in any way I can, of course." Her normally dulcet tones were brittle. "As you say, Lord Kilmaire has been like a *brother* to me."

Colin's face pinked, his nostrils flaring slightly at Miranda's words. The pads of his fingers pressed into the fabric of the chair. "Then we are in agreement."

Oh my.

The two glared at each other with such intimate intensity that Donata nearly excused herself from the room. The air between them was filled with a very real animal attraction laced with years of anger. It had been years since she'd seen such a display of emotion. They'd completely forgotten her presence.

Donata cleared her throat. "Now see what I have for you, Lord Kilmaire." She held up an embossed piece of her own personal stationary.

Two pairs of eyes flew to the creamy paper in her hand.

"Let us proceed, Lady Cambourne." The broad shoulders shrugged carelessly as Colin retreated, hiding behind those walls he'd built around himself. An icy blast of indifference chilled Donata.

"I sense your lack of appreciation for my efforts Lord Kilmaire." The cane poked Colin in the calf. "How else are you to find a *suitable and wealthy* bride?"

Miranda's body went rigid. She sat back against the cushions and attempted to look uninterested.

"Unfortunate tragedies and the madness of your mother," Donata shot Colin a look of sympathy, "will not aid you in your search."

"Perhaps I am mad as well. Is that the assumption?" Colin rubbed his chin in thought. "Mayhap I shall pass it on to any future children?"

Donata pursed her lips and gave a short nod. "And, I do not count myself impolite for pointing out that being half Irish ..."

"I thought we had agreed when I asked for your assistance that I was only one quarter Irish." Dryness laced his words. "Although the Irish is of the mad variety and I'm barely considered a Papist these days. I've not been inside a church since Thomas died."

"One quarter, one half, what does it matter? You would do well to hide the bit that slips into your words at times, for while it is charming, it reminds the *ton* that you've lived more in Ireland than at Runshaw Park. You are an English earl. Pray do remember such."

Colin shot her a rather frightening look. He did not care to be reminded that his upbringing served as a disadvantage in London and nearly everywhere else.

Donata did not scare easily. Good Lord if the Devil of Dunbar in a foul temper didn't put her off, there was little the Cursed Earl could do to frighten her.

"Now, if you are quite done interrupting me?" She stomped her cane this time more forcefully.

"I am." The words were crisp and coldly patrician. One would never know that Colin had ever set foot in Ireland. The upper-class accent was perfect.

"Good. I have narrowed it down to several girls based on your requirements. However, I feel the first two names are your best chance for expediency."

Donata dangled the bit of stationery before Miranda's nose like a carrot before a mule. "See if you agree with my assessments."

Miranda took the paper between her fingertips, holding it as if it were a poison snake. Carefully, she placed Lord Thurston beside her on the couch, all of her attention on Donata's list. Scanning the page, her eyes widened before looking up at Donata.

"Lady Helen—"

Donata snatched back the list before Miranda could finish her sentence. Settling herself more comfortably, she produced a pair of spectacles from a pocket hidden in the folds of her gown. Perching the glasses on the end of her nose, she shook the paper.

"I agree Miranda, Lady Helen *is* an *excellent* choice. She's very beautiful. Stunning, really. This is her first Season, but I understand Lord Cottingham is eager to see his daughter married as soon as possible."

"What is the urgency to see her married?" Colin said in a bored tone, eyes cast down as he pretended to brush a spec of lint from his trousers.

Donata cocked her head, not surprised to see Colin glance at Miranda from beneath his lashes.

"There are several reasons. Lord Cottingham recently inherited the title, no more than two years ago. He was formerly a dairy farmer, albeit a very prosperous one. Perhaps you can discuss the finer points of cow and sheep farming with him." Donata tried to keep the note of distaste from her words. "At any rate, Lord and Lady Cottingham seek a title for their only child."

"And?" Colin shot her a skeptical look. "I'm sure there's more."

"Don't be impertinent." Donata pushed the end of her cane against the toe of Colin's boot. "Lady Helen is a bit long in the tooth for a girl in her first Season. Most of the more *discriminating* families are not enamored of Lady Helen. Her pedigree—"

"She's considered coarse. Forward. Ill-mannered," Miranda interrupted gleefully. "Overindulged."

"Well, she is an only child, dear. And, she did not have the benefits of a refined upbringing as you did. She is quite lovely."

"With an odd fascination for birds," Miranda snapped back.

"Baron Masters," Donata interrupted Miranda's tirade of the unsuitability of Lady Helen, "as well as several other young gentlemen in much more dire financial straits then you, are sniffing around Lady Helen, no doubt smelling blood in the water. Lady Cottingham is ambitious. She wishes her daughter to be a countess. Lady Cottingham is much too practical to believe in curses, and considering her own lineage, she is not concerned with your Irish blood. Her dowry is twenty-five thousand pounds."

It would have to be, Donata surmised uncharitably. The girl was spoiled with an appalling lack of discretion. The Cottingham's sense of urgency was due to the fact that their daughter had the makings of a spectacular scandal and would ruin herself if she wasn't wed soon. Baron Masters had been the frontrunner for Lady Helen's hand, until Lord Kilmaire arrived in London.

"She sounds...*adequate*. Who is the other?"

"Miss Margaret Lainscott. A lovely girl. Considered a bit

plain and more intelligent than she should be. As wealthy as Lady Helen, she is the sole heir to father's fortune. Tin mining, I believe. Poor man died during a cave in. Since that time, she's lived with her aunt."

"You can't be serious, Grandmother." Miranda piped up.

"I am. She is the daughter of a miner, a mark against her that only a very large dowry could overlook, and of course, marrying a title." She paused for a moment. "Lady Dobson is determined that Margaret marry as high as possible."

Lord Kilmaire pinched his nose between his fingers as if striving for patience.

A wisp of a vengeful smile lingered on Miranda's lips.

Before Donata could continue, a scratch at the door announced the arrival of Bevins with the tea cart. The butler rolled in the cart, laden with a steaming pot of tea and an assortment of finger sandwiches, scones, and biscuits. Bevins leaned heavily against the cart, using the device to hold himself upright as he moved into the room.

Donata was of a mind to stand up and wheel the cart in herself. Bevins did not have the strength of a kitten and was exhausting himself in London. She really must speak to Sutton about Bevins. It was well past time for the butler to retire, but he refused all offers to spend his remaining years at Gray Covington where he would be comfortable.

Donata suspected it had something to do with Gray Covington's butler, Zander. Although she couldn't imagine how the two men even knew each other.

A maid followed behind Bevins and curtsied to the room before approaching Miranda's overturned tea tray. Silently, she bent to her task, shooting Colin curious looks while she worked. Appreciation shown from the maid's eyes as her glance ran discreetly over the Earl of Kilmaire.

Dipping again in a small curtsy, she left the room with Miranda's tray.

"Shall I pour, Lady Cambourne?" Bevins trembled as he spoke.

Dear God, they would be here all afternoon if Bevins poured, or worse. She doubted he could be trusted to hold the teapot steady. "No, Bevins, that will be all."

The elderly servant bowed, straightening himself carefully before turning toward the door. Donata watched patiently as he shuffled across the carpet, nearly tangling his feet in the deep pile of the rug before taking a firm grip on the knob.

A discreet click sounded as the heavy mahoghany closed.

Donata breathed a sigh of relief at the butler's exit. "Now, where was I? Oh, yes, Lady Dobson's niece."

"Lady Cambourne, the girl's aunt is Lady Dobson? She is —" Colin started.

Donata cut him off with a wave of her hand. "*Wealthy*. I know well that Lady Dobson has her faults. Too many for me to recite at one sitting. I am witness to them every time she calls on me. You would learn to tolerate Lady Dobson, for goodness sake. I have. There are times when I actually enjoy her company and you shall too."

Enjoy was perhaps rather strong, but Lady Dobson was *useful*.

A snort of disbelief came from the couch.

"She is a reigning matron of the *ton*," Donata continued, ignoring Miranda's rudeness. "Regardless of her past *errors* in judgement, Lady Dobson has many useful connections and could be instrumental in paving your path through society. Besides, you would be marrying Miss Lainscott, not her aunt."

Colin's gaze searched the room, probably looking for something stronger than tea. Donata wasn't surprised. The mere mention of the woman invoked fear and distaste in most everyone who knew of her.

"Are those my only choices?"

"Expediency, I believe, was one of your directives, Lord Kilmaire. Wealth, the other. We are at the end of the Season. The Cottinghams and Lady Dobson could both marry their girls to a lesser title but then you, an *earl*, fell into their laps. Lady Dobson is quite desperate, practically salivating at the thought of marrying you to her niece. I've never seen Lady Dobson exhibit joy. It was a sight I do not care to witness again. Quite alarming."

Miranda poured a cup of tea for Donata and placed it on the table. "I did not realize she exhibited any emotion other than malice." Miranda was not shy in expressing her distaste.

"Yes. Why she even tried to embrace me at Lady Hastings fete last week." Donata reached for her tea.

"Whatever for?" Miranda appeared to have regained control of her emotions. She no longer looked so despondent. She poured and handed Colin his tea.

Elegant fingers deliberately brushed against Miranda's as he took the cup.

The air fairly crackled about the two.

Donata pretended not to notice.

"I suppose it was because of the invitation to Gray Covington. She was quite beside herself at being a guest of the Marquess of Cambourne." Donata gave a dramatic pause to allow that tidbit to sink in. "I assured her it was simply a little house party. Nothing to set herself in such a state. Only an opportunity for Miss Lainscott to better acquaint herself with Lord Kilmaire. Of course, I neglected to inform her that the Cottinghams would be attending as well. It's always better not to allow Lady Dobson the upper hand."

The pot of tea hovered over Miranda's cup. "There's to be a house party? At Gray Covington?"

Oh dear. She did hope Miranda didn't spill the tea and cause another mess.

Colin placed his cup and saucer on the table without

touching the steaming liquid. "You should not go to such lengths just for me, Lady Cambourne."

"Oh," Donata laughed lightly, "not just for you, my *dear* Lord Kilmaire. But also for my granddaughter."

A stricken look on her face, Miranda set down the teapot unsteadily, nearly upending the plate of scones.

"Have a care with the tea service, Miranda." Donata flashed a brilliant smile at Colin. "In addition to the Cottinghams and Lady Dobson, I've taken the liberty of inviting Lord Ridley and Lord Hamill."

The color leached from Miranda's face.

"I'm sure Sutton's told you, Lord Kilmaire, that Miranda must make a choice herself. A house party is the perfect opportunity for either one of her gentlemen to press his suit. Miranda is determined to marry. It will be a difficult decision, I'm sure."

That wasn't true in the *least*. Ridley and Hamill were both idiots and equally unworthy of Miranda.

"Indeed." Colin sounded as if someone had just punched him and he couldn't breathe.

"I believe Lord Welles will also be in attendance along with Lord Carstairs." Well, Donata told herself, the two men would certainly be in the vicinity of Gray Covington and she thought Sutton would likely invite Welles to stay a night or two, though there was no danger of Welles deciding to court Miranda. He was a notorious rake with no interest in marriage.

"You remember Welles, don't you? From Eton? Handsome devil and still unattached."

"I should look forward to seeing Welles again." Colin didn't sound pleased at all.

"I knew Lord Carstair's mother, Lady Diana." Donata continued. "A great beauty in her day. The most startling eyes. Such an odd shade of blue, almost violet. You may have met

Lord Carstairs at the gathering hosted by Lord and Lady Marsh. I'm told Lady Marsh has settled on the sister of Lord Carstairs as a wife for her son, Rowan. The girl's name is Gwendolyn."

Donata bestowed upon Colin a benevolent smile as she imparted the information. Lady Diana had indeed been beautiful, but empty-headed, lacking in personality and had an annoying habit of tilting her head in such a way that she always looked confused. Her son had not fared much better. She doubted he was capable of carrying on a conversation in any remotely intelligent fashion. Certainly Lord Carstairs would not be in competition for Miranda's hand, though Colin need not know that.

Miranda took a raisin cake and began to systematically tear the pastry into tiny bits, carefully placing the raisins to one side of her plate.

"Malden has never mentioned Lady Gwendolyn to me. I wonder that he knows of his mother's plans for his future."

Donata frowned. "Lady Gwendolyn is an excellent choice." She didn't really believe that. The girl was as dull as her brother. "What a delightful coincidence that you and Miranda will both marry soon." Donata's voice raised an octave in delight. "It shall be quite the celebration! Perhaps we should hold *both* ceremonies at once." She clapped her hands.

Oh, that last bit was terrible of her. *Truly*.

"We shall leave for Gray Covington the day after tomorrow. Oh, how I adore house parties."

Miranda's torture of the raisin cake ceased abruptly. A loose raisin rolled off the plate.

Donata would need to ask Bevins to make sure the maids searched the couch for stray raisins.

"Sutton has asked that you escort us in the Cambourne coach, Lord Kilmaire."

Actually, Sutton had asked no such thing, as he was as yet unaware that he and Alex were *hosting* the house party at Gray Covington. Her grandson would be less than enthusiastic. His dislike of Lady Dobson was only rivaled by his dislike for Lord Ridley. Upon meeting the Cottinghams, Sutton would likely detest them as well.

"Nothing would give me greater pleasure." Colin's dark gaze slid to Miranda and the tortured raisin cake.

"We shall enjoy your escort." Donata dipped her head in acknowledgement of his offer, though she was certain if Colin could find a way to politely refuse he would have.

Miranda stood suddenly, clutching Lord Thurston to her breast as if it would protect her from the horror of the upcoming house party. "Please excuse me, but I must prepare for our journey."

Before Donata could say stay her, Miranda turned and fled the room, slippers in one hand, Lord Thurston in the other, her skirts fluttering madly about her ankles as if running from the Devil himself. Or a Cursed Earl. It appeared they might be one in the same.

Colin stood and gave a small bow. "Good day, Lady Miranda," he said as Miranda retreated. Something raw flickered in his face when his gaze lingered on her fleeing form. Hunger and longing.

Donata leaned back in her chair, satisfied. She no longer had any doubts as to the true nature of the Earl of Kilmaire's feelings. Donata felt certain Colin would never act on his emotions unless forced to. Intervention was necessary.

Colin stood for several moments, his attention focused on the open doorway. Abruptly he turned, his features carefully composed, all sign of emotion stricken from his handsome face.

"I thank you for your assistance and discretion in this

matter, Lady Cambourne. I'm sure this will result in a most suitable match."

Donata wished to reply that she had already found him a most suitable match, but she did not. Instead, she raised her cup of tea to her lips, all the better to hide her satisfaction that her intuition had been correct.

"You shall call on us two days hence for the trip to Gray Covington."

Colin bowed. "Until then, my lady. I'll see myself out. No need to call for Bevins.

Just as well, for it would take Bevins an agonizing amount of time to return and show Colin the door.

"Good day, Lord Kilmaire."

At the sound of the front door closing behind Colin, Donata poured a bit of milk into her tea and allowed herself a moment to gloat. She rarely gloated. It was unseemly, although in this instance she felt justified.

Sutton constantly chastised Donata for interfering in the lives of others but had she *not* meddled in Sutton's relationship, Alex could very well be married to that vile cur, Archie Runyon.

At the mere thought of Archibald Runyon, gooseflesh rose across Donata's forearms and the tea went bitter in her mouth. His foul legacy still permeated the lives of the Cambourne family, even though the man was dead. Thankfully. All because Miranda had learned to shoot and with deadly accuracy.

A lump formed in her throat, the words choking her as she spoke aloud to the empty room. "And yet I could not save Elizabeth from that monster."

The hand holding the teacup shook, rattling the fine porcelain against the saucer. She had not seen her youngest granddaughter for many years, not since Elizabeth was a child. Not since the death of her son, Robert.

Elizabeth had been sent far from London. To a place where given time, she would heal. A place where monsters like Archie Runyon did not exist. A convent in Scotland, on a small estate owned by the Duke of Dunbar. Elizabeth's safety was assured. She would never have to see Archie or her mother, Jeanette Runyon Reynolds, again.

"Bitch." Donata shocked herself by cursing out loud. Something she rarely did. Certainty grew within her that Jeanette had a hand in Miranda's current unhappiness. Not the unsuitability, of course, but the obvious unhappiness between Colin and Miranda. This entire affair reeked of Jeanette's machinations.

I should have had Robert send that viper he married away long before she could hurt Miranda and Elizabeth. I should never have allowed Jeanette to create such turmoil that I took myself on a tour of the continent and abandoned them to her treachery.

She took another sip of her tea, allowing the pain to linger and flow through her veins as she thought of her son, Robert, dead now nearly five years. Her eyes welled with tears and she blinked, trying to hold them back. Now was not the time to dwell on that harpy, Jeanette, a woman who destroyed everything and everyone she touched.

Six years ago, Colin Hartley had been the third son of the Earl of Kilmaire. Handsome, charming, with an air of melancholy that attracted women like moths to a flame. And poor. Not a farthing to his name. Nor hope for a title. Certainly not worthy of marrying the daughter of a marquess.

Jeanette's ambition was legendary. Miranda was only a tool to be used by her mother to make a splendid match, one that would further Jeanette in society. Colin Hartley would not have been that match. Had Jeanette witnessed the growing affection between the two and decided to make sure it didn't blossom?

"I am not," Donata said softly to herself, "about to allow

that vile creature to win." She set down her tea cup. There was much to do and little time to do it.

"Harry!" She called over her shoulder, knowing the ginger-haired footman likely stood just outside the room.

"My lady?" Harry's bright red hair popped thru the doorway.

"Will you bring me pen and paper along with my small writing desk?"

"Yes, my lady."

"And Harry. Do you recall that matter we discussed earlier? It appears that I was correct in my assumptions." She often confided her schemes to Harry, who was a more than willing accomplice. The boy was very dear to her, and she considered him to be more son to her than servant.

"Of course, my lady. You are rarely ever wrong."

Donata heard the pride in Harry's voice and smiled at it. "Very rarely."

Lord Ridley. As if she would allow her granddaughter to marry that money-grubbing dandy. Lord Hamill? Ancient. Infirm. Completely unacceptable.

A knock sounded at the door, followed by the reappearance of Harry holding a portable writing desk and ink.

"Thank you, Harry." She winked at him.

"If I may be so bold."

"You may, Harry."

"What are you about, Lady Cambourne?"

Donata chuckled as she opened the writing desk, pulling out ink, pen and several embossed pieces of her private stationery. Taking up the quill, she began to scratch away, hastily producing a letter which she sealed and handed to Harry.

"Deliver this to Gray Covington, directly into the hands of the Marchioness. And please relay to her my apologies for the late notice." She hoped that Alex would forgive her. It *was* for the best of reasons, after all. No one wished to have Lord Ridley in the family, and Sutton would never forgive Colin if he married Lady Dobson's niece.

"At once, Lady Cambourne."

"And hurry back, Harry. We've a house party to plan. Invitations to be sent." No one would refuse her. She was the Dowager Marchioness of Cambourne.

The Cottinghams and Lady Dobson would likely beat Donata to Gray Covington in their haste to visit. Ridley would immediately draw a line of credit at that gaming Hell he frequented, telling everyone he'd soon be married to the Marquess of Cambourne's sister.

"Ha!" Donata bit off a piece of her scone. "They shall all be disappointed. *Very* disappointed."

5

CAMBOURNE HOUSE 1830

"Lord Cambourne has been detained, Mr. Hartley. Would you prefer to wait in the drawing room or perhaps the gardens?"

The Cambourne's butler, a large, thin man who walked as if he had a stick up his bum moved towards the stairs and waited for Colin to respond. For the life of him, Colin couldn't remember the man's name, and the butler did not offer it, even though Colin had dined at Cambourne House at least four times in the last two weeks.

"The gardens I think."

The day was bright without a hint of the dull, gray haze that usually colored the London sky. How anyone could live in a place where the sun rarely appeared mystified Colin. Trapped as he had been the last few months amongst the tall, smog-stained buildings and constant hum of thousands of people, he longed for the pure air of Ireland and Estervale. It felt as if he were slowly suffocating in London.

In truth, he could leave London if he wished to.

I don't wish to.

Instead, Colin took the lease on a small but cozy set of rooms in a neighborhood peopled with shopkeepers and tradesmen. The partnership with Lord Wently was proving profitable and for the first time in his life, Colin had a bit of money in his pocket. Lord Wently assured him that more would be forthcoming.

Viscount Lindley was appalled at Colin's accommodations. Repulsed might be a better word. The area, Nick claimed, was unfashionable. *Tawdry*. Colin didn't even have a decent valet. And why, Nick questioned even though he surely knew the answer, did Colin insist on staying in London?

The butler strode towards a pair of French doors. "This way, Mr. Hartley."

The house was still and quiet as Colin made his way inside, only the sound of his boots against the marble floor broke the silence.

A pair of maids came around the corner, bobbing in greeting as they passed, giggling softly into their hands as he smiled at them.

The butler halted slightly, brow raised in disapproval at the two women, and they scurried off, but not before shooting Colin another appreciative glance.

Bevers? Basin? He struggled to remember the butler's name as the man lead him down the hall. The butler was a particular favorite of Miranda.

Ah, *Miranda*.

Just the thought of her shot a bolt of lust through him. He'd seen her only briefly last night at the ball hosted by the Earl and Countess of Braeburn. Sipping a horrible French wine, he'd never taken his eyes off her silk clad form as she spun about the dance floor with a young man Colin later learned was Lord St. Remy. St. Remy, Lady Cambourne had cheerfully informed Colin as she passed him on her way to the refreshment table, was the heir to the Duke of Langford. Colin's eyes had lovingly traced every generous curve, wishing desperately it was his hands touching her waist instead of Lord St. Remy. Or any of the other overly pedigreed twits in the room , for Miranda was rarely without a partner.

She had probably danced until the wee hours and was still abed.

God. Miranda in bed. Preferably, his bed. He could see her in his mind's eye, reclining back against a mountain of fluffy white pillows, her ebony locks trickling down her shoulders in wild disarray. He imagined lying next to her lush form. His fingers tugging at the silken bow on her chemise. The knot and the fabric would part to reveal her glorious breasts. He would—

"*Mr. Hartley?*" The butler raised a brow as Colin missed a step and nearly toppled a vase of moonlight roses.

Christ, this was madness.

Colin tried desperately to conjure up an image of Miranda as she had been, a chubby annoying child, with dirt on the hem of her dress as she chased frogs in the stream. But it was no use. All he could think of was the kiss they'd shared at the Dunbar Ball. The way Miranda's body had curved into his. The way she breathed his name.

Nick, you miserable bastard. You sent Miranda to me. Deliberately.

Lord Cambourne had asked him to dine the previous night, and he'd only been able to smile stupidly at Miranda from across the table.

Miranda, for her part, never gave any indication that they'd shared a kiss. Or, that she'd allowed Colin to run his hands over her body.

Colin could still feel the swell of her breasts beneath his hand.

When she spoke, in the absurd circling way she favored, Miranda had the most endearing habit of using her hands, almost as if they were props in whatever story she related.

He couldn't take his eyes off those lovely, slender hands. All he could think of was peeling back her gloves to see the swath of skin at her wrist. For Miranda's fingers to slide down the length of his chest to the waistband of his trousers, touch the buttons—

He stumbled again, and this time Bevins sniffed the air, as if trying to ascertain whether Colin had been drinking.

The butler stopped at the end of the hall, swinging open a pair of French doors.

The smell of flowers and wet earth met Colin's nostrils and he took a deep breath of the familiar aroma.

Bevins shot him a suspicious look. He'd probably count the silver once Colin left.

Nodding politely to the butler, Colin stepped onto the flagstone path and made his way into the gorgeous gardens of Cambourne House.

Stopping before a large rosebush, Colin attempted to think of something else besides the desire to bed Miranda. If he cleared his mind perhaps the raging erection straining against his trousers would abate. This was madness, this obsession with Miranda. It could not end well.

He took a deep breath, focusing on a yellow butterfly flitting around the rose buds. The butterfly, as beautiful as it was, had once been nothing more than a plump, annoying caterpillar before undergoing a metamorphosis, much like Miranda.

"Bloody butterfly," he hissed, taking out his annoyance on the insect.

"Are you cursing at the butterfly, Mr. Hartley? Whatever has it done to you?"

Anticipation coursed through him, and his heart thudded almost painfully in his chest.

Miranda.

Damn it.

They had not been alone in each other's company since the Dunbar Ball. If he visited her father, Miranda was a wisp of silk that floated by the study doors. She would greet him warmly, as one did a friend of the family. At a ball or fete, the few that Colin attended, Miranda was always surrounded by admirers, her mother hovering nearby to ensure the suitability of the gentlemen who paid her daughter court.

Colin was not considered even remotely suitable.

He turned towards her voice and found Miranda no more than ten feet from him, hidden beneath the branches of a willow tree. She was sitting on a worn patchwork blanket, her bonnet tossed to the side, a large book propped up on a pillow next to her. The title was stamped in gold across the front and on the spine - *Ancient Embalming Techniques of the Egyptians.* A small tray in front of her held slices of apple and several raisin cakes.

Colin's heart seemed to lift out of his chest to race towards her.

"Good Morning, Lady Miranda." He bowed slightly, begging his lower body to not tighten anew at the sight of her.

An impish smiled crossed her lips in greeting.

She looked impossibly beautiful. A thick braid of inky black hung over her shoulder, tiny wisps curling about her temples. She wore a simple muslin gown covered with embroidered flowers. The sheen of grass stains dotted her skirts, probably from laying out the blanket.

Or catching frogs.

Her deep green eyes sparkled in the late morning sun as she looked up at him.

"Good Morning, Mr. Hartley. What brings you to my garden? I'm sure it's not just to curse at the butterflies."

Miranda's skin was luminous, with the glow of a fresh peach. Her cheekbones were dappled with light and shadow where the sunlight filtered down through the leaves above her head. Bees hummed and buzzed through the roses in the garden and several birds fluttered off at his approach.

Colin imagined this was what heaven would be like, at least *his* version of heaven.

"I had an appointment with Lord Cambourne this morning, but he's been detained. I thought to await him in the gardens, it being such a beautiful day. I hope I am not disturbing you."

"Oh, yes. That mysterious project my father is assisting you with. The one he won't discuss with *me*." Miranda pouted a bit but her eyes sparkled. "Perhaps you'll tell me one day."

It was oddly gratifying to know she'd inquired.

"Not mysterious. It has not yet come to fruition though, and so I don't wish to make more of it than I should." Colin liked the thought of telling Miranda, she who'd adored his stories at Gray Covington. "If it does, I promise to let you in on my secret."

"I find myself incredibly intrigued, Mr. Hartley. I should adore being part of your project."

She already was, though she didn't realize it.

Miranda patted a spot on the blanket in invitation. "Sit with me. Father was called to his solicitor's. He'll be gone for a bit, I imagine. Mr. Chartwick, though a delightful man, can be quite talkative." She giggled. "Oh, I suppose that's the pot calling the kettle black isn't it?"

Christ, I want her.

"I should probably come back and return at a more convenient time." He looked toward the house.

"Don't worry. Mother has taken off to spend the day shopping, probably for a more spectacular gown than my own to wear to Lady Allister's ball next week." A rueful smile crossed her lips. "One would think it's her first Season and not mine." A note of rancor laced her words.

"Just for a moment, then." He walked over, folding himself into a sitting position on the blanket across from her. Taking off his hat, he tossed it next to her bonnet. The sun was warm and welcoming on his head.

The tail of the ribbon tied around her braid fluttered briefly in the breeze, bouncing off her bodice. He watched, entranced at the way each breath she took pushed the tops of her breasts up. To distract himself, he pretended to study the title of her book.

"Embalming techniques?"

She shrugged, and he could see she was embarrassed. Hastily, she put the book aside and covered it with her bonnet. "I suppose it's a bit peculiar."

He reached over and pushed her bonnet aside. "How often do you have the opportunity to discuss the ancient Egyptians at a ball? Between dances?"

"Stop. Now you're just making fun of me." She flushed a delightful pink and pushed her bonnet back on top of the book. "I know I'm odd."

"No. Not odd." His voice softened. "*Unique*. Think how boring the world would be if we were all the same. The only thing I do find odd, Lady Miranda, is that there is no one handy to practice embalming on. I do worry for some of your admirers. And I understand it's an unpleasant business. Don't they pull the brain out through the nose with knitting needles? Wouldn't that create a mess if one is wearing a ball gown?" He could smell the scents of lavender and honey wafting from her hair.

She laughed, low and throaty, and a tremor of longing ran through Colin. Miranda was undoubtedly beautiful, though she had none of the artifice that beautiful women generally had. She seemed not to realize the effect she had on the male species, or at the very least, did not allow it to define her.

"It is incredibly messy. Though," she continued excitedly, "the Egyptians did not have knitting needles. It was a rather long hook they shoved up the deceased's nose." She made an odd motion with her hands and his eyes followed the movement. Then a priest would move the needle about, mushing things up before pulling out the bits." Her eyes widened to see if he was appropriately shocked. "I would *definitely* ruin my gown."

"Do go on." God, he wanted to touch her.

"I find it all quite fascinating. After they removed the brain, they would then make a small incision on the left side," her hands brushed the spot just underneath her breasts and Colin's breath caught, "to remove the other organs like the intestines and liver. They put them out to dry once they removed everything. Rather like making jerky. Do you know about jerky? I read something about the Americas and the natives there, Indians they are called. At any rate the Indians dry their meat in such a way, well really, they hang bits of it on a drying rack, and they call it jerky." She shook her head, "I must apologize, Mr. Hartley, at times my thoughts wander. Mother says I'm a true featherwit as I cannot seem to hold together a conversation."

"I disagree, Lady Miranda. Continue." Lady Cambourne was a bitch who likely had never opened a book.

Miranda bestowed on him a dazzling smile.

"At any rate, I find the Egyptian version of the afterlife to be so colorful, if not a bit barbaric at times. They would sacrifice a person's household with them, to serve them in the afterlife. I'm certain that Bevins would have an issue with that, his loyalty to my family notwithstanding."

Colin couldn't take his eyes off of her. "I'm certain of it."

"My favorite is Anubis. Egyptian god, that is. Lady Sinclair has a statue of him that her husband purchased from an antiquities dealer. Most everyone finds the statue quite frightening, though I rather like it."

Miranda's lips were a delightful shade of red, reminiscent of a late summer raspberry.

"Anubis was the god of the underworld. Didn't he have the head of a dog?"

"A jackal. Which I suppose is a bit like a dog. At any rate, whenever mother begins to remind me of my unladylike behavior, I slowly work embalming into our conversation. Or tell her about scarab beetles eating the mummies flesh away." She leaned towards Colin, giving him a breathtaking view of the valley between her breasts. "It's rather...*gruesome*."

"I never realized how bloodthirsty you were, Lady Miranda. Had I known, I would have taken greater care at Gray Covington. I'm not sure I would have allowed you to bait your own fish hook. Although in retrospect, you did seem delighted at the time by the poor worm's suffering."

Colin wanted to kiss her. Touch the braid of her hair.

A very bad idea.

"Well." A pink blush rose over her cheeks and she frowned, a worried look coming over her lovely face. She stopped speaking. Always an unusual occurrence with Miranda and always directly reflective of something troubling her. Idly she toyed with the strings of her bonnet.

"I suppose you should just go ahead and do it." She nibbled a bit at her lower lip.

"Do...what?" This was torturous and unfair. He wished to be nibbling at her lower lip.

A small non-committal shrug caused her breasts to move deliciously beneath the muslin. "Don't make me say it. I'm quite embarrassed." She plucked at her bonnet again. "It's all rather awkward isn't it?"

"I'm not sure," he tore his gaze from her plump lower lip, "exactly what you mean."

"Oh, very well, Colin." Miranda dropped all pretense at formality with the use of his Christian name. An anguished look crossed her lovely face and she gave a great dramatic sigh. "You wish to apologize. For your behavior at the Dunbar Ball. For kissing me. There I've said it, and I'm horribly embarrassed. It was rather poor of you to make me say such a thing."

"Hmm." He could see the flecks of gold in her eyes.

"You didn't know it was me or you never would have done so. Kiss me, I mean."

"Possibly." That was partially true. He would have taken greater care and not pounced on her like a madman, but Colin thought he still would have kissed her. The attraction to her was like nothing he'd ever felt in his life.

"You likely thought I was an..." she struggled to find the right word and her forehead wrinkled, "an *associate* of Nick's."

"That's a rather polite way of putting things." He leaned in, inhaling deeply of the lavender and honey smell that wafted off her skin. "Nick did mention he was going to introduce me to a nice widow."

Miranda's face fell. "I knew it. You would have never-" Her hands waved, and she looked at him, unable to say what she wished. The color of her cheeks deepened to dark rose.

"Kissed you." God, she was adorable. All flustered and pink. Reading books on how to create a mummy and torturing her harridan of a mother with tales of flesh-eating beetles. The night of the Dunbar Ball he was sure he could not have wanted her more. He'd been wrong about that.

Very wrong.

"Yes, how horrified you must have been," she said, biting her lip again. "Fat little Miranda, who you had to steal raisin cakes for because her mother wouldn't allow her dessert."

"I wasn't horrified. You were chubby."

"Irritating and annoying."

"Persistent." Did she still think of herself in such a way? Looking at the regret in her lovely face, he thought she did.

"You are no longer that little girl," he said quietly. "Do not think of yourself as such. Yes, you were a bit," he gave her a soft smile, "annoying. But only because you were so intelligent. You still are. Intelligent, I mean. You cannot allow your mother to dictate who you are. I know that better than anyone."

She lay her hand on his and the touch of her skin warmed him as nothing else ever had.

"That is something we have in common, I think."

Light filled in the hollow places of Colin's soul at her touch, like the sunlight that streamed through the tree branches above their heads. Her words sent ripples of pleasure through his body.

"You were so kind to me when I was a child." A wry smile crossed her lips. "I think I may have even made you a paper crown because you were my prince. Demanded that you marry me." Shaking her head and waving her hands she said, "I should be apologizing to you. I'm so sorry I tricked you into kissing me."

"Tricked me?" He curled his hand around so that that their fingers touched.

Miranda's eyes darkened a shade, "I should have introduced myself immediately. I let you think I was someone else. It's just that you looked at me as if I were . . ." She shook her head in agitation.

"As if you were what?"

The sun flickered across her features, and her voice lowered, "You will find me ridiculous and forward I'm sure, but...I *wanted you* to kiss me, Colin. I can apologize but I am not sorry. I know that you probably regret the entire episode."

Miranda was so adorably luscious, pattering on, her fingers keeping up with her words as if she were conducting an orchestra. Surely, no man had been tempted so much. Leaning over, he brushed his lips against hers, in a brief caress, reveling in the softness of her mouth.

And to stop her chattering.

A small, blissful gasp left her lips. Her hands floated up to flatten against his chest as she bent towards him until he could feel the press of her breasts.

"Colin." It was an invitation.

He truly kissed her then, slanting his mouth over hers. He braced his hands on either side of her, afraid that if he touched Miranda he would combust. Urging her to respond, Colin teased her lower lip, imploring her to surrender to him, to open her mouth.

She tasted of tea and honey with just a bit of tart lemon.

Miranda moaned into his mouth as his tongue touched hers. Her fingers closed over the lapels of his coat, pulling him towards her as she fell back against the blanket.

Colin fell against her, adjusting so that his body was adjacent to hers, the generous curves of her body fitting into the hardness of his.

"Ouch." Miranda giggled against his mouth.

Without breaking the kiss, Colin reached behind her and tossed aside *Embalming Techniques of the Ancient Egyptians*.

"I always preferred the Greeks."

Miranda wrapped her arms around his neck, mimicking the movement of his mouth against hers. Tentatively she nipped his lower lip, sucking the bruised flesh into her mouth.

A low growl sounded in his throat. "Miranda." His voice was hoarse and heavy.

"Colin," she whispered against his mouth, "did I do that wrong? I thought that was – well you did it to me. Am I not supposed to? It's just so...*marvelous*. So much better than the dry peck on the cheek I've seen some men bestow upon a woman. Do not think I'm some green girl because I have had a kiss stolen before and—"

He took her mouth again, cutting her off, firmly and possessively. Trailing his lips from the side of her mouth to her jaw, he made his way up the slender column of her neck, marveling at the feel of her skin.

"Oh, my." She sounded blissful. "Do you feel that?"

He felt a great many things, most of which he wouldn't repeat. "What?" He nipped at the sensitive skin beneath her ear.

Miranda immediately arched against him.

"Tell me." He busied himself tracing the inside of her ear with his tongue. She made the most delightful little noises.

"When you work a puzzle, sometimes it will take days or even weeks to find the two pieces that fit together properly. Because they were made *exactly* to fit *only* each other. The pieces make a lovely clicking sound when they snap into place, so you know they fit."

Miranda took his hand in hers. The green of her eyes was the same color as the grass surrounding the blanket on which they lay.

"*The pieces fit exactly*. No other piece will do, you see."

Yes. He did see, because Colin felt the connection as well.

He pressed his forehead to hers cupping one side of her head, loving the heat of her skin beneath his fingertips. How was it possible to want something so badly but be terrified all the same?

Nick's widow friend did not exist. Of that, Colin was positive. It was rather annoying for Nick to be right once again.

"So, you do not regret kissing me," she said softly, her breath wafting against his cheek.

"Miranda, there are many things I've done, and have yet to do that I may regret. But kissing you is not one of them."

"That is a good thing, Colin, for I don't wish you to brood about it."

"I do not brood."

"You do. You have for as long as I've known you, which is half my life. Just please, do not brood over kissing me. Or anything else." Her voice lowered seductively.

"I do not brood." He whispered before he kissed her again.

6

CAMBOURNE HOUSE 1836

"Well that," Colin muttered as he dodged the rain and hastened to his waiting carriage, "was bloody awful." Frowning, he thumped back against the worn leather squabs, inhaling the familiar smell of old leather and poverty.

Tapping on the roof of the carriage he ordered curtly, "Momsby and Partners." Immediately regretting his ill humor, Colin nearly apologized to the poor man sitting atop his coach in the pouring rain. But an earl did not apologize. And God help him, he *was* the Earl of Kilmaire.

The carriage creaked forward slowly, its springs so worn that Colin imagined he could feel every cobblestone. At least the horses were of good quality, his father having spent what was left in the Hartley coffers at Tattersalls. Whatever else you might say about the deceased Earl of Kilmaire, and there was quite a bit to say, he had known his horseflesh.

Colin's finger itched at the grooved, puckered flesh that bisected his face. Miranda had appeared unmoved as she had examined it earlier. An unspoken question appeared in her eyes, but that was all.

"It doesn't matter any longer," he whispered to the moldering coach. The scar did not, but some things did. Miranda, for one.

I still want her.

Time had not healed the wound of losing Miranda. He doubted it ever would. How foolish he had been to think he could see her again and feel nothing.

"Bloody Hell."

His hand automatically went to his pocket, feeling the familiar weight of his grandmother's claddagh ring. His talisman. The ring had been in his pocket for years, so much a part of his wardrobe that he sometimes forgot he carried it. He hadn't consciously taken the ring from Runshaw Park when he left for London. Nor did he recall slipping it into his pocket as he left to call on the Dowager. Yet, here it was.

The claddagh, if the wearer committed oneself, was worn upside down on the ring finger. The Irish used the clauddagh as a token of betrothal. A promise.

Who gave Grandmother Cecily the clauddagh?

His grandparent's marriage was for land and dowry, not love, though the pair got on well enough. After Colin's grandfather died, Cecily took to wearing it around her neck, sometimes worrying it between her fingers while she looked at something only she could see. *Love*, she'd once told Colin before she passed away, *was a rare gift, one worth all the jewels and gold in the world*. The clauddagh disappeared after her death and Colin assumed she'd been buried with it, but then the ring appeared at Runshaw Park.

Uncle Gerald likely sent it to Colin's mother as a remembrance.

The heirloom languished at Runshaw Park for many years, put away in a velvet box Colin's mother kept in the library.

Not valuable in a monetary sense, Colin's father never bothered to try to sell it.

Sometimes he would take out the ring, wondering who gifted his grandmother with such a token, for it certainly hadn't been his grandfather. When his father sold the library, the ring was discovered behind a stack of books on horse breeding.

He'd given the ring to the only woman he would ever love.

Six years was not enough time to make the bitterness and anger fade.

The ring arrived with the letter. As he lay in a haze of pain and shock after his mother's attack with the left side of his face nothing but a mass of blood and bits of flesh, he'd eagerly opened the letter, desperate for Miranda, and the ring fell out. He would have stormed to London even with his face bleeding and in shreds, demanding she see him if it hadn't been for that ring.

'I've decided to accept the suit of Lord St. Remy.'

He shut his eyes against the words, as if he were reading Miranda's words for the first time today and not six years ago. Every word, every curlicue and flourish of her handwriting was ingrained in his mind.

The letter stayed in his pocket nestled against the ring for many years, to keep him from leaping atop a horse and riding to London. When he longed for Miranda, usually after the demands of Runshaw Park and his solitude caused him to drink a large quantity of whiskey, Colin would rub his fingers over the battered gold of the ring. He would re-read the words written across the creamy vellum of Miranda's stationary. Cursing her in the darkness, he would want her, wishing she were not her mother's daughter after all.

One day the letter simply fell apart in his hands, crumbling into so much dust.

The carriage rolled to a stop outside of a red brick building, lights glowing like beacons against the storm. The horses stamped their feet as the coachman swung down to open the door.

Colin pulled out the ring, rubbing the burnished gold between his fingers. The metal felt as though it were alive, warm from the heat of his body.

"My lord?" His coachman stood with an umbrella, rain dripping off of him as he waited for Colin to exit.

Taking a deep breath, Colin shook his head free of his imaginings. Stepping lightly to avoid a puddle he nodded to his coachman. "I'll be only a short while."

Why hadn't she married St. Remy?

The question haunted him. On his return to London, he expected to find her a duchess, secure of her place in society. A woman who decided to chose title and security over Colin's poverty and love.

How easy it would have been to continue to hate that woman.

Instead, he found Miranda a spinster, an unheard of state for the sister of a Marquess. Nearly on the shelf. Still lovely, but with a sadness in her eyes that bespoke of regret. He wanted to ask Cam, or even better, Nick, why Miranda hadn't married, but there hadn't seemed to be the right time. Had St. Remy broken the betrothal? That would explain the vague whispers he'd heard of Miranda's unsuitability, most of which he'd ignored until today. Unfair or not, the woman was usually blamed for a broken engagement and suffered the results of such. The thought of her humiliation did not make him as happy as it should have.

Momsby and Sons bustled with activity, even with the weather outside. A clerk approached Colin immediately and took his hat and coat, shaking the rain from the garments.

"Lord Kilmaire to see Mr. Momsby."

"Yes, my lord. The Elder or the Younger?" Momsby had

two sons, one still away at school and the other who worked alongside his father at the establishment that bore their name.

"The Younger, if you please."

"Of course, my lord. I'll have tea brought, it's quite a frightful day, is it not?"

"Frightful indeed."

※

MIRANDA FLOUNCED INTO A PAISLEY OVERSTUFFED CHAIR and pulled her shawl tighter around her shoulders. Thunder continued to boom outside as night began to fall. She said a silent prayer that the rain would continue for days, enough to muck up the roads to Gray Covington so that the ridiculous house party would be cancelled.

She had no wish to watch Colin court his future countess.

While Miranda considered herself to be fortunate in a great many things, she did not think her current plight would receive divine intervention.

Impossible. Horrible. Awful.

"I could feign sickness." She pulled a loose thread of her shawl, watching in rapt attention as the entire corner began to unravel, the yarn curling and twisting on the chair like vines. "I certainly feel ill."

Colin Hartley. Her attraction to him, unfortunately for her, had not faded with time. She'd hoped that it would. Prayed fervently to forget Colin and everything she'd once desired.

Now he had come to London and she was forced to pretend that he never made promises to her, else risk her reputation. Such as it was. If she had one more scandal attached to her name even Lord Hamill would be forced to withdraw his pursuit.

A small statue, made of porcelain so fine it was nearly transparent, sat on the side table next to her. Sutton had brought her the gift. A figurine of a woman in a long flowing robe. Her brother called the garment a kimono. The sleeves of the garment were deep, hanging from the woman's arms to pool at her feet. She was twisted at the waist, one arm held up in supplication as if pleading.

"I rather feel as you do," she said to the tiny woman, "begging for someone to stop the unfortunate swirl of events I find myself in." Her head fell back against the chair. "The irony does not escape me that I happen to be the only heiress in all of London that Lord Kilmaire has no interest in. Not even for my dowry. I'm that unlikeable." A sniff escaped her. "It's difficult you see," she touched the tip of the woman's nose, "because I've loved Colin for such a long time."

She had no choice but to marry either Lord Hamill or Lord Ridley if she didn't wish to remain a spinster. Not that anyone was forcing her to wed. Sutton was very clear that he did not care if she married or not. But Miranda did. She wanted a family of her own.

"Ridley or Hamill. Either will suit me just fine." The woman stared open mouthed at Miranda. "Oh, very well. That's a lie. My attraction to either man lies in the fact that they wish to marry *me*, despite the scandal. I'm fortunate I have any suitors at all.

The tiny woman's gaze appeared accusatory. "I see you wish to judge me." Miranda turned the small figure so it faced away from her. "But just so you know, you don't look all that innocent yourself."

Arabella would know how best to handle the situation, but her best friend was miles away in Wales. She could confide in Alex, but Miranda wasn't at all certain that her sister-in-law wouldn't then tell Sutton.

"I wonder," she mused, pulling at the yarn again, "how

one looks a man in the eye after one has shared such intimacies. There are dozens of courtesans who do such every day when they change protectors. There must be a trick to it."

A knock at the door halted her thoughts

"Come." Probably Clara, her maid, with a supper tray. Miranda had declined to go down to dinner, preferring to take a tray in her room.

The thump of a cane sounded against the floor.

"I do not care to dine alone, Miranda."

Grandmother seems determined to vex me today. "Hello, Grandmother. My apologies I did not come down for dinner. I'm a bit tired and thought it best I take a tray in my room. I'm exhausted from all the preparations needed for your little house party."

"It seems there is little preparation going on, unless you consider the unraveling of your shawl to be such."

Miranda stuffed the shawl between the cushions of her chair.

"I thought you'd be packing, or at least your maid would be. Or someone's maid. Yours is a bit flighty I'm given to understand. I'm not certain why you insist on keeping her. I don't approve."

Miranda kept her precisely because Grandmother *didn't* approve. "She does lovely hair. And her name is Clara, Grandmother."

"She is untrustworthy. I see it in her eyes. Shifty. You should sack her immediately."

"I will take that under advisement."

The Dowager thumped her cane around a chair facing Miranda. "Are you ill? You don't appear to be for all that you looked a bit green earlier during Lord Kilmaire's visit. Did something disagree with you at tea?"

A great many things disagreed with Miranda, specifically

Grandmother assisting Colin in his hunt for a suitable heiress. "No, I'm fine, Grandmother."

The Dowager sat back in the chair, sighing with pleasure as she sank into the worn cushions. "I must confess, while I insisted you furnish your bedroom with finer furniture, you were correct in your assessment of these chairs. Quite comfortable, especially for these old bones." A smile crossed the Dowager's lips, at odds with the mercenary gleam in her green eyes. "Shall we discuss the house party?"

Why couldn't she have a less Machiavellian grandmother? She should like one who sits by the fire and knits instead of constantly plotting mischief. For Miranda was quite certain Grandmother was up to something. Something more than just an unwanted house party.

"I had been considering a visit to Arabella. I thought to leave next week." Miranda countered. "She's written and asked me to visit her in Wales. It's quite solitary there. She's bored."

"You wish to visit Arabella? In Wales? And incur Nick's displeasure? The girl needs to languish a bit more and contemplate her foolish decision in conspiring to have her brother's fiancé kidnapped. Of the many things Arabella has done out of spite, that was by far the worst."

"I'm sure Nick won't mind if I visit. He's very forgiving."

The Dowager gave a short bark of laughter. "Are we speaking of the same man?" "He'll welcome her back soon enough. She's his sister."

"Doubtful, granddaughter. He is very angry with Arabella, though he loves her dearly. Your desire to visit Wales will conflict with the house party we are hosting. That will never do." Grandmother raised a brow waiting for her response.

"I knew nothing about this house party, Grandmother." Miranda allowed her annoyance to show. "And to invite Lord Hamill and Lord Ridley without my knowledge was—"

"*Appropriate.*" The Dowager waved her hand. "I wish to help you secure a husband, now that you are determined to finally take one."

Doubtful. Grandmother detested Lord Ridley. She said his clothes caused her to have dizzy spells.

"And," Grandmother pursed her lips, "I wish to assist Lord Kilmaire, of course."

"Of course." Miranda's fingers dug down into the cushion until she found the loose end of the shawl and began to tug at it again.

"Well, let's have it. What do you think of my matchmaking skills?"

Miranda stopped tugging on the shawl. Perhaps it was the timbre of Grandmother's question or the way the light green eyes narrowed on Miranda, but she had the very distinct impression that her Grandmother *knew*. About Colin. All of it. Or at the very least *guessed*. And Miranda was just as certain that wasn't possible.

"I don't think, Grandmother, that my opinion will have any effect one way or another on the choice that Lord Kilmaire makes."

"Oh, I think your opinion will matter a great deal."

There it was again. That slight, knowing tone to her words. Grandmother might suspect that Miranda harbored feelings for Colin, but if she'd any idea that Miranda was no longer a maid, she would not be sitting so calmly in Miranda's bedroom.

She is like a hound who has scented a fox.

Besides, what did it matter if the Dowager suspected that Miranda had once carried a torch for Colin? Her childish adoration was well known in the Cambourne family. She'd made a complete goose of herself years ago as a child by making Colin a paper crown and presenting it to him during a dinner party.

A speculative look entered the Dowager's eyes. "Then let us discuss *your* suitors if you refuse to discuss my choices for Lord Kilmaire. I find *neither* appropriate. Nor does your brother. I fear he will strangle Ridley before you are wed a year. Possibly abscond with your viscount, to torture him in some macabre way learned from the Chinese. I'm told they are quite skilled in that regard."

"How bloodthirsty you must imagine Sutton to be. Strangulation? Torture? I'm rather more afraid of Alex."

"Your sister-in-law does not care for Ridley either."

"You both gave me leave to decide my own fate. Perhaps Ridley is my fate."

"And Lord Hamill is only a few years my junior, Miranda. We revolved in many of the same circles. His first wife made her debut shortly after I did, for goodness sakes."

"He's dignified."

"That is a kind way to announce that someone is elderly." The Dowager cocked her head. "Lady Hamill, God rest her soul, was a complete nitwit. Loved riding. I often saw her in Hyde Park. Did you know that's how she died? She loved riding so much that she insisted doing so in a torrential downpour. She caught a fever shortly after and was dead within a fortnight."

Grandmother, much like the Duke of Dunbar, knew *something* about nearly everyone in London. At times the information proved to be useful. At the moment, Miranda found it a bit grating. "How unfortunate."

"Ridley," Grandmother continued, speaking as if she'd just bitten into a peach pit, "is beyond the pale."

"Why? He's a viscount, he's young, handsome, and educated." Ridley had once dazzled Miranda, making her momentarily forget Colin. His allure had not lasted, unfortunately, though Miranda still thought he'd make an acceptable husband.

"Dandy. Fortune hunter. Treats you as if you don't have a brain in your head. Will likely keep a mistress." Grandmother ticked off his undesirable traits on her fingers.

"Grandmother!" Miranda pretended to be outraged by the assumption Ridley would keep a mistress, though it was likely to be true. The fact bothered Miranda not a bit. She had no illusions about Ridley. He would get her money and in return she would have a family of her own. Ridley would not ask anything of Miranda as long as she produced an heir and dangled on his arm prettily when required.

"Well, it's true."

"If they are both so disagreeable then why invite them to Gray Covington? Why mention such to Lord Kilmaire?"

Grandmother's eyes slid away to look into the fire.

She *was* up to something.

"As you say," Grandmother replied, "we have given you leave to choose. Which is the reason for the house party. We should like the opportunity to know your suitors better, though I cannot imagine that anything Ridley will do could change my opinion of him. He'll likely wear something garish." Her lips pursed in distaste. "Though he is rather handsome. That *is* something."

The Dowager stood, one hand falling to her hip as she grasped her cane.

Miranda stood, reaching out automatically to assist her grandmother.

"Shoo. I've simply sat too long. My goodness, don't hover, Miranda."

Miranda flounced back to the chair. Grandmother did hate to be reminded of her infirmity.

Miranda's fingers found the end of the shawl again. "Marriage is a business contract, not a contract of the heart." Miranda's mother had often said such to her.

The Dowager pressed a kiss atop her head. "Your mother

is a foolish woman. You would do better to emulate your brother, if you can."

"Your own marriage was made in such a way, was it not? So are most marriages of the *ton*. I am only trying to be sensible."

Grandmother squeezed her shoulder. "I once thought so. Until I saw your own father choose affection rather than duty when he wed Madeline. His first marriage was for love. Convenience only came with your mother." She hobbled from the room, shutting the door quietly behind her.

Miranda sat for the longest time, her grandmother's words lingering in the air. Love. An overinflated emotion that caused young girls like herself to completely disregard their upbringing and fling themselves at melancholy half-Irish gentlemen. Or quarter-Irish.

She tasted the warm saltiness of her own tears and wondered exactly when she'd started crying. Probably six years ago. Just after Colin had left her.

7

The crowded streets of London rolled past the window of the Cambourne coach as Miranda, her grandmother, and the Earl of Kilmaire slowly made their way to Gray Covington. Miranda willed the coach to move faster through the crowded streets.

Trapped.

Trapped with the austere Earl of Kilmaire in close quarters for the remainder of the day. Since arriving to escort her and Grandmother, Colin had assumed a cold demeanor. She could be a stick of furniture or a dressmaker's dummy for all the attention Colin paid her. Unfortunately, while he seemed oblivious to her presence, it was difficult for Miranda to ignore him. Sprawled across the seat facing her Colin seemed to take up all the available space in the coach with his bloody long legs and broad shoulders."

And he's bloody ruining my joy at escaping to Gray Covington.

She sighed, clasping and unclasping her hands. Gray Covington was *home.* Not the Cambourne house in London. The estate outside London was Miranda's favorite place in the world. She longed for the peace that being at Gray

Covington brought her. Peace that had been in short supply since Colin had arrived in London.

Miranda had never been a typical debutante. Oh, she'd endured the multitude of fittings for new gowns, the constant shopping, the calls on various acquaintances every day. But it never made her happy. Rather, she mostly found herself wanting to scream for the absurdity of it.

All things being equal, she would always prefer the solitude of Gray Covington over everything that London had to offer.

The house itself was relatively new, having been built on the remains of the former manor house. As a young bride, the Dowager took one look at the outdated Tudor styled house and insisted immediately that something more modern be built.

One did not disappoint the Dowager, not even then.

The gray stone exterior was nearly hidden by the crawling ivy and wisteria that covered the walls, giving the impression of an overly large stone cottage. The gardens were enormous, winding about the grounds and filled with any manner of flowers and shrubs. The gardens were famous in London, for they contained a multitude of rare plants and were laid out in such a way that one never knew where the formal gardens ended and the rolling fields of Gray Covington took over.

The Gray Covington gardener, himself the descendent of the first gardener Grandmother had hired so long ago, was especially talented. Just before Miranda was born, the man teased a series of shrubs into topiaries. The topiaries were renowned among the *ton*, for the skill at which they were created and for the unusual animals they depicted. Three camels strode across the grass where a lion, a group of monkeys, and an elephant frolicked. As a child Miranda would climb inside those monkeys to hide from her mother's wrath. Which was quite often.

I wonder if I can still fit inside them? Probably not. How unfortunate.

Miranda stole a glance at the source of her mounting anxiety.

Did he have to be so attractive? It was rather disappointing that Colin had not grown fat. Or bald. Or *something*.

Silver now threaded through the golden wave of hair that fell to his shoulders, but the locks were still thick. Tiny lines were etched around his eyes, and the full curve

of his lips as if he frowned often. And Colin was larger, the leaner form he'd once had thicker, his shoulders broader.

Grandmother, the other source of Miranda's misery, snored softly on the leather seat beside her. Clutching a book of poetry in her gloved hands, the Dowager nodded off almost immediately after leaving Cambourne House and hadn't stirred since.

The coach hitched to the side, skimming the side of a rut in the road, and Miranda fell against the coach window.

A polished boot tip, attached to a long, lean, muscled leg, slid under Miranda's skirts as the coach rocked. The toe of that boot brushed intimately against her slipper, neatly trapping a swath of sprigged muslin skirts.

"Please remove your foot." She ignored the delicious tingle that ran up her leg at even this minor touch.

The boot slid deliberately *further* into her skirts, ignoring her command.

"How do you find Lady Helen?" Eyes the color of hot chocolate regarded her politely, as if they were engaged in discussing the weather and his foot wasn't lingering intimately against her ankle.

Spoiled. Selfish. With an odd fascination for birds. Except for her strange hobby she reminds me quite a bit of my mother.

Colin's fingers brushed down his thighs, graceful and strong. He'd removed his gloves the moment the coach lurched forward, and the discarded bits of leather sat at his side. A callous dotted one elegant forefinger that held just a shadow of ink, as if he'd been working on the accounts of Runshaw Park.

She loved his hands. They were capable of all manner of wicked things.

"Lady Helen is lovely, of course. Blonde and delicate." Heat was surging up her leg from the feel of his boot. "She's as rich as Grandmother says. Her dowry is obscene."

Colin's brow wrinkled at the mention of Lady Helen's dowry.

"There's no need to frown, Lord Kilmaire. I believe that was one of your requirements was it not? A large dowry?" She lifted a brow.

"It is." His eyes narrowed. "Please, do go on."

"Lady Helen has a huge admiration for birds. I believe she is quite enamored of our feathered friends and is an avid bird-watcher. You will find yourself with quite an education on the various species that inhabit the woods around Gray Covington. Given that her father was a dairy farmer before becoming an earl, I would rather have thought her obsession would be more of the bovine persuasion." She shrugged. "Her manners are a bit rough, but I'm sure that would not deter you from courting her."

The toe of his boot moved again, this time directly *between* her feet, or rather, her legs. Heat blossomed and rolled up the length of her body. If Colin chose to, he could easily trail his foot up her silk clad calf to the inside of her thigh. A bit of her skirt caught on the heel of his boot.

"Have a care, Lord Kilmaire. You'll ruin my dress." The words rolled off her tongue without thinking, sounding more like an invitation than the chastisement she meant it to be.

Heat flared between them. The dark gaze flickered over her breasts to trail down her stomach to her clasped hands.

Miranda's breath caught as her body responded to his gaze. Shamefully. *Wantonly*. Honey spooled between her legs and she shifted slightly, trying to assuage the sudden ache.

One side of his mouth lifted in a half-smile.

Damn him.

"I believe you've mentioned such a thing to me before." His voice lowered to a husky whisper.

Miranda spared a glance at her grandmother who continued to snore softly, oblivious to Colin's flirtation.

And he *was* flirting with her. Although she wasn't sure why. Two days ago, in her grandmother's sitting room, he'd been dreadful to her. *Brutal*.

"That was a long time ago." She paused pressing her lips together and watched as his gaze moved to her mouth. "Please, move your foot."

"Whatever happened to Lord St. Remy, I wonder?" His fingers drummed a bit on his thighs.

Why must he move his fingers in such a way. It brought to mind a great many other things, none of which were appropriate.

"You really should make more of an effort to wear gloves, Lord Kilmaire. You are no longer at Runshaw Park, but out in society." Miranda dipped her head towards his bare hands.

"I find I cannot grip things properly in gloves. Or," he said in a softly teasing tone, "touch things in a manner I wish."

A slight tremor ran through her. Oh, yes. She remembered very well the way his big hands cupped her breasts. This was a rather tortuous game he played with her. Delicious and arousing but with a hint of bottled anger.

"Will you answer me?" He said in a silky voice. "What became of St. Remy?"

St. Remy? Miranda blinked. *St. Remy.* She searched her

mind for the face of the man but found she could not. St. Remy was now the Duke of Langford. At her debut, Mother fancied a match between St. Remy and Miranda, but Miranda found him to be distasteful. He insulted Miranda for her love of books and declared, while they were dancing, that she would be a bore in other ways as well. The only one who seemed to truly like St. Remy was Miranda's mother.

"He is no longer Lord St. Remy, but the Duke of Langford."

"Yes, I'd forgotten he was the heir to a dukedom. And does he have a duchess?" His eyes narrowed, piercing her with an accusatory gaze.

"I've no idea." She hadn't thought of St. Remy, or rather, the Duke of Langford, in years. She supposed he'd married as every duke needed an heir, though why Colin would care, she didn't know. "I didn't realize you were acquainted."

A small snort came from Colin. "We are not."

"Then why this sudden interest in the Duke of Langford?"

Colin sat back against the squabs and drummed his fingers again, a rapid staccato that had her wanting to reach across the space between them and still his hand. He made as if to speak, then just as quickly pursed his lips as if he were fighting for control.

Miranda looked down, pointedly, at his boot, nudging it with the toe of her slipper. Then she attempted to pull her skirt free and found she couldn't. Not without tearing her dress.

The boot did not move.

"I rather prefer Miss Lainscott." Considering waves of heat were swirling up her legs Miranda thought she sounded rather calm. "She has a pleasant demeanor and a keen mind. Her dowry is far larger and Lady Dobson is in rather a rush to marry her off, though Miss Lainscott doesn't possess the same sense of urgency. I'm sure you could win her over with your *charm*."

Colin's mouth hardened, pulling the scar tight.

"And what of Lord Hamill? I'm told he is one of your most ardent suitors."

Ardent was not a word Miranda would use to describe Lord Hamill. The elderly lord's pursuit of Miranda was more a business negotiation than a courtship. Not that she minded terribly, for at least Lord Hamill was honest.

"He is well-regarded in Parliament and while he is a bit older than I—"

"You consider thirty years or more to be a bit?"

Miranda did not back down. "Lord Hamill's treatment of his first wife bodes well if I choose to marry him. He is a most suitable match. At any rate, I fail to see how my choice of husband is any of your business, Lord Kilmaire."

Lord Hamill's treatment of the former Lady Hamill *had* been cordial. Respectful. Their marriage was a partnership and they'd hosted countless dinners for the political elite of London. Miranda thought she'd enjoy playing hostess and involving herself in politics. Besides, Lord Hamill would allow no disparagement of Miranda's character. Once Miranda was his wife, no one would dare whisper about the possibility that she'd shot Archie Runyon. At least, she hoped that would be the case.

"Lord Hamill is not your concern."

"Old enough to be your father. Or is it your grandfather?" Colin gave her a carnal look, his implication clear. "I understand he wants an heir. Doesn't care for his sister's son, I believe. Tell me, Lady Miranda, have you taken *that* under consideration?"

An unwelcome flush crept into her cheeks. Of course, she'd considered it. She was still considering it. The biggest detriment to marrying Lord Hamill would be the actual *bedding* of Lord Hamill. He'd been very clear. While he would certainly appreciate her assistance with his political aspirations, Lord Hamill's main reason for marrying Miranda was that he wished an heir.

"My relationship with Lord Hamill is none of your concern, Lord Kilmaire. I find this conversation to be completely inappropriate."

"As someone who is *as a sister to me*," the words rolled off his tongue sarcastically, "my only wish is for you to be happy."

"Yes, your concern for my welfare is glaringly apparent. I am comforted by it," she snapped back.

"Tell me about Lord Ridley, then. I'm just curious, you see, to have you tell me what appeals to you about either man. What attributes Lord Ridley has that make him more appealing to you than say, Lord St. Remy." The scar darkened a bit across his cheek.

"The Duke of Langford," she automatically corrected, watching in satisfaction as his nostrils flared.

"If you will."

"What is *your* interest in the Duke of Langford? I do not understand the direction of your conversation. You seem unable to speak plainly to me, Lord Kilmaire."

The sharp planes of his face contorted into a mask of utter fury at her response. He looked as if he were about to commit murder.

"I think you know."

"I haven't the slightest idea." And she didn't. Not in the least. "Perhaps you'll enlighten me?"

The fingers drummed again.

She raised a brow and waited. When he didn't respond, Miranda continued.

"So I'm to guess at your motives. Well, I've no interest in doing such. So, let's move on shall we, to your question about Lord Ridley. Lord Ridley and I have been acquainted for several years. He is a viscount, with a lovely estate in Surrey."

Ridley was attractive with impeccable manners. He was a bit of a dandy and tended to dress somewhat flamboyantly but he insisted on being fashionable. Ridley could also be a bit pompous, but he did find Miranda lovely.

He *also* found Miranda to be a bit of a chatterbox. And since he openly equated chattering with a lack of intelligence, he mostly behaved as if Miranda could not grasp simple concepts. If she were honest, Ridley probably found her dowry as attractive as Miranda herself was, though she cared not to examine that last bit too closely.

A knowing smile crossed the firm lines of his mouth. "He's managed to gamble away most of his inheritance, I'm told. The duns are beating at his door. Ridley is looking for an heiress."

"Then you and he have much in common, Lord Kilmaire," Miranda snapped back, stung at being reminded that Ridley did not want her for herself.

The scar tightened down the length of Colin's face at her retort. His hands curled into fists on top of his thighs. A savage, freezing look shot from him.

Miranda didn't care. Not a bit.

"Surely, Lord Kilmaire, my brother has relayed the reason why I have a rather *limited* field of suitors. Good God, the entire *ton* is rife with gossip concerning the *incident*. One would have to be deaf and dumb," she gave him a pointed look, "not to have learned about it." Leaning forward, she peered at him across the coach, no longer interested whether or not she woke her grandmother. "You speak in riddles. You accuse and glare at me as if I were guilty of some offense." Miranda had spent several sleepless nights trying to determine the source of Colin's anger towards her. If he thought she would tell Sutton, or anyone, of their previous affection for each other, he was mistaken. Perhaps he assumed she sought to ruin his chances with Lady Helen out of spite. Absurd. Her humiliation was so acute she had difficulty evening admitting to her childish adoration for him. "Do you fear that I would inform my brother of our previous relationship and thus put your relationship with him at risk? Or are you worried I would try to hinder your pursuit of either Lady Helen or Miss Lainscott out of malice?" She gave a short bark of laughter. "Out of nothing more than a regrettable indiscretion? I'm certain I am not the only woman to have experienced such. Besides, I would not wish to harm my own chances of a suitable match. Well not completely, she thought Ridley would likely marry her regardless.

A combative look came over his face. "A regrettable indiscretion?. As you wish."

"No matter your feelings for me, Lord Kilmaire, I am *still* the sister of the Marquess of Cambourne, a powerful man and your friend. My father went out of his way years ago to assist you in some foolish venture."

"I owe your father much. And, it was not foolish."

"I don't care what it was. Likely it was the only reason you *lingered* at Cambourne House so long ago. There was certainly no other compelling reason for you to lurk around London for so long. You've made your feelings on that matter abundantly clear."

Miranda shrank back against the squabs and moved her feet to the wall of the coach, not even wincing as she heard the small sound of her skirts tearing where it caught on his boot.

"I will thank you not to insult me or plague me further with your veiled accusations. I can attend any event in London if I wish to be insulted and provoked. I'll not endure it in the shelter of my family's coach." She shut her eyes, no longer wanting to look at his beautiful, damaged face. Was he so devoid of feeling for her that he found enjoyment in tormenting her?

"Miranda." The low growl vibrated in the air of the coach. His elegant fingers fluttered against her knee.

She pulled back violently from his touch.

"Leave me be, Lord Kilmaire. I assure you, I am not your concern."

Clasping her hands tightly in her lap, she turned her attention to the passing countryside, forcing herself to focus on the beauty of the rolling hills. Gray Covington was a large estate. She could avoid Colin until this ill-advised house party was over. She had to, else she might not survive it.

8

CAMBOURNE HOUSE 1830

Miranda giggled in the darkness, the sound echoing down the parquet floor hallway. She should be more careful, but the only witnesses to her laughter were the marbles that littered the hallway of her family's London town home. Surely, the bust of a former Roman general would not complain.

Mother often traveled abroad to Italy to visit her cousin, Mr. Runyon who lived in Tuscany. Whenever she was gone, various works of art, pottery, sculpture and the like, would arrive on the doorstep of Cambourne House. Sometimes Mother was gone for months.

Father didn't mind when Mother traveled, in fact Miranda thought he was relieved, although he detested Cousin Archie. In fact, her father barely tolerated her mother. Sutton hadn't cared for Cousin Archie either.

A small ache crossed her heart. She desperately missed Sutton.

Mother's Marbles, as Miranda liked to call the statues of

Roman gods, and the odd bust of a bewigged gentleman, were exquisite though. Guests to Cambourne House raved about their beauty. Unfortunately, the statues held more warmth than Mother herself did.

Miranda halted her thoughts of her mother and smiled up into the face she loved most in the world. Colin Hartley. She adored him. Worshipped him like the Romans did the statues sprinkled around the hallway. Colin rivaled the beauty of the marbles. The candlelight lovingly caressed the sculpted planes of his beautiful face, while his eyes, the color of a burnt piece of toffee cake that Cook once made for Miranda's birthday, roamed over her in appreciation.

He caught her around the waist, pressing her up against a small statue of a satyr. The marble was cool against her back.

"You are forever pulling me into a dark corner, Mr. Hartley," she laughed, nervous and exhilarated at the same time. The most delicious sensation rolled over her skin when Colin looked at her as he did now. "Although I don't suppose he minds," she nodded at the satyr who regarded them both with a lascivious grin.

"I believe it is you who seek to pull me into darkened corners, Miranda." Colin whispered against her ear. "Though, I don't mind in the least."

Her pulse caught as his breath tickled the sensitive flesh beneath her ear. A whimper escaped her lips.

It was constant torture to sit across the table when Colin came to dine, pretending that they were no more than old family friends. She would sit and allow Mother to discuss how she hoped for a match between Miranda and Lord St. Remy. She would nod her head and agree that St. Remy, or whomever Mother found suitable, was quite wonderful, all the while knowing that the only man she wanted sat across the table, his dark eyes lit with hunger as he watched her.

Since that day, nearly a month ago, when Colin surprised

her in the gardens, they had found every moment to be together. It was amazing how many dull, boring lectures the Royal Academy presented—lectures only Colin would escort her to. Then Colin would take her for a lemon ice and debate the merits of the lecture. Or discuss the building of the pyramids. Miranda found herself saving up little tidbits of the trials of being in her First Season if only to make him laugh.

A warm finger teased her skin, slipping down the deep valley between her breasts.

Her nipples pebbled, the sensitive tips pushing up against the constraints of her bodice. Every touch between them became more intimate, more heated. Sometimes at night she couldn't sleep for thinking of the sensations Colin aroused.

"This curl will be the death of me." He wrapped a bit of her hair about his seeking finger. "It always tempts me to come closer."

"Then come closer," she breathed.

Tugging the curl, Colin pulled Miranda close and nibbled against the line of her neck and jaw. His breath warmed her skin and set her pulse racing. "Such a tempting invitation."

Honey slid down her stomach to pool at the apex of her thighs as his mouth blazed a trail against her skin. Instinctively, her hips pushed against him. Her hands ran down his chest to wander beneath his coat, catching around his waist.

A low, primitive sound came from deep in Colin's throat.

"We should go back. You are maddening," the words trailed along her neck, "and I should leave. If I were smart, I would run from Cambourne House as if the devil himself were at my heels."

"Are you suggesting I'm the devil, Colin?"

"You are." His mouth brushed hers, nipping at her bottom lip. "Devilishly beautiful. *Wonderful*. Amazing. You make my heart stop."

Miranda pressed a kiss against his lips. "I shall start it once again. Contrary organ."

"And you are quite good at catching frogs."

Miranda laughed and brought her hands up, wrapping her arms about his neck.

"You can't leave yet. You promised me a walk in the gardens."

He shook his head. "We should not. You mother watches us like a hawk. She suspects, I think."

Miranda took him by the hand, lacing their fingers together, cursing the fact that she wore gloves, although he did not. He rarely did, which pleased her, for she loved the look of his hands. Large, but graceful, sometimes with a bit of ink staining his forefinger.

"Father did not object, and my mother only suspects that I may be happy, and she does not wish me to be."

Her father, Lord Cambourne, barely looked up from the London Times as Miranda said she and Colin would take a turn about the garden before he took his leave. The Dowager was already asleep in her chair by the fire. Only Miranda's mother raised a brow, her eyes narrowed with disdain for Colin.

To be fair, her mother liked few people, and certainly not anyone that was acquainted with Sutton. Mother resented that Father's first wife had borne the Cambourne heir and her resentment festered until she hated Sutton with her entire being. The dislike of her stepson extended to his friends. Mother detested Nick especially but dared not anger the heir to Dunbar. She referred to Colin as the "Irish pauper" telling Father that Colin would steal the silver if they looked the other way. Which was preposterous. Though he might steal a kiss from Miranda.

"Your father did not object because he assumes I squire you about as a favor to your family." Colin replied as he pressed another kiss beneath her ear. "It is becoming very difficult to pretend that I only tolerate your company as I did when you were a child." A sigh escaped him. "A short walk. Then I must take my leave."

Miranda had no intention of allowing Colin to leave yet. She led him outside to the garden, her favorite spot in all of London, for it was the place that most reminded her of Gray Covington. The sun had just started to dip below the horizon, bathing everything in the entire garden with a pale golden light, including Colin.

The waves of his hair glinted as if they were lit by fire. She found Colin to be beautiful, if such a word could be used for a man.

And he belongs to me.

The knowledge filled her heart with indescribable pleasure. She cared little that he had no title, no great estates or wealth. Her ridiculously large dowry would be enough for them to do as they wished. It only mattered that she and Colin would be together.

Miranda thought how wonderful it would be to kiss under the shadow of the Great Pyramid.

Colin pulled her back to him, a tiny smirk on his lips. "What are you about, Miranda?" He shook his head and spared a glance back at the French doors. "This is unwise."

"Did I tell you, Colin," she led him to a bench well-hidden behind a rather large wax myrtle, "that I've finished the book on ancient embalming techniques?" She sat and pulled him down next to her, watching his silky movements in appreciation. Once she'd attended a lecture on snow leopards and that was what Colin reminded her of. A big, graceful cat.

"Is that why you've led me astray?" His voice took on a husky lilting quality. "To discuss ancient death rituals with me?"

Birds sang above their heads, heralding the coming night

and a frog croaked softly from the small fish pond on the other side of the garden. It was so peaceful here, so primitive. One would never know they were in the middle of London.

A gentle breeze blew across the garden, tossing a curl across the tops of her breasts.

Colin leaned forward, his attention focused on the curl. He pressed his lips against the skin above her bodice as his hand reached out and cupped the underside of one breast.

"Tell me to stop, for the love of God, Miranda."

Instead, Miranda lay back against the bench and taking his wrist, pushed her breast more fully into his hand. "I don't wish you to stop, Colin.

She heard him curse under his breath even as his thumb found her nipple beneath the silk, circling the engorged tip before rolling the peak between his thumb and forefinger. The warmth of his hand lit her skin as he pulled down the lace of her bodice to deftly free her breast.

Cool evening air blew across her nipple before she felt the flick of his tongue against the sensitive peak.

Oh, this was more wicked and pleasurable than she imagined. She twisted on the bench, her skirts rustling in the quiet. "More," she begged.

Colin gently suckled the engorged peak, his teeth nibbling against the tender flesh, the pulse of his mouth sending small waves of pleasure rippling through her body.

Miranda gasped, pushing her hips up against him, hoping to ease the ache between her thighs. She was heated, her skin feeling as if a flame had been lit to it. Miranda had the sudden desire to divest herself of her gown. Press herself naked against the large male body that held her.

It occurred to Miranda that this was why young ladies required chaperones, this feeling of wanting to throw off your clothes and rub oneself against a man like a cat in need of affection. Imagine how ruination would spread through the *ton*. Was this how the term 'merry widow' was coined? For widows could engage in such activities without a chaperone.

Her hands threaded through the silken strands of his hair, loving the movement of the molten gold waves against her fingers.

"Colin. Ruin me," she whispered. "Please."

The cool evening air again caressed her breast as he lifted his mouth from the delicious torture he inflicted upon her breast. "Dear God, Miranda, I certainly want to." One elegant finger trailed down the top of her breast to her nipple, brushing the tip until Miranda thought she would faint from the pleasure.

"Please, Colin. I wish it. I-", she didn't know how to express herself, "*want* you. So much so I fear I'll die from it."

"I would not take you on a bench in your father's garden," he said quietly, his breathing uneven. "You deserve better than that. God, you deserve so much better than me, Miranda. Every man in London wishes to court you. Had I any sense at all I would leave you alone, for both our sakes. You would do better with a man who can give you the things I cannot."

"You don't mean that," she gasped as he rolled her nipple between his thumb and forefinger.

"Miranda, you've your pick of earls and dukes. I'm a third son. I've nothing to offer you."

"Yourself. That is all I want or shall ever want. I will not change my mind." She trailed her finger against his bottom lip, satisfied when a soft growl escaped his mouth.

"This is only your first Season. You may regret such an indiscretion later." His lips twisted into a small smile.

The frog croaked again, this time sounding as if he were beneath the bench on which they sat. "Besides, think how shocked," he said teasingly, "that poor frog would be."

Miranda gave a sigh of disappointment. She pushed herself up against him.

"I said I wouldn't bed you," Colin's mouth fell against her neck to murmur in her ear, "but there are other things."

"Show me."

One of his arms fell to her lap and moved down to the hem of her dress. Shuffling through the mound of silk and petticoats, his hand trailed heat up the thin silk covering her calf, hesitating for a moment in the hollow of her knee.

"Have a care," she whispered, "for my dress."

A dark, wicked laugh escaped him. "I shall have a care for a great many things. You have my word on it."

The feel of his hands against her silken clad legs fed the ache gently throbbing between her thighs. Shyly she moved so that her exposed breast would be closer to his mouth. She should be horrified to be so exposed, but she wasn't; she was too immersed in the sensations humming through her body.

"I must be mad." His hand brushed against the slit of her underclothes to gently cup her mound possessively. "So soft," he whispered as his fingers tangled in the down that covered her.

Miranda gasped as his finger moved through the slit to touch the slick folds of her flesh. His finger circled her entrance than retreated to trail around the source of her desire. Over and over, until she was panting, ready to beg for something she couldn't name.

"Anyone could come upon us." Colin's finger continued to play against her flesh, sliding between the wet folds, brushing delicately against the tiny nub hidden within. "The gardener. A groom. The Dowager."

A lovely bit of his Irish lilt bled into his words which aroused her even more. God, how she loved the way he spoke when he wasn't trying to sound like a snobbish gentleman. She sucked in her breath as he gently thrust the finger inside of her while his thumb continued to brush against the folds of her flesh.

"She's," her heart fluttered at his touch, "asleep."

"Spread your legs, Miranda." His voice was rough as his mouth fell to her exposed breast again, suckling while his finger, now joined by a second, thrust in and out of her. His thumb rotated over her nub, now hard and erect.

Miranda complied. Torture. What he did with his fingers was sheer torture. She found herself pressing her mound against his hand, anxious for some sort of release. A small part of her was dutifully horrified by the sight of Colin's blonde head, bent over her breast while his hands moved between her legs. The properly bred part of her.

Over and over his fingers teased and swirled until Miranda was panting with need.

"Let go, my love. Welcome it. I'm here," he whispered against her breast.

A small cry left her lips as her hips moved against his hand, matching every thrust of his fingers. She whimpered and arched her back in a plea for him to release her from this exquisite torment.

"Shh. Love. Don't make a sound, Miranda."

Miranda bit her lip in an effort to hold back the cry of pleasure threatening to erupt. His fingers swirled and dipped, caressing her until she thought her heart would stop.

Then her heart did stop. Or felt as if it did. The unexpected burst of pure bliss was so unexpected, so *unbelievable* that for a moment she didn't take a breath. Her body shattered into a dozen pieces or more, every fiber vibrating with pure ecstasy.

"Colin." She cried out his name, she couldn't help it.

He pulled her tightly against the hard lines of his body, covering her mouth with his in a deep, lush kiss as her hips bucked against his hand.

Just as it she thought it would end, Colin moved his thumb again and another spasm gripped her. Her head fell back as pleasure rippled through her once again, her body tightening around his fingers. There was nothing but this man, giving her such pleasure. And she surrendered to it. All of it.

Sometime later, Miranda came back to herself, feeling Colin's breath, warm and gentle against her neck. She was firmly wedged against his chest, his arms circling her protectively.

A bird broke into song in the tree above the bench, and a smile crossed her lips. Music seemed appropriate at such a time although given the sheer magnitude of the experience, she thought the last half-hour merited an entire orchestra. Miranda, who was never without words, could find none to describe what had just happened.

Wondrous. Splendid. Amazing. *Erotic*. She finally knew the true meaning of the word.

Without her noticing, it seemed her breast found its way back inside her bodice, the lace at the edge neatly tidied. Colin's hand was no longer beneath her skirts, but instead lay on her thigh.

She looked at the instrument of all the pleasure she'd just experienced and took his hand, bringing it to her mouth for a kiss, before threading his fingers with hers.

He pressed a kiss to the tip of her nose. A small, smile crossed his lips and his eyes were dark with emotion.

Kissing the corner of her mouth, Miranda heard him whisper something under his breath.

It sounded like *mine*.

JESUS.

Had his cock been any harder he'd be considered one of the Marchioness's statues.

The wisdom of pleasuring Miranda was to be debated, for it had only made him want her more. Which he didn't think possible. Just the taste of her, the sight of her, would drive him mad the rest of his days. He thought of nothing but Miranda, and how to have her.

Few things frightened Colin. His mother. Being poor, or at least continuing to be impoverished.

Not having Miranda.

Part of him feared that Miranda's affection was only an extension of her childish adoration for him. That in time, her infatuation with him would wane and she would realize he wasn't good enough for her. That he would lose her to some fancy bit of fluff masquerading as a gentleman. The other half of him wished to claim her and stop this act of family friend.

Colin *thirsted* for her, his lovely, chattering, bit of light. A light that banished every bit of darkness that the Mad Countess bestowed upon him. It wasn't just the thought of bedding Miranda, which God help him, the events of this evening had made even worse. This was something else entirely.

The thought of leaving London, of leaving Miranda, was unthinkable.

Mine.

Nothing, and certainly no one had ever been his.

Miranda.

The chubby nuisance of his youth was this magnificent creature in his arms. A woman who begged him to ruin her. A woman who *chose* him.

Mine.

He'd grown up with two older brothers, each one more beloved by his parents than Colin could ever hope to be. His life was one of hand-me-downs, the last portion of roast past round the table. Ian's mended shirts that he'd outgrown. A pair of boots that Mother ordered for Thomas but, when proved too large were passed to Colin.

Nothing had ever been his.

Nick, who sent Miranda to Colin the night of the Dunbar ball, would be amused but hardly surprised. The Marchioness would be horrified. The Dowager he might be able to charm.

He would beg Lord Cambourne for Miranda's hand on his knees if he must.

Mine.

Something pure and wonderful blossomed in Colin's chest. A feeling he didn't immediately recognize as he'd felt it so rarely.

Joy.

The smell of a campfire and the words of an old gypsy came to him, followed by his mother's words of hatred whispered in his ear. The combined effect threatened to spread darkness in the beautiful garden, his heart's desire before him, but for the first time, he ignored both of them. They held no power here. Not with Miranda who banished the darkness as if she were the sun itself.

"Yes." The words left his lips before they could be stopped.

Miranda gave him a sideways glance, her green eyes glittering with specs of gold as the sun set. A light wind ruffled her hair. She looked well-pleasured. Sated. Her lips were swollen and her bodice just a bit crooked.

He found her to be the most lovely creature he'd ever seen.

"Yes to what? I don't believe I've asked you anything, Mr. Hartley. Unless you mean more of..." she looked skyward struggling to find the right phrase.

"Go on. You are rarely without words." He sat back

against the bench and watched as she flushed that lovely shade of pink.

"More of...*this*. If that is the case I wholeheartedly agree. Although you do not need to look so smug."

"I am not smug."

"You should hear the way the young ladies whisper and roll their eyes as they talk with distaste about the marriage bed, calling it a *duty*. As if it were something distasteful. Only good for begetting an heir. Truly, if most young girls knew about...*this*, well I would find that their opinions would be vastly different. What are you agreeing to, Colin?"

Would she always chatter in such a manner? He thought she likely would.

"You asked me once if I'd marry you." A finger traced the edge of her bodice, wishing he could once again touch those glorious breasts. "Do you remember?"

Miranda blushed, the question stopping her continuous stream of conversation as nothing else would.

"I -I was eight, if I recall correctly, hardly an age when you can make such a decision.

Colin's eyes ran up her lush form. "I brought you a half-dozen raising cakes."

Miranda looked away, the pink deepening in her cheeks. "I fear my affections do not come so cheaply now."

"Indeed?" He tugged at the curl that lay once again between the mounds of her breasts. He wished to see Miranda naked before him, her hair streaming down her body like ink against a creamy white page.

"Should you steal me a dozen," a shy smile graced her swollen lips, "I may consider my offer to still be good."

Colin bent his forehead to hers, sighing softly as he breathed in her scent. "I shall buy you an entire bakery."

9

GRAY COVINGTON 1836

"Colin, you look as if you could use a drink."

Sutton Reynolds, Marquess of Cambourne, clapped him on both shoulders, his green eyes, so like Miranda's, full of welcome. "I must thank you for escorting Miranda and my grandmother. I do hope it wasn't too much of a trial. Was the journey pleasant?"

"It was." *Not really*. He spent most of the trip lusting after Miranda. Who he ruined six years ago under the nose of the Marchioness . Being forced to watch her being courted by Hamill and Ridley would most likely incite him to murder.

Unlike Nick, who inserted himself in everyone's affairs whether they wished for it or not, Cam could be oblivious to a great many things, and one of those things appeared to be the tension between Colin and Miranda.

Satan Reynolds, as the *ton* called Cam behind his back and out of hearing of the Dowager, could be a bit self-centered. Not that Colin blamed him. Few women could resist the allure of the Marquess of Cambourne. Even Colin had to admit that Sutton possessed a face that drove women mad with lust. Since he, Nick, and Cam had attended Eton, females of every age had been throwing themselves at Cam.

Nick surmised that all that attention had gone to Cam's head. How could it not? Then, of course, there was the dragon tattoo that decorated his friend's back, which few had seen but all gossiped about. Colin *had* seen it. And he didn't understand what the fuss was about.

Cam walked across the study to the sidebar where a large decanter of whiskey sat. The jade earring he wore peeked through his ebony hair.

Colin thought the bit of jade resembled a baby, but Cam insisted it was a deity of some sort.

"Whiskey?" Cam didn't wait for his answer and instead poured two glasses of the amber liquid.

Three hours in the coach with Miranda had left Colin irritable, regretful and slightly aroused, altogether a terrible combination. First, Miranda claimed not to remember St. Remy, or the Duke of Langford, or whatever the fuck the *ton* called him. How could she not remember a man she'd been betrothed to? He almost wished the damned letter hadn't fallen apart so he could wave it in her face. It would be so much more honest of Miranda to just admit to the letter. To St. Remy. To everything.

'Surely, Lord Kilmaire, my brother has relayed the reason why I have a rather limited field of suitors. Good God, the entire ton is rife with gossip concerning the incident.'

Except Colin *didn't* know the reason. Cam had said nothing about Miranda or her lack of suitors.

"It's Irish, you'll like it." Cam held up both glasses. "Came in on one of Nick's ships. He has an uncanny ability to find the best whiskey," Cam said from his place by the sideboard. "I had a letter from him just the other day. He and Lady

Dunbar will be staying at the Dunbar family seat longer than anticipated."

"He wishes to have his duchess to himself for a while. I'm not surprised. Jemma is a rare woman to have captured Nick's affection. Truthfully, though I expected he'd marry one day, I never thought he would do so for love. I am happy for him. I'm told Jemma is rather a good shot and prefers breeches to dresses."

Cam handed him a crystal cut glass. "Yes, and I believe half the gossips of the *ton* live in fear of her, for she does not tolerate any disparaging of her husband's character. I find it quite charming that one small dog is intent on guarding the safety of a rather large, fierce wolf." He laughed, causing the jade figurine to bounce as if it were alive. "The bit with Arabella is unfortunate." Cam shook his head. "But I suppose Nick had no choice but to banish her for the time being."

"I still cannot contemplate why Arabella would do such a thing. Conspiring with Corbett, a man she knew to be her brother's enemy, to rid herself of a sister-in-law." The aroma of the whiskey wafted into his nostrils and he took a sip. "Delicious."

"Makes me appreciate Miranda all the more." Cam lifted his glass and his gaze turned thoughtful before turning back to Colin. No hint of anything other than happiness at Colin's appearance glittered in his green eyes.

Cam truly didn't know. Or even suspect. Well, he *had* been in Macao at the time of Miranda's debut.

"Tis a shame that His Grace is not here to see me paraded about like a prize steer," he remarked, swirling the amber liquid about in the glass. "Nick would find my situation humorous, if nothing else, though I expect he would have plenty to say. He rivals your grandmother with his knowledge of everyone in the *ton*."

Cam took a sip of his whiskey and regarded Colin over the rim of his glass. "This isn't necessary, Colin."

"What isn't?" The glass rolled back and forth in Colin's hand.

"For God's sake, Nick and I will both lend you what you need to restore Runshaw Park. I can send breeding stock from several of my estates. I can—"

"No."

"Damn your pride. Do you really mean to saddle yourself with one of these girls? One that my grandmother has chosen for you?"

"Well, I don't have the stomach to choose for myself." Truthfully, he wanted none of these girls, their fortunes be damned, for none of them had hair dark as ink with eyes the color of jade.

"And I'm to tolerate Lady Dobson for a week." Cam's lips curled into a sneer. "Only for you. Although my wife finds her niece, Miss Lainscott, to be a lovely girl. Much more intelligent than she lets on. If you are determined, Miss Lainscott would suit you well, I think."

"And Lady Helen? How does your marchioness find her?"

At the mention of Lady Helen, the Marquess of Cambourne laughed out loud. "Should you marry Lady Helen, you will find your visits to Gray Covington limited to holidays and the occasional hunt."

"She is that awful then?" Of course she was. The girl was bound to be bloody awful. Colin took a deep breath. Sometime during the journey to Gray Covington, between Miranda's obvious anguish and the overwhelming desire Colin still felt for her, he had lost interest in this bloody house party. Indeed, he'd lost interest in everything but Miranda, especially the girls brought here for his obvious perusal.

Which brought him back to the *incident*, as Miranda

referred to it. He was just about to ask when Cam turned to him, green eyes narrowed and speculative.

"The gypsy wasn't right, you know. You've lived your life by a prophecy given to you by a withered old crone in the woods. It did not come true for me. Nor, Nick."

"I disagree." Colin tipped his glass to his friend, the familiar feeling of dread and acceptance filling him. "Her prophecy, at least for me, has come to pass. Every fucking word."

Cam shot him a resigned look. "Why must you be so dreadfully fatalistic? She only told us what *could* be. Nothing is set in stone. It's the Irish in you. It's always made you—"

He was about to say more when the door to the study burst open.

Two dark haired toddlers with chubby fists raised in the air ran in a crazy zig zag motion straight for the Marquess. The girl, her green eyes filled with delight, giggled. Clutched in her hand was what appeared to be a tiny spray of violets. Her brother, a more serious lad with eyes the color of a summer storm, lagged a bit behind, his dark head turning back as if looking to see if they were followed.

A harried nanny, her face red from running, huffed and puffed as she entered the study. She came to a quick stop as she spotted the two men. Cap askew atop a head of gray curls, she halted in front of Cam, her round face wreathed in apology.

"My lord," the poor woman gulped air as she sought to catch her breath. "I beg your forgiveness for the intrusion. Lady Madeline insisted that she show you the violets she picked from the garden. I told her that you were attending to your guests, but," the nanny held up her hands in supplication, "well, you know, my lord, how Lady Madeline gets a bee in her bonnet."

"It's all right, Mrs. Moore." Cam sat down his whiskey and

held open his arms to the children. "Are you two looking for me?"

Lady Madeline, her head a mass of dark curls twirling about bits of ribbon leapt at her father as if Cam were a mountain that needed to be scaled. Her small mouth pressed a series of wet kisses upon his neck as she simultaneously stuck her small spray of rather wilted violets against his nose.

Lord Robert came forward more slowly. He shot Colin a curious look, studying the scar for a moment before moving forward to his father. Patting Cam's leg, he cautiously pulled himself up his father's thigh, and threw his small body against Cam's larger one.

Lady Madeline pulled her brother's hair, earning a scowl from the boy.

Cam smiled down adoringly at the pair of children in his arms. "Did you two run from Nanny again? You must obey Nanny and not send her all over Gray Covington."

"Look, Papa." Lady Madeline gave her father a coquettish grin. "Flowers." She patted his cheek with her small hand. "Love you."

Colin envied Cam a great many things, but handling Madeline when the girl came of age was not one of them. She was a natural flirt and would likely cause trouble the moment she made her debut.

"Madeline, Robert, you have forgotten your manners." Cam nodded towards Colin. "Do you remember Lord Kilmaire?"

Two pairs of eyes turned to Colin.

"Good afternoon Lady Madeline, Lord Robert," Colin greeted them. The twins were beautiful children. While he avoided Cambourne House during his stay in London, Colin had been fortunate enough to spend the day in Hyde Park with Cam and the children. They'd sailed boats on the pond and shared a picnic lunch.

Madeline waved. Robert nodded solemnly.

Cam hugged both children to his chest, his eyes closing as he whispered something to both of them, then said out loud, "Terribly bad of you to run from Nanny. Although, I am happy that you sought me out. I adore violets Maddy, how did you guess?"

Madeline preened under her father's regard. "Papa."

"There you are."

The petite form of the Marchioness of Cambourne marched across the room, eyes on her disobedient children, one brow raised in question.

The two toddlers pushed their face into their father's chest.

Colin did not know Alex, the Marchioness of Cambourne well, having only met her for the first time at Nick's wedding, but in that short time, he'd developed a deep respect for her. Cam was, well, *Cam*. Nick relayed to Colin that it was Cam who'd pursued the small spinster, only to be rebuffed. She'd been betrothed to Archie Runyon before being caught in a scandalous embrace with the notorious Satan Reynolds, much to the *ton's* surprise. Their hurried marriage had been the talk of London for some time.

'Lady Cambourne' Nick told Colin, 'is a force to be reckoned with, a small cyclone that is much more dangerous than it appears. Cam is taken with his Marchioness and much to the dismay of ladies all over London, notoriously faithful to his wife.'

Both men stood as she entered the room. Cam's children continued to cling to him like tiny monkeys climbing a great tree, all the while shooting their mother fearful glances.

Pushing an errant curl off her forehead, nose scrunched in consternation, Lady Cambourne but her hands on her hips and tapped her foot in irritation.

"Hello, Badger," Cam greeted his wife, his voice serious as if her were addressing the queen.

Colin wondered how calling one's angry wife a rodent was a wise move under the circumstances, though Colin could tell by Cam's tone that the reference was meant to be an endearment.

Cam lurched forward towards his wife, Madeline clinging to his calf and Robert with his arms firmly locked about his father's neck.

"I wondered where you'd gotten off to, Badger." Cam peeled Madeline off his leg and unwound Robert's arms. He handed both children over to the waiting nanny.

"Mrs. Moore, would you see the children back to the nursery?"

"Yes, my lord." The nanny bobbed to Cam and led the children towards the door. He turned back to Alex and took his wife's hand. His thumb ran over her palm in an intimate caress. "I've been missing you."

Lady Cambourne gave an unladylike snort of disbelief but did not pull her hand away. She stepped closer to her husband. "Liar. You were busy drinking whiskey with Lord Kilmaire while I was tasked with overseeing a tedious dinner menu and preparing for the arrival of our guests." She looked over to Colin. "Lord Kilmaire."

"Lady Cambourne."

Alex continued. "Most of whom I do not like. The guests I mean. Your grandmother has conveniently taken to her rooms to rest from the journey to avoid my displeasure."

"I've been preparing as well," Cam assured her.

Alex gave her husband an incredulous look. "Preparing for what? The headache you shall have if you finish that bottle of whiskey with Lord Kilmaire? Thank goodness His Grace is still away in Scotland. I should not survive the scandal of having *three* Wickeds under my roof *and* Lady Dobson. As it is, I expect that we are already the subject of much gossip and conjecture. I'm told all of London is agog with the news that we are hosting a house party and Lady Dobson was invited. The papers will be full of it by tomorrow." She turned to Colin. "You've made it into the betting book at White's. The *ton* is busy placing odds on who will be the next Countess of Kilmaire."

"Good God," Colin groaned and drained his glass.

"Where ever would you hear such a thing?" Cam laughed as he released her hand only to press a kiss upon her forehead. "I wonder who placed the initial bet."

"Probably, the Duke of Dunbar. Nick's sense of humor leaves much to be desired at times," Colin answered.

"Lady Dobson at Gray Covington," Alex continued. "The Dowager is fortunate I hold her in such high esteem. I'm about to flee the premises any moment. I expect the plague of locusts to follow."

"I beg your apology, Lady Cambourne, and appreciate your sacrifice." Colin bowed to Alex.

Waving her hand in dismissal, she shrugged. "I will survive Lady Dobson's visit. She may not, but I will." Alex gave a laugh. "Besides, Miss Lainscott is a lovely girl. I am more than happy to assist her in escaping the clutches of *that* woman." An impish smile crossed her lips. "At any rate, if she annoys me I shall simply encourage one of the children to unravel her turban. Miranda surmises she is quite bald beneath it. I should enjoy showing her shiny pate to the guests of Gray Covington. Now that, husband, would truly be scandalous."

Cam lifted his brow. "Surely, you can't be serious?"

"About unraveling her turban? That depends on Lady Dobson." Her eyes widened slightly. "Oh, you mean about the baldness? Miranda and I are in agreement. She's bald. She must be. I've never even seen so much as a wisp of hair escape from her headwear."

A bolt of longing shot through Colin at the mention of

Miranda. He already missed her presence. She'd fled the coach the moment they'd arrived at Gray Covington. By the time he'd escorted the Dowager through the front door, Miranda had disappeared to her room. "Lady Cambourne—"

"Please call me Alex." The Marchioness smiled up at him, gray eyes twinkling. "And I am not the least put out by you, Lord Kilmaire. Just Lady Dobson."

"Colin." He dipped his head.

"Colin." Alex smiled up at him. "I am happy to assist you in finding a suitable match."

A suitable match. Truthfully it sounded a bit awful.

'Have a care for my dress.'

The moment Miranda said such in the coach, Colin had been transported to another time.

'I will always choose you, Colin Hartley.'

Except Miranda hadn't. Nor chose anyone else it appeared.

"I think, Alex, that we can afford a bit of scandal." Adoration shone from Cam's eyes as he gazed down at his petite marchioness. There wasn't a woman in all of England who wouldn't envy such a look from the infamous Satan Reynolds.

"Humph." A runaway curl escaped the mass of pins used to restrain her hair and Alex puffed it away with an annoyed burst of air from her lips.

How wonderful to see Cam's legendary charms having little effect on his wife. Lady Cambourne's handling of her husband caused Colin to like her even more.

"I am deeply appreciative of your efforts on my behalf," he thanked her once more.

Alex raised a brow, puffing at the errant curl again. "Yes, I imagine you will be." She turned with a nod to both men and walked swiftly to the door before Colin could reply.

Mrs. Moore awaited her, the poor woman desperately trying to stay in command of her charges. The small white cap she wore tilted dangerously as she struggled to hang on to Robert and Madeline.

"Once we take the children back to the nursery, why don't you sit down with a nice pot of tea, Mrs. Moore. I fear you need to regain your strength." Alex took her daughter's hand.

Madeline wiggled like a fish on a hook. Her chin tilted at a defiant angle. She appeared to be trying to stomp on her mother's foot.

"Yes, my lady. That would be most welcome." Mrs. Moore took Robert's hand, ignoring his protest and led him from the room.

"I'll leave you to your discussion, gentlemen. Lord and Lady Cottingham will be arriving at any moment," she said pointedly to Cam, "and you, my lord, must play host. Lady Dobson and her niece have already been shown to their rooms."

Alex strode purposefully across the threshhold, pulling the headstrong Madeline with her. "Come, Maddy."

Madeline turned and blew a kiss to her father.

Cam reached out into the air, pretending to catch his daughter's kiss, and pressed it to his heart. "A tiny tempest. Just like her mother." He settled back into his chair and his voice lowered an octave. "You like the Tempest, don't you, Lady Cambourne?"

"I do, my lord." Alex replied, never halting as she sailed through the doorway. "Perhaps you'll read that to me. A bit later?"

"You may depend upon it."

The door to the study shut with a smart click, and the two men were alone once more.

"Alex adores Shakespeare."

Colin doubted that Cam actually meant to read to his wife. "Indeed?"

Cam's shoulders rippled in a careless shrug. "I read to my wife, often."

"You are truly fortunate, my friend." Colin lifted his glass in toast. "The fact that you found a woman to tolerate your dubious charm is a cause for celebration." He took a breath, wondering if *now* would be a good time to broach the subject of Miranda's *unsuitability* and the *incident* that seemed to be the cause of it.

"Miranda said something to me in the carriage," Colin started.

"Let me guess." Cam rolled his eyes. "Lord Thurston. My sister is quite enthralled with the rather torrid adventures of this mythical man and his lady love. Won't shut up about them to Alex, who, I may add, nearly swoons every time she picks up one of the damn books. Lord Wently, a friend of my father's, owns the press that publishes those ridiculous tomes. I informed him I've a mind to call Lord Thurston out for stealing my wife's affection. Except he doesn't exist. Lord Wently found my frustration quite amusing."

I imagine he did.

Colin nursed his whiskey relishing Cam's annoyance. Lord Thurston did *exist*, in a manner of speaking. It was a lark to find that the great Satan Reynolds, with his mysterious tattoo and his angelic looks, was jealous of a fictional character.

"Refuses to give me the author's name. I'm sure the books are written by some spinster living in Surrey."

Actually Runshaw Park.

"No," Colin shook his head, "she said nothing at all about Lord Thurston, though I did find her reading one of his adventures the other day when I visited the Dowager." He looked directly at his friend. "Miranda mentioned unsuitability. Namely hers."

Cam's whiskey paused halfway to his mouth, then he

tilted the glass, draining it in one swallow. The lines around his lips tightened and a shadow darkened his face.

"I thought if I gave no credence to the gossip, never acknowledged that any of it were true, the rumors would simply fade. I assumed the Cambourne name would be enough. That the threat of the Dowager's retaliation would be enough." Cam stood and walked to the sideboard and lifted the decanter. "I was wrong on both counts. Terribly wrong. The *ton* does love a scandal, especially one as juicy as my sister's."

St. Remy must have broken the betrothal. The knowledge did not give Colin any satisfaction.

"There's no proof, of course. No witness." An anguished tone entered his words. "Just the ravings of my stepmother, who no longer resides anywhere near London, thankfully."

"I BLAME MYSELF." CAM CONTINUED, HIS GAZE FOCUSED ON the flames leaping excitedly in the fireplace. "I am the cause of my sister's unsuitability. I should have protected her and her reputation. My efforts were not successful."

Colin stopped rolling the glass between his hands. Cam had been in Macao at the time of Miranda's debut. Missing. Gone heathen. How in the world could he blame himself for a broken engagement to St. Remy, if that were the case? A feeling of unease soured the whiskey in Colin's stomach. "I'm not sure I understand."

"I should have written you, Colin. Told you what happened, but I didn't wish to burden you with it. You had your brother's death and Runshaw Park to contend with. Then," Cam's brow wrinkled, "well I just assumed Nick would tell you and I wouldn't have to."

"Will you tell me now?" It occurred to Colin that the sadness in his friend's voice and face could not be because

Miranda was the victim of a betrothal gone wrong. This was not about St. Remy.

Before Cam could speak again, a soft scratch came at the door.

"Come."

A small, compact man marched into the study and executed a precise, exacting bow
before straightening with ramrod precision.

"Lord Cambourne, forgive the interruption."

"What is it, Zander?"

Zander, the Gray Covington butler, was known far and wide as the most exacting of
masters. He ran the estate with meticulousness that was legendary, much to the envy of many in the *ton*, for no lord's house was as well staffed or maintained as Gray Covington. The discipline and correctness with which Zander managed the estate of the Marquess of Cambourne would challenge the best of His Majesty's generals. Close cropped red hair with just a glint of silver surrounded a sharp, but pleasant face. Not so much as a wrinkle was visible on his uniform, nor a spec of dirt. Zander reminded Colin of a toy soldier that had miraculously come to life in order to take command of Gray Covington.

Zander's age and origin were of great debate. Sutton's father had hired Zander years ago, claiming the diminutive man was from Brussels. The Dowager, however, insisted Zander was of Russian descent. Cam claimed the butler hailed from a small town in France. Regardless of his background, Zander was intensely loyal to the Cambourne family, with the exception of the former marchioness, , a woman who was not missed by the staff of Gray Covington, or anyone else.

"My lord, Lady Cambourne requests your presence, *urgently*. Lord and Lady Cottingham, along with their daughter, have arrived from London. And Lady Dobson," a small note of distaste crept into his voice as if it pained him to say the name, "is," he paused searching for the right word, "*roaming about*."

"Good God. Lady Dobson is wandering through the halls of Gray Covington without supervision? Please inform Lady Cambourne that reinforcements are on their way."

"Very good, my lord," Zander snapped his heels together and bowed again.

"And Ridley? Zander, where have you put him?" Cam leaned in to Colin. "It's times like this that I wish my father had a guest cottage built."

Zander's face remained as smooth as glass, but Colin noticed the small tic in the butler's cheek at the whereabouts of Miranda's suitor.

"I personally saw to his comfort, my lord and have shown him to a lovely room in the *east* wing."

Colin lips twitched in amusement at Ridley's plight. Zander placed the viscount in the little used east wing, as far from the family's suite of rooms, and Miranda, as possible. The Cambourne's only ever put their least welcome guests there as the rooms all faced away from the magnificent gardens. It would take Ridley at least ten minutes to reach the main part of the house from his chambers.

"Very good, Zander."

The butler bowed, twisting his head to give his employer a rather pointed look.

Lady Cambourne's instructions were clear it seemed, and the marquess was not to delay in following them. Zander strode from the study and in a telling move, refrained from shutting the doors behind him.

"Not very subtle, is he?" Cam said. "Alex probably threatened him with a lack of starch for his shirts. He always looks *pressed* as if someone took a large hot iron to his entire form."

"About Miranda, you were going to tell me what happened." Truthfully, Colin was rather desperate to know, and he certainly couldn't ask Miranda. Not after her anger in the coach.

"Later," Cam set down his glass, running a hand through his hair as he stood. "If you'd ever seen Alex in a temper than you would know that it is in my best interests to hurry to her side. I've faced down a Chinese warlord and felt less fear."

10

Helping himself to a glass of wine, Colin winced with distaste as he took a sip. *French. Probably expensive. Still tastes like sour fruit.* He'd never developed a taste for the stuff, though he dutifully tried. He preferred whiskey or even brandy, but neither was currently being served in the drawing room.

After Zander's interruption earlier in the day, he'd had no time to resume his conversation with Cam. The Marquess of Cambourne had dutifully gone to fulfill his responsibilities as host. After being introduced to the Cottinghams and barely sparing them more than a cursory glance, Colin excused himself. He was not presentable, he explained, after the journey and needed to retire to his rooms before dinner.

Secretly, Colin wished to catch a glimpse of Miranda. And unlike Ridley, Colin's chambers *were* in the family wing.

Walking down the corridor he had paused at Miranda's door, sensing her presence on the other side. Placing the flat of his palm against the door, he willed her to open it. Since the day in the Dowager's sitting room at Cambourne House, Colin found it increasingly difficult to hold on to the anger that had sustained him for the last six years. Especially after seeing the pain in Miranda's face earlier.

Colin purposefully came down to the drawing room a bit early, hoping that Miranda would appear. Instead he found only Lord Hamill curled into a large wing-backed chair, snoring softly in his evening clothes.

The attendees of the Dowager's house party slowly filtered in and flitted about, admiring the formal drawing room of the Marquess of Cambourne. Tapestries and objects d'art were littered about, so much so that the room resembled a museum more than a place for gathering. This was not a room that the family used often for themselves. The drawing room was specifically designed to inspire awe in anyone visiting Gray Covington. Every alcove, painting, and tapestry fairly resonated with the wealth and power of the Cambournes.

It was a beautiful room.

High vaulted ceilings gave way to gentle arches through which one could spy tiled hallways. One hallway led to the formal dining room, the other, to the conservatory. The ceilings were painted by a gifted artist, for only someone with such talent could have created the scene above his head. If one were to lay on the back lawn of Gray Covington and tilt their gaze to the sky, one would see the same view. The ceiling mimicked the sky above the estate at twilight, with the sun beginning to set just over the arch to the dining room. Fluffy clouds and a flock of ducks dotted the darkening blue sky as the edges of Gray Covington's magnificent gardens could be seen.

Tapestries, ancient and mellowed with age, hung from the walls, each panel depicting a Greek myth. The designs were so intricate, Colin often marveled at the skill of those long ago Cambournes responsible for such beauty. The remains of an old castle lay entombed at the far end of the woods and

Colin imagined these tapestries once hung there. The Cambourne family stretched back to the time of William the Conqueror, holding this land since the arrival of the Normans in England. Once upon a time, Colin had fought the Battle of Hastings with Nick and Cam at that old castle.

He adored this room. When visiting Gray Covington Colin would sprawl out on his back against the Persian rug that now lay beneath his feet. Imagination running wild, he'd invent stories, only to scratch them out later in his journal. Even the tapestries spoke to him. On one wall, the Kraken threatened Princess Andromeda as Theseus, his sword drawn, hastened to save her. The trials of Hercules, including his battle with the hydra, took up most of the left side towards the entrance to the conservatory while Persephone's marriage to Hades hung at the far end of the room. A pomegranate lay next to Persephone's sandaled feet while the god of the underworld lurked over her shoulder. He could still hear Miranda's footsteps as she trailed behind him, adoration shining from her eyes as she clutched a raisin cake to her chest. She would break off a piece and offer it to Colin if only he would tell her the story of Persephone again. Just one more time.

Self-important lad that he was, Colin often shooed her away.

Loss crashed over him like waves against a rock. His anger towards her, once so fierce and thick, had softened. His bitterness still festered, but the edges frayed. Colin's gaze lingered over Persephone's beautiful, doomed face. Had Persephone truly forgiven Hades for *his* deceit?

"What a lovely room," Lady Cottingham, standing just to his left, uttered in her annoying, breathless way. "So grand and majestic. Why it's absolutely breathtaking."

Colin steeled himself for the embrace of the ladies Cottingham.

Lady Aurora Cottingham and her daughter, Lady Helen Cottingham immediately sought Colin out after entering the drawing room, reminding him of a pair of bloodhounds about to corner a rabbit.

Towering over her smaller daughter, Lady Cottingham's stout build and thick fingers betrayed her more common beginnings. Swathed in a gown of deep violet, her dimpled figure rippled beneath the thin silk. A headpiece of precious stones sat perched atop her faded yellow hair, twinkling in the candlelight.

Lady Cottingham reminded Colin of a giant blueberry. A very determined blueberry.

The descriptions of Lady Helen did not do her justice. Pale golden hair the color of spring wheat was coiled about her head with a tiny cascade of curls gently touching her perfect ears. Her features were delicate and refined, at complete odds with her mother's appearance. Cornflower blue eyes gazed at Colin with frank appraisal.

"Lord Kilmaire." Lady Helen bobbed, taking her time in straightening up. All the more to give him a view of her more than generous bosom.

"Lady Helen."

No virgin should exude such raw sexuality, if indeed she was one. Colin doubted it the moment her falsely innocent eyes ran down the length of him. He surmised that Lady Helen, if not already compromised, was well on her way to ruination. Lady Helen reminded Colin of an over-ripe peach begging to be plucked.

No wonder her parents wanted her married as soon as possible.

"I must tell Lord Cottingham how marvelous it would be to have tapestries such as these hanging in our drawing room at Crestmont. I'm in the process of remodeling parts of the estate as Lord Cottingham's cousin's taste was not our own. I imagine Runshaw Park has a room such as this." The faded gold curls at her temple wiggled in anticipation of his answer.

"I'm afraid this room is rather unique to Gray Covington. Runshaw Park pales in comparison. No tapestries of such beauty, I'm afraid." Colin bestowed a polite smile on the her.

My father sold all the tapestries at an auction before I turned twelve. And no amount of paint or plaster would hide the cracks in the ceilings of Runshaw Park.

"Oh, that is a shame, Lord Kilmaire."

Colin nodded. There was not a doubt in his mind that in addition to knowing more about the state of disrepair of his estate, Lady Cottingham could probably recite the whole of Colin's dubious pedigree. She probably fell asleep each night with Derbett's Peerage clutched to her chest like a talisman. Lady Cottingham, formerly a dairy farmer's wife, would note that the earldom was one of England's oldest and ignore the fact of Colin's mad, Irish mother. She would tell herself that Colin's scar was the result of a duel, and not a carving knife. She would strive to ignore the string of tragedies that marked the Earl of Kilmaire and his family.

Lady Cottingham's gaze traveled over his left cheek before lifting to examine the ceiling once more. "I cannot imagine how such was painted."

Oh, how she wanted to ask him about that scar. He could see it in every small twitch and shuttered glance. She was horrified yet titillated, only her determination to present herself as a woman of good breeding prohibited her from questioning him. The dairy farmer's wife that she had been not so long ago wished to gape at his puckered flesh and boldly ask if the Mad Countess were truly insane.

Perhaps I should trade her the story of the scar for some advice on the dairy cows at Runshaw Park.

Lady Cottingham looked at him with expectation, no doubt waiting for him to enlighten her.

"I'm told the artist," Colin said, trying not to sound bored, which he was, "spent the better part of a year on the project," he looked up, "lying on his back to paint it. Very much like Michelangelo."

The giant blackberry before him quivered. Confusion clouded Lady Cottingham's face for a moment.

Lady Cottingham had no idea who Michelangelo was.

Her mouth opened to reply, lips quivering, to further delight Colin with her limited efforts at conversation but changed her mind. She merely nodded in agreement before turning to examine the tapestry before her.

He could almost hear her mind working. *Have I met Lord Michelangelo at the opera?*

Lady Helen took full advantage of her mother's embarrassment and attention to the tapestry. Leaning into the space between herself and Colin, she gave a small half shrug, pushing the top of her generous breasts upward until they appeared ready to spill from her bodice. She blinked artfully at Colin her eyelashes fluttering madly. The move was so practiced Colin assumed Lady Helen rehearsed it in front of a mirror.

Colin wasn't the least impressed. Or interested.

"I'm not overly fond of Greek mythology, Lord Kilmaire. All those gods and goddesses one has to remember. The only one I can remember is Aphrodite." She cast him a seductive look beneath her lashes. Her breasts pressed lightly against his forearm.

"Romans, Greeks, Egyptians," she continued, "I can't keep them all straight, I'm afraid. It's all so much dust now, at any rate." A slightly bawd laugh left her lips. "I'd much rather concentrate on the present."

Colin gave her a courteous nod.

Lady Helen seemed not to notice Colin's lack of interest.

"I'm a bird watcher." She lowered her voice an octave as if

imparting some great secret. "I find them to be *incredibly* fascinating creatures. There are so many beautiful species, all with their own small quirks. And I *adore* feathers." A giggle burst from her lips.

A hand raised to Colin's lips to hold in the yawn that threatened. "Do go on."

"I've begun keeping a journal, a trophy book of sorts, where I track down those birds that others find difficult to spot. I am a relentless hunter, Lord Kilmaire. I record my assessment of each specimen, my observations and such. I even draw sketches. Possibly I'll share my findings with the Royal Museum at some point, or perhaps one of England's universities. I feel certain that as an expert in this field, my observations have merit and would be welcomed."

Colin found that highly unlikely, though he respected her passion. It was the only appealing thing about Lady Helen besides her dowry.

Lady Helen's eyes glistened with feverish intensity as she proceeded to relate the details of her intrepid search for a particular species of thrush. Apparently, the bird made it's home in the wooded meadows surrounding Gray Covington.

Colin reminded himself that he didn't have to find Lady Helen fascinating. He thought they would probably get along well. She'd probably cuckold him before their first wedding anniversary.

He doubted he would care.

"Few ladies, my lord, let alone a *countess,* would climb a tree to gain a glimpse of a ruby throated thrush." A pout crossed her lips as the brief brush of her fingertips pressed his forearm in a suggestive manner. "But, *I* have."

Lady Helen should learn the fine art of subtly.

"*Helen,*" Lady Cottingham turned from the tapestry to her daughter, nostrils flaring as if she were a deer scenting danger.

"I do *not* think it appropriate to mention your unladylike behavior to Lord Kilmaire."

Lady Helen shot her mother a mutinous look but dutifully took a step back from Colin.

"I'm afraid my daughter can be a bit reckless, Lord Kilmaire."

"Not at all, Lady Cottingham."

As if climbing a tree made one reckless. Or possibly Lady Cottingham assumed that the very idea of her daughter's exposed calves would incite lust in Colin. Why he might forget himself, so overcome by the thought of her ankles that he would pounce on Lady Helen and ravish her.

Lady Cottingham worried needlessly.

"Perhaps we can go birdwatching during our stay at Gray Covington?" Lady Helen murmured in a low voice.

Colin waited for Lady Cottingham to chastise her daughter again, but the lady's attention was drawn to the entrance of the drawing room. Her cheeks reddened and the fingertips of one gloved hand fluttered against her neck.

"It would be my pleasure, with your parent's permission, of course," Colin answered loudly enough for Lady Cottingham to hear. Unfortunately, Lady Helen's mother wasn't listening.

Lady Helen's rosebud mouth pursed a bit, not caring for his answer. "Of course, my lord."

Did the chit think he was stupid enough to agree to an assignation? For that was what Lady Helen implied. Her parents would happen upon them, of course, and Colin would need to do the honorable thing.

Shouldn't I want that? Cut the courtship short. Return to Runshaw Park with my pockets lined with Lady Helen's dowry?

Lady Helen wished to float about the *ton* as a countess. Colin wished to return to Runshaw Park. They were each other's means to an end. There was little shame in that, he reminded himself. Virtually every other marriage in the *ton* was cut from the same cloth. He would never care for her, nor would she care for him.

Yes. But she bores me silly. She's pretty enough and rich enough but I'm sure she doesn't know how to catch a frog. I doubt she wiggles her toes as she reads, if she reads at all.

"Lord Kilmaire?"

"My apologies, Lady Helen. I was thinking how your hair shines like gold in the candlelight. I fear it struck me speechless for a moment." I can be charming, he mused, watching the way Lady Helen preened at his compliment.

"You flatter me, Lord Kilmaire."

Her eyes slid to her mother, confirming that Lady Cottingham's head was still turned away before boldly touching his forearm with the tip of her fan. "I look forward to our bird watching, Lord Kilmaire."

"As do I," he returned.

Oh yes, I shall count the minutes until we search for the ruby throated thrush.

Lady Cottingham was still turned towards the front of the room. Her mouth opened slightly as one hand flew up to pat her coiffure. A languid sigh escaped her lips. She had totally forgotten her daughter and Colin.

Colin drained his wine in disgust.

Lady Cottingham's behavior could only be attributed to one thing, or rather, *one person*. No woman seemed immune. Once Colin saw an elderly duchess fan herself furiously at being exposed to such potent allure. The woman had to have been at least eighty.

How in the world did Alex tolerate such nonsense?

Lady Cottingham gave another heartfelt sigh as if she'd just been awarded her heart's desire and pressed her fan against the top of her chest. She was struck dumb with rapture as the Marquess of Cambourne walked further into the drawing room.

Cam strode forward, the ridiculous green baby hanging from his ear, greeting his guests with a wide smile. Alex, his marchioness dangled from one arm, the indomitable Dowager Marchioness, his grandmother, on the other.

The Dowager was resplendent this evening in a gown of dove gray satin, a small diamond tiara set amongst the silver curls of her hair. Diamonds dripped from her ears and throat, sparkling in the light.

The thump of her cane echoed in the room as she made her way forward, surveying her guests with a shrewd glance of her emerald eyes.

Alex wore a swath of shimmering blue silk, her mass of dark, curling hair twisted into an elaborate hairstyle, no doubt designed to keep her willful locks constrained. Sapphire earrings dangled from her ears, her only adornment except for a locket she wore around her neck. Alex bestowed a welcoming smile on Lady Cottingham, despite the adoration with which the woman's eyes followed the Marquess of Cambourne.

Cam seemed oblivious to the effect his appearance had on the fairer sex.

Colin knew he was not.

As he watched, Alex's gloved hand discreetly pinched her husband's forearm and whispered something for his ears alone.

Cam brought the Dowager to a large chair set in the center of the room. The position of the chair, covered in crimson velvet, as well as the chair's size, gave one the impression of a throne.

No doubt that was the Dowager's intent.

Gingerly, the Dowager lowered herself to sit, bejeweled

fingers clutching the head of her cane. She nodded to Cam in thanks before settling herself.

Lady Cambourne left her husband's side to greet Lord Hamill.

The aging lord's hooded eyes roamed over Alex's voluptuous form, settling for a moment across the tops of her breasts, before he pressed a kiss to her knuckles.

Old lecher.

Upon meeting Lord Hamill, Colin formed a very firm opinion. An elderly rake. One who still thought himself attractive to women, despite the fact his looks had long since faded. His watery eyes flickered over every woman in an assessing manner, focusing on their breasts and lips, a sure sign of his true nature. The man was reputed to be widely respected in Parliament and possessed a keen political acumen, regardless of his roguish behavior.

Miranda couldn't seriously be considering Lord Hamill as a husband. He was nearly as old as the Dowager.

"Good evening." The Marquess of Cambourne approached and slid next to Colin, nodding to Lady Cottingham.

Lady Cottingham took her daughter's arm, pulling Lady Helen down with her as she executed a small curtsy.

Cam bestowed an indulgent smile upon the two ladies.

Lady Helen struggled discreetly to loosen her mother's grip.

"Lady Cottingham, Lady Helen." Cam politely took Lady Cottingham's hand and gently pulled her up while simultaneously bowing over her hand. "How radiant you both look tonight. I trust you are finding Gray Covington comfortable?"

Lady Cottingham appeared as if she would faint from sheer delight. "My lord," she twittered, "we are so pleased at your invitation. I am in utter awe of the beauty of this room."

Good Lord, she's giggling like a schoolgirl.

Where on earth was Lord Cottingham? The man should bear witness to the way his wife was making an ass out of herself over the Marquess of Cambourne.

"My husband begs your pardon, Lord Cambourne. He is unable to join us for dinner this evening." Lady Cottingham batted her lashes.

The effect was less than alluring.

"I hope he's not ill." Cam inquired. "There is an excellent physician nearby, Dr. Merwick. I can have him sent for."

Lady Cottingham giggled again. "How generous of you, Lord Cambourne, but please do not trouble yourself. My husband sometimes becomes ill if he spends too long in a carriage. I assure you he will be right as rain tomorrow and looks forward to your tour of the estate."

"As do I. I hope you and your daughter will permit me the honor of escorting you both into dinner? I am a poor substitute for Lord Cottingham, I know."

A small snort sounded from Colin. He couldn't help it. Lady Cottingham would cheerfully push her husband off a cliff if the end result was dangling on the arm of the Marquess of Cambourne.

Cam shot him a disapproving look.

Lady Cottingham beamed with pleasure and even Lady Helen's eyes widened at Cam's words. "Of course, my lord. We would be honored." She had the decency to look askance at Colin.

Colin gave a polite nod of his head. At least he'd be spared taking the ladies Cottingham into dinner.

"And may I say, Lord Cambourne, that I look forward to walking in the Gray Covington gardens? I've long heard of their beauty, especially the midnight roses. I had the pleasure of seeing vases of the blooms once, at a ball your mother hosted in London just before her marriage to Mr. Herbert

Reynolds. Mr. Reynolds is an acquaintance of Lord Cottingham," she added.

"My *stepmother*." Ice dripped from the words.

The color left Lady Cottingham's face and her lips trembled at the rebuke.

Poor woman, she's stepped in it now. Cam detests having people assume that bitch is his mother.

Alex silently appeared at her husband's side, threading her arm through his. Her fingertips pressed lightly against his forearm in a calming gesture.

"We do not grow midnight roses any longer, Lady Cottingham," Alex said in a matter of fact tone. "Alas, the plants fell victim to a horrible infestation of aphids. Really very tragic."

"Aphids?" Lady Cottingham blinked rapidly, and two spots of color appeared on her powered cheeks.

"Birds eat aphids," Lady Helen twittered to no one in particular.

"Yes," Alex continued. "Unfortunately, the plants had to be destroyed. Each and every bush had to be ripped," her eyes narrowed rather viciously, "from the ground."

"But, surely," Lady Cottingham who doubtless knew quite a bit about gardening in addition to dairy farming said, "some cuttings could be saved? A root ball, perhaps?"

"Sadly, no." Alex shook her head which allowed a curl to loosen from her coiffure and bounce against her brow. "The aphids were *particular* to the midnight rose. Our head gardener had never seen anything like it and was quite mystified, wasn't he my lord?"

A small smile lifted the corner of Cam's mouth, his wife having dispelled his black mood. "Yes, mystified."

"We've replanted the gardens with a much more sturdy species of rose, one that can withstand an aphid attack. I'm sure you'll find them equally as lovely."

Colin knew that the midnight roses were created *especially* for Lady Jeanette Cambourne. At her command. The petals of the flowers were meant to serve as a foil for her own pale beauty. Dozens of gardeners were sacked until one lucky man produced *exactly* the right shade. Lady Cambourne had permitted only midnight roses to be planted in the gardens of Gray Covington and Cambourne House. When her ladyship hosted a ball or other large gathering, she insisted that large vases of the roses fill each room, so much so that the flower vendors of London competed for cuttings of the bushes in order to grow enough to meet her demands.

The midnight rose bushes had been destroyed at Cam's insistence once his stepmother was finally gone from London.

Alex bestowed a warm smile on the slightly bewildered Lady Cottingham who was too new to society to know of the former Lady Cambourne's venomous personality.

"I do hope, Lady Cottingham, that the chambers I selected for you and your family meet with your approval?" Turning slightly, she addressed Lady Helen. "I picked yours, Lady Helen, especially because of your fondness for birds. Your room overlooks a particularly large maple tree. A pair of robins have taken up residence in the tree and formed a nest full of lovely blue eggs. I believe they are nearly ready to hatch. I thought perhaps you would enjoy watching them during your stay."

Lady Helen's lips curled in a tolerant smile. "Robins are really rather *common*, Lady Cambourne. Why—"

"Thank you." Lady Cottingham took hold of her daughter's hand, squeezing tightly in an effort to keep her daughter from offending their hosts. "You are most considerate, Lady Cambourne. I'm sure my daughter will enjoy the view very much. May I also say again, how pleased we are to visit Gray Covington."

"My husband's grandmother would like to renew your

acquaintance." Alex tilted her head to the seat where the Dowager now held court. "She has sent me over to collect you."

Lady Cottingham swallowed nervously. "Of course. I must thank Lady Cambourne for her kind invitation."

Two men stood on either side of The Dowager paying their respects. Colin recognized the large form of Lord Anthony Welles immediately, for he'd known him at Eton. The other gentleman Colin assumed to be Carstairs. The dolt.

"Please," Alex gestured for Lady Cottingham to precede her, and took the woman's arm when she didn't budge. "I would also take the opportunity to introduce you to Lord Anthony Welles and Lord Thomas Carstairs. You may be acquainted with Lord Carstairs's younger sister, Lady Gwendolyn? She's just made her debut."

"I've met Lady Gwendolyn." Lady Helen replied before her mother could answer. "I find her—"

"Delightful." Lady Cottingham shot her daughter a firm look.

Alex guided Lady Cottingham and Lady Helen in the direction of the Dowager who sat watching their approach with an assessing gleam in her eye.

Colin leaned towards Cam. "I must remember to thank Alex for her timely rescue from Lady Helen and her mother. I was about to be treated to a very impassioned speech on the ruby throated thrush. Whatever the bloody hell that is."

A servant paused before Cam holding a silver tray holding two glasses of wine.

Taking one of the stemmed glasses, Colin took a sip and frowned. "You really should serve whiskey if I'm going to be forced to make conversation on birds."

"She's wealthy. Horribly so. Despite her eccentric hobby."

"Obsession." Colin corrected him.

Cam shrugged. "I've no wish for you to be condemned to a life of *obsessive* birdwatching. You have other options."

"Borrowing so heavily from my friends is not one of them," Colin reminded him.

Cam sighed in resignation and lifted his chin towards the group surrounding the Dowager.

"You remember Welles, don't you?"

"I do. I understand that he now uses his aptitude with numbers and business acumen on Elysium."

Cam lifted his glass. "Well, he had to make a living somehow didn't he, after refusing to marry the girl his father chose for him. Now the Duke of Baunton, surrounded by his five daughters, still waits for his heir to marry."

"The son of a duke," Colin mused, "running a club that caters to the most decadent tastes of the *ton*. I'm told there are private rooms where one can indulge and explore any pleasure one wishes."

"Welles is a silent partner. It is his half-brother who manages Elysium."

"And Carstairs? I have difficulty believing he and Welles are friends. I'm told my horse possesses more personality than Carstairs."

"No, definitely not friends. I believe there is property that Welles wishes to purchase from Carstairs and wanted to view it himself rather than send his solicitor. Grandmother invited them to stay for the house party since they meant to stop for the night anyway."

"Perhaps your grandmother," Colin bit out, hating the jealous note in his tone, "means for Welles or Carstairs to be potential suitors for Miranda."

Laughter burst from Cam's lips. "I'm glad to see you haven't lost your sense of humor. "Lord Hamill and Ridley are bad enough without adding Carstairs to the mix."

Colin ignored the fact that Cam made no mention of Welles.

Behind the chair in which the Dowager sat, a gentleman entered the room, pausing at the doorway as if waiting to be noticed, frowning slightly when he seemed to garner no attention as he made his way forward.

Beside him, Cam tensed, eyes narrowed with dislike. "I was so hoping he wouldn't be able to find his way down here until we'd already begun the soup course. The frontrunner for my sister's hand. Lord Edwin Ridley."

Colin's hackles rose immediately as he took in the viscount.

Lord Ridley was tall and slender, his dark evening clothes perfectly tailored to fit his lean form. The only distraction was his waistcoat. The garment was a mélange of colors, a crazy patchwork of blue and green shot through with gold thread. A mop of carefully teased curls hung about his face.

Christ, I can smell his pomade even from this distance.

"Just seeing Ridley makes me reconsider my earlier assessment of Carstairs. Perhaps Carstairs is only pretending to have the intelligence of a potted plant. He's hiding his brilliance for some reason and will reveal himself at an opportune moment."

"A bit colorful, isn't he?" What an utter fop Ridley was. How could Miranda consider such a man? The wine soured in his mouth just watching Ridley prance across the room.

"Carstairs a dandy?" Cam's brow wrinkled. "Oh, you mean *Ridley*. Yes. I'm told he spends more on his clothing than a girl in her first Season. I was hopeful that Ridley would lose interest in my sister, but he seems to have renewed his suit in the last few months. I still have hope that Miranda will come to her senses. I almost prefer Hamill." A pained look crossed Cam's face. "Actually, I'd rather she remain a spinster than make a foolish choice."

Colin agreed. He didn't care for either of Miranda's suitors. She couldn't possibly be serious. Again, he wished to ask about the *incident*, but now wasn't the best time.

"Perhaps my sister will listen to you?"

Colin choked on his wine. "Sorry," he covered his shock at his friend's suggestion, "you know I don't care for wine. Why," he passed his glass to a waiting servant, "would you think Miranda would listen to me?" Cam really *didn't* know, as impossible as that seemed.

"She may listen to you. Her 'prince' from childhood."

The casual remark caused his heart to contract.

"I'll speak to her if you wish." Colin ceded. "But, Cam. You need to tell me what happened. To Miranda."

Cam turned away, either not hearing Colin or choosing to ignore the question. "Ah, there's Miss Lainscott and her aunt, the esteemed Lady Dobson." He couldn't keep the distaste from his words. "Alex speaks very highly of Miss Lainscott."

Lady Agnes Dobson, so spare of form with sharp angles that one was reminded of a praying mantis, strode forward towing behind her a slight young woman. Miss Margaret Lainscott was unremarkable in every way, from the color of her hair to the pale blush of her gown. Ordinary, except for the directness of her gaze and the sheen of intelligence in her eyes.

Lady Dobson tugged her niece forward, looking as if she would toss the poor girl at Colin.

Miss Lainscott's eyes flashed with rebellion and irritation before she lowered them demurely.

Colin liked her immediately.

"Lord Cambourne, Lord Kilmaire." Lady Dobson and Miss Lainscott dipped in unison.

"Lady Dobson." Cam did not bother to take Lady Dobson's hand, ignoring it in favor of Miss Lainscott's. "May I present my friend, the Earl of Kilmaire."

The snub was not lost on Lady Dobson. The large ostrich feather atop her turban quivered a bit, though her voice showed no hint of nervousness at being in the presence of the Marquess of Cambourne. Determination gleamed from her pale eyes as she turned to Colin.

"Lord Kilmaire." Lady Dobson extended a boney, gloved hand, the stark white of her gloves giving the impression it was a skeleton's hand he bent over.

Thin to the point of emaciation, Lady Dobson's elegant silk gown hung from her meager figure, as there seemed no flesh to cling to. Everything about the woman was sharp and cutting, from the way she walked to the unseemly way she was moving Miss Lainscott closer to Colin's side. Her beady eyes took in Colin, lingering over the scar on his face before dazzling him with a false smile meant to hide her disgust at his disfigurement. After all, an earl, even one as flawed as Colin, would be more than suitable for her niece, a niece that she was quite desperate to get rid of.

The lady would make an excellent villain in a Lord Thurston novel.

"Lady Dobson, a delight." It wasn't.

Sniffing in acknowledgement of the compliment, she nodded her head in agreement. The feather in her turban bobbed, strands of it floating about her head like a feathery mist.

"My niece, Miss Margaret Lainscott." A spindly hand lay on Miss Lainscott's shoulder. "She is the daughter of my late sister and her husband." She propelled Margaret closer to Colin as if the girl were a sacrificial virgin.

"It is a pleasure to make your acquaintance, Miss Lainscott."

"My lord." Miss Lainscott curtsied, her voice so soft Colin strained to hear it. Now that she was closer, he could see the tiny spray of freckles dotting her nose. Eyes, dark and velvety like those of a doe, looked up at him.

Colin watched as Lady Dobson jabbed a finger in Margaret's back.

"A pleasure, Lord Kilmaire."

"Miss Lainscott, how did you find your journey to Gray Covington?" Cam favored her with a kind nod of his head though he clutched his wineglass so tightly Colin feared the slender stem would snap and Cam might stab Lady Dobson with the shard.

Before the girl could reply, Lady Dobson answered, momentarily forgetting Cam's frostiness towards her. "Tolerable, Lord Cambourne. Our coachman did not take great care on the road and I feared we would be jostled senseless before arriving. There is a large rut as you turn up the drive to Gray Covington. Jarring, my lord. You must send one of your servants to fill it immediately."

Cam's lips tightened. "I was speaking to Miss Lainscott."

Lady Dobson stiffened and her mouth gaped open slightly like a fish that had suddenly found itself in a fisherman's net. She quickly regained her composure, pillar of society that she was, though she likely hadn't ever been cut so directly.

A flicker of amusement lit Miss Lainscott's eyes at her aunt's discomfort, though she quickly hid it. "I found the countryside beautiful, my lord. It is such a pleasant change from London. And this room," her eyes swung around to the tapestries lining the walls, "is a work of art. I do adore Greek mythology."

"She reads overmuch, I fear," Lady Dobson said, inserting herself. "Margaret, Lord Kilmaire and Lord Cambourne have no desire to listen to your opinion on art."

Harpy.

"Then it appears we have much in common, Miss Lainscott." Colin pretended not to hear Lady Dobson and resisted the urge to swat at her as if she were a large, turbaned, housefly. "I adore Greek mythology as well."

"As do I." Cam uttered over his glass of wine, his gaze skewering Lady Dobson. "Should you decide to read *overmuch* while at Gray Covington, Miss Lainscott, I insist that you take advantage of the library. My father's collection of Greek myths is fairly extensive. I believe there is also an entire shelf on Norse mythology as well. If you would care to expand your knowledge in such things."

Lady Dobson's smile faded. It was evident she was struggling to maintain her polite façade. Clearly, the Marquess of Cambourne's dislike towards her was returned in spades. Lady Dobson might be the only woman in all of England who did not find the Marquess of Cambourne appealing.

"If you'll excuse me," Cam set his empty wine glass down on a nearby table. "I believe I have not greeted Lord Hamill properly." He dipped slightly, and the small piece of jade slid through his hair.

"Well." Lady Dobson snapped out her fan. Her eyes were riveted on Cam's earring and she muttered something under her breath. Turning back to her niece and Colin, a sly smile crossed her thin lips. "Margaret, Lady Cambourne begs my attention for a moment. Admire the tapestry and try not to bore Lord Kilmaire until I return."

Lady Dobson spun off, her skirts nearly swallowing up her meager form as she made her way to the Dowager, leaving her niece with Colin.

A sound of relief escaped Miss Lainscott at her aunt's departure. Her eyes widened, and one gloved hand covered her mouth in mortification.

Colin liked her all the more for it.

"You may breathe freely now. At least until your aunt returns. I'll test your knowledge, Miss Lainscott. What event does the tapestry before us depict?"

"The birth of Athena," she answered without hesitation. "Born fully formed from the head of Zeus." Stepping closer, the tips of her fingers reached out with hesitation.

"Go on, Miss Lainscott. I shan't tell."

Her lips turned up at the corners as she traced the outline of Athena's sandaled foot.

A melodic laugh sounded on the other side of the room drawing Colin's attention.

Miranda.

She was greeting Lord Hamill, and her brother. He could see the animation on her beautiful face from where he stood. She wore a gauzy creation of sea-bottle green edged in black piping, that floated over her generous curves. Jet hung from her ears, swaying as she spoke. She looked luscious and warm, like a summer's day.

"Lord Kilmaire?"

Miss Lainscott's gaze fell on Miranda.

"Lady Miranda is very lovely." Miss Lainscott said. "And she's very well versed in ancient history. I've had many spirited discussions with her on the building of the pyramids and their purpose." Her brow wrinkled. "Oddly enough, she knows quite a bit about the process of embalming and mummification."

"I didn't realize you were acquainted." His eyes never left Miranda. She sparkled like a rare gem from across the room.

Lord Hamill certainly took notice as he was entirely too close to her.

"I was introduced to Lady Miranda at Lady Marr's fete a fortnight ago. She's incredibly well read. There are several lectures at the Royal Museum she's invited me to attend. I believe Lord Cambourne is speaking at one. It's a recounting of an expedition through India."

"Yes, he visited there once. But Egypt is her passion." Colin frowned, watching as Ridley strode over and took

Miranda's elbow. "She has always adored ancient Egypt. Mummies. Pyramids." He could still see Miranda walking with him as they strolled through the park. She was regaling him with some horrible description of a death ritual practiced by Ramses's priests, when the breeze blew her bonnet off. The bonnet retreated out of his grasp, over and over, as if some invisible hand pulled it away from him. He'd finally resorted to pouncing on it, battering the poor bonnet and tearing off the ribbon. Instead of being angry at the destruction of her hat, Miranda had laughed in delight.

He'd spun her behind a large oak tree, out of view, and kissed her senseless.

"You seem quite intent on something, Lord Kilmaire."

Miss Lainscott was much too perceptive for her own good.

"Not at all, Miss Lainscott." He kept his tone unconcerned and blasé, as if watching Ridley circle Miranda with avarice written on his face was of no import to him. "I was just trying to place the gentleman speaking to Lady Miranda."

"Lord Ridley." Her direct gaze met his. "He seems quite taken with her."

Before he could speak, Lady Dobson reappeared behind them. "Lord Kilmaire, if you'll excuse us, I wish to introduce Margaret to Lord Carstairs."

He nodded. "Of course. I look forward to our next conversation, Miss Lainscott."

Miss Lainscott dipped in an artful curtsy. "Until then, Lord Kilmaire."

Colin bowed. He turned back to the tapestry, determined to give Athena his attention. He summoned up the anger and bitterness that raged within him for six long, lonely years, but it was no comfort. It was *natural* to be attracted to her. To want her.

The musical sound of her laughter floated to him.

Was Ridley so fucking amusing? Hamill so witty?

Mine.

Only she wasn't. Not anymore. He was here to court another woman. *Marry* another woman. Fulfill his obligation to Runshaw Park. Then he could retreat back to his family's estate and restore the lands to their former glory. That's what he wanted, wasn't it?

"I came to give my condolences at having to engage Lady Dobson in conversation." Lord Anthony Welles said as he drew near Colin. "Shouldn't she have dried up like so much dust and blown away by now instead of continuing to terrorize society? No wonder Lord Dobson met his end early. I'm sure death was preferable to their marriage."

"Welles. It's a pleasure to see you again."

"Kilmaire." Welles inspected the scar with a piercing gaze. "That must have hurt like hell, if you don't mind me saying so."

He didn't. "Like the bloody dickens." Welles rarely minced words about anything. It was one of the things Colin liked about him.

"A fine job of stitching you up." Welles dark head tilted closer to Colin and lowered his voice. "I am sorry, Kilmaire, for the loss of your family. A terrible thing. As one surrounded by five sisters, I cannot imagine."

"It was a long time ago." Colin didn't want Welles sympathy, nor anyone's. Nick and Cam were bad enough. "Tell me about your business venture, Welles. How is Elysium?"

11

"I'm sure to be seated directly between Lady Cottingham and Lady Dobson, aren't I?" I did not realize that searching for a suitable wife meant I was also to be tortured during dinner." He greeted Cam, who along with Gray Covington's guests, had stood at the announcement that dinner was served.

Cam snorted. "Then you misunderstood the nature of your request to my grandmother."

"You don't have to enjoy this so bloody much, ye smug pretty—"

Cam laughed at the insult and sauntered over to Lady Cottingham and her daughter. He bowed and extended out both arms to Lady Helen and her mother.

As Lady Cottingham took his arm she swayed a bit as if she would swoon.

Lady Helen assessed Cam with a somewhat lascivious turn of her lips.

Colin's possible future countess was definitely not completely an innocent, if the look she gave the Marquess of Cambourne was any indication.

Ridley, ridiculous dandy that he was, took Miranda's arm to lead her into dinner. He was looking down at her, lips pulled back from his teeth like a hyena or some other second-rate predator.

Colin longed to hit the man with his fist. What a satisfying crunch Ridley's nose would make as it broke.

A stomp of a cane interrupted his plans for Ridley, followed by the feel of the cane as it whacked against his shin.

"You'll escort me in, Lord Kilmaire. Do take that scowl off your features. Though *I* do not find you frightening, I would not wish you to scare the young ladies."

"I am scowling because of the feel of your cane against my leg. Who knew a woman of your—"

"Do not say *age*, Lord Kilmaire or I shall swat you again."

"I was going to say, *demeanor*." Truthfully, he had been about to say age but the lady in question was wielding a weapon. Who knew the Dowager possessed such strength? He held out his arm and made a half bow, his eyes lifting a bit so that he could watch Ridley practically *maul* Miranda.

"Hhmmph," she said, reaching for his arm. "I asked you to cease scowling."

"Apologies, my lady." Colin tucked her gloved hand through his arm and started forward, careful to measure his steps to hers.

Miranda and Ridley walked directly before him and the Dowager, so close that Colin could count the tiny satin clad buttons that wound down Miranda's back. There were exactly twenty. He longed to undo each one of them. The sweet aroma of Ridley's pomade met Colin's nose, and he grimaced.

"Well?" The Dowager said in a low voice demanding his attention.

"You look lovely tonight, Lady Cambourne."

Ridley's nose appeared to be nuzzling Miranda's neck.

"Don't be obtuse, Lord Kilmaire. I'm in no mood for games though I appreciate the compliment. Between helping you find a bride and ensuring the eligibility of several gentlemen whom Sutton approves of for Miranda, I'm quite taxed. To the point of exhaustion."

"Cam has implied that he doesn't care for *either* of Miranda's suitors." *I know I don't.*

"My granddaughter has a somewhat limited field from which to choose, but I feel certain that one of the gentlemen in attendance tonight has garnered her affections. I expect an announcement at any time."

Blinding white jealousy shot through Colin. He lifted a brow waiting for her to elaborate.

The Dowager did not. "How did you find Lady Helen?"

"She seems rather attached to birds." He almost mentioned Lady Helen's behavior but decided against it.

The Dowager paused mid step and took the opportunity to smack him again with her cane. "I asked you not to be obtuse."

"She's quite lovely."

"And Margaret Lainscott? Wealthy as well, but certainly no beauty. Rather plain but intelligent. Certainly there is also the appeal of saving her from the *ministrations* of her aunt."

"A possibility. However, I think I may like Miss Lainscott a bit too much to do her the disservice of having her marry *me*."

The Dowager's brows wrinkled. "Marriage to you would not be a disservice. She'd be a countess for goodness sakes. Ranked higher than her aunt."

Colin didn't reply. Miss Lainscott was not interested in marrying him, he'd surmised as much from their sole conversation. He wasn't sure that Lady Dobson would be able to force her niece down the aisle at all. The girl was not as malleable as Lady Dobson assumed.

"Well, if neither girl suits, there is also Lady Barbara Payne."

"Who?" Colin watched Ridley brush his thigh against Miranda's skirts.

"Lord Payne's daughter. His estate borders Gray Covington. You met him and his wife years ago, but you may not recall Barbara. Lovely girl. I've invited them to join us tomorrow for an impromptu concert. Miss Lainscott will entertain us on the piano. I'm told she's quite gifted."

Colin listened with only half his attention. The other half was focused on Miranda, who chattered away to Ridley in a low, seductive voice. At least, it sounded seductive to Colin's ears.

Ridley leaned in, his eyes not on her face but the tops of her breasts.

Bastard.

"Lord Kilmaire, are you ill? You look as if your stomach has soured. I do hope it doesn't detract from the delightful repast we are about to enjoy. Alex tells me Cook is especially pleased with the pheasant." She slowed a bit, and Colin automatically adjusted his stride.

"Perish the thought, Lady Cambourne. It's the French wine. I find I don't have a fondness for it. Is that Lord Ridley escorting Miranda? I don't believe we were introduced."

"Yes, Lord Ridley." She cocked her head. "I supposed he's handsome enough, but money seems to run through his fingers like sand. Horses, I believe."

"Horses?" Colin replied mechanically, watching Ridley's hand linger on Miranda's trim waist as he led her to her seat.

"Yes. Not buying them, of course, not like your father. Ridley is always betting on the beasts, and he's a poor judge of horseflesh. Very poor." Her lips thinned. "And he's rather extravagant, though I don't suppose it will matter if he has Miranda's dowry. Money will cease to be an issue for him."

"I doubt it," Colin hissed as he caught sight of Ridley's fingers gliding up Miranda's gloved hand. Then realizing the harshness of his reply he said, "Those who bet on horses rarely have money."

"True, Lord Kilmaire. While part of Miranda's appeal for Ridley is her dowry, I think he does bear her some affection. Enough so that she may be happy."

A pain lodged and throbbed in Colin's chest. How could any man want Miranda purely for her dowry? She was beautiful. Intelligent. Kind. *Maddening.*

"Perhaps," he started, knowing how ridiculous he sounded, "they share an interest in Egypt."

The Dowager said nothing for a moment. "I'd forgotten how much the ancient world intrigued her. I'm surprised you remember. At any rate, Ridley does indulge her visits to Thrumbadges, the bookseller. I believe she's joined a small group of like-minded blue-stockings, women more interested in studying archeology than attending balls. I expect that should she and Ridley marry, he'll allow her to continue to do so."

Allow her? His eyes flew to the dandy next to Miranda.

"I must give Ridley credit. He has accompanied her to several lectures, more out of duty than interest, of course. Miranda tells me he tends to snore through most of them."

The Dowager shrugged. "Sutton has given her leave to decide her own fate, so if it is to be Ridley, we must accept that choice. At least Lord Hamill can speak intelligently on many matters." Her tone left no doubt that she assumed Ridley could *not*.

Colin gently eased the Dowager into her seat towards the head of the table, all the while contemplating how best Ridley could meet with an unfortunate accident. It would ruin the house party, of course, if Ridley were to perish at

Gray Covington, but Colin was certain Cam would forgive him.

"Ah, and there's Lord Hamill. Where you introduced?" The Dowager asked.

"In a manner of speaking."

"I find him a bit too *elderly* for my dear Miranda. After all Hamill was only a few years younger than my husband." She laughed and shook her head. "He's quite important in Parliament and is responsible for many crucial reforms. And as I mentioned, he is at least possessed of a more scholarly constitution."

"So I've been given to understand." Lord Hamill walked with an odd, sideways step, seeming to lean more on Lady Dobson than he should. He looked a bit addled, probably from imbibing too freely of his host's brandy.

"An injury from the war I believe," the Dowager whispered, noting his interest of Lord Hamill. "Miranda is most sympathetic. A politician's lifestyle would suit her, for Hamill may travel to the continent to represent England's interests. Miranda has always wished to travel abroad."

Colin found he didn't care for the idea of Miranda traveling abroad with Hamill. *At all*.

"There's also Lord Carstairs and Lord Welles." She nodded towards Welles who escorted Alex. "Lord Welles I fear is a bit of a rogue, though a rather handsome one at that. Carstairs would be an indulgent husband and make few demands on her, though I fear her mind would atrophy."

"One of these men has Miranda's affection?" Colin bit out before he could think better of it.

"Why yes, Lord Kilmaire, I do believe one of the men at this table is the man my granddaughter will marry. I thought for the longest time that she would become a spinster, but after the birth of her niece and nephew I believe she decided she would like a family of her own. Miranda is quite determined."

"I wonder then that she did not marry Lord St. Remy." He hated that the words left his mouth with a jealous edge to them.

"St. Remy?" The Dowager gave a short bark of laughter. "Why would you ever think she intended to marry Lord St. Remy, or rather the Duke of Langford? He's inherited, you see. At any rate, Langford was never in contention for Miranda's hand, except in her mother's mind. Jeanette adored Langford."

He nearly told the Dowager that her granddaughter *had* intended to marry St. Remy, as she'd sent him a note. And returned his ring. But, just then, Ridley raised Miranda's fingers to his lips and pressed a kiss upon her knuckles.

Mine.

"I do hope you enjoy dinner, Lord Kilmaire." The Dowager bestowed a brilliant smile on him. She sounded amused.

His assumption about his seat location had been correct. Lady Helen sat to his left, Lady Dobson on his right. Much to his dismay, Miranda faced him across the table, flanked by Ridley and Hamill.

He couldn't wait for this bloody meal to end and it hadn't even begun.

COLIN UNFOLDED HIS NAPKIN WITH A FLICK OF HIS HAND and tried to stem the rise of possessiveness at the sight of another man *pawing* Miranda.

Mine.

Sitting in the darkness of his study at Runshaw Park, it was far easier to pretend he didn't still want her. At Runshaw

Park he couldn't see the glossy black of her hair, nor hear the musical sound of her voice. Nor smell lavender and honey. Alone at his estate his heart didn't feel as if it had cracked, bleeding feeling back into his body. For too many years Colin had pushed aside the depths of his feelings.

Mine.

Taking a deep breath, he motioned for the footman to bring him wine, wishing he could ask for whiskey. It would take a great deal of wine to blot out the sight of Ridley and Miranda before him.

12

How could she possibly eat with Colin sitting directly across from her?

Miranda usually had the healthiest of appetites, a fact her mother had always found appalling. Little did Lady Jeanette know that the perfect way to destroy Miranda's appetite would have been to watch Colin with another woman.

Lady Helen sat preening like one of those bloody birds she adored, a gloved hand lingering a bit longer than necessary on Colin's arm as she leaned in to ask him a question. Several feathers waved about in Lady Helen's coiffure, one of which Miranda thought resembled that of a turkey. The stupid feather would stroke against Colin's cheek as Lady Helen leaned in to murmur in his ear.

Miranda did not care for Lady Helen when first they met earlier in the year and cared less for her now. Adorning oneself with enough feathers that you resembled a bird of plumage rather than a woman was absurd. She longed to pull the possible turkey feather from Lady Helen's hair and swat her with it.

"Perhaps a walk in the garden later, Lady Miranda?"

Miranda nodded, caring little for anything Ridley said. Was it something about walking in the garden? When had she begun to find him so annoying? So predictable?

I thought Ridley to be handsome and intelligent. Once.

Her eyes slid to Colin, twirling the stem of his wine glass between his long, elegant fingers, the movement smooth and graceful. Exactly the way he'd once touched her.

Candlelight caressed the high cheekbones and sculpted planes of his face, shadowing the scar that trailed down the left side of his cheek. His hair gleamed like dark gold where it brushed the edges of his collar. Colin was devoid of ornamentation save his signet ring which glittered dully in the light of the table. Dressed all in black except for the white of his shirt, he looked beautiful and damaged, like a fallen angel.

It hurt, how beautiful he was. How he'd once belonged to her.

Hunger flickered in the dark eyes as he watched her, the pads of his fingers lingering over the stem of his glass.

Heat bubbled over Miranda's skin as if a torch had been taken to it. The tips of her nipples tingled in the most pleasurable way. As she took a deep breath, her breasts pressed painfully against the confines of her bodice.

Colin's lips twitched, his eyes no longer focused on her face.

Hamill droned on about some bill he would introduce in Parliament while Ridley regaled her with gossip from some trip he'd taken to Bath. She barely heard either one of them. Every particle of her body was focused on Colin.

Colin brought the glass of wine to his lips in a languid manner, his heavy lidded gaze catching hers, as if he were drinking her and not the wine. His tongue flicked out against the rim to lick off a drop of the dark purple liquid.

A rush of wetness slid between Miranda's thighs and she

shifted in her seat. The way he toyed with the wine glass reminded her of the stroke of his fingers inside-

"Lady Miranda?"

She turned, irritated that Ridley disturbed her from what was a rather delightful fantasy.

"I beg your pardon, Lord Ridley. I fear my mind wandered a bit. You were saying?" She squeezed her legs together. It was incredibly inappropriate to have one's body throbbing while the soup course was being taken away.

Ridley shot her an indulgent look as if she were an errant puppy.

Miranda knew he thought her simple minded, which was odd given her reputation as a blue-stocking. Few men, it seemed, believed a woman intelligent, especially if a woman was remotely attractive and titled.

Miranda wished to ball up her napkin and toss it at his nose.

"I was asking how you enjoyed Lady Willingham's fete last week?"

"Delightful." Overblown and tedious, Lady Willingham's fete had been many things but decidedly *not* delightful. She'd been grateful for the headache that erupted after an hour for it gave her an excuse to return home.

Lady Helen's laughter trilled across the table.

Good Lord, she sounds like a wounded goose.

Shooting him a flirtatious stare from beneath her lashes, Lady Helen tilted her perfect blonde head towards Colin, leaning in such a way that a plump breast brushed against his arm.

Colin spared Lady Helen a momentary glance, nodding at something she said.

What a lovely couple they made. Both golden and beautiful. What perfect children they would have. Lady Helen would probably name their children after some species of bird. Lord Osprey Hartley and his sister Lady Wren.

Miranda picked up her fork, stabbing with frustration at her turbot. This was really rather unseemly, to have to sit and watch the man she still—

The fork hovered in the air, halfway between her mouth and the plate. She forced the turbot between her lips and chewed mechanically.

Loved?

The turbot tasted like shoe leather.

With a sigh, Miranda carefully set down her fork next to her plate.

Ridley continued to ramble on, sloshing his glass of wine a bit which earned him the annoyance of the footman who stood behind him.

She should really give him all her attention. After all, she thought him the likely winner in the dubious contest for her hand. Pasting a look of interest on her face, she pretended to listen, watching Colin from beneath her lashes.

Lady Helen spoke to Colin in a low voice, forcing him to bend closer to her. Lips pouted artfully as her fingers fluttered up to lightly touch the sleeve of his coat.

Lady Helen's behavior went unnoticed, for Colin wasn't paying the least bit of attention to her. He was watching Miranda.

Miranda stabbed another piece of turbot, swirling the fish about in the delicious wine sauce it floated in before bringing it to her lips. A bit of the white wine sauce covering the turbot landed at the corner of her mouth. She caught it with the flick of her tongue.

Colin's gaze fell immediately to her mouth.

There was no mistaking the flaring hunger in his eyes this time. It was not for Lady Helen. It was for *her*.

A delicious shiver ran down her body.

Colin's eyes slid to Ridley, who unbelievably continued to speak, as unaware as lady Helen it seemed. The big man across from her frowned slightly, the dark eyes nearly going black with dislike as he watched the viscount. Colin turned his gaze back to her then, and she saw clearly the wicked, erotic things dancing in the depth of his velvet eyes.

A small gasp escaped her lips as her body arched slightly in his direction, her breasts suddenly heavy and full. Her lashes fluttered to fan against her cheeks.

The dinner party faded until the other guests were only background noise, a distant hum that did nothing to sever the connection between Miranda and the beautiful, damaged man across the table.

Colin's eyes caressed her, dipping over the curves of her breasts and following the line of her throat. A wonderful fantasy filled her, one in which Colin swept the mound of dishes, along with Lady Helen and Lord Ridley, away from the table and took her right next to the roasted pheasant.

When she found the courage to look up, Colin was conversing with Lady Helen, but one of his hands had reached to the middle of the table. Toward her.

※

DONATA ALLOWED THE BAREST WHISPER OF SATISFACTION to cross her lips. Ridley, that pompous, annoying ass, should not be counting on Miranda's dowry to pay off his extensive debts. Lord Hamill, whose limp was likely due to falling off his horse drunk, would need to find another brood mare. Seating him on the other side of Miranda was a brilliant maneuver. The old codger was so hard of hearing that if Miranda spoke to him, he had to lean closer to her, giving the appearance that he was inspecting her bosom. Which he likely was.

The Earl of Kilmaire looked torn between whom he should murder first, Hamill or Ridley.

Lord Kilmaire was ensnared between the ambitious Lady Cottingham and the desperate Lady Dobson. Miss Lainscott, with her timid demeanor on full display, looked as if she wished to fade into the wall paper of the dining room. Well, possibly the girl wasn't timid but bored. She made a mental note to engage the girl in conversation at another time and take her measure.

Lady Helen was an *embarrassment*. Why in the world did her mother allow her daughter to go about garnishing herself with feathers that looked as if they'd been plucked from some farmer's henhouse. The girl's only redeeming attribute, in Donata's mind, was that she was quite beautiful. Beautiful but with a vain personality that would grate on Miranda's nerves. And Lady Helen was entirely lacking in decorum. She even ogled Lord Welles during dinner. Not that Welles didn't enjoy being ogled, but that was hardly the point.

Lady Helen had been an inspired choice for Lord Kilmaire.

Miranda was miserable. She'd attacked her turbot as if the unfortunate fish had insulted her, stabbing at her portion until it resembled a pile of stones swimming in wine sauce, all while shooting Lady Helen looks of distaste.

Alex, her adored granddaughter-in-law, had created the seating chart *exactly* as requested.

A *most* successful evening.

Donata took a small sip of her wine and wondered at Colin's assertion that Miranda had been betrothed to St. Remy. Contrary to what both her granddaughter and Colin assumed, Donata had *not* been sleeping on the journey to Gray Covington. Well, at least not all of it for she'd heard every word uttered, some which made her blush a bit. Colin seemed very certain that Miranda had meant to marry St.

Remy, which was preposterous. Miranda hadn't cared for the future duke, only Jeanette had been in favor of the match.

St. Remy. The *crux,* it appeared, of the situation.

Donata drummed her fingertips against the fine linen that covered the table.

"*Rainha*, what are you about?" Sutton, seated just to her left at the head of the table, leaned over and whispered. "I can almost hear your scheming."

"Whatever do you mean, my lord?" She wrinkled her brow as if confused by his statement and sliced the pheasant on her plate into tiny bite-sized portions. Donata found that as one got older it became increasingly *easier* to pretend one was addled. "And you must cease referring to me as *Rainha*. Our guests may not understand the Portuguese word for queen and will assume you are calling me an awful name in a foreign tongue. Some might think you are making fun of an old woman."

The ghost of a smile crossed her grandson's lips. For a moment, he looked so much like his father, her beloved son Robert, that Donata's breath caught. How fortunate that the Duke of Dunbar had assisted her in bringing Sutton back from Macao. If Sutton hadn't returned...*well it didn't matter.* Sutton *had* returned. And, now she had dear Alex and those adorable children. *You would have scolded me for meddling as well, Robert, but you see, it has all worked out for the best.*

"Do not think I am ignorant of what goes on at my own estate, *Rainha.*"

"Of course not, my lord," she murmured, as she popped a piece of pheasant in her mouth.

Dry. The pheasant was *dry*. Reminiscent of overly seasoned parchment.

Sutton snorted in amusement, glancing down the length of the table to catch his wife's eye. "Subservience does not suit you, nor is it believable."

Alex was holding court at the other end of the table, laughing as Lord Welles entertained her. Carstairs was dutifully chewing his food and nodding as Welles spoke. The poor boy looked completely lost.

Not an intelligent thought in his head. Just like his mother.

Alex's eyes caught Donata's, and she tilted her head slightly before turning her attention to back to Lord Welles.

"And you've involved Alex," Sutton hissed under his breath while waving for more wine.

"Goodness, my lord, you make me sound rather Machiavellian. I assure you that all I have done is arrange a house party so that your sister and your dearest friend may make suitable matches." Donata took the opportunity to glance down the length of the table.

Colin appeared to be strangling his napkin while glaring at Lord Ridley, probably imagining the napkin was the viscount's neck.

Splendid.

Donata did wonder if she should worry over Ridley's welfare as the Earl of Kilmaire looked quite intent on doing the viscount bodily harm. There was also the matter of a rather large blade Donata knew Colin carried on his person. He never went anywhere without the weapon. Ironic considering what a knife had done to his face. Ridley would do well to give the Earl of Kilmaire a wide berth.

Or not. I cannot wait until that man has served his purpose and we can be rid of his presence. Donata speared another piece of pheasant.

Ridley had been assessing the value of Gray Covington and its contents from the moment he arrived. Just before dinner, she could see the greed gleaming from his eyes as he mentally tallied up the wealth he assumed he would soon have access too. Donata had the inclination to hide some of the more valuable works of art least Ridley try to abscond with them in his saddlebags when he departed. She would need to have Zander watch Ridley very carefully, for the young man was desperate. That much was apparent.

Hamill looked in vain amongst the ton for a brood mare. The former rake had affairs with many of the older ladies whose daughters he now attempted to court. Hamill was politely refused by them all. Then Miranda, with her unsuitability, landed in his lap. Donata had no doubt Hamill would use his influence at Parliament to staunch some of the gossip concerning her granddaughter, but she doubted he would stop the flow altogether. *Certainly* not enough to merit wedding him.

Lady Cottingham was terribly uninteresting. Donata continued to ignore the prattling woman on her right who would do better to rein in her daughter than bore Donata.

She placed her fork down. *Atrocious.* Zander *must* be told about dinner. Mushy, overcooked potatoes. Dry pheasant. Only the sauce for the turbot had been acceptable. The meal was well below the usual standards of Gray Covington.

She doubted anyone invited to this house party, save Lady Dobson, would realize such.

Donata found the whole of it very *satisfactory*.

"Lord Ridley," she said down the table to the dandy, I'm so happy you could join us."

13

Dinner, *thankfully,* was finally over.

Colin now knew the meaning of Hell. Hell was listening to Lady Helen drone on about the specific migration habits of something called a blue cockerel all the while batting him in the face with a feather she'd decorated herself with. He was so annoyed that he said nothing when the tip of the feather skimmed across the top of her soup.

The Dowager regarded Lady Cottingham with dismay, her lips pursed as if she were sucking on a lemon.

The Harpy, whom most of the *ton* referred to as Lady Dobson, recited all of Miss Lainscott's accomplishments to Colin, pausing only to sip her wine with delicate precision. She had waved her fork around in circles, thrusting it towards Colin when she felt the need to emphasize her point. Which was often. He should be grateful she hadn't carved up his other cheek.

Miss Lainscott kept her gaze firmly on her plate, as if the peas rolling around were the most interesting thing she'd ever encountered. Two red spots appeared on her cheeks while

Lady Dobson listed her niece's most favorable attributes as if Miss Lainscott were a horse Colin was considering purchasing.

That was not the worst of it.

The *worst* was watching Ridley salivating over Miranda and her dowry while the elderly lecher to Miranda's left, Hamill, eyed her bosom. Colin considered it an act of true discipline that he hadn't murdered either man before the dessert course appeared.

He had spent the entire meal irritated with his dinner companions and wanting Miranda with a cockstand so fierce it could have toppled the table. That damned curl. Tempting him from its place between Miranda's breasts. Begging for his touch. He was only human.

Damn it.

He saw the way she arched her back as if he were touching her, as if she could feel the stroke of his fingers deep inside her. He'd never known such passion. Such desire for anyone or anything.

Such longing.

I miss her so much.

A horrible cruel ache filled Colin. He forced himself to remember her duplicity and the return of his ring. And St. Remy.

I want her chattering at me like a crazed magpie. I want to hear her tell me to not tear her dress in my haste to touch her. I want her to tell me how to make a fucking mummy.

I just want her.

As the gentlemen withdrew to the library to enjoy their port and cigars, Colin found himself moving away from the group towards the enormous fireplace that took up one wall of the room. He slid into a secluded leather chair, craving a moment of solitude, his emotions unsure. This was not how he'd imagined things when he'd left Runshaw Park for London.

Cam, Welles, and Carstairs stood to one side of the room. Welles and Cam were engaged in a quiet discussion while Carstairs tried to follow. Based on the vacant look in the man's eyes whatever Welles told Cam was beyond Carstairs's limited comprehension.

"My lord?"

Colin waved away the port a servant attempted to press upon him.

"Whiskey, if you please."

"Of course, my lord." The servant scurried off with barely a second glance at the scar. Within moments, Colin held a glass of fine, smoky whiskey, the very same he and Cam indulged in earlier. Inhaling the welcome aroma, he took a sip and closed his eyes in satisfaction, allowing his body to sink back into the cushions of the chair. He willed his heart to slow and his mind to clear.

"I believe I'll have one of those as well." The scrunch of padded leather met his ears as a body settled into the chair next to him. "I've no liking for port either."

Bloody Hell.

Was there no end to his torture this evening?

Ridley. The scent of his pomade wrinkled Colin's nose. What man walked around smelling like the inside of a lady's wardrobe? He opened his eyes only to be met with the sight of Ridley's waistcoat. Horrifying. A ruby, probably quite valuable if it were real, glittered in the pin affixed to his lapel.

Probably paste.

"I hope, my lord, that you do not mind me joining you." It was a statement rather than a question.

Since a reply was not required, Colin merely closed his fingers tighter around his glass.

The viscount sat back in the chair with a grunt of pleasure.

"Kilmaire." Ridley nodded politely and he smoothed down the lines of the thin mustache that graced his upper lip.

Those same fingers had run down the length of Miranda's back. Something dark and brutal curled in Colin's belly. He embraced it. "Ridley."

Silence descended upon he and Ridley, which was just as well for Colin didn't trust himself to speak yet. A light drizzle pattered against the window panes, and the fire hissed and popped as rain found its way down the chimney.

He studied the viscount from beneath hooded eyes.

Weak chin. A slight paunch as if he ate to often and too richly. Brown hair artfully styled about his head to match the bit of hair above his upper lip. Expensive clothing. Gloves from the finest kid.

Overindulgence emanated from Ridley, as if he were an overgrown boy whose parents had spoiled him terribly and who assumed the rest of the world would do so as well.

Up close, Colin liked Ridley even less than he had before.

"I have been looking forward to meeting you, as we are of like minds." Ridley chuckled. "I understand you are an old acquaintance of Lord Cambourne's."

Colin did not care for the reminder that he and Ridley were both seeking an heiress.

"I am." He should have asked the servant circulating the room to bring him the whole bottle of whiskey. He'd need it to tolerate the presence of Ridley.

Ridley's gaze flickered over the scar on Colin's cheek. "The Dowager speaks so fondly of you."

The Dowager did not speak fondly of Ridley, and the edge to the viscount's words told Colin Ridley knew it.

"How kind of Lady Cambourne."

The twit was already imagining the flood of invitations at his door when word got out he'd attended a house party with the Cursed Earl.

"You and the Marquess attended Eton together."

That was no great secret. *Get to the point, Ridley.* "Yes, along with Dunbar."

The viscount's features tightened until he resembled a terrified rodent. That wasn't unusual. Most gentlemen held a healthy fear of the Dunbar family.

Ridley leaned over the arm of the chair. his whiskey-soaked breath bathing the air around them. Bloodshot eyes stared at Colin from a face already lined with dissipation, as if being in his cups were a fairly regularly occurrence.

"Is it true? What the gossips say about him?"

The whiskey made Ridley bold. He assumed a friendship with Colin where none existed. Another mark against the man for sheer stupidity.

"I do not hold much with what the gossips say, Lord Ridley. You would be wise not to do so."

The viscount did not care for the rebuke. He sat back in his chair. This time he didn't bother to hide the examination of Colin's scar, studying the jagged line long enough that a lesser man would be uncomfortable.

Colin didn't give a damn.

"How did you manage to find favor with the Dowager Marchioness? I confess, it has been difficult to earn her regard."

Colin shrugged. "I've known Lady Cambourne half my life. I am honored that she holds me in affection."

"She is very highly thought of in *most* circles." Ridley snapped his fingers above his head and a waiting servant rushed to refill his glass. "As highly thought of as the esteemed Lady Dobson." Ridley threw back the amber liquid in one swallow, shaking the empty vessel as a plea for more.

Besides being pompous, Ridley didn't appreciate good

whiskey, especially one so fine as Cam kept at Gray Covington. Another reason to dislike the *ass*, as Colin was beginning to think of him.

"Lady Helen is very beautiful, Kilmaire. I'm given to understand that Lord Cottingham is quite insistent that his daughter marry before the end of the Season."

"Indeed?" Colin saw no reason to enlighten Ridley.

"Lady Cottingham, of course, wishes a title for her daughter, and as there are no dukes available this season, nor a marquess in sight, she set her sights on the next best thing and has determined not to go lower. How fortunate for you."

Miranda is not the only heiress you considered wedding. How upsetting it must be for you that Lady Cottingham would rather an earl than a viscount.

Just when he thought he couldn't dislike Ridley more, the man inferred Miranda was a consolation prize for having lost Lady Helen.

"Lady Helen is quite lovely, with a curiosity about the world around us which never ceases to fascinate me. Charming, and so sophisticated, is she not? I believe she possesses a rare wit. Lady Helen would make any man a wonderful wife."

Ridley was joking. He had to be. Lady Helen was one of the most boring individuals Colin had ever met.

"Her understanding of birds and their habits speaks well of her intellect. It is good for a woman to have interests outside of her husband and family. It *is* unfortunate that her father's humble beginnings reflect on her in some degree, but her beauty and substantial fortune still make Lady Helen a prize for any man."

Colin sipped his whiskey and declined to comment. Lady Helen's humble beginnings, he feared, were the least of her flaws.

"She needs only a firm hand," Ridley continued, "to lead

her into society, a society that will welcome her with open arms if she has the proper patronage."

Much as he hated to agree with Ridley, Lady Helen would get nowhere unless she married well. *That's where I come in. The Cursed Earl, but still an earl.*

"I alas, have a much more difficult path ahead of me." The last word slurred just a bit.

The pompous dandy was already foxed. Colin found it incredibly annoying that while he declined to engage in conversation, Ridley continued to talk to him. The Dowager would label the viscount, oblivious. Obtuse.

"I fear that the Marquess of Cambourne does not hold me in the highest regard, through no fault of my own, of course."

Colin really wasn't sure where the conversation was headed, though he was rather certain that he wasn't going to like it. "I've no doubt."

"Surely, he realizes that I am Lady Miranda's *best* choice. Goodness she's been out for quite some time and is rapidly approaching spinsterhood. One leg on the shelf and all that," he chuckled.

Colin said nothing, he simply allowed the raw anger he felt towards Ridley to rush unchecked through his veins. The man *actually* believed he was doing Miranda a favor? This insipid twit?

"And of course with the *incident*, and the resulting *scandal*," his words trailed off to hang in the air between them. "You would think Lord Cambourne would be more welcoming of my suit. Hamill is far too old even though he's a well connected and respected in Parliament."

"Yes, the *incident*." Colin would rather hear about this mysterious incident from Cam, but Ridley would have to do.

Ridley smiled, showing a flash of crooked teeth. "I had a feeling that you would agree. Lady Miranda is lovely, of course," he lifted his glass to Colin, "quite lovely, though a bit more rounded than I prefer. Beautiful eyes."

Miranda was perfection. Could he quietly bloody Ridley's nose without causing too much of a scene?

"And regardless of the *incident*, she is from one of the best families in England. The Cambourne family has a long and ancient lineage. Her bloodline is impeccable."

I will do more than bloody his nose. He's describing Miranda as if she were one of the horses on which this idiot gambles.

"It's a pity that even the Dowager cannot make the scandal go away. That would be preferable. Lady Miranda is still received *everywhere* of course, for no one would dare cut her, but it will be rather difficult to have my wife continually gossiped about." Ridley gave a put-upon sigh.

Colin's hands clenched into fists.

"Rather like her friend, Lady Arabella, although Lady Arabella's disposition does not lend itself to being welcomed." A hiccup escaped Ridley. "She will undoubtedly stay *very* firmly on the shelf."

"Perhaps." Nick's sister was at best considered prickly. It was the only thing Colin found he could agree with Ridley on.

"The lack of suitors does help clear the field for my suit. I've even been told I'm considered brave for courting her. After all, what man wishes to marry a woman who might very well shoot him over breakfast one day? Can you imagine?" Ridley chuckled as a bit of whiskey dripped down his chin. "The gossip," Ridley lowered his voice to a whisper, "that she killed her mother's cousin is ridiculous, of course." He looked at Colin for confirmation.

"Of, course." Colin replied numbly. He'd gone cold at the information Ridley so nonchalantly relayed. Miranda *killed* Archie Ruynon? This was the *incident*? Impossible. Runyon was shot by a tenant farmer at Helmsby Abbey, the estate

Alex inherited from her aunt. Cam awarded the man a large sum of money as a reward for saving the lives of the Marquess and Marchioness of Cambourne.

"There are many in the *ton* who believe the rumors, of course. Rather silly if you ask me. I find the whole of the tale to be pure fiction. Lady Miranda is simply not capable of such a feat."

Colin's mouth went dry. He struggled to recall the letter he'd received from Nick with the details of Archie Runyon's death.

A farmer was hunting for one of his calves that had wandered away from the herd. He was searching for it in the woods when he chanced upon Archie Runyon threatening Cam and his wife. The farmer, luckily, carried a weapon. I heard the story from Cam myself.

Why hadn't his friend told Colin the truth?

Because I told Nick six years ago that I never wished to hear her name nor ever see her again. That I wanted to forget Miranda ever existed.

"What makes you think," Colin said quietly, "Lady Miranda incapable of such an act?"

"She's a bit empty-headed. Even if she had the intelligence to learn to load a pistol, I can't imagine she'd have the presence of mind to actually shoot someone. No matter what the gossips claim."

Colin disagreed. Miranda was nothing if not determined and her intellect far exceeded that of Lord Ridley. He looked over at Cam who was laughing at something Welles said. How much money had he paid that farmer to take the blame for shooting Runyon? Miranda's scandal was much more serious than being jilted by St. Remy. No wonder the *incident* pained Cam so. His sister killed Runyon in an effort to protect Cam and Alex.

And it ruined her reputation.

Miranda. So brave. And apparently an expert marksman. A surge of protectiveness mixed with pride rose in his chest.

"Don't you find her a bit *flighty?*" Ridley chuckled.

Ridley was oblivious to a great many things, including the fact that his life was currently in danger.

"Not in the least."

"No? She's always insisting on dragging me to lectures on topics far above any woman's knowledge. I believe she is just parroting Lord Cambourne when she relates such tales to me. Her incessant chattering is like the buzzing of a thousand gnats in my ear. I fear I shall grow quite deaf once we're wed." Ridley frowned as the movement of his arm spilled a bit of the whiskey on his lap. He cursed under his breath.

"So, you are certain that Lady Miranda will accept you?"

"Yes. I told you. I'm her best choice." He winked at Colin and reached into his pocket for a tin of peppermints. "Do you really think she wants to marry that old reprobate Hamill? She's just attempting to make me jealous." Popping a peppermint into his mouth he stood rather drunkenly and set his glass on a side table.

Colin regarded Ridley blandly, careful to conceal the revulsion he felt. There was absolutely no way in hell Colin would allow Miranda to marry this revolting, gold-digging dandy.

"Good evening, Lord Kilmaire. If you'll excuse me, I must speak to Lord Cambourne before I retire."

The viscount steadied himself against the arm of the chair while he ran his hands down his arms, releasing the small wrinkles in his coat. Moving a bit gingerly, as if to maintain his balance, Ridley moved towards Cam, Welles, and Carstairs.

"Whiskey," Colin hissed to a nearby servant. "This time, just bring the bottle."

14

"Don't you think so, Lady Miranda?"

Truthfully, Miranda had no idea what Lady Dobson was speaking about. Her thoughts were on Colin and the way he'd looked at her over dinner. She hadn't imagined the heat that flowed between them. But what did it mean?

Lady Dobson bestowed a toothy smile on Miranda, her turban dipping slightly as she nodded her head.

Miranda watched the turban tilt, silently begging the headgear to slide.

"I was saying that it is gratifying that *this* Earl of Kilmaire," Lady Dobson trilled, "will not seek a bride from Ireland. The former earl as well as several of his predecessors showed an odd preference for women who were not English. Highly unusual."

She winced as Grandmother pinched her forearm. "Indeed, Lady Dobson."

"You've known Lord Kilmaire since you were a child. What traits do you think he values in a future wife?"

"I – well that is to say – Lord Kilmaire values intelligence." Miranda spared a glance for Lady Helen who sat with her hands clasped demurely, a distant look in her cornflower blue eyes.

I bet she's thinking of birds. Or feathers. Or possibly nests and eggs. She's really rather strange.

Miranda bestowed a polite smile on Lady Dobson.

"Yes." Lady Dobson smiled again. "And, Margaret," she patted her niece's hand, "has that in spades. I did despair that her love of books would prove a detriment. It is a happy occurrence that it will not."

Miss Lainscott flinched slightly from her aunt's touch, though her face remained passive.

Lady Cottingham pursed her lips, rising to Lady Dobson's challenge. "He has promised Helen a walk so that she may introduce him to the joys of birdwatching. Isn't that right, my dear?"

Lady Helen nodded, her eyes narrowing to slits. "He *insisted,* Lady Dobson, on assisting me in my search for the ruby-throated thrush. I'm told the thrush lives in the woods surrounding Gray Covington."

Lady Dobson's nostrils flared. "How lovely. I know that several gentlemen have mentioned to me how they've enjoyed birdwatching with you."

A small puff of disbelief came out of Lady Cottingham at the comment.

Lady Helen paled slightly, but she lifted her chin defiantly.

Lady Dobson continued in a mellow voice, knowing her barb had met its mark. "Have I mentioned Margaret's talent at the piano forte? She will showcase her talent for us tomorrow evening."

Miranda wondered if Lady Dobson and Lady Cottingham would go at each other like two dogs fighting over a scrap of meat, with the Earl of Kilmaire in the role of the scrap. She stood, rather abruptly, a faux pas at which her grandmother, as hostess, would likely chastise her for tomorrow. But, if she retired now, Miranda could avoid both Lord Ridley and Lord Hamill. The gentlemen would soon be joining the ladies in the drawing room and Miranda was certain she could not pretend interest in either man again.

"Pray excuse me." She put a hand to her head as if she were about to faint. "Much like your husband, Lady Cottingham, I am prone to sickness after long carriage rides. I beg your forgiveness, but I must retire."

"A wonder you did not succumb to this affliction earlier," Grandmother murmured, one grey brow raised in question. The green eyes, shrewd and knowing, took in Miranda's slightly flushed features. "You do look a bit ill, granddaughter. Alexandra and I will entertain our guests."

Alex nodded. "Pray get some rest, dearest."

Miranda nodded to the circle of ladies as she made her way from the room. At least the sickness was not completely feigned. The entire conversation had made Miranda sick to her stomach.

It had been hours since Miranda fled the drawing room and the discussion of how best Lady Helen or Miss Lainscott could ensnare the Earl of Kilmaire. Upon arriving in her room, Miranda ordered a warm bath. A bath always soothed one's nerves and aided in sleep.

Except that sleep did not come and her nerves were far from soothed.

"A book," she murmured out loud as she hastily slid her arms through a robe left on the back of a chair. "Something dreadfully boring, may help me sleep. I think Sutton just received a package from Thrumbadges. There's bound to be something tedious in there." Mind made up, she left her bed.

Miranda's dressing gown flowed about her ankles, tickling the tops of her bare feet. She probably should have put on slippers, but really, this was her home and surely no one would be about at this hour. Even the footman who always stood ready at the door had sought his bed.

Quietly, she opened the doors to the library, shutting them behind her with a soft click. This was her favorite room at Gray Covington. The library smelled of old leather, ink and paper. The lingering aroma of a cheroot touched her nostrils as did the smell of the fire, now banked. Her toes sunk into the thick rug covering the floor as she made her way toward the window. The package from Thrumbadge's was bound to be on the long table that ran aside one tall bookcase.

Halfway across the room something stopped her. A sound, like someone taking a breath alerted her to another's presence. She froze, praying that Lord Hamill wasn't hidden in the dark somewhere drinking her brother's brandy.

"I didn't know, Miranda." The words, soft like velvet, with just a slight lilt to them, flowed across the room to her.

Carefully, Miranda turned towards the fire and the pair of wing-backed chairs that flanked the hearth.

Two long legs, crossed at the ankle, stretched out from one chair. A hand dangled over the side clutching a glass of amber liquid.

Whiskey, probably.

Miranda walked towards the hearth and turned to face the chair. Firelight glinted off hair the color of faded gold, to frame a face all the more handsome for the damage done to it.

"What are you doing here?" She clutched her robe around her, suddenly feeling very small and vulnerable in front of the large male sprawled in the chair before her.

"Brooding." He held up the crystal glass in his hand and gave her a crooked smile. "You always insisted that I liked to brood. I suppose you're correct. Your brother's excellent whiskey is assisting me in my melancholy. I'm grateful that Hamill prefers brandy else we'd be fighting over it. Did you know I found him asleep in that chair," he pointed somewhere to the left, "before we'd even gone to dinner? You'd end up his nursemaid, feeding him gruel with a spoon."

"You're foxed."

"A bit, perhaps." He raised a golden brow at the dressing gown and her bare feet. "Are you having an assignation?" The words growled from between his lips before he took a large swallow of the whiskey and glared at her. "Have I interrupted?"

"No." She shook her head. "And if I were it wouldn't—"

"Matter? You're mistaken on that point. It shall always matter." His face softened a bit, but the intensity in his eyes didn't lessen. "I would hear all of it, Miranda, for I didn't know." His voice lowered to a delicious whisper. "I would not have you think I baited you deliberately. I am not that cruel."

He leaned forward and tried to catch her hand. Fingers brushed against hers as he tried to pull her to him. "Tell me. Of Helmsby Abbey and Archie Runyon."

Miranda looked down, loving the feel of his skin against hers. She'd always adored his hands, for they were possessed of a certain masculine grace. Not soft, like so many gentleman's hands, not like Ridley's. Instead, Colin's hands were rough, probably because he didn't care for wearing gloves. "I don't think now is the time, Colin."

"There is no better time." He pulled her down to him.

Surprised, Miranda didn't object, but allowed herself to be drawn down next to Colin. She perched on the arm of the chair, her feet against his leg and her knees pressing against the upper part of Colin's thighs. The heat of his body seeped through the dressing gown.

Colin did not release her hand. Instead his thumb moved

back and forth over the base of her palm. It was an intimate gesture meant to comfort. Or possibly arouse. Miranda felt both emotions equally.

"Miranda," he urged softly, looking up at her from beneath those ridiculously long lashes he sported.

He didn't sound as if he were aroused. Or attempting to seduce her. Possibly he was trying to be her friend, something he had not been since arriving in London.

She took a long shuddering breath.

What, exactly, should she say? Grandmother instructed her never to speak of it. Pretend the incident had never occurred. Alex and Sutton were so guilt ridden that the mere mention of that day left them both anguished for hours. Which left Miranda with no one to talk to about the thing that had forever altered her life.

Her mother's cousin had been a *terrible* human being. Archie caused her family nothing but pain. He was to be blamed for the indirect death of her father, and the continued absence of her sister Elizabeth. But it was no small thing to end another's life, even if that person were Archie Runyon. She'd prayed of course, begging forgiveness from God, but she felt no relief in doing so.

"I don't regret that he is dead," she finally said.

Colin's eyes deepened to near black. "I do not either. The world is a better place without Archie Runyon. Go on."

"I'll have a bit of that, if you don't mind." Miranda nodded to the glass of whiskey Colin held in his hands.

Her hand shook as she reached for the glass. "I don't wish your pity."

"Good, for I have none to spare." His hand covered hers to steady the glass. Gently he tipped it up to her lips. "You've taken to drinking whiskey?"

The liquid burned down Miranda's throat and her eyes immediately watered though she managed to keep the cough moving up her throat from erupting. "No," she choked. "But I find it difficult to talk about the *incident*. I thought perhaps the whiskey would help."

Colin moved the whiskey glass back, but not before wiping at an amber drop that fell from her lip with his finger.

"I – I'm not sure where I should start." Her lips burned both from the whiskey and the movement of his finger over her mouth.

"At the beginning. That is the best place to start." He moved across the chair and in doing so, pulled her off the arm of the chair until she half sat in his lap.

Warmth emanated from him. He smelled of clean linen, cheroot, and the whiskey, a delicious combination that sent tendrils of longing through her.

"I – I did shoot him, Colin." Her heart began to race, as much from his closeness as the remembrance of that horrible day. "He was going to kill my brother. Hurt Alex. I really had no choice." A shudder ran through her as her body bent towards him, seeking the solace he offered.

"You absolutely had no choice, Miranda. No one, in the same situation would have done otherwise."

His arm came around her shoulders to press against the middle of her back. The slight pressure brought her body against the length of his. "Continue. I'm here."

He's only trying to comfort me. "Sutton left Alex. When she was with child. Or, children, I suppose I should say, although she didn't realize, of course, that she'd have twins. No one did. But, he left, I'm not sure he–"

As if it were the most natural thing in the world, Colin leaned over and brushed his lips against hers. "Slowly, Miranda."

Traitorous body. She was about to recite the most horrible moment of her life and her body was paying her mind no heed. The tips of her nipples were hardening to pebbles beneath the nightgown and an ache started low in her belly from just the merest touch of Colin's mouth on hers.

His arm slid down until it rested on her waist.

"Sutton left because Mother," she couldn't keep the venom out of her words. "You know that Alex and Sutton had a scandalous start to their marriage. Alex was once engaged to Cousin Archie. But of course, after Sutton and Alex were found together, her betrothal to Archie was over. Thank God.

"He told me." Colin's fingers moved lightly against her.

"Everything was fine. Then Mother filled Sutton's head with nonsense about Alex. That she had married him for other reasons. Even though Grandmother and I told him differently, he took off to be part of some ridiculous expedition. He left Alex with barely a word. He didn't know about the child yet. I mean the twins." She waved her hand. "Maddy and Robert."

Colin brought the whiskey to her mouth again, allowing her a sip. He took it back from her and tossed back the remainder before setting the glass down on a table next to the chair. He turned her hand and laced his fingers through hers. As he used to. Before.

"Nick did not intervene?" Colin's fingers squeezed hers. "I'm somewhat surprised, because he has a strange propensity for doing so. He enjoys meddling in the affairs of others." His voice hardened. "I'm a bit surprised Nick didn't rid the world of Archie Runyon himself as a favor to the Dowager."

"He wasn't here. Bermuda." Miranda whispered. "Nick left for Bermuda, but he dispatched several men to watch over Sutton. He knew of Mother's desire to harm my brother. Several attempts had been made on Sutton's life since he'd returned from Macao. We all knew, deep down inside, that the attempts were somehow Mother's doing. Without Sutton's knowledge, Nick instructed several men to watch over my brother as he was being an idiot. Thankfully. Though

Grandmother and I didn't know then. About the men, I mean. My mother and her merry band of assassins." A small choking laugh came from her. "God, she's horrible. I don't even know what she expected to accomplish." Her mouth held a terrible bitter taste that she felt certain only more whiskey would dispel.

"I don't suppose I could have some more whiskey?"

"In a moment. Thank God for Nick's meddling. He's as bad as the Dowager. Inside the Devil of Dunbar beats the heart of a matronly busy body."

Miranda gave him a weak smile. "Alex was alone in Hampshire at her family's estate. At Grandmother's urging, I went to visit her. She was nearly ready to give birth and big as a house. You should have seen her. At any rate, I didn't want her to be alone just because my brother is an idiot. Just before I left for Hampshire, I received a note from Sutton. He'd finally come to his sense after being such an—."

"Ass."

"Yes. Sutton was being an *enormous* ass. And he finally realized it. He arranged to surprise Alex and beg her forgiveness. I was to take the carriage and pick him up in the village on the outskirts of Helmsby Abbey. I told Alex a package had arrived from London."

He brought her hand to his lips and pressed a kiss against the knuckles. "A bit of the truth, then."

She remembered every detail of that day, for she dreamt of it often enough. Her gown was of light blue muslin with daisies gracing the skirt. The slippers she wore matched, with tiny daisies decorating the toes. Of course, the slippers were ruined. Blood splattered the daisies, dotting the tiny fabric petals. The blood on Archie's lapel. He'd looked so surprised.

"I -I had a new bonnet. With green ribbon. I'm not sure why that seems so important, but I can still see that ribbon trailing in the wind. My bonnet fell off, you see, when I shot him."

The stone façade of Helmsby Abbey loomed again before her as she sprinted up to her rooms to retrieve the pair of pistols in her valise. The smell of her own sweat filled her nostrils as she cursed those ridiculous slippers, wondering why she hadn't worn a sturdy pair of walking boots for her trip to the village.

"When – when," she took another breath, remembering the smoke that had billowed out of the barn that day. "When we arrived at the house, the servants were struggling, *screaming* to get out of the barn. He'd locked them all inside. He meant for them to burn. Sutton yelled for the groom that accompanied me to the village to open the barn doors. We heard Alex scream," she shook her head slightly, "and that's when Sutton took one of the carriage horses and rode into the woods."

The servants of Helmsby Abbey, many of them elderly, fell through the barn doors, choking and gasping for breath.

"I almost didn't bring my pistols. They were a matched set. I was so proud of them. I meant to show Alex how I could hit the tip of a tree branch from several yards away. At the time, I thought I was being foolish." Her voice was shaking. Her mind often relived the what ifs of that day. What if she hadn't brought her pistols? What if Sutton hadn't come to Hampshire and instead stayed in Macao?

She still smelled the scent of the forest, felt the way the wet leaves slid beneath her feet as she ran toward the sound of Alex screaming. The thought that she would never be able to wear the pretty daisy slippers again for the mud ruined them. Before the blood.

"Who taught you to handle a pistol?" Colin's hand trailed along her thigh to pull her closer into the shelter of his arms.

"Sutton. I begged him, when Archie returned to London.

Nagged him every day until he took down one of Father's old pistols and showed me how to clean and load it. He allowed me to shoot in the garden when Mother was out. I destroyed the birdbath." Her eyes began to fill with tears and she couldn't stop it. "My father's favorite birdbath. The only thing my mother ever brought from Italy that he loved."

"Sutton is a terrible shot." A kiss pressed against her temple. "It was Nick, wasn't it?"

Miranda nodded slowly. "Sutton taught me to shoot, but Nick made me practice, until he left for Bermuda. He worried because he was leaving, and he had to go. Grandmother told him he must. After that, I practiced on my own. Sometimes Bevins helped. Did you know that Bevins had been in the army? He fought in France."

"I have renewed respect for Bevins." His pulled her closer until her head lay against his shoulder. "I have you, Miranda. It's all right."

Wetness slid down her cheeks at the gentle words. She hadn't cried truly, about the *incident*. Not really. In fact, she'd cried more over Colin than shooting Archie Runyon. A deep heaving gulp of air filled her chest.

"Miranda," the sound of her name was gentle. "Few men would ever have been as brave as you, love. I am in awe of you."

She trembled, her fingers playing at the collar of his shirt, plucking at the fabric. The words tumbled from her lips as she gasped and sobbed.

"Alex was begging for my brother's life, Colin. Pleading with Archie to spare him even as that- that *monster* threatened to cut the baby out of her womb."

"Oh, Miranda." He pressed a kiss into her hair. "That's enough, love. Enough."

Colin's fingers trailed up and down her back, rocking her

gently against him as she wept. One hand moved to thread through her hair as he murmured words of comfort.

"I knew what Archie was capable of. When I came upon them in the woods, Archie was *laughing*. He thought my brother was dead. I – I thought Sutton was dead. And Alex-" Miranda wiped at her eyes. "That bastard was so busy taunting Alex, saying horrible things to her, that he never heard me approach. I didn't hesitate. I shot him."

"Shh."

"My bonnet flew off my head when I shot him. He was so surprised. He shook his head at me before he poked his finger in the hole I'd made with the pistol. He always told me I was just an ornament to be hung on some gentleman's arm. I think that's why he was surprised." She wasn't making sense, she knew it, and still she could not stop talking.

"Yes." He wrapped his body around hers, as if to shelter her from the horror of that day. "It's all right now. I have you."

"I'm an excellent shot." The words barely left her mouth before she began to sob violently, her entire body shaking. She cried until there was nothing left, pouring out her pain and fear until Colin's shirt lay damp beneath her cheeks.

It felt so good to finally tell someone everything. "I think I've ruined your shirt."

"I have others." He released her hand, but not his hold around her waist.

The light of the fire threw Colin's features into shadow, hiding the scar and for a moment he looked as he did years ago.

Reaching up, he gently tucked one errant, ebony curl back behind her ear, allowing his finger to linger against her cheek.

"Breath, Miranda. It's over. You are safe."

Snuggling closer to Colin, her entire body gave a sigh of pleasure. This was where she always wished to be, safe in the warmth of Colin's embrace, with his heart beating strong beneath her cheek.

He whispered something into her hair and gripped her tighter.

Miranda lifted her head and looked up at the man who held her as if she were a cherished object. Though she'd long since stopped crying, his hold on her had not lessened.

Light blonde bristles stood out against his jaw, glistening as if he'd been sprinkled with fairy dust.

Her fingers lifted to his face, brushing against the bristle of his night beard before moving to trace the line of the scar. She pressed her lips to his ruined cheek

Come back to me. Her heart whispered to his.

"No matter what Miranda, I hope you know that I do care for you." Colin's eyes were closed, the length of his lashes dark streaks against his cheeks. His breathing slowed and his grip on her slackened.

"I care for you as well," Miranda swallowed and summoned her courage, "does this mean that you will not marry Miss Lainscott?" Her heart was beating rapidly but not with passion.

"I have no intention of marrying Miss Lainscott." His voice drifted off.

That was only part of Miranda's question. "Will you then end your pursuit of Lady Helen?"

A wry half-smile twisted his lips. "I would not call it pursuit, *exactly*. More duty, I suppose."

She didn't move, nor flinch at the words that broke her heart. Devastation filled her. She should not have asked a question she didn't really want an answer for.

A small snore sounded from the man beneath her.

Miranda was desolate. Humiliated. *Pained*. Gently, so as not to wake him, Miranda stood. How peaceful Colin looked as he slept, his face relaxed and open. She supposed he did care for her, as much as he was capable. Perhaps he did not so much leave her as run away from her, away from love and all it entailed. He didn't want to be loved. Maybe he should marry Lady Helen.

Miranda supposed she should pity Colin, but instead her heart broke for them both. She made her way carefully from the room, her robe clutched tight about her, forgetting the book she'd meant to retrieve. Nothing would allow her to sleep this night.

15

CAMBOURNE HOUSE 1830

"Nonsense, Colin. I insist you stay the night. The street is beginning to flood. You'd be risking your life just stepping off the sidewalk."

Colin regarded his benefactor with a smile. Lord Robert Cambourne was a generous host indeed, inviting him to stay the night, especially when the marchioness had made clear her abundant dislike. Even if the marchioness welcomed him with open arms, his lordship's invitation should be declined. It was akin to putting a fox in charge of a hen house.

"The roast was excellent tonight, was it not? I think Cook outdid herself."

Colin wouldn't know. With Miranda sitting across from him, every movement she made calculated to drive him mad with lust, he'd barely tasted the food.

"My lord, I would not wish to impose." Dear God, he didn't think he had enough self-control to spend the night under the same roof as Miranda.

"Colin, your presence is never an imposition." Lord

Cambourne settled into a tobacco-brown leather chair across from Colin with a deep sigh of pleasure. "I do love this chair. It goes back and forth with me from Gray Covington to London. Battered, old, worn." He gave a bark of laughter. "Much like myself."

"My lord—"

"You will stay." The older man's tone brooked no further discussion on the matter.

Sweet Jesus. How would he ever survive the night with Miranda only a few doors away? Still, he dared not offend Lord Cambourne.

"Thank you, my lord. I would be delighted."

Hopefully, Miranda had retired for the night and need never know Colin was ensconced in a guest room. Miranda was bent on ruination, and Colin steadfastly refused to bed her before they could be formally betrothed. He also wished to be sure he could support a wife, though he would never be able to support Miranda in the extravagant way she lived as the daughter of a Marquess.

Miranda argued that Colin was being stubborn. Her dowry was *ridiculously* large. Any other gentleman wouldn't blink at the thought of all that money. It was normal, ordinary even, to expect a large settlement from a titled young lady.

Colin didn't feel right about it. If that meant he wasn't a gentleman, then he wasn't. He wanted Miranda for herself. Not for the wealth she would bring to him, nor the connections her family provided. He only wanted *her*.

Thankfully, after nearly three months in London, his financial situation had finally improved. Somewhat.

"Wently tells me that Thrumbadge's has had to replenish their stock twice and that's not happened before. I am very proud of you, Colin."

"Thank you, my lord. I had no idea that a story I wrote to

entertain my uncle in his sickbed would prove to be so popular. Lord Wently has already urged me to write the second book while the demand remains strong."

'Lord Thurston Begins', the saga of a young lord lost at sea for ten years, who returns to London to claim his estate and marry the woman he loved, had become *the* novel of the Season. The book was full of daring and frothy romantic escapades. No one would ever suspect the author to be a gentleman.

He'd never thought to actually profit from telling a story though he'd long kept a journal. *Lord Thurston* began as a way to entertain his ailing uncle when the man's illness left him bedridden. The servants of Estervale would sneak to sit outside of Uncle Gerald's bedchamber to listen as Colin spun the tale for his uncle. They were his first critics, often adding bits and pieces he would later incorporate into the story.

"You were right, of course."

Lord Cambourne reached over and patted Colin's arm in affection. "How well I remember seeing you on your visits to Gray Covington, sitting under that giant oak tree. I could spy you from my study as I attended to business. You were always scratching away in that red leather notebook."

"A gift from you, as I recall, my lord, one Christmas when you invited me to come to Gray Covington." That had been a wonderful holiday, the best Colin ever had. Christmas for the Earl of Kilmaire and his family was a much more somber affair. No gifts were exchanged. No sweets or other treats prepared. Christmas at Gray Covington was something else entirely. Even Lady Cambournee took part in the merriment.

"And the stories you used to tell Miranda! I've you to thank for the mornings I spent hunting for leprechauns and wee folk in the gardens. I believe you convinced her a family of fairies made their home in the topiaries. She's told those stories to Elizabeth, you know. I'm now looking for gnomes down in the basements, a candle clutched in one hand and my youngest daughter in the other."

Elizabeth was a beautiful, gap-toothed child who lisped a bit. Colin could not enter the Cambourne House without the youngest daughter of the Marquess of Cambourne tugging on his sleeve. Yesterday Elizabeth informed Colin that a troll lived under her nursemaid's bed.

"Your daughters share a vivid imagination. Miranda is spinning her own stories I think."

"It's kind of you, to escort her about. With Sutton's absence. . ." Lord Cambourne's words trailed off and his handsome features took on a pinched look. Clearing his throat he continued, "I do appreciate you stepping in."

"It's no trouble at all, my lord. It's my pleasure." Lord Cambourne had no idea how much. It was a useful ruse. Pretending to be a somewhat put-upon family friend, it allowed Colin to escort Miranda to the bookstore or the museum. Sometimes they would take walks in the park.

A small smile tugged at Lord Cambourne's lips. "Miranda can be challenging. Always chattering on about this and that. I've no idea how her mind works; it remains a constant mystery to me. Her current obsession appears to be ancient Egypt and mummies. I'm not sure it's proper reading for a girl of her station, and Lady Cambourne despairs that Miranda's interests will put off suitors." Lord Cambourne shot Colin a rather pointed look and sipped his drink. "Do *you* think Miranda's eccentricities would deter the *right* suitor?"

"I believe, my lord," Colin said quietly and firmly, "that the right gentleman will appreciate Lady Miranda and encourage her interests."

"Such as escorting her to museums and lectures?" Lord Cambourne's green eyes sparkled in the dim light of the study.

He knows.

"Yes, my lord. A man of honorable intentions who appreciates Lady Miranda for herself."

"Very good." Lord Cambourne nodded. "Very good indeed. I shall welcome this suitor with honorable intentions. I do hope he does not delay, for my daughter grows impatient."

Colin took a small sip of the brandy he held and allowed the warmth from both the brandy and Lord Camborne's approval to sink in. "I feel certain, my lord, that he will make an appearance quite soon."

The conversation moved to other things as the storm raged outside, until the hour grew late, the clock striking midnight.

"Goodness," Lord Cambourne set aside his glass and shot another look at the storm outside. "I believe I should retire. Bevins had prepared you a room." He waved his hand as if anticipating Colin to protest again. "I cannot in good conscience send you out in this weather and well you know it. I'll see you at breakfast."

"Thank you, my lord. For everything."

"You are most welcome, Colin. Most welcome. And I am incredibly pleased by developments," he chuckled in a low tone, "since your return to London. In all respects." He stood a bit unsteadily. "Stay and finish your brandy. One of the footmen will show you up when you're ready. Perhaps the storm will give you creative inspiration."

Colin sat and watched the fire for the longest time, sipping his brandy and listening to the rain dripping down the windows. He thought of the royalty check he'd received from Lord Wently. Of the kindness of Lord Cambourne. Of the gypsy in the woods and how wrong her prediction of Colin's life had been. But mostly he thought of Miranda.

"Colin?"

Miranda was lying next to him in the gardens of Gray Covington, her glorious ebony hair fanning out on the soft summer grass. Clad only in a very thin, very sheer chemise, her generous breasts were barely covered. She beckoned him with a seductive tilt to her lips as her fingers fell to the thin satin ribbon holding the garment together. Green eyes sparkled with promise as the ribbon slowly unfurled and the chemise opened.

Sun lit her naked body as Colin leaned forward to trail his lips across the top of breasts.

"Colin."

Miranda writhed beneath his touch, her hand reaching up to caress his shoulder. She pressed her lips against his mouth.

"Colin, wake up."

A soft, female body settled next to Colin. Tiny nips at his earlobe and the press of lips against his neck shot sensation down his body to his already throbbing cock.

"Mmm. You taste good. Not as good as a raisin cake, of course, but altogether quite delicious."

Christ. Colin's eyes shot open.

Miranda pressed her body against his back, curling her smaller form over his. Her hair trailed in wild disarray tickling his nose as she looked down at him. She was grinning from ear to ear as if she'd accomplished some magnificent feat. Pressing a kiss to his naked shoulder, she peered at him in curiosity, her face bathed with the soft light of the fire. "You haven't any clothes on, do you?"

"Not a stitch."

Miranda bit her lip. "Don't gentlemen wear something to bed? I ask because once I saw Bevins late at night sneaking down to the kitchen. He had a nightshirt on and-"

Colin rolled over on his back and pulled her atop him.

"I'm not at all interested in what your butler may wear to bed."

He positioned her hips so that she straddled him, watching in fascination as the nightgown rode up her thighs. He could feel the warm press of her mound through the sheets and his erection throbbed painfully in response.

Miranda made a soft sound of pleasure. The long curling strands of her hair floated over his bare chest like a dark cloak.

"I saw you once," her gaze ran over his torso, "when you and Sutton swam in the pond at Gray Covington. I do not remember this." A fingernail grazed his nipple and trailed through the mat of hair on his chest. Miranda's eyes turned thoughtful. "I don't suppose I've ever seen a man without his shirt."

"You shouldn't be here, Miranda." Colin was quite sure Lord Cambourne's approval of their courtship didn't extend to bedding the man's daughter beneath his own roof.

"I wanted to see you. You ignored me all through dinner." She wiggled atop him again, pushing herself against the thickening of his groin. "And don't worry. Everyone is asleep. Even Bevins. I locked the door."

"You were teasing me, deliberately, all through the meal. The way you licked the pudding off your spoon, for instance."

"I wasn't." She leaned down and brushed her lips to his. Her breasts hung down, the plush warmth pushing suggestively against his chest. "It was only pudding."

The nightgown, some sheer bit of cotton that aroused Colin more than deterred him, gaped open at the neck. Nipples the color of summer cherries pushed impudently against the nearly transparent material, begging for his mouth.

"I've tried to be good, really I have, Colin. I know I'm terribly forward. Wanton, even. I supposed I should be ashamed, but . . ." A soft gasp escaped her as Colin nosed his way inside the gaping neckline and flicked his tongue against one nipple.

"Oh." Miranda made a lovely little squeak.

The problem, Colin thought as he took the cherry red peak in his mouth and his hand cupped her breast, was that Miranda possessed not an *ounce* of shyness around him. She begged for his touch with every glance and swish of her hips, until Colin thought he would become mindless with lust.

A tortured gasp parted her lips as he drew her nipple between his teeth. She arched her back, pushing her breast more fully into his mouth as her fingers found their way to the base of Colin's skull. Her hips rolled back and forth over his rock-hard erection.

Colin released the nipple, his breathing harsh as he lay his head on her breast. His hands gripped her hips, holding her still. How many men could withstand such an assault?

"Miranda, leave now, I beg you."

"I cannot." Her hands fell to his shoulders and she lightly traced his collarbone. A light kiss pressed the corner of his mouth. Then his shoulder. Then the hollow of his neck. She sat back.

A whoosh of air left his chest at the feel of her flesh rubbing against him through the sheet.

Cheeky, magnificent woman.

Miranda watched him, a curious look in her eyes, then she moved again.

Colin pushed up as she did so, letting her feel the rigid heat of his cock.

Miranda's mouth parted in surprise, then her lips curled seductively.

"*Christ*, you should leave."

Suddenly, she slid down his body, so that her face now hovered just above his stomach.

His cock twitched beneath the bedclothes. Colin was certain he wouldn't survive the night.

Miranda's eyes widened even more, her gaze glued to the movement beneath the sheet. A fingertip toyed with the edge of the linen.

"Go on," he whispered, fascinated by the way the tangled mass of her hair traveled down his torso.

The sheet pulled away from his stomach until the edge lay just below his navel. Her touch was light as she explored the breadth of his chest, tracing the muscles of his stomach. She pressed her lips to the skin just above the cover of the sheet. Her palms flattened over the mat of hair on his chest as her fingers tickled the lines of his ribs.

"You resemble one of mother's statues," her voice was soft, "except for the hair, of course. I wasn't expecting that."

"You weren't?" He struggled to keep his voice even as she touched the rim of his navel with her tongue.

In one fluid move, Colin rolled Miranda over, as the sheet fell from his body.

"Oh." She blinked at him. Her hands trembled slightly as she reached up to run her fingers over his arms to his bare hips. "You're so much better than one of mother's statues. I find that I am speechless."

Smiling, he kissed her skin through the nightgown until he came to her hips. "At last." He pulled up the edge of her nightgown.

God, she was lovely. A perfect mound of dark curls nestled between the soft curve of her thighs, begging for his touch. Colin's fingers danced over the soft down, lightly blowing against the curls and watched as her legs opened like a rose unraveling it's petals. Her flesh glistened, wet and beautifully pink.

"Shall I kiss you?" He breathed against the warm, wet

softness, eager to have the taste of her on his lips. Colin didn't wait for her to answer.

A soft whimper came from her lips as his tongue found its way to her center, sliding between the silken folds.

"You're very wet, Miranda." He inserted a finger while his tongue licked and tasted her.

"Colin," she whimpered. "This is very wicked."

"Mmm," he growled from deep in his chest. He inserted another finger, feeling the clench of her muscles. His tongue roamed over her, seeking out the tiny nub of flesh that was the source of her pleasure, teasing and coaxing, until it became swollen and engorged.

Miranda began to pant. Nonsensical words spilled from her lips as the sensations began to build within her. He felt every small tremble. Every soft sigh. He adored the way her body tightened as his ministrations intensified. Her hands fell to his head and shoulders, holding him against her.

His mouth closed over her, drawing the bit of engorged flesh into his mouth, sucking gently but relentlessly. His fingers moved within her channel, curling back and forth, searching for exactly the right spot.

Miranda cried out when he succeeded. Her fingers dug into his shoulders as she arched against his mouth.

A deep seductive moan came from her as she bucked against his mouth, the muscles of her body clenching around his fingers as she climaxed.

He held her firmly against his mouth, his fingers moving out of her body to spread the pink swollen flesh. Taking the tip of his tongue, Colin laved only that sensitive nub, enjoying the way the flesh pulsed.

Miranda's hips came off the bed as another orgasm rocked her body. Her legs trembled against his shoulders as each waved ripped through her. He continued to lick and suck until the last tremor subsided and a deep sigh of satisfaction left her lips.

Mine.

Miranda felt absolutely decadent.

The things Colin had just done to her with his mouth and tongue were nothing short of wicked.

Delicious.

She looked down, pushing back the shyness that suddenly engulfed her at the sight of Colin's head still between her legs. His chin was settled on one thigh, watching her with a tiny smug lift to his mouth. He was very pleased with himself.

"I am the most fortunate of men."

Colin's eyes had gone nearly black, almost feral, as he slowly moved up on all fours. Like a beast about to devour her. Ravish her. A tingle of excitement ran through her.

Miranda's eyes lowered, looking at his manhood jutting proudly from a wild thatch of dark blonde hair. Had it always been so large? She'd often felt the hard length of him, pressing against her skirts, and again tonight through the thin protection of the sheet, but how in the world would that fit inside her?

Colin's beautiful face looked down at her with concern and something else. *Hunger*.

"Don't tell me you've lost your courage?" He followed the track of her eyes.

"No." She wasn't afraid, exactly. At least not of Colin.

"We can stop now, love." He pressed a kiss to her lips. "I would not wish you to regret the loss of your virginity." The Irish lilt she so adored rippled against her skin.

"I will regret nothing."

Love for him suffused every nerve in her body. It nourished her as she awoke every day. Made her long to be with him, always.

I want him. For the first time, Miranda actually understood the meaning of desire. Desire was Colin, the firelight making his skin glow gold as he looked down at her with heat in his dark eyes. She felt the touch of his gaze across her aching breasts down to the center of her, still throbbing from the ministrations of his mouth. Her hand reached out and she touched the length of him, marveling that something so hard could also feel like silk. Her fingers tightened.

Colin groaned. His eyes fluttered shut for an instant.

Miranda was not *completely* innocent of the act between a man and a woman. For one thing, she read quite a lot, even scandalous things that she shouldn't. Books were marvelous for gaining knowledge about all manner of things. She'd found such a book in her mother's sitting room, hidden beneath the seat cushion and read the whole of it before Mother returned from paying calls. It had been a very stimulating afternoon.

She stroked him, back and forth, gratified when his breathing intensified. "Am I doing this right?"

"You know full well you are." He moved further over her and her hand fell away. His teeth fell to the ribbon of her chemise, pulling free the knot. Impatient, he tore at the ribbon with one hand.

"Have a care, Colin."

"Take it off, Miranda," a rough whisper left him, "least I rip it from you."

She sat up and pulled the nightgown up and over her shoulders, tossing the discarded bit of cotton to the floor. The cooler air of the room caused goosebumps to bubble over the skin of her breasts and arms. Her nipples pebbled, hardening almost painfully beneath the intensity of his gaze.

"Magnificent." Colin's eyes ran over the length of her. One hand fell to her breast, a finger hovering over the nipple, before leisurely circling the peak. The hand moved, lightly skimming her stomach, before pushing her down on the bed. Possessively he cupped her mound, looming over her like some great golden cat.

Miranda arched as a light touch glided through her still throbbing flesh.

Colin leaned down to brush his lips against hers even as his fingers began to tease again.

She opened her mouth at the pressure of his lips, allowing their tongues to twist about each other. Her hips pushed up against the insistent probing of his fingers.

Colin seated himself firmly between her thighs, his fingers disappearing as she felt the length of him slide back and forth against the aching folds of her flesh. He reached down between their bodies, took himself in one hand and gently moved himself into her entrance.

Her hips immediately pushed towards him, seeking to draw him in deeper.

"Always so impatient," he whispered. A big hand cupped one buttock. "I've no wish to hurt you."

"You won't". Miranda wrapped her arms around his neck. "Ravish me."

Colin thrust forward slowly, as if Miranda were made of the finest china.

"It doesn't hurt." Miranda shifted so that Colin sank deeper into her flesh.

"Love, wait." Colin swore under his breath.

She gasped sharply at the painful burn that heralded the loss of her maidenhead. Though she'd been expecting some pain, the pressure and the sensation of tearing still took her by surprise. Her entire body screamed in response to his invasion.

Colin didn't move, and he closed his eyes. "Wait, sweetheart." He pressed a kiss to her lips, her cheek, the tip of her nose. "Let your body accept mine."

"What if it—"

"It will, my love," he pressed his lips to hers.

Miranda took a deep breath and relaxed, allowing her body to stretch and open. Already the pain, so sharp a moment before, began to recede. It was actually a rather wonderful feeling, to be joined. Like puzzle pieces. She tipped her hips up and Colin's body slid deeper into hers.

"*Christ,* Miranda." Colin sounded pained. He took her hand and laced his fingers with hers. Turning her hand, he pressed a kiss to her palm.

"Mine," he murmured, nipping her wrist.

"Yes." Miranda inhaled sharply as Colin pulled back, only to thrust more firmly inside her, burying himself. He stopped again, waiting.

"Again." She pulled her hand from his and placed in on his hip.

Colin moved back, and thrust into her, pressing the bottom half of her body up to match his movement. Teaching her what to do.

Honey coiled between her legs, the exquisite need building again with each stroke. Clumsily, she pushed up to meet his rhythm until their bodies moved in unison. Colin thrust again, catching his body against hers.

"Oh!" A bolt of pleasure shot through her.

"There?"

"Yes." The way Colin moved, twisting himself so that he would briefly tease her still swollen flesh sent a deep throb through her body. Her hunger grew with each stroke until Miranda thought she'd go mad.

A rough kiss pressed her lips. "Tell me what you want, Miranda.

"More, Colin," she panted. "I want more." Ripples of sensation ran riot over her entire body.

"Greedy." His mouth moved to her neck, nipping at the lobe of her ear. Wicked, erotic things whispered from his lips.

She cried out as his fingers moved between them, touching her with a lingering caress as his movements became more forceful. Miranda heard herself beg. *Plead.* If only he would give her what she needed.

"Colin," she implored. "Please."

Miranda climaxed suddenly, almost violently. She threw her head back as the most intense bliss shot through her, sharp and fine, where it bubbled underneath her skin. It was the most glorious feeling, to float on a wave of pleasure with Colin's body buried within hers. Such pleasure. She wished it would never end.

Colin thrust once more, burying his face in her neck as he spilled into her, murmuring her name.

Miranda welcomed his weight as he collapsed against her, her own breathing as ragged as his. She could feel the pulse of his climax still beating inside her, and she smiled, wrapping her arms around him.

I love you. Her heart beat against his. *You belong to me. Always.* She pressed a kiss into his hair and stroked his back, slick with sweat. They were part of each other. Mated. More firmly joined together than any ceremony performed by a vicar could make them.

Colin moved to lay on his side, taking her with him so that he remained inside her. His breathing was still ragged, and his eyelids fluttered down to fan his cheeks, before looking back at her. That smug smile was back, hovering about his lips.

Miranda grinned at him like an idiot. She was ridiculously happy.

I am well and truly compromised. Ravished. *Ruined.* The

word had a delightful sound to it. There could not be any objection to Colin's suit *now*.

Mother would be furious.

A long, elegant finger trailed down the side of her cheek, to rub gently against her bottom lip.

"You belong to me," she whispered and placed her hand over his heart.

The intensity in his gaze took her breath away.

"Always."

16

GRAY COVINGTON 1836

Oh, my. Miss Lainscott seems to have forgotten to be timid and demure.

At the urging of her aunt, Lady Dobson, Miss Lainscott was coaxed into being this evening's entertainment. The piano, one that Miranda's father once played, seemed to come to life beneath the ministrations of Miss Lainscott. She was known to be skilled at music, but Miranda had no idea she played so well. Or with such unbridled emotion.

Most young ladies learned to play a piano or some other instrument passably well, even Miranda. Usually these same young ladies were trotted out to showcase their skills in the presence of potential suitors, to mild, polite applause. Blushing, the young ladies would bow and hopefully catch the eye of a young man who admired the musical skills presented.

In no way did Miss Lainscott's playing tonight resemble those tepid performances.

Miss Lainscott's slight form bent back and forth wildly, as if caught in a torrid embrace with a lover, while her fingers, gloveless, flew over the keys. Lashes flickering against her cheeks, her mouth widened in a beckoning smile as a deep rose suffused her cheeks. Her feet moved in time to the music beneath the bench on which she sat, skirts flipping up to expose trim ankles. The raw sensuality with which Miss Lainscott played completely transformed her. No longer plain and ordinary, she'd transformed into a siren. A seducer of men.

Lady Dobson, thin lips curled in disapproval, regarded her niece with something akin to distaste. Angrily fluttering her fan from one boney wrist, she narrowed her eyes at Miss Lainscott, no doubt already thinking how best to punish the girl.

Miranda really could not wait for Lady Dobson to depart the premises.

On the other side of the room, Lady Cottingham and her daughter stood guard over the Dowager, monopolizing her attention. Lady Helen wore a gown of pale lilac adorned with ornately tied bows around the skirt. In her hair she wore an enormous feather suffused with jewel tones. The feather wafted gracefully about her cheek as she spoke to Grandmother.

It looked suspiciously like a peacock feather. She should tell Zander to check tails of all of the peacocks that made Gray Covington their home.

Lady Helen appeared to be discussing something of great importance with Grandmother, although it did not appear that the Dowager felt the same. Grandmother's eyes held a faraway look as if she wished she were somewhere else. She turned slightly trying to catch Miranda's attention over Lady Helen's shoulder, possibly to beg rescue from the ladies Cottingham.

Miranda ignored the plea in her grandmother's eyes.

Mrs. Cottingham and her daughter seemed unaware of the Dowager's lack of interest. Lady Helen in particular seemed very agitated, even moving her perfectly gloved hands in order to make some point. Birds, probably. The action caused the feather she wore to become unmoored. It was tilting, the nib began to point up as the plume turned to caress Lady Helen's neck.

It would be kind of Miranda to inform Lady Helen that her headdress was coming undone. The girl looked ridiculous with her hair adornment listing across her face.

Just then, Lady Helen stopped speaking, her mouth curling into a seductive smile as her attention was taken by the Earl of Kilmaire making his way around the room.

Miranda's thought to inform Lady Helen of her mounting disaster with the feather was immediately discarded. She was not feeling especially kind towards Lady Helen this evening.

Lord Ridley and Lord Hamill were circling around Miranda like sharks smelling blood in the water. Each man constantly espoused their individual virtues while she nodded and pretended to carefully consider their suit. Lady Helen stalked Colin about Gray Covington as if he were a rare species of bird, even going so far as to boldly brush her breasts against him repeatedly at the breakfast table yesterday morning. The only person whose company Miranda enjoyed was that of Miss Lainscott.

Every bit of this nightmare was Grandmother's fault.

Miranda's eyes rested on Colin as he wandered about the room, greeting first her brother, then Alex. Again, he wore not a bit of color, his formal attire all black except for the snowy white shirt and neckcloth he wore. The scar flashed across his cheek, peeking through the waves of his honey-colored hair. She watched as he dangled a glass of wine carelessly from one hand, laughing at something Alex said to him. He hated wine.

She looked away, not wishing to be caught ogling the Earl of Kilmaire.

After telling Colin the whole of her scandal and the death of Archie Runyon, Miranda felt immeasurably better. The burden of carrying the tale of that day within her took a toll Miranda hadn't acknowledged until she was free of it. She'd never discussed that day with anyone. Not her brother, nor Alex. Not even Arabella, her dearest friend.

A wave of sadness washed through her. Colin had always been at the very center of her world. First, during her childhood at Gray Covington, then later, as the young woman she'd once been. His rejection pained her. Was he incapable of love? Did he only seduce her for sport? Last night, as they sat together in the library, Miranda had allowed herself to hope, only to have that hope thrown back in her face. The worst part was, she didn't know why.

I may never understand. Perhaps I am better off not knowing.

Her eyes followed Colin's form as he made his way through the room. Miranda inhaled, imagining she smelled cheroot and whiskey, two things she would always associate with the Earl of Kilmaire. The physical attraction between them had not dimmed with the passing of years. Even being in the same room with him caused a prickling of sexual awareness that frightened her. As it had in the library.

She'd been avoiding him ever since.

After her *discussion* with Colin the night before, Miranda had gone down to breakfast in a rather poor mood. Lady Helen's behavior that morning, practically throwing herself on Colin's plate like a serving of kippers, only increased Miranda's annoyance. She declined to join the other guests for a picnic near the ruins of the ancient Cambourne keep, insisting she needed to pay a call on the vicar's wife, who was ailing.

Over her grandmother's objections, she'd taken a basket of freshly baked bread and some cheese to Vicar Paulson's wife. The simple task of visiting Mrs. Paulson and catching up on the village gossip had done Miranda a world of good. And Mrs. Paulson as well. The poor woman had been laid up for several weeks with a broken ankle after tripping over her dog.

Upon her return, citing exhaustion, Miranda took a tray in her room and did not go down for dinner, only joining the party to hear Miss Lainscott's performance.

A crescendo of music echoed through the room as Miss Lainscott launched into another piece on the piano, a rather erotic and sensual sounding piece.

Lady Dobson snapped her fan loudly, clearly announcing her irritation to the room.

Lord and Lady Payne sat near Lady Dobson and her annoyed fan. Miranda had known the Earl of Payne for many years, as their land bordered Gray Covington to the east. Their daughter, Lady Barbara, had been a childhood friend of Miranda's, though Miranda was several years older.

Lady Barbara's copper hair caught the light as she leaned in to say something to her mother, her profile delicate and refined. Lady Barbara was slender, athletic and renowned for her horsemanship. Everything Miranda was not. Miranda was far from athletic, except for her excellent marksmanship, and she didn't think that actually counted. She was also not "willowy" a description one often heard in conjunction with Lady Barbara.

She would at least be a better choice for Colin than Lady Helen.

Lord Payne was notoriously protective of his daughter ever since his son and heir, Lord Benjamin, disappeared in the wilds of America. Miranda's father and Lord Payne had often shared a bottle of scotch together, each mourning the loss of their sons.

Except Sutton came home, and Benjamin has not.

Miss Lainscott's passion appeared to have dissipated. She bent low over the piano, slender fingers caressing each key with infinite sadness. The melody slowed, becoming cheerless and forlorn. A thin sheen of sweat coated Miss Lainscott's forehead and cheeks.

Miranda turned and caught sight of Welles, leaning against the wall, his form nearly hidden in the shadows lingering in the corner of the conservatory. He watched Miss Lainscott with a bemused look on his face.

Lady Dobson suddenly stood, the veins in her neck sticking out like the strings of a violin. Approaching the piano and her niece, she leaned her skeletal form forward, shaking her head in admonishment. The angry vibration of Lady Dobson's chastisement could be heard, if not the actual words she used.

Miss Lainscott's fingers left the piano rather abruptly. Her mouth opened as if she would challenge her aunt, but she quickly looked down, and nodded obediently to Lady Dobson.

A light airy tune soon filled the room as Lady Dobson made her way back to her seat, smiling like a crocodile who had just taken a bite out of an especially tasty water buffalo. She made a great show of smoothing her skirts before laying the fan in her lap.

"Lady Miranda." Lady Helen, unfortunate peacock feather still untethered, perched herself next to Miranda. "I'm so sorry you missed our outing to the ruins. Your cook prepared a most marvelous picnic." The feather dipped until it dangled near her chin.

"Unfortunately, I needed to pay a call on the wife of our

vicar. She's been ill. I wished to assure myself that she was on the mend."

Lady Helen waved her hand, dismissing Miranda's words, not at all interested in Miranda's visit with the vicar's wife. "Lord Kilmaire escorted me, of course. I was so grateful for his assistance as the ground was strewn with stone. Why, I nearly stepped into a hole, but luckily Lord Kilmaire caught me."

Miranda could just imagine. Lady Helen blithely sailing about the ruins, probably in a pair of slippers more suited for dancing than for climbing. Tripping gracefully to allow Colin to catch her in his arms.

Ugh.

"How fortunate for you that Lord Kilmaire was in attendance."

"Indeed." Lady Helen allowed a satisfied smile to creep across her lips. "Fortunate for Lord Kilmaire as well." She laughed at her own cleverness before tilting her head toward the piano and Miss Lainscott.

"She plays beautifully, doesn't she? Though I fear it won't help her in finding a husband. Only her enormous dowry will assist with that. Perhaps if she weren't so *terribly* plain."

Mean-spirited little twit. "Musical talent of such magnitude," Miranda's voice hardened, "is a gift. When Miss Lainscott plays, her beauty shines through. Every man in the room was in awe of her."

Lady Helen's fan stilled for a moment at Miranda's defense of Miss Lainscott. Or perhaps it was the thought that the gentlemen in the conservatory paid attention to someone else *other* than Lady Helen. She cocked her head, considering her rebuttal, then shrugged her small, perfectly formed shoulders.

"I'm told the grounds at Gray Covington are absolutely splendid for bird watching. In fact, perfect for all *manner* of things." Lady Helen purred, eyes hardening into bits of flint. "After dinner last night, Lord Ridley took me for a turn around the garden so I could hear the evening bird song." She blinked at Miranda in pretended innocence.

Miranda regarded her blandly. Waiting.

"Oh, please," Lady Helen spouted in false apology. "Do not misunderstand me. He only escorted me as you were absent. I'm *sure* Lord Ridley is quite taken with you. I do hope I haven't distressed you in any way."

"Perish the thought," Miranda replied, her tone neutral and polite.

"Lord Kilmaire, of course, was not pleased." Lady Helen fluttered her lashes, lowering her voice as if exchanging a confidence. "He's quite enamored of me."

Miranda's heart constricted painfully, though her face remained serene. "How could he not be?"

The girl was deliberately baiting her. She doubted Lady Helen was astute enough to sense that Colin and Miranda had a past together. After all, no one else had. No, it was more likely that Lady Helen needed to be the center of attention, particularly masculine attention.

"I consoled Lord Kilmaire with the promise to accompany him on a walk to search out the ruby-throated thrush. I'm quite passionate about him." She covered her mouth in mock horror. "Oh, dear, I meant to say the ruby-throated thrush, Lady Miranda."

Lady Helen deserved a good spanking. What a rude *child* she was.

"I am not a bird watcher myself, Lady Helen, but with the immense parkland that surrounds us, I would assume that your efforts would not go unrewarded. I am sure if you consult our steward, Mr. Smythe, he could tell you where many of the birds you seek can be found. He is more familiar with the grounds than anyone."

Lady Helen tilted her head closer to Miranda's, the feather she wore tickling across Miranda's cheek. Her perfume, something so sweet it made Miranda's stomach roil, floated in the air.

"Lord Kilmaire tells me there are many paths that lead to more isolated parts of the woods, "she said pointedly, leaning back. "That is where we'll find the ruby-throated thrush, I'm sure. Or perhaps, something else."

Miranda wanted to slap Lady Helen for her outlandish behavior. What young lady speaks of seduction in such a manner? Or speaks of seduction at all?

"I keep a journal of my birds, documenting those I see with notes and drawings," Lady Helen continued in a breathless voice. "Lord Kilmaire is *fascinated* by my hobby. Absolutely fascinated." She gave a practiced shake of her head so that her blonde curls fell artfully to her shoulders. "I find Lord Kilmaire to be quite handsome, in spite of that dreadful scar, don't you? He's quite infamous. As his countess, I suppose I would also have to tolerate scrutiny."

Lady Helen would no doubt thrive on Colin's infamy. Who wouldn't wish to dine with the Cursed Earl's wife? Or pay a call on the Countess of Kilmaire?

"I'm sure you will manage," Miranda replied wondering how much longer Lady Helen would feel the need to engage her in conversation.

"I shall tell you a secret," Lady Helen giggled. "I'm *certain* a proposal is forthcoming. Why, he's even told me that I may call him Colin." She pressed a gloved hand to her lips. "It's rather exciting."

Miranda again resisted the urge to bat Lady Helen away as one would do an annoying gnat.

"I do hope he won't try to steal a kiss." She looked sideways at Miranda.

Of course, Lady Helen wished Colin *would* steal a kiss.

"Lord Kilmaire will make an excellent tour guide," Miranda murmured, allowing her disinterest to show. "I daresay he knows the woods around Gray Covington as well as any member of our family. He visited often during holidays from Eton with my brother, Lord Cambourne. I'm sure you will enjoy your outing together immensely."

"Oh, I am *certain* of it." Lady Helen waited for Miranda to say more, snapping her fan impatiently when Miranda turned her attention back to Miss Lainscott.

If Lady Helen sought to intimidate Miranda, the girl would need to do better than that. Miranda had years of experience dealing with vain, cruel women who felt they were superior to others. Mother had been an excellent teacher.

Lady Helen's perfect pink lips pursed together. She didn't care at all for being ignored.

"I do hope you'll forgive me, but I quite admire you." Lady Helen's face took on a look of innocence.

Miranda turned, knowing what would come next.

"I apologize if I speak out of turn, for I have *nothing* but admiration for the way in which you have handled," she hesitated as if it pained her to continue, "the *circumstances* that surround you. Gossip and rumor do such terrible things to a lady's reputation."

Miranda clasped her hands in her lap and waited politely for Lady Helen to continue. If the girl thought she could ruffle Miranda with a mention of the scandal, she was sadly mistaken.

"Why it's *terrible*." Her pretty face appeared mournful. "Mother and I have spoken at length about it. We nearly did not accept the Dowager Marchioness's invitation."

Miranda wanted to laugh at the blatant lie. No one declined an invitation from the Dowager Marchioness of Cambourne, especially a social climbing harridan like Lady Cottingham.

"You understand, with it being my first season and my father's title fairly recent, that we cannot have an *ounce* of scandal attached to us."

"Of course." Miranda replied. "One wonders then, why you would entertain the suit of the Cursed Earl."

Lady Helen's perfect brow wrinkled as if she were wrestling with some inner dilemma. "Well it's quite different for a gentleman, obviously. Scandal only makes some men, like Lord Kilmaire, that much more attractive. Women, however, become unsuitable. I've often thought it unfair. You're so terribly brave to withstand such talk and still go about in society."

What a little *bitch* Lady Helen was. "What makes you so certain," Miranda said softly, "that *you* are not considered unsuitable?"

Lady Helen's perfect composure faltered. She reddened, rather unattractively. "You are—"

Miranda turned in her seat abruptly and leaned forward, her nose nearly touching Lady Helen's. "I am the *sister* of the Marquess of Cambourne, *your* host. My lineage and that of my family would never be in dispute, nor would I need to marry to gain social standing."

Lady Helen fell back as if slapped.

"I would consider what you say next, Lady Helen, *very* carefully. My circumstances, of which you have very *kindly* offered your sympathy, will be *nothing* compared to the circumstances you will find yourself in should this conversation continue further. I would beg you to remember who my grandmother is and the damage she can inflict with only a few, well placed words. I fear neither you nor your family could withstand such an assault."

Lady Jeanette Cambourne had not been much of a mother to Miranda, but she had imparted some useful lessons to her daughter. Namely, how to give a *set down* to a malicious little bitch.

Lady Helen's lips moved as if she would speak but could not. She now resembled a sputtering tomato with an atrocious hair ornament.

"And since you are so *terribly* fond of gossip, I would remind you that there is always a grain of truth in every rumor." Miranda straightened her gloves. "Most of it is conjecture, of course, except the part in which I am a *crack* shot. I often practice in the woods. Pray be careful as you walk." She stood and looked down her nose at the younger girl. "I've enjoyed our conversation, Lady Helen, but if you will excuse me, there are other guests who I must attend to."

Standing, she strolled away from Lady Helen, listening to the poofs and squeaks of outrage the girl made. How dare that social climbing little twit insult her.

Everyone's attention, thankfully, remained on Miss Lainscott. Miranda doubted anyone had seen the exchange between she and Lady Helen. Still smarting from the girl's snide remarks, Miranda took a deep breath. She needed a moment alone to get her wits back and the conservatory was not the place to do it.

Out of the corner of her eye, she spied Zander who nodded back, seeming to understand Miranda's unspoken request.

Grandmother had rebuilt Gray Covington, and her first request, besides the completion of the gardens, was that as many rooms as possible have a view of the magnificent parkland surrounding the estate. A terrace had been constructed along the entire back of the house that overlooked a maze of paths all leading into the gardens. Each room that faced the gardens also contained large, floor to ceiling doors that opened to the grounds.

A footman immediately opened a pair of those doors and

swung them wide, inviting the evening air to filter through the conservatory. The scent of moist earth and the delicate aroma of roses filled Miranda's nostrils.

Peace. The gardens of Gray Covington offered sanctuary to Miranda, as they had when she was a child and sought to escape her nanny, or as she grew older, the constant scolding of her mother.

Laughter sounded from across the room, low and deep.

Colin, his hair shining like a beacon in the candlelight, tilted his large form over the arm of the couch on which Lady Barbara sat. He laughed again, his eyes crinkling at some joke the pair shared.

Lady Barbara lifted her chin and gave what looked to be a saucy reply.

Jealously Miranda decided, was an awful, dark emotion. It made one wish to stride across the room and punch her childhood friend right in her lovely face.

Almost as if she bade him, Colin turned.

Their eyes caught and held. His lips moved, speaking to Lady Barbara, though his gaze never left Miranda.

Miranda blinked and looked away.

She barely felt the touch of Lord Ridley at her elbow, agreeing to his suggestion of a walk in the garden without thinking.

Anything to get her out of this room and away from Colin.

***

COLIN SPENT THE BETTER PART OF MISS LAINSCOTT'S performance longing for Miranda. To be fair, he'd spent nearly every moment since coming to Gray Covington wanting her. But the passionate playing of Miss Lainscott seemed to enhance his desire. And her playing was quite passionate. He wondered that Miss Lainscott didn't burst into flames before their eyes while at the piano.

Miranda seemed not to notice him, perched as she was upon a damask settee, her powder blue skirts draped provocatively about her generous curves. Curves he had felt through the thin protection of her dressing gown as she'd confessed her role in the death of Archie Runyon and the ensuing innuendo that followed. No one would ever be able to prove the truth, but the suggestion that Miranda had been involved was enough to tarnish her.

He'd awoken in the library as the sun was barely lighting the sky, his mouth dry as parchment and his head aching. As the sun rose higher and the sound of the maids making their rounds met his ears, Colin struggled to unwind his form from the leather chair, wincing at the slight twinge in his neck. Lavender and honey permeated his shirt, along with several, long inky black hairs. His heart ached for Miranda, along with the thought that had he not been holed up at Runshaw Park, he could have protected her somehow. Which was ridiculous.

I only wished to comfort her. I'd had too much whiskey.

He recognized the thought for the lie it was. Once Miranda sat in the circle of his arms, nothing else mattered to him. Not St. Remy, nor the damned letter with his ring rolling out. Certainly not the amount of whiskey he'd had. None of it.

Loss created a giant aching pit in his stomach, an abyss that widened and became more immense with each passing day. He sat for the longest time in the library, ignoring the maids, who in turn pretended that there wasn't a large man with a scar looking as if he'd slept in a chair all night with a decanter of whiskey at his elbow.

The two maids dusted around him and carefully removed his empty glass.

As he sat thinking, the maids rubbed beeswax into the table next to him, Colin pondered the insanity of the situation he found himself in.

I am planning on marrying a woman I don't want to restore an estate I don't care about.

He was deeply conflicted where Miranda was concerned. Colin was not the most trusting of men to begin with and Miranda had betrayed that trust in the most terrible way possible. His mind insisted that she beg his forgiveness. Admit her mistake. Express her regret.

By the time he decided to find Miranda and speak to her, Colin was reminded, gently by Zander, of a planned excursion to view the Cambourne ruins. The Cottinghams swallowed him up as soon as he came down the stairs.

Miranda did not join the excursion, much to Colin's disappointment.

Lady Cottingham and her daughter stuck to him like burrs. Clothed in some ridiculous pink confection, completely inappropriate for an exploratory walk through stone ruins, Lady Helen resembled an extravagant cake topper.

She immediately took Colin's arm as they alit from the carriage in a death grip.

He resisted the urge to shake her free.

Miss Lainscott and her aunt settled themselves on a blanket, placed according to Lady Dobson's instructions by one of the footmen.

Lady Dobson spent her time ignoring the repast of cold chicken, cheese and an assortment of fruit prepared by the Gray Covington cook in favor of shooting hot scathing looks at the Cottingham's.

Miss Lainscott watched Lady Helen's antics with laughter glinting in her eyes.

Lord Hamill wandered off, probably to drink the brandy

Colin knew he'd been stealing from the sideboard in Cam's study.

Lord Ridley jarred the senses with his coat of bright yellow, looking like a large, mustached, canary. He wandered off to smoke a cheroot and was joined by Lord Cottingham. Which was just as well because Lord Cottingham rarely spoke and was not known for saying anything interesting when he did.

Four agonizing hours later, Colin thankfully found himself back at Gray Covington.

Now he stood in the conservatory, pretending *not* to watch Miranda when in fact he could look at nothing else. Lady Barbara, a gorgeous redhead, failed to hold his attention, even though under ordinary circumstances he would find her quite attractive.

Something beckoned him to look up.

Green eyes shone like emeralds from across the room to meet his. She wore her hair down this evening, the ebony strands falling in a heavy mass of curls to her waist. Small diamond pins held the inky tresses back at her temples to reveal tiny diamonds glinting in her ears.

The punch of desire to his gut was swift as he caught her eyes. He could not remember a time when he didn't want Miranda.

You belong to me Colin Hartley.
Always.

His lips formed the word even as he watched Ridley make his stumbling way over to Miranda, a toothy smile on his face. The viscount consumed a considerable amount of wine at dinner and it looked like he was still imbibing.

Ridley cupped Miranda's elbow and pulled her towards the doors open to the gardens.

Miranda did not shake him off.

"Lord Kilmaire?" A hand lightly touched Colin's arm. "Are you feeling well?"

Colin gave a polite nod of his head. "Lady Cambourne."

"You'll pardon me for saying, but you look a bit green." She turned her head towards the terraced doors. "The wine sauce for the quail was perhaps a bit rich?"

"Dinner was delicious, my lady, though I feel the need for some air. Perhaps a cheroot. A walk around the gardens should set me to rights."

"I do not think a walk in the gardens will prove as beneficial for Lord Ridley," her voice was polite, but her eyes glinted with mischief. "He's had a bit more to drink than is wise and it *is* dark. I do hope he doesn't trip."

"If you'll excuse me, Lady Cambourne, Lady Barbara." Colin executed a small bow before leaving both women, his attention taken with the crawl of Ridley's hand on Miranda's back.

"Enjoy the air," Alex said as he walked away.

17

"I find Bath a most delightful escape from London, Lady Miranda," Ridley droned in her ear. "Lady Radford is a dear friend of my mother's and often invites our entire family to visit." Ridley mentioned his association with Lady Radford, a wealthy duchess to whom he was distantly related, at least once a week. The constant name dropping was meant to impress Miranda. Unfortunately for Ridley she couldn't care less where he visited. Or to whom he was distantly related.

She gave a small dip of her head as if she were listening. She wasn't. Not in the least.

Miranda allowed her mind to wander while Ridley prattled on about Lord Montieth's hunting lodge. She knew from past experience that she need only blink and nod while he spoke, for he rarely asked her opinion. Not that she had an opinion about Lady Radford or Lord Montieth.

Her anger at Lady Helen had cooled somewhat in the peace of the garden. She should tell Grandmother to put the Cottinghams out on their ears for Lady Helen's behavior, but then chastised herself for allowing the girl to get to her.

Miranda had weathered worse. It was simply because Miranda knew that Colin was intent on marrying Lady Helen.

"Do you know who I saw riding, just the other day on Rotten Row?"

Goodness, she'd nearly forgotten about Ridley.

"I've no idea."

Rotten Row was something Miranda tended to avoid, as riding there had been a favorite activity of her mother's. She did love Hyde Park though. Colin used to take her there after they'd visited the museum or attended a lecture. Once he'd taken her for a lemon-flavored ice, laughing as she took a bite and succeeded in getting some on her nose.

Then he kissed her, his mouth cold and tasting of lemon.

Ridley continued to speak, the smell of wine on his breath quite noticeable. The peppermints did not mask the scent of his overindulgence at dinner. She thought it ironic that Ridley always informed anyone who would listen that *she* was a chatterbox.

Would he allow her to retire to the country after they were wed? She studied his profile as he continued his recitation of the people he'd seen riding on Rotten Row.

Probably.

He would want her dowry, and an heir of course, but mostly Ridley was concerned with money. She heard whispers before leaving London that Ridley's latest mistress was an actress at Covent Garden. Very beautiful and very expensive.

I could always change my mind and choose Hamill.

Lord Hamill offered her his standing in Parliament, and Miranda thought it likely the elderly man would allow her to maintain her independence. The stumbling block, of course, was that she would have to give him an heir. Which meant sharing a bed with the man. Had she been a complete innocent, she may not have balked at the marriage act with Lord Hamill.

The unfortunate thing, Miranda mused, was that she was *not* innocent. Her ruination at the hands of the Earl of Kilmaire had been very thorough.

Too damn thorough.

Miranda stumbled, catching the heel of her slipper in her skirts.

Ridley deftly caught her about the waist, pulling her close against him.

She realized as she apologized for her clumsiness, that Ridley had maneuvered her into a secluded area, right beneath a large weeping willow. The gardeners lit torches along the gravel path, but Miranda noticed with some trepidation that none glowed along this section. She hadn't yet accepted Ridley's suit, and Sutton would not accept the viscount until she did.

The moon peeked from behind a cloud, shining enough of its pale light to discern the desperation on Ridley's face.

And determination. He's very, very determined.

A cold trickle of dread ran down her spine. It appeared Lord Ridley would attempt to force her hand.

His fingers dug into the soft skin of her elbow as she tried to wrench away from him.

"I think we should turn back, my lord," she stated primly.

"Now, Miranda," his eyes narrowed, "it's not as if I've never stolen a kiss from you. There was a time when you fairly threw yourself into my arms."

Miranda felt herself redden and was grateful he couldn't see it. She'd once been so sure that Ridley could make her forget Colin. That she could fall in love with him. Her plan hadn't worked of course, for Ridley's kisses left her cold.

"Come now, it's time for you to accept my suit. You've

been dangling yourself in front of me for years, Miranda. Teasing me." His hand moved possessively against her back.

He was right of course. She *had* been leading him around.

I didn't mean to.

"Lord Ridley," Miranda began, unsure what she should say. Did she have any other choice? It would be Ridley or remain a spinster. Just now, watching the wolfish glint to his features, Miranda thought it would be best to remain a spinster.

"Edwin." A waft of alcohol soaked his words. "We will soon be wed. You should call me by my Christian name. Little tease." His hand fell to her hip and he squeezed hard enough to make her wince.

"*Lord Ridley*," she emphasized, "you are a bit foxed. I think it would be wise to return to the house." Miranda stepped back, freeing herself and picked up her skirts. She would leave Ridley in the garden.

Ridley would not be deterred. He pulled her toward his chest, caressing the curve of one breast as he did so.

Miranda gasped in outrage. He'd never been so forward before. A couple of stolen kisses, little more than a peck, was all he'd bestowed on her up until now.

I should tell him I'm already ruined, though it's likely he won't care.

"Let go of me, Lord Ridley. You forget yourself."

"Miranda," his voice was silky and warm in her ear. "I've enjoyed the chase, truly I have, but I believe," he pulled her against him roughly, "it's time I finally caught you."

"Let go of me. If my brother-"

"I should love nothing more," he slurred, "then to have your brother find us. Please, scream out for him or that annoying butler you have. I'm sure the entire house party would come running. I expect Lady Dobson would lead the pack. She doesn't care for you at all, by the way" he murmured. "You'd have no choice but to marry me. Let's make sure that we *are* found in a compromising situation, shall we?"

His hand shot out pawing the front of her bodice. The fragile lace edging her neckline pulled away, making a soft tearing sound. A sloppy kiss, tasting of sour wine, pillaged her mouth.

Miranda put her palms on Ridley's chest and tried unsuccessfully to push him away. Surprisingly, he was stronger than he looked.

"Lovely night for a walk isn't it?" A voice, angry and laced with an Irish lilt, floated through the garden.

Ridley's hand froze in the assault of her breast. "What the bloody hell is he doing out here?"

Miranda heard the scratch of a match before a flame burst to life, flashing light over the scar that ran the length of Colin's cheek. With an elegant turn of his wrist he touched it to the tip of the cheroot.

Ridley let his hand fall to Miranda's waist.

"Kilmaire."

"My apologies if I've interrupted. I was just havin' a smoke." All traces of the upper crust accent Colin usually affected had fled.

Miranda inhaled sharply. It was rare, if ever, that Colin allowed himself to slip in such a manner. It was her father, who after witnessing Colin lose his temper once said, *'his uncle has not done him a favor in the regard of his speech for he sounds like an Irish dockworker.'*

"Do you think it wise to be here, out of sight of the house, with Lord Cambourne's sister? Trying to steal a kiss, are you?" Colin blew another smoke ring. "Most unwise."

"We are nearly betrothed."

"Nearly? That's akin to a horse losing a race by a nose or less." Colin gave a deadly chuckle. "But, you'd know all about that, wouldn't you?"

Ridley's entire body stiffened at the insult, incensed by Colin's slur. "Your speech betrays your common blood," Ridley spat back. "The Irish are such an emotional race. Take your mother, for example. Crazy as a loon. One wonders that you are not cut directly in polite society, Kilmaire."

"*Earl* of Kilmaire." Colin took a deep drag of the cheroot. "Which is bit *less* common than a *mere* viscount." He stepped forward and blew a gentle puff of smoke at Ridley. "Even Lady Cottingham is aware of the difference between the two."

Ridley pushed Miranda to the side, his handsome face contorted in anger. He took a deep gulp of air through his nose which made the hairs of his moustache quiver. He resembled a frightened mouse more than a viscount at that moment.

And Colin was the large, golden cat who had trapped his tail.

"You . . ." Ridley's cheeks bulged. "I should call you out."

"No!" Miranda shouted.

Both men looked at her as if they suddenly realized she was still standing there.

"Let us all return to the house. Lord Ridley, *Edwin*," she said softly, "you've indulged overmuch. We will leave Lord Kilmaire to enjoy his cheroot in peace."

Ridley *had* behaved badly but Miranda didn't think that was worth one losing one's life over. And Ridley would certainly be killed or maimed. Never mind that she was probably going to marry the man. Colin, though he preferred a knife or swords, was, in his youth, a much better shot than Miranda. She thought it likely his skill had only increased over time.

"Yes, *Edgar*, listen to Lady Miranda." Colin butchered Lord Ridley's name before flicking an ash off the cheroot. "I'd hate to put a wee hole in you."

Ridley thrust out his chest like some bantam rooster, "I'll have you know—"

Colin cut him off with a graceful wave. "Let me explain something to you, Ridley. Even *if* you were very lucky and killed me, which is highly unlikely, you'd never survive what the Devil of Dunbar would do to you if your aim was true." Colin shrugged. "Lady Radford aside, I fear my connections are much better than yours." The patrician accent returned, his words sounding as if they were cut from stone.

How long had Colin spied on she and Ridley? *Long enough to hear about Lady Radford.*

Ridley paled and swallowed. He stepped back and his stance became less threatening. Sweat beaded his upper lip, shining above the ridiculous mustache he wore.

Miranda detested that mustache.

"That's unfair to threaten him so," she said in a low voice to Colin.

The broad shoulders shrugged, and he blew a row of smoke rings into Ridley's face.

Arrogant Irishman. She clamped her lips shut to keep from hurling the insult out loud.

Colin clenched the cheroot between his teeth and gave Ridley a scathing look. "Now, out of consideration for Lady Miranda's reputation and yours, I'll not share this little incident with Lord Cambourne." Colin sniffed the air. "You've had a wee bit too much to drink, Ridley. I'll overlook your behavior and your insults. You're not yourself."

Ridley pushed back a piece of hair that had fallen against his forehead. He straightened his sleeves, brushing them off as he composed himself. Turning to Miranda he bowed. "My apologies, Lady Miranda. I fear that I may have enjoyed your brother's wine more than was wise during dinner. I believe I shall retire early this evening."

"Of course, my lord," Miranda gently touched Ridley's arm. "We shall not speak of this again."

Colin winked and slapped Ridley on the back. "No harm done, Ridley. I'll see Lady Miranda back to the house."

Ridley stumbled a bit, his shoes slipping on the gravel path. He gave Colin a hard look, but he wisely said no more.

Colin watched until Ridley vanished from sight before turning to her.

"That was not necessary." Miranda's cheeks burned with embarrassment at being caught in such a situation with Ridley. *Edwin,* she reminded herself. *I've decided that despite his boorish behavior this evening, I'll marry Ridley.*

"Was I to allow you to be mauled in the gardens of your own home and not come to your aid? What were you thinking?" The upper crust accent slipped.

Miranda lifted her chin defiantly. "Quite frankly, Lord Kilmaire, it is none of your business whom I take walks with in the garden."

As he stepped closer, moonlight fell over his shoulders, bathing the left side of his face. The scar stretched like a bolt of lightning on his cheek.

Unexpectedly, he reached out to touch her hair.

"I never told you, but I think of you when I write her." His voice was soft and low, vibrating through Miranda.

He wrapped an ebony curl about his finger. "I adore this curl."

"Don't." Miranda gave his hand a half-hearted slap. She felt the brush of his finger against her chest as he tugged on the curl, sending a burst of fire down her breasts. The awareness of him silenced the world around Miranda, as it often did, leaving nothing but Colin. She could no longer hear the night song of the birds nor the gentle ripple of the breeze through the tall grass, only the sound of Colin's breathing as he watched her.

He tossed the cheroot to the ground and put it out with a twist of his heel. "I don't know what to do," he murmured, bringing the curl to his lips.

Miranda's breath caught. "About what?" Her body leaned towards him, begging for his kiss.

"I think you know." He released the curl. One elegant finger trailed along the neckline of her gown, his face hardening as he noticed the torn lace. He moved no closer, but his finger continued the inspection of her person, moving slowly down the side of her breast to circle her hardening nipple through the silk.

Heat radiated through her.

Colin looked down at her, his eyes dark and half-lidded as his finger continued the circular motion around her nipple before lightly brushing the tip of the engorged peak. He watched the path of his finger as it left her nipple to wander across the valley between her breasts then down to her stomach.

The muscles of her stomach contracted delightfully beneath his touch. She had to bite her lip from moaning out loud, the pleasure was so intense. Her lips parted in expectation.

The brush of his lips against hers was featherlight. The tip of his tongue ran along the seam of her mouth, tracing her lower lip. One large hand splayed possessively against her stomach, holding her in place, while his other hand seemed to wander aimlessly over her body.

Miranda's toes curled inside her slippers.

Colin's mouth left hers, moving up the side of her jaw, even as she felt the press of his fingers against the underside of her breast.

She swayed towards him and tilted her head, an invitation for his mouth to tease the soft skin of her neck.

Colin did not deny her. His lips leisurely explored the

column of her throat, coming to rest just beneath her ear. Gently he pulled the plump lobe of her ear between his teeth.

"You'll not marry Ridley," he whispered.

"No," she agreed.

"Chose another."

Had he thrown a bucket of ice water over her, Miranda could not have been more surprised. Surely, he was joking.

"But you want me." Miranda said stupidly.

"Yes. So much so that I continue to make a fool out of myself."

His hand moved from the side of her breast to thread through her hair to the back of her head. "In spite of everything."

Again, Colin referred to something she had done, some error in judgement, perhaps. "In spite of everything?"

He stepped back. "I'll not lie and say I don't care for you, but–" He shook his head.

Miranda pushed back the pain his words caused. Had she thought he would say anything different? What an unmitigated ass he was. "The words of a gypsy and your mother's own coldness mean more to you than I do. They always did."

A hiss escaped his lips at the mention of the Mad Countess.

"Why," he snapped, all control gone, "must you pretend? Why can you not admit what you did?" His voice lowered to a ragged whisper. "I wish to forgive you, Miranda. I *need* to forgive you."

"Since I continue to remain ignorant, will you not at least tell me of my transgressions?" Miranda's anger matched his own. If I am to beg," she snarled back, confused and hurt, "for forgiveness, I would at least know the reason."

Colin's lips drew tight and he shook his head.

"You would parade your suitable heiresses in front of me as punishment and not at least tell me what I am being punished for? You would kiss me, hold me, and then marry another?" Her breath hitched as she spoke. "And you cannot even say why?" She balled her hand into a fist and struck Colin in the middle of his chest.

"Coward. You are a bloody coward."

He caught her hand as she made to hit him again. "Enough, Miranda."

Wrenching violently away from him she spun, her hair flying about her shoulders.

One of the diamond clips flew out of her hair to land in a nearby rose bush.

Damn him.

"*I* am your bloody heiress, Colin. *Me*." Miranda lifted her chin. "You would rather marry the likes of Lady Helen than admit to it? After you ruined me?"

"You wished to be ruined. You *begged* me as I recall and came to my room in the middle of the night. Crawled into my bed. What should I have done?"

Anger and pain, the likes of which Miranda had never felt, coursed through her. And shame. Shame that she had once behaved so wantonly. That the most beautiful moment of her life meant nothing to him.

She slapped him, hard, the sound cracking through the silence of the garden like the shot of a pistol.

"You cold, *unfeeling* bastard. Go on. Go back to Runshaw Park. Marry the beautiful Lady Helen and have your marriage of convenience. Live your life alone. You aren't capable of love, nor do you value the emotion. Whatever it is you accuse me of, Colin, I've no doubt you deserved it."

Colin's eyes widened in surprise as her words hit home. He shook his head, backing away from her with a deep gasping breath as if she'd punched him in the gut. Desolation flickered across his beautiful face, and anguish so deep that Miranda nearly felt sorry for him.

Almost.

He took a deep ragged breath and turned from her. When he faced her again, the coldly polite mask he'd worn since his return to London had dropped back over his features.

"This conversation is over. You are overwrought." The clipped words were full of icy disdain. He turned his back, dismissing her. The crunch of his boots filled the air as he began to walk back to the house.

How *dare* he dismiss her. To leave her alone and bleeding from the wounds he inflicted.

"You were right years ago, Lord Kilmaire," she said to his retreating figure, wanting to hurt him. "You don't *bloody* deserve me. In the future, I will thank you not to disturb me when I am taking air with my future husband."

Colin halted at the mention of Ridley, and Miranda silently begged him to come back to her.

He did not.

A lone tear slid down her cheek as he resumed walking, his steps echoing in the silence of the garden.

Miranda fell to her knees, unmindful of the sharp stones that tore at her hands and gown. A deep mournful sob left her throat as she stared at the gravel of the path, her heart refusing to accept the inevitable.

Tomorrow she would betroth herself to Lord Ridley.

18

"Oh look, Lord Kilmaire, I do believe that's the ruby-throated thrush." Lady Helen's voice raised another annoying octave in her excitement at discovering her quarry.

Colin couldn't tell the difference between a golden finch and the ass of his horse, but he resigned himself to his situation and followed the intrepid Lady Helen.

"Do keep up, Lord Kilmaire. It's rather important that we don't lose sight of him." Clutching her notebook, Lady Helen neatly sideswiped a thorny bush.

God, he wished to be anywhere but there, traipsing through the woods with Lady Helen, who seemed intent upon convincing Colin to compromise her.

Lord and Lady Cottingham also seemed intent upon the ruination of their daughter at Colin's hands. The pair trailed several paces behind Lady Helen and her suitor.

Lady Cottingham, overdressed for an outdoor excursion, greeted Colin warmly as the quartet set off. A straw bonnet sat atop her head was held in place by ribbon wound underneath her double chin. She giggled prettily as Colin took her hand, ignoring her husband's frown.

Lord Cottingham grunted, the cigar clamped between his yellowed teeth wobbling as he did so. Ham-fisted and beefy, Lord Cottingham was not known for his skill at polite conversation. A brutishness emanated from the newly minted earl, as if he'd recently done something unsavory.

Colin did not doubt that he had.

"Watch for that stump, Lord Kilmaire. I don't wish you to become injured."

Were he a man bent on the seduction of a much too forward virgin whose dowry was the talk of London Colin may have responded to her saucy remark with one of his own.

Unfortunately for Lady Helen, he'd already been seduced by a beautiful virgin. One he still wanted.

He should have found a plausible excuse and begged off this intolerable excursion with the Cottinghams. Lady Helen and her dowry no longer interested him.

His interests lay in another direction.

At least the air was crisp and cool in the shadow of the trees. He could smell the earth and hear the scamper of small animals scattering before him. Taking a deep breath of the pine scented air, Colin saw his past behind every tree.

He'd stolen a kiss from one of the chambermaids underneath the weeping willow to his left, charming the girl with his Irish accent. Lord Cambourne had taught him, Nick and Cam to fish in the small stream trickling in the distance. All three of them had proudly held up their small catch to be admired by the Dowager, while she congratulated them on their skill before ordering a servant to take the fish to Cook for supper. Cam bragged over dinner that the entire household was eating due to his skill at fishing, while the Dowager smiled quietly into her napkin, and Lord Cambourne applauded each boy's efforts.

Colin doubted the trout they ate that night was the same they'd fished out of the stream for their catch had more closely resembled minnows than trout.

Lady Helen entered a small clearing, but as Colin watched, her form changed into that of a small, chubby child, determined to follow her older brother and his friend, no matter how they tried to dissuade her.

Miranda stared up at Colin with eyes the color of leaves, proudly holding a frog out to him, a token of her childish affection. Then he saw her again as she'd been last night, the same hand reaching out to him as he walked away, leaving her in the garden. Colin had stopped before a hedgerow at the sound of her weeping, each sob tearing at his soul, but his stubborn pride held him back from her. She'd accused him of being unable to love. And he was too afraid to tell her, even after he'd taken her virginity. He'd left his grandmother's ring for her but didn't have the courage to place it on her finger himself. Was that why she'd written the letter? To force a declaration from him?

Christ. I never even fought for her.

"Over here, Lord Kilmaire. I think I've run him to ground. Little devil." Lady Helen turned and waved a gloved hand at her parents who paused on the path, pretending to examine a profusion of wild violets.

Colin had the distinct impression it was *he*, and not the ruby throated thrush, being run to ground.

"I understand your seat, Runshaw Park is in a rather wild area of England. I've even heard there are wolves to be found in the surrounding woods." Lady Helen took a reluctant stab at conversation.

"A few, none so much as to be a problem to the livestock. But, you are correct, Runshaw Park is a bit isolated. The distance and the demands of my estate are such I don't often visit London." He could think of nothing but speaking to Miranda, a need that was suddenly urgent after so many years.

Lady Helen climbed over a rotten log. "The distance?" Her nose scrunched in a most unbecoming manner as she contemplated how in the world, she could avoid Runshaw Park.

"Three days ride. Longer if you are in a carriage."

That tidbit did not sit well with Lady Helen. "I've no love of the country, Lord Kilmaire. I grew up hearing the sounds of crickets and the cows as they moved around the pasture. Bugs everywhere. Dust on every bit of clothing. And, you'll forgive me for saying, the smell of dung."

Apparently, Lady Helen hadn't smelled the Thames recently. The smell of cow dung would have been an improvement.

"I much prefer London to the country.."

Her declaration didn't surprise him in the least.

She paused and pointed into the branches of the enormous oak looming before them. "Pity there are no footholds on this tree." She walked around the trunk, studying the gnarled bark with a look of concentration on her pretty face. Pouting, she put a hand up to her forehead and looked up into the limbs of the oak.

How could I have left her weeping in the gardens?

"There he is, Lord Kilmaire! My goodness, do you see him? He's beautiful." Lady Helen cried in excitement, rapture lighting her face. "Do you see him? He's just there." She pointed upward into the branches.

Colin looked up to spy a tiny bird no bigger than Colin's fist. A flash of red showed on the bird's breast, but otherwise didn't look remotely interesting. Probably only a robin. He spared a glance at Lady Helen staring up at the ruby-throated thrush. Is this where his obstinance would bring him? Boring days spent wandering the woods with his pretty, wealthy, *uninteresting* wife? Endless dinners sitting opposite the length of a long table with Lady Helen, eating in silence? Spending his wife's dowry to repair Runshaw Park while his countess flitted around London taking lovers?

He would doubt the paternity of every child she bore.

But the letter, his mind shouted. *If Miranda loved you why did she return the ring?*

Miranda would marry Ridley and produce a tribe of children who dressed in a garish manner and used too much pomade. He would have to see her at various family gatherings, or perhaps at the opera, with Ridley's arm around her waist. He would live with the knowledge that she shared another man's bed. He would drink whiskey in the dark halls of Runshaw Park and dream of her, with only his stubborn pride to keep him company and not Miranda. Would he be grateful then, that he'd not put the past aside?

Colin couldn't breathe for a moment. The thought of spending the remainder of his life, alone without the sun, was not in the least appealing. *Would I rather be wise or right?*

The ruby-throated thrush flew off, disappearing into the canopy overhead.

"Come, we must follow." Lady Helen posed, her breasts thrusting forward. The bonnet she wore slid gracefully from her head to expose the perfect oval of her face. Cheeks pink from her exertions, with the sunlight streaming through the trees upon her golden hair, she remained still for a moment so that Colin could appreciate her lovely form.

He had to admit, Lady Helen painted a pretty picture. But her posturing was wasted on him.

Taking hold of her skirts in both hands, she stepped over a large rock in the path, giving Colin a view of her ankles, clad in half-boots.

"Oh no," she batted her eyes and kept her skirts raised, "I've dropped my sketch book. Would you mind fetching it for me, Lord Kilmaire?"

Stooping, Colin bent to pick up the notebook as she bid, wondering that the girl hadn't been ruined many times over. Her every action spoke of practiced flirtation and artifice. Most men would respond willingly to the temptation she offered. Just not Colin.

For the love of God, he ruined Miranda and the least she expected was that he speak to her father. Instead, he'd only left a note with a promise and a ring.

"Lord Kilmaire, I don't mean to be rude, but is your attention on our excursion? I feel certain it is not," Lady Helen said, her lips pursed.

"My apologies, Lady Helen." *Where were Lord and Lady Cottingham?* "I think we should wait for your parents."

"Whatever for?" The blue of her eyes shone with feminine calculation.

Apparently, his assumption earlier was correct. The small bird flitting about the thicket before them was not the only thing Lady Helen stalked this morning. Colin had the urge to follow the creature to safety.

"We can sit here and watch the ruby-throated thrush." Lady Helen spun about and carefully sat herself on a nearby tree stump, arranging her skirts as if she sat on a throne. She looked up at him expectantly.

"May I have my notebook, Colin?"

The use of his given name set off warning bells. Any woman of good breeding knew better than to call a gentleman by his Christian name on such short acquaintance. Lady Cottingham and her husband were much farther down the path than Colin originally thought. In fact, all he could see of Lady Cottingham was a large flash of color among the trees.

Maintaining a proper distance, Colin held out the slim leather notebook to Lady Helen.

A frown crossed her pretty face, crinkling her brow in an unappealing way, before her features smoothed. A winning smile crossed her lips.

"Come, sit next to me, Colin." Her fingertips brushed his as she took the notebook from him.

Ignoring her invitation, Colin made his way to a large tree, leaning back against the pitted trunk. It was rapidly becoming apparent that the Cottinghams grew impatient waiting for Colin's proposal. Surely it could not be only that the girl was headed for a scandal? He eyed her waist.

"You are so far away," Lady Helen pouted, "that I shall have to shout at you to make myself heard."

Lord and Lady Cottingham finally rounded a bend in the path and came into view.

At the sight of Colin, a good distance from their daughter, defeat clouded the faces of Lady Helen's parents. Lady Cottingham shook her head in resignation and looked as if she might weep.

Lord Cottingham said something to his wife and she nodded.

"You've known the Marquess of Cambourne for quite some time, haven't you my lord?" Lady Helen's fingertips stroked the top of her notebook, tracing the design that decorated the cover.

"We attended Eton together. I spent many summers at Gray Covington before leaving to live with my uncle in Ireland. I've known the Marquess and his family for many years." Colin crossed his arms and wondered what Lady Helen's parents were discussing.

"I had only met Lady Miranda before arriving here" Her mouth turned slightly as if the taste of something bitter happened upon her tongue. "But I understand Lord

Cambourne has two sisters. The younger, I'm told, is at a convent in Scotland. Imagine, the sister of a marquess languishing in a convent."

"Yes, Lady Elizabeth is Lord Cambourne's younger sister." He offered no more information. Lady Helen was not only spoiled, but ill-mannered to say such a thing.

Well, I was warned.

"No one speaks of her. It's as if she were a ghost." Lady Helen paused and put a finger to her lip. "Unlike Lady Miranda, who *everyone* knows about." The blue eyes grew wide and innocent. "Does Lady Elizabeth reside in Scotland so as not to be tainted by the *scandal*?"

Colin resisted the urge to take Lady Helen over his knee for saying such, though the little twit would probably imagine it as foreplay and not punishment.

"Perhaps it's time we joined your parents." He pushed away from the tree and nodded to the couple standing some distance away.

Lady Helen pretended not to hear and instead opened her sketch book. She took out a small charcoal pencil from a pocket in her skirt. Her hand hovered over a blank page before saying, "I'm given to understand that Lord Ridley and Lady Miranda will soon be wed. It's fortunate, of course, that someone will offer for her. She's nearly on the shelf. A spinster."

"I would hardly call Lady Miranda a spinster."

"Well, I certainly would." She leafed through her journal. "How relieved her brother must be to know that Lord Ridley will save her from such an embarrassing fate. She had literally dozens of offers during her first Season and refused them all. Too picky." The small shoulders shrugged. "At least, that's what Lady Dobson says."

"Perhaps Lady Miranda found no one to suit her." Colin's chest tightened, and breakfast soured in his stomach. He knew with certainty that had there actually been an engagement to St. Remy, Lady Dobson wouldn't have resisted gossiping about its demise.

"I find it odd," Lady Helen continued in a catty tone, "that the Marquess didn't arrange a marriage for his sister before now, or at least," she lowered her voice, "before the *scandal*."

How many suitors had Miranda rejected before the death of Archie Runyon? His heart thudded dully.

I am your heiress, Colin. Me.

"Very tragic. I don't know how Lady Miranda goes on. Why, if I were the subject of such conjecture, I'm not sure I could show my face in London. I fear I would retire to the country and give up all hope of marriage."

"Indeed." He needed to return to the house. *Immediately*.

"I find her incredibly brave," Lady Helen continued, "to attend balls knowing that she will not be asked to dance. I've seen her," Lady Helen shook her head as if saddened by Miranda's fate, "standing with the other spinsters against the wall. Outside of Lord Hamill and Lord Ridley, I've only ever seen the heir to the Earl of Marsh dance with her. I can't remember his name but he's very handsome."

"Lord Malden," Colin said quietly.

An ugly snicker left Lady Helen's pink lips. "You'll forgive me for saying that Lady Miranda is a bluestocking as well and she's—"

"Wonderful." He watched, delighted, as Lady Helen's nostrils flared in annoyance. "Educated. Amusing."

Lady Helen's lips thinned in disapproval. She carefully placed her charcoal into the sketch book and slapped it shut. "You deliberately provoke me, Lord Kilmaire. I realize you've known her since she was a child but how can you not be horrified by the shame she's brought to her family?"

"She's brought her family no shame. You are jealous of her because she is beautiful and intelligent."

Lady Helen stood abruptly. She swatted at her skirts. "I don't care for your tone."

"Nor do I care for yours."

That rebuttal earned him a curled lip from Lady Helen. She raised a gloved hand, summoning her parents. "Have a care, Lord Kilmaire, I have other suitors."

"I don't doubt it." Colin did not offer Lady Helen his arm as they rejoined her parents.

19

CAMBOURNE HOUSE 1830

Thank goodness she was taking matters into her own hands.
Lady Jeanette Cambourne schooled her face into concern, even wrinkling her brow a bit. Something she rarely did. "Oh there you are, Mr. Hartley."

The Irish pauper stopped as his boot hit the last step, looking a bit chagrined. He likely hadn't expected to see her waiting for him at the bottom of the stairs. He looked past her into the breakfast room and frowned slightly.

Probably looking for his free breakfast.

"Good Morning, Lady Cambourne." He bowed slightly over her hand. "I didn't realize the time. I'm not accustomed to sleeping so late. You have need of me?"

Hartley was obviously disappointed to find only herself in the breakfast room, despite the hour. He didn't really care to speak to *her*, that much was certain. Pity, for she had so much to tell him.

Jeanette held out a note, still damp and mud-stained. "A messenger came to the kitchen door this morning. I was having tea when Bevins brought the note to me. You were still abed. The messenger didn't wait for a reply."

A complete and utter lie. The letter had arrived the previous night and the messenger had, indeed, been instructed to wait for a reply, but Jeanette made sure one of the footmen sent him away.

Hartley took the missive and ran his fingers over the elegant seal of the Earl of Kilmaire. He looked at it for so long that Jeanette was afraid he would be able to tell she'd already steamed the note open when it first arrived.

Tearing open the note, she was pleased to see Hartley's eyes widen in surprise and concern.

"Is something amiss, Mr. Hartley?" Jeanette let her voice tremble as if concerned. *Of course something was amiss.* One of Hartley's brothers had fallen ill. Hartley was being called back to Runshaw Park immediately as the brother wasn't expected to live. Tragic, really, and quite fortuitous. She'd long been racking her brain trying to figure out how best to rid herself of Hartley. She nearly wept with relief after reading the note.

"My brother. Ian." He looked up, worry and fear in his eyes. "He's quite ill. I need to leave London immediately for Runshaw Park."

"Oh dear." Jeanette placed her hand on his arm in what she hoped was a consoling manner. "Is there anything I can do?" At his nod, she continued, 'I'll instruct the footman to ready your horse immediately and have Cook pack you something for your journey."

She'd actually already told Paul, her most loyal footman, to have Hartley's mount readied, a small basket with bread and cheese attached to the saddle's pommel. She wanted the Irish pauper out of the house as soon as possible.

"I must make haste. Excuse me." Hartley bounded up the stairs towards the guest room he'd slept in last night.

Jeanette waited at the foot of the stairs, tapping her foot

as she watched the clock. Hopefully he wouldn't take too long. She was not disappointed. He reappeared almost immediately.

"My lady." Hartley cast another look over her shoulder into the breakfast room, still hoping, no doubt, to find Miranda, or even Robert. But Jeannette was thorough. She'd worked hard to make sure Hartley would see no one else before his departure. Even the Dowager, old bat that she was, always breakfasted in her chambers and rarely appeared before luncheon. She'd tell them all that Hartley had left in great haste. Miranda especially would be distraught.

"Is Lord Cambourne in his study?"

Lord, he sounded so hopeful.

"I'm so sorry, Mr. Hartley, but Lord Cambourne and Miranda ran out for an errand. I will express your regrets that you had to leave without saying goodbye."

"My lady." Hartley bent over her hand, his eyes dark with dislike.

"Safe travels, Mr. Hartley. Godspeed." Jeanette gave him the sincerest smile she could muster, under the circumstances.

Hartley gave her one last look and strode out of Cambourne House.

***

"My lady."

Paul, her most devoted footman, handed her two envelopes. One was addressed to her husband. She put that one aside. The other was addressed to Miranda and bulged at the corner. She eyed the small bump with distaste.

Dear God. He's given her a token of affection.

"Hartley gave these to you?"

"Yes, my lady. Mr. Hartley was very adamant that I deliver

the letters directly to Lord Cambourne and Lady Miranda." The footman held up a coin. "And gave me this to do so."

"He wasted what little coin he has." She smiled as she tore into the note for Miranda. "I'll have something for you to post tomorrow, for Runshaw Park. The *only* mail that is to go to Runshaw Park. No matter who writes the letter. That includes Lord Cambourne. Am I understood?"

Another bow. "Yes, my lady. And incoming mail?"

"Bring me anything posted from Hartley or Runshaw Park. That is all."

The footman stepped back out of the breakfast room. Paul would do as she asked. He didn't *dare* not to.

Someday Miranda would thank her, especially once she was safely married to St. Remy, or perhaps the Earl of Kent. Jeanette hadn't really made up her mind who Miranda should marry, only who her daughter would *not* marry. Hartley.

20

GRAY COVINGTON, 1836

"Perhaps you are wrong." Alex motioned for the servant to place the tea service on the table separating herself and Donata. "You could be, you know. You are not infallible."

Donata declined to answer and instead turned towards the long windows that lined the family's private drawing room at Gray Covington. The sky was rapidly darkening as the clouds again threatened rain. Even now, the servants moved through the room to stoke the fire and light the lamps littered about. She and Alex had fled to the drawing room earlier, seeking a welcome respite from their guests, who all reeked of desperation of one kind or another. That included poor Miss Lainscott who'd incurred her aunt's wrath by not snaring the Earl of Kilmaire. Donata made herself a mental note to help the girl.

Alex raised a brow at her lack of response, her eyes as stormy gray as the threatening sky outside. The artful coiffure, designed to restrain the mass of curls atop her head, was no match for the dampening air. Several tendrils had already come lose and more would follow. "Perhaps your intuition has finally deserted you." Absently she swatted a curl off her cheek.

"I am never wrong, Alex. *Never*."

"There is a first time for everything, Grandmother."

Donata snorted. She *was* beginning to have her doubts, however, that the house party would force Colin to declare himself. He seemed intent on pursuing the obnoxious Lady Helen, even taking the chit and her parents for a bird watching expedition.

Miranda disappeared directly after Miss Lainscott's slightly scandalous display on the piano and refused to leave her rooms. Even the threat of a physician could not budge her. Nor would she speak to anyone, including Donata. That had been two days ago.

Welles departed, looking vastly relieved that he would return to London on horseback and not share a carriage with Carstairs.

Carstairs remained to wander aimlessly about Gray Covington. She'd found him having tea with Lady Dobson in the conservatory, while Miss Lainscott embroidered and longed for the piano she was forced to look at but not permitted to play.

Agnes Dobson was a spiteful old bitch.

Lord Hamill could not be induced to leave even though he'd surmised that he would not be Miranda's choice. Instead, the elderly rake seemed intent on consuming the entire contents of Sutton's liquor cabinet. Last night, the old reprobate had to be carried to his room by two footmen.

Ridley casually asked Sutton for the use of a carriage citing an urgent business matter in the village. The viscount had yet to return. Whatever his "business" matter was, Donata thought it likely consisted of a woman of low morals and a pint of ale.

Unfortunately, she expected him to return at some point.

"She's not sleeping." Alex lifted her cup of tea to her lips.

Donata leaned forward hopefully. "You have spoken to her?"

"No." Alex shook her head. "Her maid has imparted the information to me. Miranda sits in a chair, gazing into the fire. She barely touches the trays that Zander sends up, not even the raisin cakes. Only, tea, it seems."

Donata pondered that bit of disturbing information. Things were far worse than she'd originally assumed if Miranda refused to touch a raisin cake.

"Something happened after Miss Lainscott's rather scorching performance on the piano," Alex informed her. "Miranda walked with Ridley into the garden."

"Perhaps she found Ridley offensive. I know I do."

"*Followed* by the Earl of Kilmaire, Grandmother. Ridley returned to the house, a short time later and retired immediately to his room. Lord Kilmaire, according to Zander, then appeared, asked for whiskey and closeted himself in the library. According to Sutton, Colin could only drink a thimbleful of liquor before becoming foxed while they were at Eton. It appears Colin's tolerance has improved since then."

Donata put her finger to her lip. "Well, Lord Kilmaire doesn't care for wine."

Alex frowned. "Miranda slipped back into the house and has remained in her rooms ever since. Zander caught sight of her and told me her eyes and cheeks were red. From crying, Grandmother." A curl popped over her forehead and she puffed it away in annoyance.

Donata mulled that bit of information. "Are we *certain*

Ridley did not say something cruel to her? He's become quite impatient in his pursuit. He dares not return to London until Miranda accepts him. The duns beating on his door won't allow him any peace."

"I do not think Miranda is concerned with Ridley or anything he does. When I mentioned that he'd been seen with an actress from Covent Garden, Miranda didn't so much as blink. I don't care for the man. He is garish, boastful and," Alex wrinkled her nose, "free with his hands."

Donata lifted a brow in question. "Please tell me he has not made lewd advances."

"A maid has complained, and Zander has given the girl duties in another part of the house. I believe he has assigned a much older woman to freshen the linens in Ridley's chambers."

"He should be horsewhipped. We do not tolerate such behavior at Gray Covington."

"Indeed not." Alex nibbled at a scone. "At any rate, I have been adamant with Sutton. Even though," she hesitated, "I fear that Miranda is determined to marry the dandy anyway."

Sighing, Donata turned her attention back to the windows. Green, rolling hills tapering off into dense woods filled the panes. How lovely the wildflowers were at this time of year, like a brightly colored blanket. She could still see Robert as the child he'd once been, marching toward the house, his small bag of toy soldiers clutched tightly in his hands. The image faded to be replaced with Robert and Madeline, his beloved first wife, Sutton's mother. Robert would swing his new bride up in the air, the love he felt for the vicar's daughter so apparent that Donata's breath caught as she watched. Having been forced to give up such a love herself for the sake of a suitable marriage, Donata did not want the same for her son. She'd been adamant that her husband, Lord Cambourne, give his blessing to Robert and Madeline's marriage.

Sutton had followed in his father's footsteps, marrying for love. Was it so wrong that she wished the same for Miranda? And dear sweet Elizabeth?

How she missed her son. Terribly so. Eyes misting over, she blinked to stay the tears that threatened to fall and brought the steaming cup of tea to her mouth. She had failed Robert, miserably, by not recognizing the danger that Jeanette Runyon Reynolds posed, but she would not fail his children.

Alex, seeing her mood, clasped Donata's hand, her fingers tightening around Donata's. "Grandmother, are you well?"

"Don't fuss at me so, Alex. I'm quite all right.," she responded, more curtly than she meant. "Am I not allowed a moment to think?"

A wisp of a smile danced around Alex's lips. She wasn't at all put off by Donata's curt reply.

Donata sipped her tea to keep from smiling in return. How grateful she was for this *darling* girl that Sutton married. Her grandson, the former rake, brought to heel by one tiny spinster, whom the Marquess of Cambourne adored. Women still threw themselves at Sutton, they probably always would. But, much like his father, Sutton would never stray because he loved his wife. As Robert had loved Madeline.

Alex shifted, putting down the scone she'd been nibbling. One of her hands fluttered down to touch her stomach.

Donata caught the movement but said nothing, even though she was delighted. Alex would make the announcement she was with child again in her own time.

Turning back to the large window Donata spotted a group leaving the woods and enter the path back to the house. . The Cottinghams appeared. Even from this distance Donata could see that Lord Cottingham was puffing and red-faced. Lady

Cottingham looked stricken. Lady Helen resembled a small child about to throw a tantrum.

The tall, broad shouldered form of Lord Kilmaire strode out of the woods, his agitation apparent as his large form paced back and forth while speaking to the Cottinghams. His head turned abruptly in the direction of Gray Covington, specifically to a particular row of windows.

"Grandmother, perhaps—"

"Not now, Alex." Donata sat up taller, her gaze riveted at the sight of Colin who continued to pace while speaking to Lord Cottingham. "How interesting." She pointed, directing Alex's attention to the scene unfolding outside.

Colin bowed stiffly and turned away, leaving the Cottinghams open mouthed. They resembled a trio of owls, blinking in confusion.

"Watch closely, Alex. I believe you are about to see just how right I am."

Colin strode towards the house, his long legs making haste across the manicured grounds. Honey colored hair fluttered about the scar as he moved purposefully towards Gray Covington.

"What in the world are you talking about?" Alex's eyes widened as she regarded the figure of the Earl of Kilmaire, marching with determination towards the house. "Lord Kilmaire seems in a bit of a hurry. Why—"

Her words were interrupted by the Earl of Kilmaire himself, flinging open the door to the drawing room without being announced.

"My lord," Zander sputtered. "You cannot just march in." Zander bowed to Donata and Alex. "My lady, I apologize."

Colin waved his hand at the butler. "Yes, yes. I'm lacking manners. I must speak to Lady Cambourne." The chocolate-colored eyes landed on Donata. The scar slashed dark pink across his cheek as he moved closer, like a stalking panther.

Goodness, Colin was very *intent* on speaking to her, wasn't he? Well, she had no intention of making this easy for the Earl of Kilmaire. From his manner, Donata surmised that Colin had experienced something of an epiphany during his walk with the Cottinghams.

"My goodness, Lord Kilmaire," she said, welcoming him, "you look as if your little excursion was most taxing. All that running about in the bush chasing Lady Helen's ruby throated thrush."

Big, angry man that he was, Colin scowled at her.

"Would you like some tea? You seem distressed."

The elegant hands, free of gloves as usual, clenched and unclenched in agitation at his sides. "No, thank you." A tic appeared in his cheek.

"Perhaps you'd like something stronger? It's a bit early in the day, however I'm sure we could have some whiskey brought. You certainly look as if you could use it. Perhaps it wasn't the ruby throated thrush that you found taxing but the company of Lady Helen."

"If she was once betrothed to St. Remy, why didn't she marry him?"

My goodness, she'd forgotten how Colin sounded when that carefully controlled upper-class accent slipped. He'd need to be reminded to mind his speech when agitated or angry. No one, including Colin, should ever suspect he wasn't exactly who he appeared to be. That particular revelation, however, could be saved for another time.

"St. Remy?" Alex sat back on the settee, regarding Colin as if he were a dangerous animal. "Oh, you mean the Duke of Langford. Why should Miranda ever have been interested in him?"

"You are the only person, Lord Kilmaire, to assume my granddaughter ever betrothed herself to Lord St. Remy."

"The Duke of Langford." Alex corrected.

Donata nodded. "Just so."

Pushing back the thick strands of honey-colored hair, Colin scowled a bit more. He was altogether quite handsome, especially when he looked a bit anguished as he did now. While Colin was certainly aware that the female sex found him attractive, he had not a hint of the conceit her grandson did. Any woman seeing him at this moment would do whatever necessary to comfort him.

Except Donata. She felt he needed a stern hand just now.

"Don't you dare frown at *me*, Lord Kilmaire. Nor behave in such an impolite manner or I will have you removed." Donata adored Colin, but she would not tolerate his rude outburst, nor his scowling. She was trying to help him.

"Was she?"

"Tell me why you would think such a thing. Surely, it did not come from Miranda's lips."

Colin looked away, refusing to meet Donata's eyes.

"Miranda never betrothed herself to St. Remy or, for that matter, anyone else. At the end of her first Season, she declined all offers for her hand and her father supported the decision. Her mother was livid as I recall. Jeanette *wished* her to marry St. Remy, but there was never an agreement of any sort."

"The Duke of Langford," Alex muttered into her tea. Her eyes on Colin were not especially kind.

Colin turned to face them. He looked so *beautifully* distraught. That urge to comfort him rose up in her again and Donata pushed it aside.

"That's impossible," he choked. "She wrote me a letter telling me she wished to be a duchess."

"I don't believe it. Miranda detested the man." Calmly, Donata sipped her tea as if Colin weren't raging about the room. "You'll forgive me for saying, Lord Kilmaire, but I fail to see who Miranda was or was not betrothed to could possibly be of interest to you. Especially now, when you are about to offer for Lady Helen."

"I saw it in her own hand."

"*Impossible*," Donata thumped her cane for emphasis. "You say you received a letter. So be it. But are you positive it was Miranda who wrote it?"

"She told me she wished to be a duchess," he insisted.

"I still do not know why this interests you-"

"Of course, you *do*." A stricken look fell over his face. "That's why we're all here at this house party, isn't it?" His lips tightened. "Please. I need to know."

"Very well." Donata ignored his accusation knowing that he would forgive her machinations. Eventually. "You are sure that you would recognize Miranda's hand if you saw it?"

The blonde head nodded. "I should not ever forget it. I remember every flourish."

"Alex, I believe that Miranda was writing to Arabella just the other day in this very room." Donata waved a hand towards the small desk hidden discreetly in an alcove. Donata often wrote her correspondence there as well for the position of the desk offered a lovely view of the gardens. "Let Lord Kilmaire see if this letter is written in the same hand he remembers."

"Of course." Alex rose and quickly made her way to the delicate mahogany desk and opened the top. The sound of shuffling papers echoed through the room until Alex held up a creamy piece of vellum. She looked down at it and nodded. "Her signature is at the bottom."

Colin stood frozen as Alex approached Donata and held out the paper.

Donata examined the letter. "It's to Arabella. That and her signature is all I can decipher." She sighed and handed the letter to Colin. "You are so incredibly stubborn, Colin. Refusing to see what is before you."

A mulish expression crossed his face, pulling the scar down in an ugly line. He took the letter from Donata, his expression never changing though his fingers trembled.

"Far from elegant, wouldn't you say? Barely legible in fact. Miranda is naturally left-handed. Jeanette didn't care to have a left-handed daughter and forced Miranda to use her right. Did she write to you of her desire to be a duchess in this hand, Colin?"

"No," he whispered. "It was Jeanette, wasn't it?" His skin went deathly pale as he shut his eyes. "Jesus." His voice cracked with emotion. "I always thought she was too good for me. I saw her with St. Remy, dancing. I knew he called on her repeatedly. Miranda was so young and I thought…What have I done?"

"You've believed the worst," Alex snapped, "and not trusted the one person you should have, leaving you both miserable. That's what you've done."

"Alex." Donata nodded her head to stop.

"I was lying in bed when the letter came," Colin said in a low voice, perhaps more to himself that either Donata or Alex. "The surgeon was sewing up what remained of my cheek and I read her letter and…" A choking sound came from him.

"And you assumed the worst," Donata added unnecessarily. "Had you been in your right mind, Colin, perhaps you would not have jumped to such a conclusion."

"I have something I need to do." His face offered no insight to his thoughts or emotions, for his features had become as smooth as glass, though Donata sensed the effort it took to hide his pain.

Making a short bow to both of them, and ignoring Alex's poof of outrage at his dismissal, Colin stalked out of the room.

"I do not care for the Earl of Kilmaire just now, Grandmother. If I were Miranda, I'm not certain I'd forgive him. I'm not even certain he is *going* to Miranda. How can one know? What if he still marries Lady Helen?" Alex bit her lip. "What if it is too late? Miranda may have already betrothed herself to Ridley."

"It is never too late, Alex."

Donata prayed that it wasn't.

21

Miranda sat before the fire, her much abused copy of Lord Thurston discarded on her lap. She'd tortured the poor book, tossing it across the room several times in her frustration and anger. A page was torn, and the fine leather scratched.

"He truly means to marry Lady Helen." Staring at the bottle of whiskey stolen from Sutton's study, she wondered if Sutton noticed her theft of his liquor yet. Even if he did notice that a bottle of his very finest whiskey had disappeared, Sutton would likely blame Ridley. Her future husband possessed not an ounce of decorum, assuming everything in Gray Covington belonged to him. Including Miranda.

I haven't married him yet.

She'd almost taken some sherry but that seemed rather staid. Boring. Sherry was something the perfect Lady Helen would drink. Miranda equated whiskey with power. After all, her brother and his friends drank the amber liquid. So, had her father. Especially when faced with an unpleasant situation. Whiskey *fortified* you.

"God knows if anyone at Gray Covington deserves to get

properly foxed it's me. Trapped at this hideous house party, watching Lady Helen flutter her eyelashes and wear atrocious feathers in her hair. Panting after Colin in her breathless forward way. I am forced to watch this terrible play unfold while politely escaping the roving hands of Lord Hamill. I cannot believe I considered the old goat as a potential husband. In comparison Ridley comes out ahead, if one isn't first greeted by one of his garishly designed waistcoats. Or minds that he makes no effort to hide the fact that he has a mistress. Well, I suppose he does, it's not as if he's brought her to Gray Covington. Lady Dobson just delights in informing me of such things for my own good." Miranda ended her tirade with a large swallow of whiskey that left her coughing.

"I don't care if Grandmother's guests find me rude for staying in my rooms. Lady Dobson is already very clear in her opinion of the entire Cambourne family. The Cottinghams are barely presentable. Lord Cottingham addresses my breasts when he greets me, and Lady Cottingham is too busy being in awe of the great Satan Reynolds to watch her daughter launch herself at any man who will allow it."

Miranda took a deep heaving breath, pausing for a moment to take another sip of whiskey. It felt good to unburden herself. Even if it was to an empty room.

"Lady Helen is a tart. Colin deserves to be burdened with her. She'll probably decorate him with feathers."

Just the thought of Lady Helen made her stomach roil.

After Miranda's rather pathetic loss of control in the garden the other night, she'd hidden in her room. Ashamed and heartbroken, Miranda didn't feel she was quite up to facing the house party again. Nor did she want to pretend false happiness when Colin's betrothal to that twit was announced. She would tell her brother as soon as the guests left Gray Covington that Ridley would be her husband.

Miranda took another sip of whiskey and sighed. "I can't come down for dinner because the thought of marrying Ridley makes my stomach hurt. Oh, dear, how shall I ever bed him?" She took another healthy swallow.

Ridley was really her only option. After witnessing Hamill's drunken lechery, she found him a less than desirable candidate.

Sutton would not be pleased. His opinion of Ridley was no secret, especially not to Ridley.

"I don't bloody give a fig whether Sutton's nose is out of joint or not. I've got to marry Ridley, not my brother. Besides, had Sutton not been Colin's friend none of this would have happened. A toast," she raised the glass of whiskey and noticed how little of the liquid remained.

"Oh dear, this will never do." Pouring another finger of whiskey into the glass she held it up again. "A toast, to Edmund Ralst, Viscount Ridley and my future husband." She frowned. "Goodness, it's *Edwin*, isn't it?"

Edward – no *Edwin*, she corrected herself, wasn't really a terrible sort. True, he was mainly after her dowry, but that could work to her advantage. He'd probably allow her to retire to the country after they wed. She was reasonably sure he found her attractive and would give her children.

"I'll raise them away from London, in a place where we can chase butterflies and catch frogs. Ridley is welcome to pursue his life uninterrupted. I shan't bother him." There was a certain amount of freedom in that.

She shook her head and looked down at Lord Thurston, noticing with dismay that a page was torn. Looking at the page the name *Marcella* stood out. There was something important about Marcella, but she couldn't quite remember. Lord Thurston and Colin. Colin would make an excellent pirate.

"*Damn*. Why can't I accept that we are not meant to be

together?" She sipped her whiskey. "I was so sure, you see. Positive, in fact. I've been waiting all these years." She took a deep breath to keep the tears at bay. "It's all rather tragic, if I must say so."

Miranda slung one leg over the side of her chair, shivering slightly. The room was cold, even though a fired blazed cheerfully in the hearth. Probably because she was wearing only a robe and nothing else. Proper ladies didn't lounge about in a silk robe with one thigh exposed, and no undergarments. But Miranda wasn't feeling especially proper. She'd brushed aside her maid, Clara, earlier that morning stating she'd spend the day in her robe.

Clara's look of utter distress had been very gratifying.

Miranda wiggled her toes as she gave serious study to the flesh of her thighs. Taking another sip of the whiskey she turned her leg back and forth.

"Mother was right; my thighs are a bit plump. And these," she looked down the top of the robe to the deep valley between her breasts, "are larger than they should be. Oh, I know that gentlemen seem to admire my breasts, for whatever reason," she took another drink, "but I find them a bit of a bother. I wish they were less full. More like the drop of a pear. My bosom is a bit...*overwhelming*."

Lady Helen's breasts were just the right size.

This morning, as she bathed, Clara informed Miranda that the below stairs gossip involved the impending proposal of the Earl of Kilmaire to Lady Helen Cottingham.

Today was the day, Clara's voice was wistful. *He's to propose to her after a walk in the woods.*

Miranda swished the whiskey around her mouth, liking the way it made the flesh of her gums tingle. Grandmother would be shocked to find her drinking whiskey in the middle of the afternoon, in nothing but a robe.

She rather hoped Grandmother *did* find out. Or possibly

Lady Dobson. That would give the old harridan something to gossip about.

A tray bearing a bowl of soup and tea sat beneath the window. When had that arrived? She stood a bit unsteadily and stuck her finger in the soup. Cold. And, Miranda didn't especially care for pea soup. Especially *cold* pea soup.

She wandered back to her chair and sat down with an alarming thump. "Goodness, I'm feeling a bit," she put a finger to her lips, "*airy.*" Slinging her leg again over the arm of the chair once again, Miranda looked down the length of her thighs. "Good Lord."

Whiskey, Miranda surmised as she pulled the decanter unsteadily off the side table, forcing her hand to remain steady as she poured it into her glass, made one positively *euphoric.* No wonder gentlemen retired to partake of spirits.

"They don't wish us to be happy. That's why women are relegated to ratafia and sherry. I shall demand whiskey on my wedding night to Edward. No *Edwin.*"

Miranda leaned her head back. "At least I know what to expect."

Did she? While Miranda was certain the basic mechanics of the act remained the same, it would not be Colin in her bed, but Ridley.

Edwin would not cause her skin to tingle. She could not imagine his touch between her thighs.

She looked down and pulled the robe aside until she saw the dark thatch of hair that covered her mound. Colin had touched the core of her with his tongue. Tangled his beautiful fingers in the soft hair. Her hand slid down her thigh, pretending it was Colin's hand and not her own.

A knock sounded on the door and she jerked, almost spilling the whiskey.

"Go away," she said, holding the glass tight against her breasts. "I'm ill."

Satisfied that whoever lurked in the hallway had departed, Miranda closed her eyes again. Colin. A guilty pleasure this was, to envision his naked body bathed in the light of the fire.

Another insistent knock.

Had she rung for her maid? Called for another tray? She didn't think she had.

At the sound of the knob twisting she congratulated herself on remembering to lock it before indulging in the whiskey. "I'm terribly ill. The door is locked. Please, just go away."

A series of clicks met her ears, followed by the sound of the door opening.

Miranda sat up, shocked that anyone would disturb her. Zander must have given her maid a key. Could she not have a moment of peace? Possibly it was the Dowager. Or Sutton. And here she was wearing nothing but her robe and drinking whiskey. And possibly foxed. No, *definitely* foxed.

The door shut with a discreet click.

She sat up and clutched her robe around her breasts, though she didn't move her leg. It seemed like too much effort.

"My door was locked for a reason." Relieved she didn't hear the thump of a cane she continued, "I'm not sure, Clara, how you found a key to my room, but I do not wish to be disturbed, no matter what reason Lady Cambourne gave you."

Footsteps sounded behind her, approaching the chair.

"Did you not remember my skill at picking locks?"

22

Christ.
Colin expected to find Miranda sipping tea and calmly reading a book before the fire.

Well, at least she was in a chair before the fire, though the book she'd been reading, probably Lord Thurston, lay on the floor. And she wasn't sipping tea, but whiskey.

One gorgeous leg hooked over the arm of the chair, the robe she wore, a frothy peach confection, split open to expose the creamy skin of one thigh. He could just make out the shadow of her mound in the firelight.

Christ.

Inky black locks spilled over the tops of her shoulders to slide down over the peaks of her magnificent breasts. Which were barely covered by the robe. He could see the tiny mountains of her nipples beneath the silk.

Her eyes widened. "Bloody hell."

The scent of Sutton's fine Irish whiskey rose in the air.

She stood, clutching the arm of the chair to steady herself. Her breasts rippled beneath the silk, and the robe opened to display another flash of her legs.

Colin's mouth went dry. Everything he'd planned to say to her as he made his way upstairs immediately fled from his mind. The letter, still clutched in his hand, fell to the floor. Lust slammed into him.

"What are you doing here?" She seemed completely oblivious to the fact that she was half naked. "Shouldn't you be traipsing about the woods with Lady Helen looking for some stupid bird?" Miranda waved the glass of whiskey at him. "Did she accept your generous offer to become the Countess of Kilmaire?" Miranda lifted her chin defiantly. "Well, I don't bloody care. I'm marrying Ridley. You may," her body swayed a bit, "call me Lady Ridley."

The dusky circles of her nipples shown beneath the robe as she came closer. Her hair, the color of a raven's wing, hung in spill of curls to her waist, begging him to plunge his fingers through the heavy mass.

She raised one dark brow at him, waiting for him to speak.

Instead, one arm reached out to snake around her waist, pulling her lush body against his own. The warmth of Miranda flamed beneath the thin silk of the robe and sent a rolling wave of heat down to the toes of his boots.

Miranda gave an angry gasp, and the glass she held tilted dangerously.

Gently, he took the whiskey from her and swallowed the remainder of the liquid before setting the empty glass on the table. His eyes closed, inhaling the scent of lavender and honey while his lips sought out the nape of her neck. Miranda's scent enticed him, tempting him press his mouth against the scented flesh.

Miranda put up no resistance. Her head fell to the side with a soft whimper. She pressed herself against him even as her hands reached up to thread through his hair.

"You are bloody well *not* marrying that imbecile Ridley,"

he murmured harshly against the column of her throat. "Nor Hamill, nor any other idiot who comes calling." The words of apology he'd meant to utter, the admittance of what an ass he'd been stuck in his throat. He meant to claim her. *Finally*.

"Forgive me," he whispered against her hair as his lips found hers. "Forgive me, Miranda. *Please*."

Well, this was rather unexpected.

Miranda thought at first it was the whiskey. Alcohol gave one delusions. Hallucinations. At least, she'd read that once in a book, or, maybe Grandmother mentioned it.

If this is an illusion, it's remarkably realistic. The hard length of Colin swelling against her thigh did not *feel* as if it were a figment of her imagination. Figments didn't feel hot and warm and press between one's thighs.

A delicious vibration slid across her skin as he drew her more firmly against his chest. Her curves molded perfectly to the hard lines of his body, knowing instinctively where they fit together.

Dreams did not smell this amazing either. Leather and the citrus soap he'd used that morning filled her nostrils. His presence gave her the same euphoric feel as the whiskey, only she wished to drink more deeply of Colin.

I should probably demand to know what he is doing in my room.

If anyone found him there, even Ridley would find her unsuitable. Miranda didn't find that thought as terrible as she should have.

His lips were moving along her throat, his breath tickling the inside of her ear. Teeth nipped the sensitive lobe and she immediately sank more fully into his chest.

Colin's mouth left her neck to move against the line of

her jaw. When he reached her plump lower lip, his tongue ran over the crease, then he pressed his lips to the corner of her mouth, coaxing her to kiss him.

Miranda's fingers flowed through the honeyed strands of his hair, loving the feel of his skull beneath her fingers. She dragged his mouth down to hers, pent up longing surging through her. The silk of the robe chafed against her nipples, and the small peaks tightened, waiting for his touch.

They tasted each other, testing, asking, remembering. No kiss, especially in recent memory had ever stirred Miranda so. She surrendered so completely to Colin that she clung to him, her mouth opening as his tongue twined around hers.

One big hand cupped her behind, pulling her up against the solid length of him.

The back of her legs bumped against the side of the bed. Her fingers flew to his shoulders, trying to push off the coat he wore.

He broke the kiss, his breathing heavy and ragged against her ear. "Wait." Then he gave a sigh of resignation. "I can't help myself around you. I never could. I meant for us to speak first." The cool patrician accent he usually affected had completely disappeared, and Miranda allowed the Irish lilt to wash over her already aroused body.

"Forgive me." He brushed his lips against hers slowly, dragging out the sensation until she reached for him again.

"No," he caught her hands and drew them down to her sides. "I've waited what feels like a lifetime."

The robe fell from her shoulders, sliding down her already heated skin in a sensual caress to pool at her feet.

Miranda stood naked before him, her nipples peeking through the dark locks of her hair. Immediately, she put a protective hand over the small bump of her stomach, wishing she could hide her thighs as well.

He raised a brow in question, the chocolate of his eyes dark and unfathomable.

"I'm not as slender as I once was, Colin." Miranda bit her lip and looked away. Would he find her wanting?

Reverently, Colin ran a fingertip along the line of her jaw, moving to slide along the delicate rise of her collarbone.

"Shush, Miranda. Just this once."

His hand opened, the palm resting on the rise of her breasts before moving to cup the underside, as if testing the weight. With a graceful slide, his hand splayed against her stomach, before possessively cupping her mound.

"I'd forgotten," the deep tenor grew rough with longing, "how beautiful you are. All of you." His fingers threaded down into the heat of her, sliding through the slick, wet flesh. Rubbing back and forth until Miranda arched her back and thrust her hips forward.

"Mine."

"Yes," she moaned as he teased his finger between the folds.

"You're very wet, Miranda," he whispered. "I want you so very much."

He was torturing her, his fingers gliding back and forth sending ripples of sensation across her skin.

"I find it unfair," her voice caught as he slid a finger inside her, "that you are still clothed." If she were being truthful, it was incredibly erotic to stand naked before him, while his fingers did the most amazing things.

He blew air across one nipple, eliciting a soft cry from her. His tongue flicked out to circle the tip.

"Open your legs, my love."

Miranda fell back against the bed, her legs parting. He pressed against her until she lay down, settling his large body between her thighs.

Colin leaned over and sucked one taut nipple into his mouth, fingers curling up inside of her as he moved in and out.

Miranda moaned, reaching out to grab his hand and push it shamefully against her.

His mouth left the throbbing nibble. "Right there? I remember." Then bent to his task again, his mouth sucking and nibbling her breast until she was near mad. He allowed the pressure inside her to build, then retreat, until she heard herself beg him.

Drawing his tongue over her tortured nipple, he murmured. "Now, my love." He rotated his thumb over the engorged piece of flesh he'd so far ignored.

A cry escaped her lips as Miranda came apart. She bucked against his hand, her head falling to the side as her body moved with each wave of pleasure. Miranda floated up and then fell again as another tremor wracked her body, the whiskey giving her release an even more dreamlike quality.

He entered her suddenly, in one thrust, embedding himself deep in her body before she'd even realized he'd discarded his clothes. A soft moan came from his lips as he sank into her.

Instinctively her trembling legs hugged his hips. Reaching up, she ran her fingers down the length of the scar, tracing the puckered flesh to the place where it met his lip.

"I love you," she whispered. "I will always love you."

Colin turned his head and pressed a gentle kiss to her palm.

He moved inside her, thrusting slow and deep as Miranda rolled her hips. He kissed her eyes, her cheek, the corner of her mouth. "Here?" he asked as he turned his body, catching hers.

"Yes," Miranda whispered, surprised at how quickly the

pleasure built again. She didn't wish this to ever end. "I think perhaps I am dreaming from overindulging in Sutton's whiskey. But, it's such a beautiful dream. Go slowly, for I don't wish it to end."

Colin smiled and kissed her. "You are not dreaming, my love."

"Say it again. Not the dreaming part."

"My love," he said in a ragged voice.

Flames cascaded over Miranda as her body moved with his. She wanted him deeper, harder. Miranda ran her hands down the sides of his torso, her fingertips dipping into the hollows of his muscles, until she reached his buttocks. "Harder."

A growl sounded from him. "I'm afraid I'll hurt you."

Miranda squeezed the firm cheeks beneath her hands. "Bullocks."

"*Christ*, you'll be the death of me."

The intensity increased until Miranda writhed beneath him, as if her body was on fire and Colin stoked the flame. When she arched against him, unable to wait any longer, he pinned her hands above her head, lacing his fingers through hers.

Miranda's body tightened, the damn breaking apart within her. She cried out, feeling the clench of her muscles around the length of him. This time her release was deeper, more intense and the waves shifted and crested madly.

Colin thrust once more, burying his face in her sweat-damp hair, saying her name over and over.

They lay together, entwined on the bed, as their breathing slowly returned to normal. Colin was still buried inside her, his hips pressed against hers. Afraid to break the spell brought about by their lovemaking, Miranda remained silent. Instead, she listened to the beat of his heart, and took in the way their bodies fit together so perfectly.

"Puzzle pieces." She mouthed the words but did not say them.

Her fingertips traced the outline of every supple muscle on his back, to the hollow at the base of his spine, to the curve of his hip. *Gorgeous man.*

Colin pressed a kiss to her nose and took his weight from her, ignoring the small squeak of protest she made.

"You're no good to me if you can't breathe, Miranda." His fingers traced the line of her cheek as he pressed a gentle kiss against her lips. "My Marcella."

"You're not so heavy. Though you seem to be bigger than I remember."

Colin wiggled his eyebrows.

"Not *there*." Miranda giggled. "You just seem larger. More imposing." She smiled against his chest. "If I am Marcella then you must be Lord Thurston," she joked.

"In a manner of speaking." He gave her a deep languid kiss that Miranda felt to the bottom of her feet and made her toes curl in pleasure.

"You taste of whiskey. And ravishment." The big hands lazily moved over her body, possessively, caressing every curve and hollow. He worshipped her with his mouth and hands until she begged him for release.

Colin took nothing for himself, only murmuring beautiful wicked things to her as he coaxed her body to pleasure again until Miranda lay limp and boneless. Her body still throbbing from the aftermath of his attentions, Colin pulled her into the shelter of his arms and pressed a kiss to her brow.

"I wonder if we've missed dinner."

Colin merely smiled at her. Picking up a curl that lay across her breast, he absently toyed with it, wrapping it and unwrapping it about his finger.

"Colin." She was so sleepy. "Don't leave again."

Colin gathered her to him and pulled the bedcovers up around them. "Sleep."

She snuggled closer to the large, warm male next to her, thinking she had never been so happy.

Always.

23

Sunlight glared through the curtains and Miranda swatted at it. She gave a small groan as her muscles protested moving from the bed. Carefully opening her eyes, she took in the rumpled bed clothes and the fact that she was naked beneath them.

Goodness.

A persistent knock sounded at the door.

"A moment." Her throat was dry as the desert. Temples aching, she wished desperately for a headache powder, but she supposed she would need to answer the knocking at her door first. Whiskey, she decided was not something one should overindulge in often.

Cautiously she turned her head, smiling at the indentation of a man's head on the pillow next to hers.

Not a dream.

Another knock. "My lady?" Clara, her maid whispered through the door.

Quickly, she smoothed the bedclothes with her palm and reached down to the floor to grab her robe. With a roll, one that sent the room spinning, she managed to slip on the robe and tie the sash, even as her maid, Clara, cracked open the door.

Miranda slid back under the covers, pulling them up to her chin. Only an idiot would miss the smell of sex that permeated the room. Fortunately, Clara was known for doing hair, not being intelligent.

Clara bustled in with a breakfast tray, setting it on the bed. She efficiently poured out tea and placed a small plate of warm raisin cakes next to it.

"Cook made a fresh batch just for you. Just out of the oven. I do hope you're well enough to eat."

"How kind of her." Miranda's stomach grumbled. She *was* hungry. Ravenous in fact.

"Should I lay out your clothing?"

"Please." Miranda couldn't wait to leave her room.

The maid nodded and began to straighten the chamber and lay out Miranda's gown for the day. Walking before the fire, she stooped to pick up the discarded Lord Thurston, carefully placing a slip of paper to mark Miranda's place, before putting the book on the table.

Smearing freshly whipped butter on top of one of the raisin cakes, Miranda took a bite, relishing the taste of the fruit and butter. As she munched away, pausing only to take a sip of tea, her eyes fell to the spine of the Lord Thurston novel.

"My Marcella." And what had he said the night in the garden? *"I think of you when I write her."*

Surely not. The idea was absurd.

Or was it?

The author of Lord Thurston remained a mystery, the initial "J," the only clue to his or her identity. Several things flashed through her mind at once. Colin's forefinger often sported an ink stain. He was a gifted storyteller. He used to scribble away in a red leather journal her father gave him one Christmas. His middle name was James.

And my father was close friends with Lord Wently, who publishes Lord Thurston.

"You'll wish to bathe, I imagine. Shall I draw you a bath?"

Miranda nodded mutely at Clara. It had been in front of her the entire time and she'd never noticed. *This* was the business venture her father had helped Colin with so long ago.

"It makes perfect sense," she giggled. "Marcella. I do rather resemble her. Or she, me."

Clara gave her and odd look and raised a brow.

Miranda waved her hand. "I'm muttering to myself, Clara. Pray ignore me."

Clara moved into the dressing room and began to prepare Miranda's bath. The aroma of lavender and honey filled the air in the bedroom as steam from the water rose in the air.

All she wished to do was see Colin. She needed to know that last night had been real.

"I must hurry, Clara. I need to speak to Lord Kilmaire. About a book," she added. How *rich* that Colin was the author of *Lord Thurston*. Wait until she told Alex. Miranda pushed aside the tray and made her way to her dressing room where a steaming tub awaited her.

"Oh, my lady, I fear you're too late." Clara's head popped through the doorway, her hands full of soap and towels. "Lord Kilmaire left for London early this morning, just before Lord and Lady Cottingham departed. One of the grooms saddled a horse for him. I'm not sure why he'd prefer to ride rather than enjoy the comforts of Lord Cottingham's carriage." Clara shrugged her shoulders and turned back to the bath.

Miranda froze, her toes curling into the patterned carpet that covered the floor of her room. Her fingers wiggled, begging for something to hold onto as her legs sagged, threatening to drop her to the floor. She backed up to clutch at the bedpost.

"Lord Kilmaire has left Gray Covington? With the Cottinghams? Why," her voice cracked, "I did not have the chance to say goodbye. What a poor hostess I am."

Forgive me.

"Lord Kilmaire was in quite a hurry to get to London. One of the footmen overheard him. Apparently Lord Kilmaire had an urgent matter that needed attended to immediately." Clara blushed. "Begging your pardon, my lady. I shouldn't like to gossip."

"You aren't. And the Cottinghams?" Miranda fell against the bed. The pain in her temples intensified.

"Lord Cottingham met with your brother in the study before he and Lady Cottingham departed for London. Lady Helen," Clara lowered her voice to a whisper, "was discussing wedding gowns with her mother."

"I see." The raisin cakes threatened to leave her stomach.

Forgive me.

He'd whispered it into her hair. Repeated it to her the entire night. She'd been so absorbed in bedding Colin, so caught up in her desire for him, that she'd never asked him what brought him to her chamber.

I fell on him like some sex-starved widow.

"Clara, the washbasin please," Miranda gestured wildly. *How stupid I am. How utterly pathetic of me. He was begging my forgiveness for marrying Lady Helen.*

The raisin cakes did not taste half as pleasant when they came back up.

24

Colin flung his reins to a waiting groom and raced up the front steps of Gray Covington. The sun had begun to descend across the sky and twilight was gathering. Even leaving as early as he had, the ride to London and back still took most of the day. His hasty departure was borne of urgency. The need to claim Miranda, immediately, and end Ridley's courtship was paramount in his mind. Pressing a kiss on her forehead, he left the soft warmth of her body and dressed as the sky lightened to pink. After quietly leaving her room, he washed and requested a horse be saddled. Cook pushed a fresh biscuit in his hand as he strode out, only to glance back at Miranda's window.

A light, heady feeling coursed through him as he rode. The sun shone on him for the first time in six long years. Happiness, he mused, was something he meant to get used to.

It was not until he reached the outskirts of the city that Colin remembered that in his haste, he'd neglected to leave Miranda a note. It was rather careless. And he had promised himself that he would never again be careless where Miranda was concerned. Nor take her for granted.

During the entire ride to London, he'd thought of nothing but the fact that he would need to tell Miranda about her mother's machinations and in doing so, confess his own sins.

Bloody Jeanette. I hope to never set eyes on the woman again.

He *should* have done the honorable thing. Explained the letter and begged her forgiveness for having doubted her. Instead, he'd ravished her. Made sure that she would have no choice but to marry him after he ruined her yet again. For hours. Ruthlessly.

She was well and truly compromised. While he was certain no one saw him leave her room, the same could not be said for entering her chambers. But then, he rather hoped Ridley had witnessed Colin entering Miranda's rooms.

Standing for a moment on the step, his hand went to the inside pocket of his waistcoat, to assure himself that the items he'd brought from London remained safe.

"I'll make her happy. I swear that I will."

The door opened before Colin could knock.

"Good evening, Lord Kilmaire." Zander, Gray Covington's butler, narrowed his eyes at Colin, taking in his dusty coat and muddy boots. "I'm afraid you've missed dinner."

"Where is Lady Miranda?" Colin stepped inside, his eyes immediately going to the staircase as if his words would cause her to appear.

Zander lifted a brow. "Lord Cambourne instructed the staff that if you returned to Gray Covington you were to be escorted directly to his study."

"I would see Lady Miranda first. Is she in the gardens?" *What did Zander mean if I returned?*

"I do not know the current whereabouts of Lady Miranda, my lord. However, as I've explained, I have very specific orders that you be escorted to Lord Cambourne." Without waiting for an answer, Zander started down the hall towards the Marquess of Cambourne's study, marching away as if a stick had been shoved up his arse.

Bloody little tyrant.

"I should at least change clothes. I've been riding all day." Colin said, waving a hand down his wrinkled riding coat. "And I smell of horse."

"This way, Lord Kilmaire." Zander's tone was curt. Stopping before the large mahogany doors, Zander rapped with his knuckles and poked his head inside. He said something in a low tone, then ushered Colin through the doorway, before stepping deftly to the side.

The first blow from Cam's fist hit Colin squarely in the jaw, splitting his lip and knocking his head back.

"What the bloody—"

The next punch landed in the middle of his stomach, doubling Colin over and knocking him to the floor. He fell sideways, his head lolling against the fine Persian carpet.

Blinking to clear his vision, Colin attempted to focus on the pattern of blue and green swirls he lay upon, stupidly wondering whether the swirls were supposed to be flowers. He thought they looked like teardrops.

"You bastard." A pair of boots landed squarely before Colin's nose. "Get up."

It occurred to Colin as he studied the carpet, that while it was certain that his friend had not known of Colin's relationship with Miranda *before*, Cam sure as hell did *now*.

Zander's lack of welcome should have given Colin ample warning. His observation skills aside, Colin was mainly concerned that one of his closest friends was about to beat him to death.

Christ, he hits hard.

Blood trickled down the corner of his mouth as he pushed his tongue against his lip, wincing a bit at the pain. He'd been in many a brawl. After all, he'd grown up with two older brothers, but he was not going to fight Cam. Cautiously Colin stood, bracing himself against the door.

Cam rolled back on his heels, fists clenched, ready to beat Colin to a bloody pulp at the slightest provocation.

"Cam," Colin held up his hand in a gesture of supplication. "Where is Miranda? I can explain—"

Pain exploded in his temple and cheekbone. Colin's head swam a bit, and for just a moment, he saw two furious Lord Cambournes standing before him.

"Bloody hell, Cam. Stop for just a moment."

"No." Cam's grunted with a snarl. "Stand up. Fucking Irish—"

"There's no need for insults," Colin replied a bit flippantly. "Besides, even your grandmother agrees I am only a quarter Irish." He wiped at the stream of blood dribbling down his chin, anger flaring at Cam's words. "Are you trying to ruin what's left of my looks? You never could tolerate any man being as pretty as you."

Cam made a sound like an enraged bull and moved forward but halted as a voice emanated from the large leather couch facing the fireplace.

"Sutton," the imperious voice commanded, "I insist you stop this instant. I'll not have Lord Kilmaire's blood all over the carpet. The rug was quite expensive and a favorite of your father's. As it is, I fear Zander will never be able to get the stain out. And your language. You've forgotten yourself speaking so in front of me."

Colin stared in disbelief at the couch.

The Dowager peeked around the side, her gloved hands wrapped around the head of her cane, expression bland as if she watched Cam engage in fisticuffs every day and tolerated the spectacle. A silver brow raised as she noted Colin's regard, and there was no welcome for him in her face.

He moved a step towards the couch.

Cam snarled at him.

Next to the Dowager, sat Miranda. He swayed with the urge to go to her.

The ebony locks of her hair were pulled back and tied with a ribbon, allowing a cascade of dark strands to curl over her shoulder. She was busy twisting the sprigged muslin of her dress, wrinkling the fabric. Deep emerald eyes gazed at him without the slightest hint of mercy.

"My God, were you both going to allow him to beat me to death? Miranda?"

She turned away from him.

Bloody Hell. I should have left a note.

The Dowager pursed her lips in disapproval. "You are impertinent, Lord Kilmaire."

"Why did you come back to Gray Covington? Did you forget something in your haste to follow the Cottinghams to London?" Cam hissed.

"Why would I follow the Cottinghams anywhere? Let alone to London? They were here when I left Gray Covington."

"The Cottinghams returned to London this morning. Lord Cottingham admitted that he would soon have a titled son-in-law." Cam grit his teeth. "You bastard."

Colin struggled to sit up and removed a handkerchief from his coat pocket to dab at his battered lip. His eye was already swelling. "Well, it's bloody not me. I have no intention of marrying Lady Helen. I have an aversion to birds."

"You glib Irish—"

"I thought we all agreed I was barely Irish. Quit flinging that about. It's insulting."

Cam took a deep breath and shot him a murderous look. "I don't care if you've promised to marry Lady Helen."

"I didn't. I'd never..." God his ribs hurt. "...marry that peawit."

"You will marry Miranda. You've ruined her. Her reputation is—"

"Already in tatters," Miranda said quietly from her place beside the Dowager. "Besides, Lord Kilmaire did not seduce some virginal spinster under your roof last night. I have not been a maiden for some time."

Cam turned the most disturbing shade of beet. Had the situation not been so serious, Colin would have laughed out loud.

"Who . . ." Cam sputtered and turned wild eyes on Colin. "I'll kill you."

"And I will not be married to a man who doesn't want me." An anguished look shadowed her green eyes. "Whether he decides to marry Lady Helen, or any other woman, is not my concern. I would not have him marry me out of misguided duty. Lord Kilmaire has made his feelings toward me abundantly clear."

"Apparently, I haven't." He'd held her all night, worshipped her as he had nothing else in his life, and still Miranda didn't know what was in his heart.

"I will marry Ridley," Miranda continued calmly, her voice barely hesitating as she said the viscount's name. "I'm sure he's still lurking about Gray Covington."

"Miranda." The Dowager took her hand. "The man is a disaster. A bounder."

Stunned by her declaration, Colin found he couldn't speak. Was she insane?

"I'm certain he can be convinced to overlook my indiscretion," her voice caught, "in return for my substantial dowry. Grandmother can put out the story that it was not Lord Kilmaire leaving my room this morning, but was in fact, Ridley. Lady Dobson's eyesight is a bit poor, is it not, Grandmother? There will be a tad of scandal, but it will not be insurmountable."

Lady Dobson had seen him leave Miranda's room? That certainly explained the welcome he'd received from Cam.

"Miranda, have you lost your mind?" Colin spat blood onto the handkerchief he'd found in his pocket. One of his lower teeth wiggled. "*No.* Absolutely not. You *will not* marry Ridley. I did not leave you to go chasing after Lady Helen. She's an insipid twit."

"Colin," she looked at him, lovely and resolute. "You do not have to do the honorable thing. I did not hold you to it years ago and I will not do so now."

"Yes, he does." Cam growled.

Another punch to his side, drove Colin down on one knee. Wincing with pain, he tried to take a deep breath. He'd be lucky if he could explain about the letter before the entire damn family murdered him in the drawing room. The Dowager refused to say a word, even though she knew full well what happened. God, even she believed he'd left Miranda for Lady Helen.

He needed to be the one to tell Miranda.

"Stop," he looked at Cam, "doing that. Miranda," he implored, "please listen to me, for just a moment. I did not leave you six years ago. Well, I did, but not for the reasons you assume. Ian fell ill, and I had to return to Runshaw Park. I left you a note with one of the footmen and one for your father. After my mother's attack I received a reply, from you."

"My God. I thought you were my friend. While I was in Macao you ruined my sister?" Cam raised his fist again. "I will call you out, I—"

The Dowager thumped her cane. "You will do no such thing, Sutton. I forbid it." "Allow Lord Kilmaire to speak in his own defense. You were about to say, Lord Kilmaire?" This time, her eyes twinkled with a bit of encouragement.

For someone who usually had command of the spoken and written word, Colin found himself at a loss to explain his own role in the end of his relationship with Miranda. He'd seen the love in her eyes last night and the fact that he'd ever doubted her shamed Colin to the core.

"I never would have. . ." Colin took another breath trying to find the right words. "A letter arrived at Runshaw Park announcing your intentions to marry Lord St. Remy."

"The Duke of Langford," Miranda automatically corrected.

"The letter stated, rather bluntly, that you found me incredibly unsuitable for marriage. That the," he hesitated, "*affection* that lay between us was no more than a mild flirtation. I wasn't myself," he said by way of apology. "and the token I had left for you was enclosed with the letter. I assumed—"

Miranda sucked in her breath, her hand pressed against her stomach. "You thought I would say such a thing to you, after...after..." The dark locks spun about her shoulders as she shook her head in disbelief. "We have been apart for six years because you received a letter? You never even tried to find out if it was true, did you? Never sought me out to hear such a thing from my own lips? Anyone could have written that letter. And what token? You gave me nothing."

"Miranda, love, I'm so sorry." Colin said. "Please, can we discuss this alone?"

"It was my mother, wasn't it?" Miranda swiped at her eyes as the Dowager took her hand. "She did this."

"Yes," the Dowager stated. "I cannot imagine that anyone else would have done such a thing deliberately. And your mother," the Dowager's shoulders sagged, "well, she did wish a different match for you."

"Bitch," Cam hissed.

"Yes, we all know what my mother is, Sutton. God knows, she could never allow me any happiness. I'm not surprised she would do such a thing. But, you, Colin, should have known better."

Miranda was angry. Furious. Hurt. He saw every emotion play along her beautiful features. Disappointment. That was the worst of all of them. She may never forgive him.

"I told you how I felt about you, Colin Hartley. You chose to believe the ravings of the woman who bore you and some ridiculous curse an ancient gypsy sprouted, but not *me*." A tremor entered her words. "*Not me*. Who loved you. I've loved you all of my bloody life, and yet it was *me* you chose not to believe."

"I never received another letter from you. Not even after the Mad Countess carved me up like a Christmas ham. Why did you never write me?" Even to his own ears the defense sounded weak. "And the ring—

"I did." Miranda shouted. "You *left* me a bloody ring? You couldn't be bothered to give it to me and declare yourself?

She strode over to him, angry and so hurt it broke Colin's heart. A lone tear ran down her cheek and she wiped at it furiously. "I wrote you nearly every day. I begged you to allow me to come to you when Father told me what happened. You never replied. Nor did you reply to any of Father's letters. It broke his heart, Colin." She swiped at another tear. "I even tried to bribe a groom to take me to you, but Mother caught me."

"Miranda," Colin wanted to weep himself. This was not going at all as he'd planned. Miranda was not going to forgive him. He may as well allow Cam to beat him to death in the study. The Dowager would no doubt assist in Cam's endeavor by using her cane. He reached his hand out to Miranda in a silent plea.

"Don't," Miranda stepped back, pulling her skirts behind her. "Six years, Colin. *Six years* and you never once tried to see if I'd actually married. Hiding away at Runshaw Park, brooding. Probably sitting alone in your study, drinking in the dark. Did you ever even think of me?"

God, she knew him so well. "Jesus, of course I did."

She flinched. "When did you find out that I did not write such a thing?"

"A sherry, Sutton. Please," the Dowager said quietly.

"Yesterday," he winced and wiped another trickle of blood from his lip. "Your grandmother and Alex showed me a letter you were writing to Arabella. The handwriting did not match."

Her brows raised. "I wondered why I found my unfinished letter to Arabella in my chambers as I swore I'd left it in the drawing room." Her face didn't soften. "So, once you realized you'd made a mistake, you came to my chambers."

"Miranda," he implored. "I had already decided that it didn't matter, that St. Remy didn't matter. I told Lord Cottingham I would not marry his daughter before I knew the truth about the letter."

The look on Miranda's face told Colin he had said *exactly* the wrong thing.

"You idiot." Cam muttered under his breath, handing the Dowager her sherry.

Miranda's eyes hardened to bits of flint and her lush mouth grew taut with anger. "What a grand gesture for you to make. You assumed I wrote the letter but forced yourself to overcome your disgust and forgive me. How fortunate I am that you decided to overlook such a large flaw in my character."

"Christ, that's not what I meant. Don't you want to know why I left this morning?"

"No. I find it doesn't matter. Now, if you will all excuse me."

She spun from Colin, her entire body vibrating with anger as she left the room, slamming the door behind her.

A choked sound came from Cam as if he found amusement in the horrible situation. He sat down next to his grandmother.

"You should bear in mind, Kilmaire," he said, his voice still hinting at his earlier rage "that my sister is a crack shot."

25

"Detestable man. Coward. *Ass*."

Miranda sat back against a stone bench before the topiary garden, not giving a fig if the moss covering the ancient stone stained her dress. "A flirtation? Did he think I ran around London telling every man I loved him? Or gave my virtue so lightly?"

The three topiary monkeys making their way across the rolling lawn before her didn't answer, of course. Perhaps the monkeys were more concerned about the topiary tiger that seemed poised to attack them. The tiger was her brother's idea. Sutton hunted tiger in the jungles and described to Gray Covington's master gardener, exactly what he wanted.

How often had she come to the topiary garden to hide from her mother?

The revelation that Mother went to such lengths to determine Miranda's future was actually not that shocking. Not really. If one were listing all the terrible things Mother had done, ruining Miranda's life would have been towards the bottom of the list. She'd been nothing more than an accessory to Lady Jeanette Cambourne, like a hat or a parasol. A tool to be used to further Mother's own ambitions.

"God, she's a bitch," Miranda uttered bitterly into the breeze ruffling her hair. Her heart pinched for a moment, as it often did when she thought of Mother, but it came less these days. Sometimes Miranda envied Sutton, for his mother, Madeline, *had* loved her child.

"I shouldn't complain. You loved me and Elizabeth, didn't you Father?" she said to the wind, hoping that somewhere, Lord Robert Cambourne heard her. "I miss you. I could certainly use your counsel now."

Miranda swallowed back the tightening of her throat, attempting to banish the tears she felt certain would pour out of her at any moment.

"He would tell you that Colin Hartley is one of the most foolish men alive." The words came from behind her.

He'd approached without a sound. Colin would have made an excellent Indian scout. She'd read about those in a book on America her brother lent her. "It's not polite to sneak up on someone in such a manner. I find it's something else about you I don't care for."

Colin was right behind her, so close that his breath moved the hairs at the base of her neck. She could feel the brush of lips against her skin and she shivered slightly.

"I know you are angry."

"Furious," she spat back trying not to enjoy the feel of his mouth against her neck.

"Rightfully so." He pressed a kiss on her shoulder.

"I don't wish to speak to you. Go away. I must contemplate my marriage to Lord Ridley. After all, you seem to believe I can allow one man to bed me and still marry another."

A hand fell to the top of her head, the fingers trailing through the strands of her hair and down the length of her back. "I deserved that." Warm fingers ran up and down her spine. "I knew six years ago that I wasn't good enough for you. I was out of my mind Miranda, after Mother sliced my face. The pain was unbearable. I longed for you, my touchstone. The thing that kept me sane," his voice grew raspy with emotion. "Then the letter came."

"I don't know if I can forgive you." Tears fell from her eyes.

Colin came around the bench and sat beside her. "I know. But, I pray that you will. I'm lost without you, Miranda."

The skin around his eye was rapidly turning a shade of deep purple as was the bruise along his jaw. His eyes had deepened to chocolate, so dark she could barely make out his pupils. He took her fingers and pressed a kiss to the palm of her hand. "I would marry you."

"Because you've compromised me?" She pulled her hand away. "Because you feel guilty?"

He looked away to study the topiaries, his gaze lingering on the tiger. "Stop, Miranda. You know I do not wish to you wed you out of honor." He took her hand again. "I'm not the least bit honorable."

Miranda bit her lip and looked down at the larger hand enfolding hers, unsure as to what to say.

"I have *never* wanted anything as much as I have wanted you, Miranda Reynolds," Colin's voice was thick with emotion. "My life is empty without you in it. I merely exist, and not well, as you've probably guessed. I'm a bad bargain for you, I always have been. I brood. I drink whiskey. I have nothing but a crumbling estate and am the author of a series of lurid gothic novels."

"They are my favorite." Miranda said in a quiet voice. "That was the only pleasant surprise I've had in the last twenty-four hours."

A very determined, possessive look crossed Colin's poor

bruised face. "You are free to refuse, of course. But it won't matter."

"It won't?"

"Not in the least. I am willing to be quite ruthless. Six years? I refuse to go even six more minutes without claiming you. I will kidnap you and take you to Scotland for a hasty marriage. Ridley will meet with an unfortunate accident to prevent his interference."

"How very Lord Thurston of you."

He brushed a kiss against her lips, his hands, warm and ungloved as usual, cupped both sides of her face.

"I am hopelessly and madly in love with you, as I shall remain until I have passed from this life. I know you may never forgive me. I don't blame you. You may no longer love me, but I will take you none the less. I'm that selfish. And I'm a bit disfigured to boot."

"Colin." Miranda pressed a finger to his lips, blinking back tears.

The chocolate eyes were warm on her. "Did I mention the brooding?"

"Yes." God, she loved him. And she would forgive Colin. Eventually. The alternative would mean misery for them both.

"And the whiskey?"

"I'll share a glass with you." Miranda leaned forward and pressed a kiss to the puckered scar that split his cheek. *Gorgeous idiot*. "You do not sound appealing in the least." She wrinkled her brow. "I really have no choice in this matter?"

"No." The large body slid closer to her, and she was enveloped by his warmth. He smelled of horse and dust. "I promise, Miranda, that I will never doubt you again, nor give you cause to doubt me." He lifted his hand to trace the outline of her jaw. "I love you, and I promise to tell you so. Every day."

She could clearly see the stain of ink on his forefinger. Sometimes one cannot see the truth when it is right in front of them.

"You belong to me," she whispered.

"Always."

His lips met hers in a slow, lingering kiss that sent Miranda's blood racing. The kiss also brought her peace. This was where she belonged, with Colin. She'd know it since she was eight years old.

"I should have left you a note this morning. I didn't realize you would jump to the wrong conclusion. When I asked you to forgive me last night it was for-"

"Doubting me. I know that now. What was in London?"

Colin gave her a lazy smile. "I am a foolish man, Miranda. I never thought your mother would go to such lengths. When I left Cambourne House six years ago I wrote you a letter with my intentions and left you this. I should have put it on your finger right after—

"You ruined me."

"Yes. I left a note for your father as well, declaring my intentions." His fingers held up a battered gold ring. "It was my grandmother's, the only thing I have left of her. I know it isn't a great jewel. To the Irish it means," his forehead touched hers, "that is to say, it's a traditional way to announce one's betrothal."

"I know what it means." Miranda's heart ached with love for him as he slid the ring on her finger. "I accept your claim on me, Colin Hartley."

"Good. As you've little choice in the matter." His lips brushed hers again. "Oh, I almost forgot," he pulled a piece of paper from beneath his coat. "I went for this as well."

"A special license?" Miranda wrapped her arms about his neck. "I still haven't said yes."

"Haven't you been paying attention? If I have to debauch

you in full view of those topiaries to make you agree, I will." Elegant fingers slid beneath the silk of her bodice to caress the top of her breast. "One hopes that your brother will not murder me before the wedding."

Miranda pulled his mouth to hers. "Have a care for my dress."

EPILOGUE

"Colin," Miranda giggled. "Have a care for my dress. You'll tear the lace if you aren't careful. I can hardly return to a ball given in our honor with my bodice torn."

A frustrated look crossed her husband's handsome face. "Good God, Miranda," he kissed the side of her neck, as his hands moved possessively down her back, "I am constantly being warned about ruining your wardrobe. It's annoying. I've never once so much as ripped a seam."

Colin spun her around so that she faced the arm of the plump, overstuffed couch.

The small drawing room, barely bigger than a closet, was one that was little used at Cambourne House. A perfect spot for an assignation. Miranda could see a thin layer of dust on the side table. She'd have to inform Bevins.

Miranda could just make out the musicians tuning up after taking a break, along with the humming of dozens of voices, the sound of the *ton* gossiping and swirling across the floor of her brother's ballroom like a hive of vicious bees. Thank Goodness they would leave for Runshaw Park in the morning. Once estate matters were handled, Colin was taking her on a tour of Egypt.

"Your brother threw me a dirty look as I followed you down the hall," Colin muttered as his hand ran up the length of one silk clad leg.

Miranda trembled with anticipation as she pressed herself against the arm of the couch. "Perhaps he overheard the very wicked thing you said to me."

"Doubtful." Colin nipped the back of her neck and whispered against her ear "Bend over, Miranda, my lovely wanton wife."

She complied without a second thought, wondering if she'd locked the door behind them. It really wouldn't do for someone to find them here. "I don't think we locked the door."

Colin's hands moved up to the juncture between her thighs. "It appears, my love, that you've become absent-minded since our marriage. You've forgotten your undergarments." His fingers slipped between the folds of her sex. "Very naughty, Miranda."

She moaned softly. "I thought you'd like the surprise."

Her gloved hands ran over the cushions of the couch as she pushed her bottom towards Colin.

Colin leaned over and murmured roughly. "Grab the arm and spread open your legs. Christ, you've a lovely ass."

There were many wonderful things about being married to Colin, the least of which was that her husband's fertile imagination was useful not only for his writing. Colin, Miranda thought as she grabbed the arm of the couch and listened to her husband undo his trousers, was quite creative when it came to marital relations. Or possibly the word was adventurous.

"Do you think all husbands and wives are so daring? I'm asking because I do wonder about Lady Hemley and her husband. They're newly married and. . ." The movement of Colin's fingers was rapidly cutting off all coherent thought.

"Hemley is an idiot. I doubt he knows what to do. But I do. Good thing," his finger slid into her as she whimpered and pushed back in response "that I had no knowledge you'd neglected your underthings else we never would have made it through the first dance."

"It was a small oversight," she panted. "Please, Colin."

"You're very wet, Miranda."

Miranda gasped as Colin thrust into her, pushing her forward across the arm of the couch. She could already feel the climax building inside of her, painfully urgent and intense. So far in the last fortnight, they'd made love in the Cambourne gardens, in a carriage moving slowly through Hyde Park on Rotten Row, in the kitchen at their recently purchased townhouse after the servants had gone to bed and discreetly against the wall in a darkened alcove during the opera.

Colin put one hand on the back of her neck, his strokes long and even. His breathing was ragged and choppy. She could feel her body tightening around his.

"Harder, Colin," she begged. "Please."

The couch squeaked in protest as he moved in and out, pausing only to kiss the place beneath her left ear.

Miranda pushed back her hips and Colin's fingers found her, stroking her until she forgot where they were, her body focused only on the mounting pleasure. The world held and shattered as Miranda cried out her release into the couch, hoping to muffle the sound.

Colin thrust twice more, and with a quiet groan, found his own release, before he collapsed to lay his head against her back.

"Jesus, you'll be the death of me, Miranda."

"You'll die happy," she replied tartly.

A quarter of an hour later, they stood outside the door of the sitting room. Colin smoothed her skirts and tucked a stray hair behind her ear. "You're all pink, a sure sign you've been tumbled." He looked toward the ballroom. "I suppose we have to return," he said regretfully, pressing his lips to hers. "Though I would rather not."

Miranda concurred. She and Colin were much happier in the cozy library of their town house. She would curl up on the sofa to read, while he scratched away at the latest escapade of Lord Thurston.

It was the Dowager who insisted on a ball to celebrate the wedding of the Earl of Kilmaire to her granddaughter.

"Don't be angry at Grandmother. We did cheat her out of a grand wedding. First Sutton married in scandal, and then myself." She reached up and smoothed his cravat. "You look a bit pink yourself, Lord Kilmaire," she gave him a saucy smile.

"Wicked little thing." He kissed the tip of her nose. "Very well. Lead me back to the den of lions."

"I do wish Nick and his duchess could have been here." His voice lowered else he'd be overheard as they entered the ballroom. "Though Nick assures us that Jemma is well, I know he is worried over the child. At least he has released Arabella from her banishment in Wales. I expected to see her dour, frowning face this evening."

Miranda swatted his forearm. "She's not dour."

"She always appears as if she were sucking on a lemon."

"Perhaps she didn't welcome the news of our marriage. Nick assured me that he'd given her permission to leave Wales and come back to London." Miranda shook her head sadly. "I hoped she'd be happy for me."

"Wales is a long way off, my love. Quite possibly she's run into poor weather and will surprise you at any time. I'm sure she wouldn't miss such an event intentionally."

"I suppose not." Miranda wasn't so sure. At times, Arabella could be difficult.

They wound their way back to Sutton, Alex, and the Dowager Marchioness, who was holding court over the room.

Sutton was scowling as he took in Miranda's color, but wisely said nothing.

Overprotective, Miranda mused.

Her brother was still coming to terms with her marriage to Colin and all that preceded it, but his relationship with Colin was slowly repairing itself.

Colin went to speak to her brother, declining a passing servant's offer of wine with a grimace.

"You were gone quite a long time." Alex took in Miranda's appearance.

"The ribbon on my slipper came loose and needed a stitch to repair it."

"I didn't realize the Earl of Kilmaire had a way with a needle." Her sister-in-law raised a brow. "What talents he possesses."

"It's not the same as being read Shakespeare, I suppose," Miranda reminded her sister-in-law of the way in which Sutton and his wife often excused themselves in the evening.

"Mmph." Alex puffed a curl off her cheek.

"I fear Lady Dobson means to betroth her niece to Lord Carstairs," Miranda pointed discreetly with her fan to Miss Lainscott, who smiled wanly as the dimwitted lord twirled her about. "I do hope it's not true, for Margaret's sake, though Carstairs does seem to be nice enough, which makes up for his lack of intelligence. And he is attractive.

"If you say so," Alex replied. "I still do not buy Sutton's excuse that Lord Welles was traveling only with Carstairs to look at a hunting lodge. There is something not quite right there though I cannot put my finger on it."

"You're overly suspicious I think. Is Lady Gwendolyn lost?

She appears to be." Miranda nodded towards a lovely ash-blonde who meandered about the edges of the room rather aimlessly, apparently searching for someone.

"I would imagine she's looking for Rowan. Lady Marsh is hoping for a match between the two. He's yet to arrive." Alex tilted her head. "You did," she lowered her voice, "hear the latest about Lady Helen?"

Miranda pressed a gloved hand to her mouth to keep from laughing out loud. Lord Ridley and Lady Helen Cottingham had married in some haste not long after the ill-fated house party. Apparently, Miranda was not the only woman who welcomed a man to her chambers at Gray Covington.

"Yes. I understand she's become quite plump while Ridley gambles away her fortune."

"My lady." A discreet inquiry sounded from behind Alex.

Alex and Miranda turned to find Zander, who'd been brought to Cambourne House for the express purpose of the ball, bowing to them both.

"A note has arrived from Lord Malden." He held out a silver plate bearing the missive.

"I bet Rowan is sending his regrets, if only to escape Lady Gwendolyn for the evening." Alex smiled and picked up the note. "How odd. Are you sure this isn't from His Grace?

Miranda caught sight of the Dunbar coat of arms against the missive. "That's Nick's personal stationery."

"Yes, my lady. I was to deliver it to Lord Cambourne, but he is not in the ballroom."

Alex looked to the spot Sutton and Colin had been only a moment ago and shook her head. "Gone to smoke a cheroot I suppose. Very well, as I said, it's probably Rowan apologizing for not attending tonight, though I'm not certain Nick would approve the use of his stationary. Thank you, Zander."

The butler bowed and disappeared as silently as he'd arrived.

"I don't blame Rowan" Miranda said behind her fan. "Lady Gwendolyn, while certainly lovely, is a bit bland."

Alex smiled in agreement and tore open the note.

"Rowan, I think, would prefer a more intelligent woman for a wife. Don't you agree? I've always thought he harbored an affection for Arabella. There is something in the way he looks at her."

Alex remained fixated on the missive she held. "We must find Sutton and Colin."

"Alex? What's wrong?"

Miranda's sister-in-law looked up at her, all gaiety gone from her face.

"Arabella has gone missing."

"What do you mean, missing?" Miranda immediately feared the worst had happened to her dearest friend. The roads from Wales to London could be treacherous, especially in bad weather. The coach could have thrown an axle, or the horses gone lame.

"I mean she's been taken." Alex began to move purposefully towards the terrace where Sutton and Colin must be.

Miranda followed closely at her heels, her hands shaking with fear as she rushed to keep up with Alex. "You mean kidnapped?"

"Yes," Alex took Miranda's hand. "Lady Cupps-Foster was escorting her niece back to London. When the Dunbar coach stopped to change horses Arabella disappeared. She's been taken. And Rowan has gone after her."

Thank you for reading Miranda and Colin's story.

If you enjoyed My Wicked Earl I would greatly appreciate you leaving a review.

Read Rowan and Arabella's story in Wickedly Yours.

If you just started getting Wicked...start here with Alex and Sutton's story in Wicked's Scandal then meet Nick and Jemma in Devil of a Duke.

ABOUT THE AUTHOR

Kathleen Ayers has been a hopeful romantic since the tender age of fourteen when she first purchased a copy of Sweet Savage Love at a garage sale while her mother was looking at antique animal planters. Since then she's read hundreds of historical romances and fallen in love dozens of times. In particular she adores handsome, slightly damaged men with a wicked sense of humor. On paper, of course.

Kathleen lives in Houston with her husband, a college aged son who pops in to have his laundry done and two very spoiled dogs.

Sign up for Kathleen's newsletter:
www.kathleenayers.com

Like Kathleen on Facebook
www.facebook.com/kayersauthor

Join Kathleen's Facebook Group
Historically Hot with Kathleen Ayers

Follow Kathleen on Bookbub
bookbub.com/authors/kathleen-ayers

ALSO BY KATHLEEN AYERS

The Wicked's Series

Wicked's Scandal

Devil of a Duke

My Wicked Earl

Wickedly Yours

Tall, Dark & Wicked

Romancing the Vegas (Novellas)

Trust Me

Kiss Me

Printed in Great Britain
by Amazon